From The Sea TO THE STARS

BAEN BOOKS
by
ANDRE NORTON

Time Traders
Time Traders II
Star Soldiers
Warlock
Janus
Darkness & Dawn
Gods & Androids
Dark Companion
Masks of the Outcasts
Moonsinger
From the Sea to the Stars

From The Sea To The Stars

BY

ANDRE NORTON

BAEN

FROM THE SEA TO THE STARS

A Baen Book

Baen Publishing Enterprises
P.O. Box 1403
Riverdale, NY 10471

ISBN 13: 978-1-61129-507-8

Cover art by Bob Eggleton

Distributed by Simon & Schuster
1230 Avenue of the Americas
New York, NY 10020

Printed in the United States of America

Contents

Sea Siege

Part 1
PROJECT SEA SERPENT

Chapter One
ONE DUPEE—BEACHED

"Perfect opportunity—chance of a lifetime!" Griffith Gunston exploded to the empty reaches of the wide blue sky. "I don't think!" he added forcibly.

He was standing defiantly, his hands on his hips, breasting the trade wind. It was blowing steadily, pushing the booming surf against reef and rock, sounding an organ's deep notes, bending the bushes and trees with the flail of its invisible current. Griff knew that down on the beach one could hear another song, the tuneful whisper of sand on the move, as restless under the push of the wind as he now was under the lash of his personal frustration.

There were few real heights on San Isadore. It was an island born of the sea, not of volcanic eruption. But the coral block building, once part of the old saltworks, which his father had turned into a combined laboratory and home, was on the cliffs. And from this vantage point of headland Griff could now survey not only the sleepy indifference of dying Carterstown but look across the wide sweep of Frigate Bay to the waves smashing on the barrier reef—that division which separated the shallows he had explored, during his exile of the past few weeks, from the depths into which a skin diver dared not venture.

Below him, the *Island Queen* swung at her moorings, her spars bare to the pull of the wind. And beyond her the rich aquamarine of the water was split by a wedge of silver flying fish. It was a world of color—the sea. But, on the other hand, the island hues were muted, ghostly. Here was none of the gaudy luxuriance of the tropics that one might find elsewhere in the West Indies.

San Isadore was truly a sea island—encased, encrusted in salt. Gray-white crystals gathered not only in the beds of the old saltworks but about the trunks of the trees, at the roots of shrubs, and lay in crusts on the thin soil. The vegetation was largely silver-gray, some leaves glinting metallically in the sun. Among the plants were the pointed, brittle fingers of cacti and the menace of skeleton thorn trees, with only the darker sheen of lignum vitae and sea lavender to break the salty sweep. Men had their gardens on San Isadore, but they were planted and reaped in defiance of nature, not with her cooperation.

Griff strode into the full drive of the wind. He wanted to fight something. His impatience, repressed for days, had come to a head with his father this morning—disastrously. He had advanced his plea to be allowed to return to the States, advanced it, as he thought, with reasonable restraint. And what had happened? Griff's fists clenched until his nails bit into the palms of his hands.

He wasn't ten years old and he was not going to be treated as if he were. To be spoken to like that with Hughes sitting there on the other side of the table! The perfect assistant, Hughes, Dr. Ramsey Gunston's shadow and alter ago. The calm good sense of all the answers Griff's father had marshalled had only added to the humiliation and disappointment of that scene—every one of Griff's own points demolished without any real understanding of how he felt, what he wanted to do!

Run away little boy and play—find some way to amuse yourself—that was about the sum and substance of Dr. Gunston's reply. But Griff wanted his own life—to follow the plans he had been making for years. Did his father believe that he had existed in a sort of vacuum, growing no older, doing no thinking for himself for the past five years? True, his father did not know him well—how could he? Ramsey Gunston had been out in the East Indies chasing fish all over the place, writing scientific papers that might be in an obtuse code as far as his son was concerned. What did Griff care about the diseases of fish—Fish! He couldn't be less interested!

His father had turned up again just after Griff had graduated from Emmsly, swept him off to this West Indies salt pot, as if his son had no right to a life of his own at all, and settled in for another season of prying into stinking messes of seaweed, of analyzing scum.

Oh, he supposed it was important—at least some of the magazines and papers back home had said that it was—this study of the Red Plague, of the strange new death in southern waters that had appeared without warning a season ago and was making great inroads in the profits of the fishing industry, sending the dead bodies of fish floating ashore by the millions along the lower coast of the United States and among the West Indies. Dad's job was backed by both the American and the British governments. He'd been brought halfway around the world to do it. But there wasn't one small piece of it his son could help with. And Dr. Gunston had the perfect Hughes always at his elbow, making Griff's first fumbling but honest attempts to help seem so childish that the younger Gunston soon stopped trying.

So—why should he be chained here, on an island even tourists did not visit, so far off the shipping lanes that the *Island Queen* was their only link with civilization when she made her biweekly trip to Santa Maria. And what was Santa Maria, in spite of its government house and port for freighters, but a dirty flyspeck on some out-of-date charts? Let him go home and try out for the Academy. For a moment Griff saw not the blue sea—but the blue sky. Jets—those were the future—not fish! He didn't know one fish from another and had no desire to be formally introduced either.

But there Griff was belittling his own curiosity, a curiosity that he had no intention of admitting to either of the two men now at work in the building behind him. His diving adventures along the reef during the past few weeks, his companionship with Christopher Waite, the mate of the *Queen*, had taught him more than he realized about the finned and shelled inhabitants of the bay—including some lore that might have surprised Dr. Gunston. But Griff took a perverse and childish delight in keeping to himself the results of his own underwater explorations. After all, both Dad and Hughes must have forgotten more than he would ever know. Why babble about such kindergarten stuff to them?

He wanted to get away. If he didn't, he had a vague fear that he might fall under the same spell that doomed Carterstown, that inertia that had sapped the energy of the islanders since the closing of the saltworks. They fished; they planted a few grains of corn, melon seeds, some garden truck in those tiny potholes of real soil to be found at such intervals that a small garden patch might cover several acres; they caught conch and dried them to sell in Santa Maria for the only cash they ever saw. But no one worked regularly or cared much about the future.

Griff, some of his hot resentment cooled by the press of the wind against his sun-browned body, considered languidly his own plans for the day. He could take out the underwater camera and try for some shots along the reef. He could strike inland to the plate-shallow salt lake and study the flamingos. He could try to find the bat cave Le Marr said was back in the desert strip. Or, he could again tackle the books he had flung aside last night with a petulance more suitable to someone half his age. He ought to sweat out that course sometime, in case he could ever take the Air Force Academy exam—if Dr. Gunston would even consider allowing him to try it!

Once more that stab of irritation. Lord, he didn't *like* fish, he never would! Moodily he stared down at the *Island Queen* without really seeing her at all.

There was a stir of life on her deck. A figure wearing only ragged dungarees pattered barefooted on the snowy-clean boards. That would be Rob Fletcher, his white-blond hair identifying him even at this distance. The islanders were an oddly mixed lot. Some "red-legs," rebel-convicts of the eighteenth century political wars, Scottish clansmen after '45, or the Monmouth rebels, had been sent here by their planter-masters to start the first of the salt beds. Then the pirates of the cays had added men from time to time, marooned free-booters or shipwrecked buccaneers. There were Negro slaves and a few Indians—and now the islanders were a mixture of races, colors, heritages—Saxon names wedded to black skins, blue eyes beneath thick fuzz, startling blond locks now and then. And among them was a very small core of families who had not altogether slipped back to the semisavage existence of the rest, a core that produced from time to time an island leader or a man able to better his condition and try for some degree of civilized living.

Angus Murdock, the captain of the *Queen*; Fletcher; and Chris Waite, his mate; Dobrey Le Marr; Braxton Wells who managed the one store in Carterstown—you could count their number on the fingers of one hand. But they were there, distinct from their fellows, with a measure of energy, a degree of curiosity and of solid belief in themselves, and some ambition for the future.

Griff made his decision about the day's employment. He'd join the crew of the *Queen*, give them a hand as he had so often done before. Chris had just come above deck, his darker bulk looming over that of his slighter companion. The date of their scheduled trip to Santa Maria was still two days away, but there was something in that sudden appearance of Chris that suggested action, and Griff hurried down the winding cliff path.

He followed the rutted path, which could not be termed a road, between the tumble-down ruins of Carterstown. From one house in five he caught the sound of life. The rest were left now to the lizards and the spiders. As he trotted into the main street, he almost ran into Angus Murdock.

"Slow you down." White teeth showed in a wide friendly grin, and a rich slur of voice somehow soothed the sting left from the curt interview in the lab house.

Griff grinned back happily. "Care to sign on a new hand today, Cap'n?"

"You aimin' to go worryin' them fish 'long the reef?" was Murdock's counter question. His well-muscled shoulders moved easily under his loose and very clean white shirt. The officer's cap, its captain's insignia carefully rubbed into winking brightness, was cocked over one eye in a way that gave his square-jawed face a rather rakish cast. Murdock traced his lineage back to another captain, one whose reputation at the time had been far from savory but over which modern romance cast a softening glow. There are few modern sea-rovers who can state with truth that their great-great-great-great-grandfathers were highly successful pirates.

"Not unless you do—" Griff returned, matching his stride to the other's rolling gait. "Is something up?"

"Up? What you mean, mon?" Murdock was at the dingy, preparing to launch out to the *Queen*. "We ain't sailin' today—"

But an impatient hail from the ship interrupted him. Chris was waving from the deck, his arm a whirlwind of summoning, and Murdock, with Griff, pushed off, to swing through the water at an oar speed much greater than usual. It was clear that something had happened, something actually drastic enough to excite the usually placid Waite.

"They's found the *S'Jawn*, Cap'n!" Chris blew out his news in a mighty blast almost before his superior officer clambered over the rail.

Murdock paused, pushing back his cap. Then, with a frown cutting a deep line between his brows, he confronted Waite as if he were accusing the islander of being personally responsible for bad news.

"Where they find her?"

"Driftin'—" Chris waved an arm to indicate the vast expanse beyond the reef. "She was driftin'—without no mon 'board her. Jus' like the *Neptune* an' *Flyin' Fish*!"

"On the wireless you heard dis?" Murdock asked.

"Aye, Cap'n. They say it from San' Maria. She was found this mornin' by the Dutch freighter. No mon 'board her—driftin'—"

Rob Fletcher had a single comment, which he made with the sullen persistence of one who had said the same thing before and did not expect to be attended to any more this time than he had been the last.

"Dupee—"

Murdock rounded on him, and the frown became even deeper. "A dupee? A ghost thing from the sea, eh? That's what you say, mon? Me, I don't believe in no ghost dupee thing without I see it with these two eyes—"

Rob shrugged. "So you don't believe, Cap'n? Then tell me true—what takes the mons from those ships an' leave them sailin' without no mon on board? Tell me that? No storm, no fire, no thing bad, jus' ship sailin' without no mon on her—that dupee work, that is!

"No mon knows what things be in the deep sea." He expanded his argument. "There's this red death what be killin' off the fish, ain't there? And Buzzy Defere, he saw that debble thing a-swimmin' off the reef in the moonshine—"

"All right," Murdock countered. "So there be things in the sea what be strange. But they're no ghostes—They're things a mon can see—like barracuda or shark. I don't believe in dupees—no ghost thing is gonna climb on the *Queen* an' push us off!"

It seemed to Griff that Rob did not look at all convinced. But he had a question of his own.

"What do you think *does* happen, Cap'n?"

Murdock was staring at the distant reef, to the deeper blue of the wave-ruffled water beyond.

"I think—subs!"

All the rumors of the past months, the tall tales that had passed from island to island, that had been mentioned on broadcasts from the States, were summed up in that one word—for not only had the red scum come to plague the sea but also this other lurking menace.

Several years before, similar tales had come from the far islands of the Pacific. There, too, small craft had cleared port with full crews and passengers for short runs between one landfall and the next—only to be entirely lost in a calm sea or to be found drifting days or weeks later, deserted by any living thing, with no evidence of any disaster such as fire or storm. And there had been rumors then of a new type of shark prowling the lanes, a sub that struck, killed, and struck again for no gain anyone could fathom.

Because the tension between the Eastern bloc of nations and the West had been building, so that they were on the brink of a holocaust, which both sides knew might put an end not only to the actively warring nations but to perhaps the whole world, the story of an underseas scout, a lurking, unnamed enemy, had been readily accepted and believed. And only because the mysterious attacks had suddenly ceased had real conflict been averted then.

Now within the circle of the Caribbean and the Gulf, the same game was being played once more. Three small island ships, the *Neptune*, the *Flying Fish*, and now the *St. John*, had been plundered of life and left to drift after the familiar pattern. And the affair of the *St. John* struck close to home with the men of San Isadore. She was a small vessel with the usual crew of three—twin to the *Island Queen*—and her home port was Santa Maria.

"Cap'n Luis, an'Sim, an'Marco." Chris was reciting the roll of the missing.

"An' Florrie, Sim's woman," Rob added. "She be 'long this time—do cookin'. Dupee done caught hisself big mouthful!"

"Them Reds." Murdock's voice lost much of its warmth. "They's gonna find out that they's got some real mons on their tail this time! We ain't gonna be gobbled up like the hound fish gobble up their dinner 'long the reef. We gits us some teeth like a shark an' then we goes 'til we can use them right!"

There was a menace in that last, though Griff wondered how Murdock proposed to face up to a modern sub, probably atomically powered and armed, with only three diver's knives, a shark gun, and the automatic that was the captain's own prized possession, those being the total sum of all armament he had ever seen aboard the *Queen*.

"They's give out a warnin'"—Chris's slower drawl was a cushion to the captain's heat—"do any ship see something, they say it by the wireless. Government boat, it be all ready steam out an' help—"

Rob shook his head. His long face was all solemn disagreement. "No government boat ain't gonna find no dupee. Get Papa-loi make a gris-gris charm—That's the only thing send dupee back where he belong. I speak Le Marr—he make gris-gris for the *Queen*—"

Murdock shrugged. "Gris-gris—an' guns! We git them both. Then we see who bigger—this thing in the sea or we."

"Ahhhh—" The hail echoed over the waters of the bay, and the four on the deck of the *Queen* turned to look at the dilapidated boat that was approaching under oar power from around the point. Its two man crew was putting on a better burst of speed than Griff had yet seen any of the islanders produce, and their excitement was manifest. Had the mysterious jungle "telegraph" that operated on San Isadore spread the news of the *St. John's* discovery this soon—or was it something else?

"Mosely Peeks." Chris identified one of the oarsmen without much concern, Mosely being on the bottom rung of the island's social ladder and of little consequence to the more solid citizens now represented in the gathering on the *Queen*. "Whyfor that mon make all this noise?"

"Got him a conch pearl an' think he be rich for all days," suggested Rob. "He talk, talk pearl all the time since Joise find that one last month."

Murdock walked to the rail. "Mosely!" His hail held the ring of command. "Whyfor you yell your throat sore that way? What big thing you have to say, mon?"

"Dupee—!" The word echoed over the water, rising above the boom of the surf. "Done found dupee lyin'out there!"

Rob spat disgustedly into the water. "Done got sun in the head," was his verdict. "Dupee don't go 'round lettin' hisself be foun'—"

"Sub!" Griff and Murdock snapped the word out almost together. And when the captain swung down into the dingy, Griff was only seconds behind, his heart beating fast. Could a sub actually be in these waters after all?

Murdock sent the dingy toward the wallowing, weed-hampered boat of the two conch fishermen. He put out a strong brown arm and anchored them to its side, looking into the excited faces before him.

"Where this dupee?"

"On beach—Daid Sailormon's Point. The birds, they's peckin' it. That dupee's sure daid, sure is—"

"Whale." Griff lost his keen interest of the moment before. No birds would be pecking at a sub, even if the underseas vessel had grounded. But at his explanation both of the fishermen shook their heads vigorously.

"Ain't no whale, nosuh," they chorused. "Ain't never seen this thing. It be dupee for sure—for sure—"

Murdock, after a careful study of their expressions, settled back at his oars, and under his stroking the light craft swung into a course that would bring the dingy and its passengers to Dead Sailorman's Point, where the outer reef ended and a jumbled mass of coral boulders stuck out into the raging surf of unchecked waves.

"Surely it's a whale," Griff repeated, surprised at his companion's action.

Murdock was frowning again. "Mosely—that mon, he be mostly no-'count. But he know daid whale. He say this ain't no whale, it ain't. An' I want to see this dupee for my ownself."

There was certainly something grounded on the rocky point, something dead, a loadstone for all the winged scavengers on the island. During all his months on San Isadore, Griff had never seen such a large gathering of screaming birds. And, as the dingy neared the place where they must land to advance on foot, avoiding the smashing surf rolling in from the open sea, he was aware of something else, the sickly stench of rotting flesh. Yes, whatever had beached here was very dead.

He struggled after Murdock across the sharp ridges of broken coral, feeling the bite of the razor-edged stuff through his sneakers—

though the captain's bare and callused feet took the same path with apparent ease. They pulled up to the cliff top together and looked down into a small cove where something lay half buried in the sand.

Not only birds had been to the feast, but a multitude of crabs, so that the beach itself crawled with snapping life. But it was what was being torn by those busy beaks and claws that brought an exclamation out of Griff. In those few seconds his lifelong belief in the omniscience of science was rudely shaken—he was seeing legend clothed in sloughing flesh.

Mosely's dupee—the vicious ghost of voodoo folklore—was a creature out of the fairy tales of Griff's own heritage. The fanged and grinning head, turned up by some freak so that the empty eyepits stared at the two men above, bore a photographic resemblance to the dragons of his childhood reading!

Chapter Two
OCTOPI REEF

Half the population of Carterstown was assembled to beat the feasters off their malodorous banquet as Dr. Gunston and Hughes took photographs feverishly, measured, dug to free the carcass from the sand. They had something new right enough—or old enough if one wanted to recall the very ancient legends and later accounts of "sea serpents." An unclassified sea animal some twenty feet long, a snake's supple neck planted on a barrel body equipped with propelling flippers, a toothed alligator-like head. The stench of the rotting, rubbery flesh did not appear to bother the fascinated ichthyologists, but Griff, at last, climbed to the headlands once more to gulp in cleaner air.

"That thing"—Chris Waite dropped down beside him—"be a bottom thing."

Chris waved a big hand seaward. "Bottom—far down bottom out there. That thing come up from the bottom—"

"Why, do you suppose?"

"Maybeso something chase he."

Griff surveyed the length of the beached thing. Something from which that monster had fled would indeed be formidable. Shark? But if so—an outsize in sharks.

"Did you ever see anything like it before, Chris?"

The islander shook his head. "Never no time. But some things in the big bottom—no mon ever see them! An' Defere, he see something swimmin' two-three weeks ago. Might be this here—"

"Wonder what killed it?" Griff mused.

Chris shrugged. "Birds, fish, crabs, they nibble, nibble 'til a mon can't tell that. But the doctor, he be pleased!"

"I wonder how old that thing is—or was?" Another thought had struck Griff. Memories of fantastic stories spurred his imagination—the "lost world" where prehistoric monsters still lived, waiting to be discovered. Did that lump of decaying matter down there come from such a place? Did it represent a species that had inhabited the swamps of an earlier continent? He had browsed enough in the laboratory library to know that odd discoveries had been made of survivals from the unreckoned past. There was the Latimeria, the monstrous armored fish caught in the net of a trawler off the tip of South Africa back in 1938, a fish that rightly should have been dead a hundred and thirty million years like its carefully preserved fossils of the Devonian period.

However, this time they had photographs, measurements, careful observations to back up their report—proofs the unfortunate ships' officers and earlier travelers could not offer in testimony when they had tried to explain what they had seen, and so suffered the ignominy of complete disbelief.

Later that night the Americans learned another fact—one which was almost as great a shock as the original discovery had been. Hughes burst out of the laboratory, his tousled hair glued to his sweating forehead, his eyes wide with excitement. And the very impetus of his entrance brought him a full audience at once.

"That thing was 'hot'!" he exploded.

For a bemused second or two neither Griff nor his father understood. Then it was the younger Gunston who answered, "Radioactive!"

"Certain?" Dr. Gunston asked with schooled detachment.

"The counter says yes. It's about double that of the last batch of scum, too. I'd say that thing caught a good blast—maybe enough to kill it!"

Griff followed the others back to the laboratory workroom, hovering near the dissection table, listening to the fatal clicking of the Geiger counter. But he knew better by now than to ask for an explanation. The creature had somewhere, somehow absorbed enough radiation to make its carcass "hot."

"We must report in tonight—"

Hughes shifted his weight from one foot to the other. Griff believed that he wanted to protest that decision.

Then Dr. Gunston added, "I don't think it is necessary to go into too much detail as yet. Just say that we found a new marine life form, a large one, dead on the shore and that it registered exposure to radiation."

"Yes, sir!" There was plain relief in that prompt reply. "I'll code it and send it short wave to Dr. Langley's office at Key West—"

Griff waited until Hughes had gone. "D'you suppose this thing"—he indicated the remains on the table—"came out of the depths—what Chris calls the big deeps?"

Dr. Gunston looked tired. He ran both hands through his stiff brush of gray-brown hair. "Well, it certainly wasn't hatched, born, or spawned on that beach. And we haven't been able to get our claws on its like before. There'll be a regular consultation over it when the news gets out."

"And 'hot' too—"

His father stiffened. "That you'll keep quiet, Griff." He was no longer speaking equal to equal, but giving an order. And hearing that tone, Griff's old resentment awoke. Stubbornly he voiced another question.

"So the plague scum is radioactive, too?"

"Hughes had better keep his mouth shut!" Dr. Gunston exploded and then added, "That's another point to forget, Griff."

The younger Gunston leaned back against the row of shelves with their jars of bottled specimens. "Is somebody experimenting with atomic stuff out in the Atlantic, Dad?"

Dr. Gunston stood very still, his mouth thinned into a grim, straight line. His eyes were bleak. Griff had a second of something close to panic under that keen scrutiny.

The doctor's hand shot out. His fingers closed with a pinching and compelling grasp on his son's upper arm, and he propelled the young man before him down the short corridor to his office. There he released his captive and went to the desk. From his pocket he brought a cluster of keys fastened to his belt by a length of chain. Selecting one, he unlocked a drawer. He did not open any of the folders that lay within, merely shuffled through them, glancing at the notation on the front of each as if making sure that they were in some special order. Then he relocked the drawer and turned to his son.

"So that was just a good guess, Griff?"

Griff's Indian-brown face was impassive, but his hands locked together in a tight clasp behind his back. So, his father dared to think that—that he had been—spying!

"It would seem so, sir." He was proud of his control.

Dr. Gunston did not appear to notice any change in his son's attitude. "You've been around with Murdock, with these other islanders. You heard them say anything?"

"Nothing about atomics—" But his father was not going to let him off that easily.

"Maybe nothing about atomic experiments—but you have heard something that made you think?"

"Murdock believes the 'mystery sub' story about the trouble with the ships. Well, there're atomic subs, aren't there? And I don't think one of ours could have turned pirate. So if there is one patrolling, or observing about here, there's a reason for it—"

Dr. Gunston sat down in the desk chair, fumbled with the pipe he picked up, and sucked at it unlighted. "Logical deduction, Griff. But such bright ideas are not to be peddled outside of here, understand?"

"Yes, sir." Mentally Griff shrugged. Three warnings in three minutes or so—did his father think that he habitually ran off at the mouth?

Hughes appeared in the doorway. "Report through and acknowledged."

The doctor put his hands over his eyes and then pushed them upward through his hair. Under the garish light he suddenly looked very tired. "Good enough. Time we locked up for the night, Frank. That'll be all, Griff."

So dismissed, the younger Gunston went on to the room that housed his cot and foot locker. But he did not make any move toward going to bed. Tiny brown lizards, which could have curled comfortably inside his class ring, flashed across the ceiling and walls in the glare of the unshielded light bulb dangling from an electric cord. And outside, the nightly chorus of hermit crabs, their claws clicking on the rocks, their stolen shell houses clanking as they scuttled, was an under-note to the high squealing bray of one of the wild donkeys come down to raid garden patches in the town.

Griff pushed aside the netting and lay down on the cot, his fingers laced behind his head. The constant roar of the surf under the rising wind beat in his ears as a low boom. But he was trying to forget one thing, that his father had been willing to believe that he had rifled that desk drawer. Had everyone working for the government become so "security" conscious that now they suspected everyone else? Or—

Five years was a long time, and even before Dr. Gunston had left the States on his first trip, they hadn't been together very much. Griff had lived with his Aunt Regina after his mother's death—until he went to school. His relationship with his father had always been on a visitor basis. So maybe it was natural that Dad could believe him capable of a trick such as that. But—Resolutely Griff tried to think of something else.

So the red plague scum was "hot"? That was an interesting fact. Atomic experimentation of some kind under the surface of the Atlantic? Near enough to the West Indies so that traces of such activity could be detected there? What kind of experimentation and who was doing it? Somehow Griff was sure that it was not his countrymen, nor their allies, unless the various "security" precautions, which were growing more and more irksome, had taken to concealing one government project from another, leaving it that one finger could no longer learn what the other was dabbling in.

And if that atomic research was *not* the concern of friends—then what? It was hard to lie in the dank heat of this island night, listening to the vociferous life outside in the dark, a life that had nothing to do with the concerns of bipeds such as himself, and think of the cold, thin fear that had lain on the horizon of his world as long as he could remember.

Griff got up. There was an adventure he had in mind—perhaps this was the night to try it. He stripped and pulled on swimming trunks. The rest of his equipment was in the second locker. He strapped on the watch protected against moisture, the wrist depth gage, and buckled about his waist the weighted diving belt, fastening his knife in place. The aqualung, the mask, a rubber-encased flashlight—he gathered them all up and a few moments later was going down the cliff path. Chris would be willing to take him out to the reef. This was a plan they had discussed for some time.

Here and there lamplight shone warmly yellow from unshuttered windows in the dying town. But there were few other signs of life.

And then the steady beat of a drum, to be heard above the surf, told him why.

Le Marr—Dobrey Le Marr—was drumming up the spirits. Nominally the islanders were Christian. There was a church they attended on Sunday, a vicar who came over from Santa Maria twice a month to hold services.

But underneath that shell of the civilized world there had always lurked something else. And in late years—perhaps because of the world-wide unrest—it had bobbed once more to the surface. Dobrey Le Marr was no witch doctor of the jungle, but he claimed some of their ancient powers. His knowledge of herbs had confounded Dr. Gunston, and his psychological understanding of his fellows, shrewdly used, had made him the most powerful man on the island, though he made no open display of his power. Luckily, Le Marr was a benevolent despot. And the Gunstons believed that he had a better education in the field of civilized learning than he now admitted. He was a racial mixture, as were all the islanders, but when he had been ten, he had gone off island, not to return until he was a man in his thirties. From then on he lived quietly among his fellows, saying little for five years or more, until he began to practice medicine as the men of San Isadore knew it, with potions and spells. But he refused utterly to use his skill to kill. A gris-gris fashioned by Dobrey Le Marr was always for a man's protection, not his neighbor's damnation.

He had held aloof from the Gunston laboratory when the Americans had arrived and started their work. But Dr. Gunston had deliberately sought him out. And when Le Marr discovered that the scientist from the north was willing to listen without impatience to his theories and explanations, he had fallen into the habit of coming in once in a while in the evening, sitting for long silent moments turning the American cigarettes they gave him in his long, artist's fingers, his thin hawk face—with the features of an Andalusian grandee—composed, until at last he told some fantastic tale that they could accept as true. Le Marr always used the idiomatic speech of the island, but he did it with the precision of one who speaks a foreign tongue, and Griff suspected that he could have spoken as an off-islander of education had he so desired.

For a minute Griff hesitated on the path. He longed to watch Le Marr at his business—see a voodoo gathering. But he sensed that that was one place where he would not be welcome. And his presence there might undo all the friendliness of past relations. The Gunstons were interlopers here, and there were parts of island life that could never be open to them. Anyway he was sure he would not find Chris in that audience. Though Rob Fletcher was a devoted follower of Le Marr, Captain Murdock and Waite held aloof from the calling drums and the dark belief born in an older and hotter jungle land.

Griff's feet, clad in rubber-soled sneakers, made no sound on the road. He came to the three-room coral block house set in a garden patch and turned in.

"Who there?" A dark shadow detached itself from the doorway and moved out, to be outlined against the cream-white of the wall.

"Griff Gunston. That you, Chris?"

"This me. Ha—" The other had a cat's eyes in the gloom. "You gonna dive now?"

"Can you take me out, Chris?"

"Sure. But you mighty teched in the head, mon. The fishes, they eat your skin offen you some day, you do this fool thing."

"You ought to try it, Chris."

The other chuckled. "Me, I ain't gone in the head yet, mon. I'll pull the crazy one out—afore the crabs eat him to little pieces—"

Inside the reef the water was calm, not the blue-green of the day, but a purple-blue. And Griff, looking down into it, began to wonder about the wisdom of his plan. But he knew that the world below him, in which man could only be an intruder for short spaces of time, had two separate lives—that the activity that filled it by night was not the activity that it knew by day. And he had long wanted to observe the difference for himself.

As they rowed out along the reef, Chris was full of news.

"The wireless, it go war, war all evenin'," he remarked. "Big talks here, there. They talk bomb, bomb all the time. Say, 'You do what I say, mon, or I blow you up.' Think that they do that, Griff—blow us up?"

"They've been talking that way ever since I can remember," Griff remarked somewhat absently, his attention more on the water into which he was going. He kicked off his sneakers and adjusted swimming flippers.

"Sometimes"—Chris's powerful oarswing shot them forward—"I think that maybe this world's gonna get powerful tired of mons. Spit us out like we ain't no 'count no ways. There's things on this world mon ain't never seen, no matter how big he talk with the mouth. Your father, he know many things, but he ain't never seen that there dupee afore, had he?"

"No," Griff admitted as he adjusted his tank between his shoulders.

"New things comin' outta the sea. Maybe new things comin' other places, too. Mon, he mess 'round, start things comin'. But what if they don't stop? Back there"—in the light of the lantern his chin pointed to the land behind them—"they ask voodoo for gris-gris. Me, I think better ask for good wits in mon's head—so he learn he maybe ain't top cap'n afore it be late!"

Some of that sunk into Griff's mind, past his preoccupations of the moment. But now he made ready to dive and slipped over into the weird world, the existence of which he had suspected, but the reality of which completely bewitched him.

He was familiar with the fairy tale seascapes that confronted the daytime diver—the rich color of live coral and sea fans, the butterfly tints of the small fish, the dusty patches of sunlight that filtered down through the waves to dazzle the diver and upset his judgment of distance.

But this—this was very different. His finger moved on the torch button beneath its rubber coating. A beam of light cut through purple murk, struck coral into life, brought into its cone furious fish, their colors all altered so that Griff had to reidentify them. Then the light caught and centered on what he had come to find—that crevice in the rock wall with its telltale pile of shells beneath it.

The octopi clan had long furnished a boogy man for the ocean. Since the days of the legendary Great Kraken—said to arise from the depths to wreath its arms about the mast of a ship and draw it down into darkness—there had been horror stories of the cephalopods and their cold-blooded enmity to his kind. Yet most of those tales were sheer fantasy. When man faced octopus, he was facing a creature that, had native conditions varied only the slightest degree, might have been this planet's ruler in man's place. They were the keenest witted creatures in the ocean for the same reason that man had been forced to develop a brain in order to survive on land. If they possessed thumbs and fingers instead of tentacles armed with suckers, the whole history of the world might be different.

Organic evolution had left them, as it had puny man, without adequate physical protection against the dangers of their world. What were man's teeth and nails against the talons and fangs of the creatures he faced—until he lengthened and strengthened his arm with a stick and a rock and learned to build fires in the night? And the cephalopods, mollusks that had lost their shells in the dim past, became streamlined in action, used a smoke screen of ink to mask their escapes, and lived in houses of their own contriving.

That pile of shells outside the door was in itself remarkable, testifying to the fact that the owner of the dwelling was unlike other water creatures. They were not all empty shells—a goodly portion were still living, stored in anticipation of a hungry morrow.

Griff had located this largest inhabitant of the reef some days earlier when he had been about to steady himself with one hand against a coral boulder, only to see two black eyes regarding him bleakly. Then the rock had separated, and the larger portion had oozed away into the crevice, from which at last only the point of a single tentacle trailed as if to wave him good-by.

Now he picked up those eyes again. The octopus was enthroned on the same rocky vantage point, its stare into the flare of his torch unchanging. Would it change color? He watched for the livid white shade, which he knew meant that it was alarmed. But that alteration did not come. Instead Griff felt a queer sensation—as if hundreds of tiny wet and clammy hands pulled at the skin on his thigh. He looked down. A tiny edition of the large mollusk clung there, spread starfashion, less than eight inches across.

In that moment Griff lost his taste for night exploration. There was something about those unblinking eyes—that touch from which his flesh shrank. He tore at the infant on his leg. It slipped across his skin, but he could not pry any one of those arms loose from their sucker clutch. It was as if the small mollusk was determined to go into the air with him!

Then the large octopus moved. With the lightning speed usual to its kind, it swam away out of the light, leaving Griff staring at the rock where it had been only a second or two earlier. He had decided now about calling an end to this adventure. He wanted above all to lose the baby thing that clung so persistently to him. With a practised flip he swam up toward the dark shadow of the boat and the waiting Chris.

Chapter Three
BASE HUSH-HUSH

Griff sat cross-legged in the scrap of shade thrown by a single wind-warped palm tree, regarding intently the drama in his own private pool jungle. It was on the top of the cliff, a depression hollowed out by the beat of falling spray through the centuries, filled drop by drop by that same moisture, kept heated by the sun to blood temperature.

Without any clue as to how they had made the journey up the cliff from the sea below, hundreds of small rainbow-colored fish flashed their vivid blues and golds, their gleaming silver, their flamboyant purples and reds, their black and yellow stripes, as they wheeled and sped or hung suspended on quivering fins. Shrimp and prawn, which might have been ghosts of themselves, so transparent that one could see their lunch being digested inside their frankly revealed interiors, scuttled across the sandy bottom.

Amid all these was the newcomer introduced by Griff in the early hours of the morning. A strangely streaked rock gave resting place to the baby octopus that had clung to him, refusing to be parted even when he had climbed into the boat. And true to its nature, the lurking cephalopod was now the same shade as that rock, only visible to Griff because he had seen it anchor itself on that point. In the light of day it was quiescent. But two tiny crab shells, emptied of their lawful contents, marked activity in the last hours before dawn. And if it allowed a rainbow fish to brush a tentacle with a careless fin, it was because that was its period for rest.

Griff thought of what he had seen the night before—at least ten of the shell-heaped crevice doors along the reef—an octopi town.

And Chris admitted that at the other end of San Isadore there was an even larger colony of the creatures. The law of the sea, supply and demand of food—Griff frowned at his small specimen in the spray pool. Why so many of them about here now? Was hunting so rich hereabouts that the cephalopod population was going up? Were more of the young surviving than was usual? An octopus was a noted mother, protecting her eggs as they lay concealed in some carefully selected crevice, sending the water moving in currents over them by sweeps of her arms so that algae and other tiny plants and animals could not root on them, refusing to leave them even to hunt for food. But, with the prodigious wastefulness of sea life, for every one that hatched and reached adulthood, perhaps hundreds of others died. Conditions must be unusually favorable to bring such large colonies to settle about the island at this time.

A shadow fell across the pool startling the fish, which fled in rainbow bands. Griff glanced up.

"Dobrey Le Marr—"

In the freshness of the morning it was hard to connect this thin tall man, possessing the air and features of high-born Spain, with the drumming of the night before, with Le Marr's acknowledged—could you term it?—profession?

"The reef—how it be at night?" Le Marr asked abruptly. As usual he spaced his words as if he spoke in a foreign tongue.

"I didn't stay long." Griff wanted to explain that sensation he had had of menace, of being cut off from his own world, which had sent him out of the water and back into the boat last night, but somehow the words were missing.

"You bring something from the reef?"

"Baby octopus—" Griff pointed to the new occupant of the pool.

Le Marr leaned over, his odd yellowish eyes finding the small mollusk quickly.

"It came to you, you did not hunt it?" There was a new note in his precise voice.

"It clung to my leg—"

"It came to you. Now it stay—an' watch—" Le Marr's head lifted, and he looked down out over the sea. "Other things come soon. Life change—mons change too maybeso—"

"You mean—the sea monster—?"

Le Marr shook his head. "First come mon. Then—" He brought his slender hands together in a smacking slap, which sounded almost like a shot. "Then—all the trouble in the wide world!" His gaze flickered to Griff and became more human as the seer faded into the man. "We go inland—see things—"

Griff was ready to agree. Since the incident of the night before, he fought shy of his father. And anyway both the elder Gunston and Hughes had been shut up in the laboratory almost since dawn. Also, Le Marr was none too generous with invitations to explore the wasteland that was the interior of San Isadore, and this might just be the time when he would reveal the site of the bat caves.

"Thanks!" The American went in to gather up a canteen, a pair of shoes suited to scrambling over coral rock, and a broad-brimmed hat to keep off the sun.

He joined Le Marr, who had a donkey on a rope, on the faint path leading inland. No islander ever showed any interest in the passing of time, an hour more or less made little difference to their plans. But there was something in Le Marr's attitude that suggested he was eager to be on his way.

The heat increased, and Griff did not relish the thought of emerging from the shade to the open country about the shallow salt lake, where the flamingos fished and water birds were thick. Their trail wound through the type of jungle peculiar to San Isadore, a matted growth of tangled thorn trees and stunted bush. Now and again Le Marr paused with an unerring sense to scrape loam and brown leaf mould out of hollows, allowing the murky liquid to gather so that the donkey could suck at it noisily, easing the tongue that lolled, foam-flecked, from its mouth.

They came out at last on what Griff considered was one of the weirdest of all the island features—a hard floor of gray rock. The hoofs of the donkey, the tread of his own heavy shoes, even of Le Marr's hide sandals, caused low booming sounds. San Isadore was in reality a vast stone sponge, eaten into, channeled under, by the sea. This flooring was hollow, probably covering some vast cave or series of caves in which the sea washed. Loose slabs were piled here and there, and these, Griff knew from earlier experiments, gave off the sound of bells. To cross the strip was to tread from key to key on some giant piano.

And always, the drift of salt, the soil that was 90 per cent shells and the remainders of sea life. Above them wheeled flamingos in formation. A wild clatter of sound heralded the retreat of some wild donkeys across the hollow rock.

Le Marr plodded on around the edge of one of the sea pools, deep, blue, leading down to unplumbed depths with some outlet to the ocean. Such wells rose and fell with the tides, and Griff saw anemones and scarlet sponges growing along its sides. Doubtless other marine life lurked in the underwater, but it was also a good place to meet a moray eel.

The islander paused. This was one of the big wells, a good sixty feet in diameter. Le Marr stared into it with the same measuring intentness with which he had regarded the surf pool on the cliff. After a long moment of silence he asked a question.

"Could you dive down there? Like you do by the reef?"

"I suppose so. But it might be dangerous—"

"Some day—maybe you have to," was the reply. Le Marr went on, across a dried-up lake, where the bodies of tiny fish, desiccated because of the high salt contents, now made a silver carpet of scales. They did not proceed to the flamingo lake but cut over to come out on San Isadore's nearest approach to a real headland.

Beneath them was a knife-sharp valley, which might have been on another planet. Some hurricane of the past had scoured brain coral, massive chunks of it, free from the sea floor, the surf tossing it high enough against the outer cliff for it to be seized by the wind and brought over that obstruction to lie here, a weird monument to the horrors of wind and water unleashed.

The mass of boulders and coral were embedded in sand, and that sand was patterned by the tracks of countless wild pigs. This appeared to be one of their favorite hiding places. But Le Marr was interested in neither the evidence of the forgotten storm nor the prospects of good hunting. Instead he pointed seaward, as if he sighted there something he had been waiting to see.

And Griff was completely surprised when his gaze followed the line indicated by the other's brown finger.

The *Island Queen* linked them with Santa Maria. There was also a Dutch freighter, which called at widely spaced intervals. But this ship, coming to anchorage now beyond the ruffle of the reef, was neither island sloop nor small freighter.

"Mons come—" Le Marr's voice held a hint of satisfaction as if some prophecy of his own was about to be fulfilled.

"But who—why? And why not come to Carterstown? There's no landing point here."

"These mons—they make their own landin' place. They think they can move the world. Maybe so—maybe no."

Griff watched the amazing activity beyond the reef with a faint feeling that somewhere he had seen its like before. Surely that wasn't a boat they were slinging over the side of the ship—Yet when it hit the water, it did not sink, and the men aboard it, hardly distinguishable dots at this distance, flung off the slings and started the queer craft. It made straight for the reef, and then, turtle-like, it actually crawled through the pounding surf, up over the exposed coral ridge, and slid into the quieter waters of the lagoon, heading for the shore as if those who piloted it did, indeed, have no fears of their mastery over both water and land. And reading the insignia painted on the crawler, Griff understood a little of their confidence. They had built and wrecked around the globe in their time and done it well. But what were Seabees—American Seabees—doing on San Isadore?

Within three days the first foundations of the mysterious buildings of Base Hush-Hush were being erected. The men from the north with their wealth of machines and supplies worked feverishly around the clock, in the daytime under the torrid sun, at night under floodlights. But as far as the islanders were concerned, what they slaved to create remained a puzzle. The commander had come armed with papers for the resident commissioner, and guards patrolled the area the newcomers had selected, keeping all sight-seers away.

Naturally wild rumors circulated. Griff, lounging on the deck of the *Island Queen*, heard a collection of the choicest from Rob Fletcher. As usual the islander's long face mirrored a worried expression, and his hand fondled the small bag hanging on a cord against his bare chest.

"They done bring the bomb—the big bomb. An' they's gonna bust it right here."

Griff shook his head. "They're working too hard to build whatever it is to smash it with an atom bomb."

Chris came along the deck and dropped down beside the other

two. He lighted one of the coarse island cigarettes, and the blue smoke floated lazily on the air. Rob turned to him.

"They's gonna bust the big bomb right here!"

But Chris also disagreed with that. "No bomb, I think. Maybeso make place to hide sub—"

Griff sat up. Now that made sense. A sub base! But why all the hurry? Those Seabees were putting to it as if they had a time limit imposed.

He caught sight of the dingy, with Angus Murdock aboard, headed for the *Queen*. And when the captain came over the rail, his good-humored face was very serious.

"Chris, you been harkin' to the wireless?"

Waite got up. "Bad news, Cap'n?"

Murdock took off his peaked uniform cap and rubbed the back of his hand across his forehead.

"They's another ship amissin'—the *Rufus G.*—down at Nassau. They got the government cutter out cruisin' 'round. She had the governor's aide 'board her."

"So?" Chris moved toward the radio cubby. "I done listened to all the talk 'bout the big no-war meetin'. Seems like every time they talk like that things gets worser. But they didn't say nothin' 'bout the *Rufus G.*"

"Just come on the wireless at the Government House ashore." Murdock waved an explanatory hand. "Do you think these here Navy mons are buildin' a place for subs?" he asked Griff. "They gonna send out subs to hunt down this thing what gits the mons on the ships?"

"I don't know any more about that than you do, Cap'n," Griff was forced to admit.

"They's sure in a hurry 'bout whatever they do," Murdock commented. "An' they's not lettin' any mon see what they do—They warned Mosely to git outta there when he went out for the conch."

Rob roused at that. "How come they think they can say where a mon do fish? The best conch, they lie 'long there. They ain't *own* this here water!"

"They's got 'em a paper from the government—say they do what they want. They don't care water good for the conch. Why, they cut right through the reef—change all that part of island. Ain't never seen nothin' like that before—" Murdock gazed toward the scene of activity now hidden from the *Island Queen* by miles of curving and recurving shore line, for the site of Base Hush-Hush was the northern tip of San Isadore.

So far, save for the bafflement and irritation of some conch fishermen and the unrewarded curiosity of the islanders at large, a wonderment at the energy of the northerners and speculations concerning their purpose on San Isadore were the substance of the comments Griff overheard. Le Marr, after his initial sight of the task force, had withdrawn to some hidey hole of his own and had not been seen. And the Gunston project had had no reason to contact the Naval party, the doctor and Hughes being intent on the problem of the "sea serpent" as represented by the bones and remains over which they labored in the laboratory.

The *Island Queen* cleared for her scheduled run to Santa Maria with the mystery still unsolved. And it was that evening that Project Sea Serpent had its first brush with the Navy. It was time for the sample testing along the reef, and Hughes went out in the small motor launch, Griff ready with diving equipment. They took four or five samples at selected sites, and then Hughes pointed the course farther north to a section where the reef broke, near the promontory where the carcass of the monster had lodged.

Griff shrugged on the tank, made sure of the easily released clasp of his weight belt, the presence of his wrist depth gauge and watch.

"Get a sea fan," Hughes told him, "and water samples. Three or four small plants ought to be enough. Then we'll take another about a mile or so to the north—"

But as Griff started to descend the small diving ladder, they were both startled by the ear-piercing shriek of a siren. On a course headed straight for them was a neddle-slim cutter, slicing through the waves at a dazzling speed. With masterly seamanship it pulled up in a circle about the project launch while one of the three men on board called across, "This is closed territory. Do your fishing down-reef!"

Hughes stood up, and there was a snap to his voice as he answered, "No closed territory for our work. We're from the Gunston laboratory—Project 914-5. Now get out before you stir up the stuff we're collecting—"

"Don't know anything about your project," the other replied

brusquely. "You get out and stay out—this is a security order. Can't you get that through your thick heads? We have to run you blasted fishermen off the lot every time we turn around—"

"We represent Project 914-5," Hughes repeated. "Our orders are to prospect this reef. We'll take this up with your superiors—"

"Do!" The other sounded as if he hoped that they would. "We have *our* orders—they're to keep all unauthorized persons out of this area. Now get going, and make it snappy!"

Griff climbed back in the outboard and took off the air tank. Hughes raised their anchor line. And the Navy launch continued to circle them, escorting them out of the disputed area of lagoon. Hughes headed back to the lab anchorage, making no comment to Griff, but every line of his stiff shoulders, his set mouth, suggested his inward seething. In Hughes's estimation the project was second to nothing in importance, and Griff guessed that he now lived to make that clear to the interlopers from the base.

He left Griff to gather the equipment and headed up the cliff path at a pace which seemed excessive in that heat. Griff wondered what his father's reaction would be. But he was not to learn then. Both his elders remained in the laboratory, and he ate alone, turning his attention to the collection of shells he had been driven by boredom into assembling.

Afterwards he wandered out to the surf pool. A carpet of empty crab shells in one corner testified to the skill and appetite of the newest settler therein. And he watched the octopus feast now, marveling at the neatness and dispatch with which the cephalopod acted. A crab snared in the tentacles was turned bottom-side-up as one might hold a soup plate, while the miniature parrot beak of the captor pierced the soft lower shell and the file tongue inside that beak rasped out the contents.

The patch of bitter aloe blossoms by the path had attracted a flock of humming birds, and they sipped and hung fearlessly almost within Griff's grasp. It was close to sunset, and the sun was a vivid cherry-red.

There was a flurry in the pool as the octopus made another kill. But it seemed to the spectator that those black beads of eyes were now staring up over the body of its victim, straight at him—as if the new master of the pool had some plan of its own—some plan into which it was fitting the man who could crush it in one hand. As that fantasy crossed Griff's mind, he shivered. The spray borne inland by the wind, flicking his shirt and salty on his lips, was for the moment icy cold.

"Hello there!"

Griff got to his feet. There was a tall man on the cliff path, a man now outlined by the odd flash of greenish light that was the island phenomenon at the setting of each sun. His white shirt and slacks were vivid, but his face under the shadow of an officer's cap was partly concealed.

"Dr. Gunston here?"

"He's in the lab."

"Tell him Breck Murray's here—Commander Breck Murray. I'm from the base—"

"So you finally got here, did you?" That was Hughes. He was standing belligerently on the path leading to the building. "What's your explanation for this afternoon?"

"Dr. Gunston—?"

"I'm Hughes, his assistant. Dr. Gunston is occupied."

The commander made as if to turn. "When he's free, he can find me at the base—" His retort was pointed.

"Who's there?" Dr. Gunston called through the dusk. The sky above them was now gray, deepening to the purple of the quick-falling tropical twilight. "Commander Murray? Your people said you would get in touch with me. Come in, sir—"

Hughes stepped aside, and Griff knew he was not pleased. But both of them followed the other two men inside.

Chapter Four
COOPERATION—ENFORCED

The harsh light of electricity, which always seemed alien to the houses of San Isadore, drew lines in Dr. Gunston's face, pointed up Hughes's irritated twist of mouth, highlighted the creases about the outer corners of Commander Murray's eyes. His peaked cap had been thrown on the small table; his long legs were stretched out before him. He should have been at ease, but he wasn't as he turned his tall glass with nervous little jerks. However, as he looked at the doctor, his expression was faintly amused.

"I assure you, Dr. Gunston, that we were not landed here just to provide difficulties for Project 914-5. In fact, three months ago I was peacefully engaged in erasing a few hills preparatory to building a dam out in Arizona. Then they grabbed me back by my reserve commission, gave me a briefing, and sent me down here to do my worst. You don't argue with top brass—" For a second his amusement flickered out, and a hint of other emotion took its place. "Understand that you haven't spent much time back in the States recently, Doctor." He took a sip from his glass.

In contrast to the commander's controlled tension, Dr. Gunston appeared as relaxed as one of the islanders.

"I've been in the East Indies for the past five years. And I gather that while we were not informed about you, you know a great deal about us—?"

"Security can probably tell you right now how many grains of sand lie down on the beach!" That exploded from Murray with a force that appeared to have nothing to do with the subject. "Well,

Doctor, while you were back of beyond, a lot of things have changed stateside. The race is nearing the finish line." He stared ahead of him at the wall, and the muscles about his mouth tightened visibly. "We're running it too fine, much too fine—"

"War?" It was Hughes who asked that. Dr. Gunston frowned and shifted uneasily in his chair.

"We can pray not. But it's getting close—too close!"

"They're meeting in Geneva tomorrow—the Peace Conference—" Dr. Gunston's protest was eager.

Murray laughed, and there was no amusement in that sound. "How many peace conferences have they had in the past twenty years? And has any one of them led to as much as laying down a single gun? Though guns are outmoded now!"

"This base—you seem to be working against time here—"

Murray put down his glass, and the click of the crystal against the wood of the table was unduly loud.

"I think our time is running out fast, gentlemen, very fast. But there is nothing we here can do to alter that. We have our own problems." He achieved the light touch once more. "As you have pointed out, it is necessary to your work that you have samples from along the reef, even in the now restricted area. Gentlemen, as far as I am concerned you can cart off the whole blasted reef piece by piece if you wish. But"—he was openly smiling now—"very unfortunately I do not have the final word on the subject!"

Hughes bristled. "I understood that you commanded here—"

"One would think so, wouldn't one?" the question was sardonic. "But in the new setup, we have our little problems, too. And a major one is Lieutenant Charles Holmes—our security officer. Security has declared Base Hush-Hush to be strictly that, and I can do nothing about it. You've already protested to *your* high brass—" He paused and glanced at Dr. Gunston, who nodded. "Well, now it depends upon just how much weight they can throw about in certain circles stateside. I'll send in my report, but I must be frank with you. My word against Holmes's orders doesn't weigh at all. However, there is one thing I can do—ask you to give Mr. Holmes a demonstration—"

"Demonstration?" Hughes was wary.

"Who does most of your diving?"

Dr. Gunston answered that. "Griff does the ordinary work. Hughes and I take over if we have to see something for ourselves."

"Suppose I detail Holmes and Bert Casey—he's one of my own men, an underwater demolition expert I brought on this job—to go out with you tomorrow and watch how you do your stuff? Then Holmes will see for himself that you are working on a project, that you are experts. I'll make him file a report of all this to his department. It may help—you can never tell."

Surprisingly Hughes laughed. "And it gets Holmes out of your hair for a while—"

Murray grinned. "I won't answer that. But is it a deal?"

Dr. Gunston answered. "We're merely doing some routine sampling; it may be dull. And your men aren't to dive unless we say so—indiscriminate exploration might upset our observations—"

"I don't think you could get Holmes under water. And Casey'll abide by your orders. Shall I send them around? Believe me, Dr. Gunston, if you want to make a stiff protest through channels, I'll not be upset. This is not my decree. By the way—" he got to his feet and picked up his cap, but still lingered—"know anything about the country inland? I have the official charts and the material the briefing crowd assembled, and if what they say is true, this place is a weirdie. Any of the native sons willing to help us explore?"

"You'd better contact Dobrey Le Marr on that. If there is anything to know about the interior, he has it filed away in his brain."

"Native?"

Hughes snorted. "Very much so. He's the local witch doctor!"

A shade of annoyance shadowed Dr. Gunston's face. "Le Marr is an unusual man. Yes, he's a native and practices what the islanders recognize as medicine—of a sort. But if you can establish a friendly relationship with him, you might discover it to be to your advantage, Commander."

When Murray had gone, Dr. Gunston continued to sit, sucking at his empty pipe. Hughes broke the silence first.

"So we put on a show for the Navy?"

The doctor smiled wryly. "Murray's laid his cards on the table. I don't think he likes his orders any better than we do. Yes, we'll give a demonstration for the Navy. But not just our usual job. How about it, Griff?" For the first time he spoke to his son. "You've been haunting the reef. Where can we really show them something of interest?"

"According to Chris there's a stretch of reef to the northeast where there's an octopi town—big collection of them. I was going to take a look at it anyway. Think that might be impressive enough?"

"Octopi—" Dr. Gunston considered the point. "You haven't dived there before?"

"I haven't. Chris did—straight skin diving without a lung. Take it with a lung and we might get some good camera shots—"

"All right. Make it this octopi paradise and do just that—take the movie camera—"

They made ready in the early morning of the next day, taking diving apparatus enough for three in case their guests decided to share in the exploration. And the Navy cutter was on time, coming smartly in to drop two passengers. The shorter of the two cast a knowing eye over the equipment Griff was carefully stowing in place and, without a word, stepped down into the motorboat to help him with the ease of long familiarity with such gear.

"Bert Casey," he introduced himself casually. "You've got some good stuff here." He handled the tanks with open approval.

"All the latest. I'm Griff Gunston."

"Pleased to meet you, kid. You the regular diver?"

"I do a lot of it. My father's the real expert, though."

"Don't see any harpoon or spear gun—"

"We don't hunt," Griff returned a little shortly. He liked to stalk with a camera only.

"Nothing you have to worry about? No sharks?"

Griff laughed. "That shark boogie has been pretty well exploded. As long as you aren't killing fish and there's no blood in the water, you're safe nine times out of ten. Barracuda's worse. But if you really want to make trouble for yourself, plant a foot on a sea urchin—or get tangled up with a Portuguese man-of-war! For the rest—" he patted the knife in his sheath, its cork hilt in easy reach of his hand—"moray's bad, but you have to tickle them up before they jump you—keep an eye out for their heads sticking out of rock crevices—"

Hughes came down the wharf carrying the under-seas camera, paused at the sight of the other officer standing there, and then nodded stiffly.

"Lieutenant Holmes," the other introduced himself. "You are in charge?"

A smothered noise came from Casey. It sounded suspiciously like a snort. The lieutenant, it was very apparent, desired neither to win friends nor to influence people.

As abruptly, Hughes replied, "I'm Frank Hughes, assistant to Dr. Gunston. This is his son, Griffith."

The lieutenant favored Griff with a disapproving stare, and he realized that in his trunks and burned brown by the sun, Holmes had taken him to be an islander and so not worthy of notice.

"All ready, Griff." Hughes passed the officer to hand down the camera, and his voice was far more cordial than usual. In face of a common enemy Hughes was closing ranks. He took his place at the motor, leaving Holmes to get aboard by himself, and they headed out into the bay without another word.

Casey looked about him with frank curiosity. "Lots of color," he commented to Griff.

"You've dived here?"

"Not yet." Casey pushed the cap with its Lieutenant, J. G., insignia to the back of his bullet head. "I've been down mostly in the north. During World War II I was a demolition man. That's how I met the skipper—he was running a show in Alaska. But that was frogman stuff, and we wore suits—"

"I understand that your project is connected with the collection of marine specimens." Holmes cut across Casey's reminiscences.

"Collecting and observation." Hughes was curt.

"What bearings, Griff?"

Griff squinted back at the curve of the shore. "Clear around the bay, Frank. It's near Finger Cay—opposite the mangrove swamp—from what Chris said."

White water boiled in their wake. A line of flamingos etched across the sky, and they passed one of the weed-grown conch boats wallowing along, exchanging hails with the island fisherman.

"What do they get out here?" Casey wanted to know.

"Conch. Sometimes a pearl or two," Griff answered.

"No kidding! I didn't know that they did pearl-diving here—"

"Conch pearls. They're supposed to be turned in to the commissioner when they're found. But precious few are. There's not much market for them—they're colored, apricot, lavender, rose, and mostly baroque. But they are pretty. And conch meat, dried, sells over at Santa Maria. It's used to make fertilizer, I believe."

"Deep water out there?" Casey pointed to the darker hue beyond the reef.

"Dips to two thousand fathoms or more." Hughes answered that. "We haven't tried there; our kind of diving doesn't reach such distances."

"There's Finger!" Griff hailed their landmark. The tiny island, hardly above sea level, was unique. There were three wind-worn palms on one end, but the major portion of the land mass supported a single tree—only, what a tree! A mangrove that had several hundred separate trunks, stemming from some thousands of kneed roots on a platform well above the wash of intruding waves. And, above, the branches and leaves had entangled in a canopy of dark green leaves, covering well over an acre. Bobbing in the water at the shore line were drifting coconuts and another spear-pointed mangrove seed trying for a rooting, to increase the holding of land over sea.

Hughes sent them between the island and the mainland and brought them to anchor behind the reef, while Griff got into his diving kit. He turned to ask Holmes politely: "Care to go down, Lieutenant?"

"Perhaps later." Holmes was making a point of noninterest, preserving the attitude of one carrying out boring orders.

"You, Mr. Casey?"

"Yes, sir!" The other was already stripping off his shirt. Holmes looked as if he might protest, but he remained silent on that point if not on another.

"What is your research here?" He spoke to Hughes, who was rigging the over side glass through which those in the boat could watch activity below.

"Octopi settlement—or an alleged octopi settlement."

Casey paused in the process of shucking his slacks. "Octopi?"

Griff laughed. "Not dangerous at all—and these are small ones. Most of the stories about them are in the same class with shark tales—only more so. They're intelligent after their own fashion and don't go around picking fights. You let them alone, and they won't even give you the ink treatment."

He slipped his mask into place, made sure of his air, and climbed down the short diving ladder, shivering a little as the chill of the sea hit his sun-warmed skin. Then, instantly, he was in another world. Above him was the bottom of the boat, festooned with feathery green stuff. Golden spears of sun struck down to be swallowed up by endless blue. The distance became hazy, overspread with an almost pearl luster. For perhaps a little more than fifty feet he could see clearly, the fantastic forest of yellow coral trees into which he was descending standing out with the sharp relief of a silhouette. Sea fans, brilliant blood-colored sponges, and then the dark caves in between. And always the flights of gemmed fish in brilliant array of every shade and color. He judged his distance and took off in one of the slow-motion bounds, which cleared a hedge of purple sea plumes. The flooring, which, from above, had looked so smooth and flat, was in reality a hillside, jagged and torn with crevices and outcrops, pitted with hidey holes and caves, each of which, Griff knew from his past experience, housed a varied collection of inhabitants. He jerked his hand back from a careless grip on a pinnacle of smooth, brownish coral, which stung hotly.

Drifting, he made a feather-soft landing some twenty feet from the point where he had taken off. But in doing so, he dislodged a growth of anemone, and within seconds he was the core of a whirling pool of fish, all feeding or attempting to feed on the crushed and drying flower-animals. A flounder crawled on a patch of white sand and dug in, its eyes rising on stalks above its chosen ambush.

As usual Griff had to drag his attention back to the job on hand. He progressed along the line of sea fans, watching for the telltale piles of shells, which marked octopi dwellings. And with mounting excitement he saw that Chris had been right—this section of reef housed more of the cephalopods than he had ever seen gathered together before. He jerked the signal line for the camera to be lowered.

A weird shadowy form moved toward him with deceptive slowness, and the sea-monster head turned so that he recognized Casey. He reached out to draw the other down beside him and indicated the crevices. Whether the other understood or not, he could not tell. But the Navy diver helped him steer the camera around to face that stretch of wall. Now if he could just get one or more of the creatures out of their holes to put on a real show—

He caught the sign of an octopus at home, the end of a tentacle issuing from a crevice, a slit in the porous rock, which seemed too narrow to house a creature of the size he knew lurked there. Would a current of water set up by waving hands entice the things out of hiding? He flipped tentatively in the direction of the nearest, and the result was spectacular.

Accustomed to octopi that were retiring, who fled from man rather than courted him, Griff was not prepared for the sudden eruption of some five of the species, who oozed out of their homes and appeared to be intelligently waiting for him to declare his intentions. Advancing with their arms pointing to the bottom, the ends curved slightly, their head-bodies erect, they presented the curious aspect of walking on tiptoe. And that concentrated move was so unlike the habits of their kind that he gaped at them for a long moment while Casey withdrew with a quick flip of his fins.

A five-foot, sucker-adorned arm curled lazily through the water as if its owner wished to drag to it this out-land monster for a closer inspection. Griff, alert to an opportunity he had never had before, was busy with the camera. Five—no, six—seven—he counted as he watched a new big-eyed dome crawl across an outcrop of brain coral, shooing before it a wave of parrot fish.

An azure Beau-Gregory, jealous of its homestead rights as always, flashed down to defend its chosen section, but, baffled by the cephalopod, merely darted about the bulbous head, which was also body, as a bee might dart about a bear. Griff worked feverishly, intent upon filming the scene. But when a hand fell on his shoulder, urging him back, he became aware of something else, that he now floated in a ring of solemn mollusks, the center of attention for a whole circle of dark, expressionless eyes. And for the first time, his belief in the relative harmlessness of octopi was shaken. In all his observation, in all his reading, he had never seen nor heard of any such move on the part of their species. It was as if some strange being from another planet had landed on San Isadore and the natives had ringed the new arrival around, not menacingly—as yet—but curiously, intent on discovering just what the thing was and why it had come to disturb their peace.

Casey was tugging at his weight belt, signaling with exaggerated jerks of his arm for a quick retreat. But Griff, though uneasy, was intrigued. He knew that an octopus could move fast, but he was also sure that it was possible to escape that steadily narrowing circle when he wished to. He was still busy with the camera, getting what he hoped was a clear and detailed shot of the scene.

A sharp warning tug on his signal cord broke his absorption at last. No diver dared ignore such a summons. He was being paged from above. Those three stiff pulls meant to surface. Casey was already spiraling up, the splashing of his flippers stirring the floating plumes. Reluctantly Griff released the camera and followed. Holding onto the lowest rung of the boarding ladder, he waited for Casey to precede him out of the water.

"What is it—?" he pushed up his face mask and demanded in annoyance. Then he heard the beat of a motor. Around the mangrove-covered cay and straight for their anchor launch came the Navy cutter. It couldn't be another warn-off. They weren't in the disputed territory. And what was his father doing in that cutter?

"Hughes, Griff." As the Navy craft came alongside Dr. Gunston called to them. "Take a tow—we're needed!"

They retrieved the camera, stowed their gear temporarily, and took up anchor to accept a towline.

"What's the matter, sir?" Hughes asked for them all.

"Diver in trouble at the base. I don't know the particulars, but apparently Murray believes we can help. And it's a rush job."

It was Lieutenant Holmes who protested. "That's restricted territory, Doctor. You haven't been cleared to enter it—"

Dr. Gunston favored him with a grim stare. "I gather that there's a life in danger, Lieutenant. Your commanding officer has asked for our assistance, and he's going to get it."

Holmes did not answer as they trailed along behind the cutter. But Griff had an idea that he would not accept the rebuff so easily and was planning to take steps of his own. In the meantime, since diving would probably be required, Griff knelt to check his apparatus carefully.

Chapter Five
DEPTH SCOUT

The muddle of clashing machinery and visibly rising foundations, which marked the site of Base Hush-Hush, meant little or nothing to Griff. There was activity unleashed over a wide section of territory where the cliff wall had been graded down, where the whole face of San Isadore was in the process of being drastically altered. And not for the better was Griff's secret thought.

However, the cutter did not point in toward this anthill of action but swept on farther north, coming in to a wasteland Griff had never explored and which even the islanders avoided, there being nothing to draw them to the desert of curdled rock and salty sand.

Here, at some time in the past, a large slice of cliff had broken loose, to fall outward, forming a roughly surfaced natural wharf, over the lip of which spray was flung in rainbow bubbles. It was probably almost beneath the surface at high tide, Griff judged by the lengths of vivid yellow sea moss that clung to it in ragged patches.

Breck Murray was easy to note among the three men who stood there awaiting the cutter and its tow. His khaki shirt was plastered to him by the spray, and his stance suggested impatience. Griff remained in the laboratory launch, content to await developments, but Casey and Holmes went ashore.

Hughes stared down into the water at the edge of the rocks.

"Not too good a place for a dive—"

Griff chose to believe that was addressed to him. "Have to take it easy," he agreed. "This surf could smash you before you got under."

Hughes leaned back, studying the broken cliffs with narrowed eyes. The rock was pitted and creviced all the way along. There could be innumerable caves and crannies below as well as above. A diver swept into one of those by some freak of current might well find himself in dangerous difficulties. This was no place to dive alone, nor without all the safety precautions possible.

"What are they trying to do, anyway?" Hughes mused. "They couldn't have picked out a nastier place to work."

"Frank—Griff—" They both turned at Dr. Gunston's call and scrambled over the greasy footing of slimy waterweed to the rocky platform.

"What about it?" The doctor motioned along the edge of the surf.

Hughes was scowling. "No place to play the fool. Not a place to dive unless you are pushed into it." He gave his verdict frankly. "Most of it is an out-and-out death trap—"

Now Murray was frowning, too. "All right. We understand that. Only there's a job to be done here. Jim Lasalles, my expert, is down under there somewhere and"—he looked at his watch—"time's about run out for him. Those cylinders hold just so much air, remember? How can we work to get him out?"

Dr. Gunston paced closely along the edge of the natural wharf, studying the boil of the waves. "You know where he went in—but he may be half a mile from this point now. We can at least take a closer look." His fingers were busy with the buttons on his shirt as he spoke.

"Chief—let me go down!" Hughes was at his side, while Griff simply slid back into the launch and reached for a tank harness.

But the doctor shook his head firmly. "I'll do it, Frank. After all, I've had the most experience—and I've had time to learn my way around down there. You'll keep a line on me, I promise that!"

Griff, silently rebelling, was forced to accept that ruling. He strapped on his father's weight belt, made sure that watch and depth gauge were safely in place, testing each fastening. But when he turned to pick up the tank, he discovered that Casey, too, was making preparations to enter the water. And almost side by side, the two used the same trick of an expert diver, catching the exact moment to slide into an advancing comber. Frank was crouched over the water glass, watching their descent, while Griff stood with Murray, paying out the lifelines, feeling the pull with sensitive fingers, the pull that meant all was right below.

Seconds seemed hours long during that period of waiting. Griff would gladly have surrendered his hope of returning to the States to be making that dive himself. It was easier to battle the actual dangers lurking along the broken shore line than to sweat it out up here.

"Sharks—" He caught the mumble from one of the attendant Seabees.

There was little to fear from sharks here. But morays—this was just the type of coast line to attract the deadly eels. And barracudas had been sighted in island waters from time to time. Resolutely Griff tried to curb his imagination. He had dived without fear for himself, but now he discovered it was very easy to know anxiety for another.

"Can't see him!" Frank's head lifted from his glass watch.

Griff's grasp on the signal line tightened. He must have given it a noticeable twitch, for a reassuring tug was telegraphed back.

"He signals 'all right'!"

"Where's Casey?" Murray demanded.

"Working his way around the point, sir." The Seabee pointed north. "Must be rugged down there, he's taking it mighty easy—"

Disaster struck so suddenly that for a moment they did not really understand what had happened. A low swell of water, which did not seem alarming from their viewpoint, hit the rocks, dashing up with a volume of spray that betrayed its force. And in that moment the line spun between Griff's fingers, burning flesh. Instinctively his grasp on it tightened, but he had followed it almost knee-high into the water by then.

"Hughes!" He cried the warning. What was happening down there? His father must have been swept away. Griff pulled the cord, praying for the return signal. But the line was now stiff, as if it were hooked upon some projection of rock. And he dared not exert any more pull for fear it would snap.

A nightmare span of time followed. Casey was recalled to trace Dr. Gunston's line as Hughes made ready to dive. And then came the paralyzing answer. The cord was fouled, right enough, about a sharp spur of coral even as Griff had dreaded. And beyond drifted a frayed end. His father might have been sucked into any one of half a hundred cracks and caves, caught there unable to win free again.

Griff fought panic. The island was a porous sponge, carved out below sea level. And a cave big enough to admit the body of a diver might run back for some distance. There were the sea wells dotting the interior—they were fed through such breaks in the cliff wall. Here the combers would endanger a diver, give him a limited chance for search. But if a man might go down one of those pools—

"The wells!" He must have said that aloud, for Murray had spun to face him. But Griff was staring inland, trying to remember all he knew of the sea pools.

"You have an idea?" Murray pushed.

"The sea pools, inland—they have their outlets." He didn't want to explain too much, and he stopped before he had a chance to even try.

Murray was startled and then thoughtful. "There's a large one, about a quarter of a mile due west—"

Before he could elaborate, the head of a diver broke water, and Hughes climbed up the weedy verge. He shoved up his mask and squatted, panting, a pinched look about his nostrils.

"I think maybe I've got it—" But there was little exultation in his voice. It was plain he did not consider his news good. "Traced in from where the cord fouled. There's a cave there—reaches pretty far back. The chief may have been jammed in by that wave. I need a lamp—"

"We've got that." One of the Seabees produced an underwater lamp of the latest design. As he rigged it under Hughes's direction, Murray spoke again to Griff.

"About that pool—"

Griff leaned over the busy pair before him. "Frank, in which direction does that cave run?"

Hughes sat back on his heels, glancing from the surging waters to the cliff front. "From about there"—he indicated a point some hundred yards to the south—"west. It's pretty long, that's why I have to have the lamp—goes straight in."

Murray was obviously thinking. "Could be—just could be—" was his verdict.

Griff was willing to accept that. He waited until Hughes submerged once more, and then he assembled his own equipment from the lab launch. He'd probably need extra weight on his belt. With care he tested its latch, making sure it would release at a touch. Too many divers had been drowned because of faulty belts, and what he proposed to do was the trickiest bit of underwater work he had ever attempted.

"You've dived the inland pools?" Murray asked the question Griff dared not answer with the truth. As far as he knew, no one had ever invaded the mysterious depths of one of the sea wells, but that fact was not going to stop him now. He nodded, rather than spoke.

The blistering heat of the sun dried the last remaining drops of sea spray from Griff's half-naked body during that trek across the upper reaches of the cliff. One of the Seabees helped him with his equipment. They crossed a stretch of heated rock, found a gully running back in the general direction, and dropped thankfully into the thick white sand that drifted there. The well, when they finally came to its lip, was no different from the others Griff had seen. The deep blue surface, the scarlet sponges growing along its walls, seemed to add to the secret, closed-in quality, a quality the waters along the reef never had. To slide over into that and to allow oneself to spiral down through the liquid that appeared from above to be thicker, less like salt water, was going to be an ordeal.

And the reasoning behind Griff's recklessness was so flimsy a guess. Griff could not have explained it—had no wish to put into words his feeling that there *was* a connection between this deep sapphire well inland and the cave on the coast. He was going by hunch now, and a kind of inner stubbornness kept him to his decision. It was good that Murray believed he had done this before—no use asking for complications.

Griff inspected his equipment with the care of a veteran diver who knew only too well that a single slip or rash lack of examination might mean his life. The depth gauge was his special protection now. If the blue hole before him was too deep, he would have warning and be able to drop his weight belt and pull out in time.

But, even as one part of his mind thought that, he was looking about for a piece of coral of the right size to add to the weight about his middle. Holmes had followed carrying an underwater lamp, and Commander Murray dropped from his shoulder a coil of lifeline.

Griff slipped his feet into his flippers, made them fast. He shrugged into the tank straps, felt the weight of that precious supply of air settle into place like a knapsack, wriggling muscles until he was sure of the right balance. He wouldn't try a straight dive here;

instead, he used the lifeline to lower himself slowly into the water. The surface, warmed by the sun, was at blood temperature, but as the water closed over his head there came a chill.

He made the descent, using the line as a check. Someone with a good sense of timing was lowering the lamp at a speed almost equal to his own. And, as the murk around him deepened, he flashed it on. Fish swam here, came to gather in the beam, goggling in stupid bewilderment.

Another object came dangling down, and Griff identified a light fish spear. He used it to fend away from the broken surface of the wall, keeping a watch for a crevice or hole from which the flat, evil head of a moray might project.

Down, down—now he was in a twilight, which might have been more disturbing had he not had that experience of diving after nightfall. The ray of the lamp gave him an excellent picture of his surroundings, and it might keep at a distance the larger creatures of the deep.

A sea urchin clung to a ledge, its poisonous spines thrown into high relief by the light. Anemones, crabs, other life flowed, swam, crawled about him as he kicked his way down. Time ceased to have meaning as it always did under water. He would have said that he had been a half hour in the leisurely descent, when his water-protected watch registered only minutes.

Then he saw what he was searching for, what the hunch had told him did exist. But as he clung to the line, drifting, he swallowed, and a prickling chill, which was not born of the water, ran along his spine. Opposite him was a black hole, a hole into which the full light of the lamp beamed to show no inner wall. If this wasn't the entrance of the sea passage, it was more than just a cave.

Now he must enter that hole, swing along into the dark unknown, where he could be trapped, where a lifeline fouled about a rock, as his father's fouled in the sea, would not help him. But this was what he had come to find—and inwardly Griff knew that there was no returning.

He fastened the spear in his belt loop. Then he gave the agreed signal of the line. Unhooking the lamp from its cord, he flipped his way into the hole.

Ragged rock, sea things—He flinched from stinging coral, trying to watch for any unpleasant surprises, animal or vegetable, which might lurk there. The passage sloped downward, to Griff another proof that this was what he sought—it must drop to below coast level. He kept his attention on what lay ahead, tried not to remember that he was making his way down an enclosed vein in the rock. Now and again he gave a tug to the line. It was free, untrapped by the rocks.

Just as it was difficult to judge time under water, so did distance cease to register properly. Perspective under the surface was warped, and Griff could have been inches from what he saw ahead—or feet. But the steady, unfailing beam of the light showed him what obstructions to avoid. It was a journey that could not have been made in darkness—too many projections, and once a turn, which he negotiated with care.

Then, all at once, the walls of the tunnel fell away, and Griff swam out into open space. The sea? But it couldn't be! Beyond the path of the lamp was darkness. He flapped up until his head broke surface. Where in the world was this?

Treading water, he pulled up the lamp and swept it around. He was in a vast pool, and to the left were rocks with their tops above water. Griff made for these and clung there, one arm across a slimy surface in support. The lamp displayed a ledge a little above, and he pulled himself up on that.

Gingerly he pushed up his mask. There was air—but it bore an odd and disagreeable musky taint. The walls were glistening with weed to a point well above his head—they must be covered at high tide. He turned the light out over the surface. It centered on a rock some distance away.

"Helloooo—"

Griff started, almost lost his grip on the slippery ledge and went back into the water. That hail, distorted by the echoes that magnified and dehumanized it, was the last thing he had expected. Bracing himself against the wall, having taken the precaution of snapping down his mask again against an involuntary descent into the flood, he got to his feet and flashed the ray of the lamp in a slow crawl along the opposite wall of the cavern.

Then the light picked up and held a waving arm, found the head and shoulders of a weird, masked monster, who apparently could not move but lay on water-washed rocks.

Griff went into the water and swam, the light beam before him pinpointing that figure. Then he fetched up against the tiny rock island, and a hand closed with convulsive tightness about the wrist he lifted for a hold.

"Snap off that light!" Griff knew his father's voice, hoarse, low, and hurried, as if they were in some danger that could be drawn by that core of hard yellow radiance.

Griff pulled up on the islet and levered up his mask. They were crowded together in the dark, and he heard the click of metal against metal as his air tank struck against some part of Dr. Gunston's equipment. His father was breathing heavily, as if half-winded from some exertion.

"How did you get in?" The question came with queer pauses between words. "It's waiting out there in the other cave. If it hadn't had that poor devil to amuse it, *I* wouldn't have escaped—"

Griff felt a shudder pass through the body so close to his. He drew a deep breath of the tainted air. His father didn't sound hysterical, but there was an odd note in his voice.

"I took a chance on one of the inland pools. Just followed a hunch—"

"The wells!" Dr. Gunston was honestly surprised. "A back door. Then there *is* another way out of here! We don't have to pass it—"

"Pass what, sir?"

"The monster—the thing, whatever it is, that's laired up in the outer sea cave here. I was swept in by a wave. It was—busy—" his father's voice again slid up scale a tone or two—"with the Navy diver when I caught it in my lamp. Then the light drew it. I dived, dropped the lamp to the bottom to interest it, and came up in here. The Lord only knows where 'here' is! But there's no going back with that thing doing sentry—"

"A dupee—?" Griff used the only term he knew for the dead monster of the beach.

"I didn't get a good look at it. But it's something which has no right to be alive in this day and age! One of Le Marr's voodoo nightmares!"

"We can make it back to the pool," Griff said confidently. "The passage is fairly easy."

But to his surprise his father did not agree at once. There was a lengthy pause, and then Dr. Gunston spoke.

"I've a game leg—gave it a scrape on something when I dived to get away from the thing's rush."

Whether it was wise or not, Griff used the lamp, training the lowest wattage beam on his father. Across his thigh was a line of red dots, and about them the flesh was already puffing into ugly swelling. Griff could guess the agony of pain that must be knotting muscle and flesh. And that must be seen to at once! It could be the mark of any kind of wound from a coral scrape to breaks left by the poisonous spines of some fish.

"We'll get out!" From somewhere he found that confidence—making his voice sound firm even in his own unbelieving ears.

A length of the snapped life cord was still at his father's belt. With that linking them together, he should be able to win back up the vent to the well and safety. At least that was their only chance now.

Chapter Six
TOO LITTLE, MUCH TOO LATE

Years afterwards nightmare memories of that journey back up to the inland pool awoke Griff bathed in a cold sweat. Dr. Gunston, with iron endurance, had held on to consciousness. But for much of the trip back Griff was supporting a limp body. He dropped his own weighted belt, the spear, every bit of extra equipment he dared abandon.

A coral graze on his shoulder set blood to staining the water and brought a dryness to his mouth. What if that summoned the mysterious nightmare from which his father had fled—or any of the other carnivora that might lurk in the circle of day beyond the lamp? He could only force himself to swim at that steady pace which would mean their eventual salvation.

The tunnel walls opened out—he was in the well. And someone above had sense enough to rig a ladder over the lip of the rim. He clung with one hand to the rungs, supporting Dr. Gunston's weight with an arm that felt as if it were being pulled from its socket. A splash of water in his face—then the weight was gone. Hands, locked in his armpits, pulled him up. But it wasn't until he lay on a blanket on the sand, his face free from the mask, tank and flippers stripped from him, that Griff realized he had made it.

He sat up. "Dad?"

A Seabee grinned at him. "They're carting him down to the base—where Doc can get to work on him. He's got a bad leg—"

Griff pulled himself up. He knew just how bad that leg could be! And there was Hughes and Casey. If his father's story were true, any seaside diver might be in trouble. He had to get moving. But he was plowing heavy-footed through the sand as if weights were on each foot. A hand slipped under his arm.

"Go small, mon—" The soft slur of island speech brought his head up.

"Le Marr!"

There was something reassuring about the voodoo man. Griff had a queer feeling that alone of those around him now Le Marr could believe in that weird world beneath them, take at face value his father's report of the menace that had killed the Navy diver.

"Debble thing—" It was as if Le Marr read his mind. "Mon go in debble thing's house-hole—come out. You have the gris-gris in here." His long ivory finger tapped Griff lightly on the breast.

"There *is* something in there?"

Le Marr nodded, his face serious. "Debble thing."

"Has it been there long?"

The other answered in the negative. "Come lately. Sign—bad sign—"

They had crossed the sandy desert and were following a line of tracks back to the base.

"What kind of sign?"

Le Marr did not answer that. Instead he spoke over his shoulder to the Seabees trailing them with Griff's diving apparatus.

"Tell mons that dive—debble thing down there—"

"Sure, pop." The cheerful American voice rang loudly over the softer speech of San Isadore. "The commander's already passed the word to stop."

The glare of the sun and his own fatigue blurred his surroundings for Griff. He had a vague idea that he had been half-carried over the last section into the base, and only when pain pricked his upper arm did he come around. He was lying on an examination table while a medical corpsman cleaned and treated the coral graze.

"—you'll fly him out then?" Murray's deep voice came from the hall.

"It's a matter of time, Commander. Yes, I'd say his only chance was the mainland. Hooker can take a stretcher in the cabin, and I'll make the trip with him. Frankly—I've never seen anything like it. Some kind of poison and a very virulent one. It's amazing he's lasted this long. We've got to learn what it is before we have another case on our hands."

"All right. I'll alert Hooker. You want to leave at once?"

"As soon as it is humanly possible."

Who were they going to fly out? As the corpsman walked to the supply cupboard, Griff sat up.

"Hey, fella—"

The man turned, but Griff was already on his way to the door. He reached that vantage point just in time to see a stretcher being borne past. And his father's face, flushed and swollen, puffed eyes half-open but unseeing, his father's voice muttering in a thick, senseless whisper flashed before him. The corpsman had caught up with Griff and could not be shaken off when the younger Gunston tried to follow the stretcher down the corridor.

"Take it easy, kid. Doc's flying your old man up to the States—they'll be able to fix him up. We aren't equipped to handle it here. They'll have him under treatment in three—four hours. Lieutenant Hooker's a hot pilot and knows how to get speed out of that bus of his—"

So Griff had to watch the seaplane off, blinking as it disappeared into the bright blue of the afternoon sky. Hughes reached the landing stage just as the plane lifted.

"How is it with the chief?" Beneath his tan, his face was greenish white and drawn. There was a moment of silence, and it was Griff who replied, steadily enough:

"He got some scratches—"

"Poisoned?" Hughes demanded sharply, almost as if Griff had been responsible.

"Something new—at least Doc can't diagnose it," Murray cut in. "That's why he's flying him north. He needs an expert opinion."

"Something new," Hughes repeated savagely. "Yes—we're up against something new all right, Commander. Your man is gone, you know—"

Breck Murray's mouth set grimly. "So we pieced out from some things Dr. Gunston said. What did he tell you?" He rounded on Griff. "Or what did you see down there?"

Griff described the underground cave but added that all he knew about the menace that guarded the sea entrance was what his father had told him—that some unknown sea dweller had killed the Navy diver and that Dr. Gunston had only escaped from it by chance.

"And what did *you* see?" Murray swung now to Hughes.

"I got in far enough to spot the torch the chief dropped. Then it was caught up by something. I didn't get a good look at it—"

"Shark?" Murray hazarded.

Hughes replied to that with a firm negative. "I'd take my oath it's nothing we know. You heard of the thing that was found on the beach before your arrival?"

"Some garbled stuff about a sea serpent." Murray looked perplexed.

"Not a sea serpent in the snake sense," Hughes corrected. "But it was an aquatic mammal, large, unknown, and we still are trying to classify it—"

"Man-eater?"

"It was a flesh-eater, yes," Hughes admitted. "And it bears resemblance to the most recent reports of the so-called 'sea serpents' that have been sighted from ships."

"And now we've another of the things roosting down there in that cave!" the commander burst out. "It's liable to make things hot for any diver!"

"How can I tell what it will do?" Hughes shouted back. "We don't know anything about it. But it did get your diver this morning, and it attacked Dr. Gunston. I'd say you'd better get rid of it if you want to feel safe under water here. It may hunt only at night, keep under cover during the day. But we can't be sure of that—"

"What we need, skipper,"—Casey, looking as tired and drawn as Hughes, had come up to join them—"is a bomb planted down there."

"Maybe you're right. Look over our stuff, Casey, and see what we have which will be a good answer to a sea serpent—" Murray rubbed his hand wearily across his sweating face.

Griff sat down in the half-finished mess hall. The food, which had just been placed before him, was good—it smelled like home. But, though he hadn't eaten since early that morning, he did not pick up his fork. There was something wrong. The same hunch that had led him to venture into the inland pool was working. He could agree that they had no way of enticing the mysterious monster out of its cave, nor could they be sure that it *would* come out. There were sea dwellers content enough to remain in self-chosen prisons from which they never emerged, allowing the water currents to supply them at random with food. Perhaps Casey's suggestion was the only possible answer, and he was a demolition expert, used to such tricks under water.

Only Griff could not rid himself of a feeling of foreboding, a feeling that was not born of the worry connected with the plane beating its way north. They had had two radio reports in flight. Dr. Gunston was still holding his own, and as long as life remained they had hope.

"I will speak with the commander now—" The voice was soft over a core of iron. Griff glanced up to see Le Marr.

The islander was at ease, a man with a mission, and he manifestly was in no way influenced by Holmes's scowl and refusal.

"This is restricted territory. You'll be given an escort to the edge of the zone and then—you'll beat it!" But in spite of the authority of those words, there was uncertainty below them. Holmes had been briefed in the routine of his job, was zealous in its duties. But there were no regulations to cover the happenings of the past few hours. Nothing in security files taught a man to stand up to an unknown carnivore at the bottom of the sea, nor did it prepare one for tactfully handling a voodoo priest, the unofficial ruler of the island. Griff cut in.

"I think Commander Murray wants to see Le Marr."

"And that is the truth!" As if the mention of his name had been a conjure spell to summon him, Breck Murray materialized just within the doorway. "Glad to meet you, Le Marr." He held out his hand. "Yes, I know, Mr. Holmes, he hasn't been cleared by security. Le Marr, I'm told you know a lot about this island and what makes it tick. There's some sort of a wild thing down in that sea coast hole. It's taken my diver, and now Dr. Gunston's out of the picture, too. Have you any idea of what it is or how we can get it out of there?"

Dobrey Le Marr's ivory hands fluttered in a quick gesture. "This debble thing be new to the island, sir. It comes up from the deeps—"

"Why?" Murray demanded flatly.

"Who knows? Maybeso trouble there—I think that. But I know it not fo' true. Debble thing run from trouble; it 'fraid, it hungry. It find hidey hole an' wait. Pretty soon maybe it forget—it not like mon." He tapped his own chest. "Then maybeso it go—"

"Well," Murray shrugged. "We can't afford to sit it out. But you haven't hunted these things then?"

Le Marr shook his head.

"What killed that one found on the shore?" Holmes asked the question as though trying to force Le Marr into some damaging admission. Again Griff struck into the conversation. The circumstances, he thought, released him from the promise he had given his father.

"The Geiger said it was 'hot.' Maybe radiation got it."

He was amazed at the result of his perfectly truthful statement. Both of the officers froze, almost as if the thing they discussed had appeared in the center of the floor. Holmes opened his mouth and then closed it tightly. But Murray strode to the table and glared down at Griff.

"That the truth?"

"Ask Hughes. He discovered it during dissection. It was 'hot'—so's that plague scum—"

Murray ran both hands through his thick brush of hair and then glanced over his shoulder at Holmes. "D'you know that?"

"I have nothing to say," snapped the younger officer in return.

The commander bit off a forceful word. "That answers me." He was curbing his temper with a visible effort. "Maybe someday they'll give a man all the facts before—" He swallowed. "So this menace may be radioactive along with all the rest! That's pleasant. I guess Casey's answer is the only one."

"Bomb it out?" Griff's earlier uneasiness awoke as he saw Le Marr give a start.

"You put bomb down there, sir? That be bad thing—very bad thing!"

"Why?"

"Sea run under the land—far, far." Le Marr's hands moved in graphic motions. "You break that—land fall—into the sea."

"You've got a point. But we can't lie around here waiting for that thing to move out. We've got to get it out and fast! We're working against time—"

Out of the tail of his eye Griff saw Holmes make a warning gesture in a vain attempt to stop Breck Murray's explanation. But Griff, remembering a problem of his own and how he and Chris Waite had solved it, dared to interrupt once more.

"Look here, sir—could you rig some sort of small explosive which could be planted in bait. If we could get that thing to eat it—"

"Hmmm—" The commander stopped pacing. Even Le Marr looked thoughtful. "You tried something like that before?"

"Chris Waite, he's the mate of the *Island Queen*, and I got rid of a big moray in that way. We baited a hook and pulled the eel out of its hole—though we had to use a block and tackle to do it. We couldn't hope to drag *this* out of hiding, not if it is the size of the dead one we found on the beach. But supposing it was eating and a small charge blew up in its face—that ought to kill it."

They held a conference, Hughes, Casey, the commander, another demolition man, and Griff. A party went inland with rifles and returned before the hour was up with the rangy carcass of a wild pig. The scrawny frame now occupied the position of honor in the center of the table while Hughes examined the bristly corpse and asked questions of Casey and his second-in-command.

"We may be able to do it," was Hughes's verdict, "assuming that the thing doesn't like its dinner alive and kicking when it gets it and assuming that you can measure out a charge which will answer the purpose." He glanced out of the window to where evening shadows were purple-black and thick. "A lot of the big ones feed at sunset—"

Griff, remembering octopi activity, nodded at that. Now that they had made up their collective minds, he was eager to get into action. Anything was better than to sit in this half-finished building listening to the clatter of work without, waiting for the arrival of a messenger with a new radio report—

But there proved to be little that he could do except watch the evisceration of the corpse and the rigging therein of some complicated wiring and grenades dreamed up by the demolition people. Casey straightened up at last from the gory table with a tired ghost of a grin.

"That ought to do it, skipper." He spoke across the smelly board to Murray. "Just let the whatsis get its back teeth into that and whamo!"

They could not depend upon the sea to deliver their prize package. It must be introduced by hand into the ominous cave opening. And it was Casey who overrode all the others in his demand to be the one for that job.

Armed with a harpoon gun-spear, a lifeline fast to his harness, his face very sober behind his mask, he entered the combers and hung, one hand anchoring him to a rock, as his assistant gingerly lowered the bait into his reach.

With the pig bomb in hand he went under water. And those above had to depend upon the reports from Hughes and Murray, crouched by the water glass, as to his movements. Almost immediately he was beyond their point of vision, and they could only stand on the natural jetty, the spray soaking through their clothing as the dusk with its odd greenish glow gathered fast.

Griff's fingers were on the lifeline. He caught the signal and he shouted, "He's in the cave!"

The commander's hand fell heavily on his shoulder. Griff nursed the line, now taut, waiting for the second pull, which would mark Casey's escape. It was far too long in coming.

"What's Bert doing!" That was his superior officer, tossing away a half-smoked cigarette in order to light another with hands that shook a little, "Shoving its dinner right into the thing's teeth?"

"Now!" Griff caught the "mission accomplished" twitch.

Casey had better make it fast. If he had waited to see the bait seized, he might have waited far too long—for, in spite of all their care, the charge might be too strong and would bring the cliff down as Le Marr had warned. Yet the islander did not appear to heed his own warning. He was teetering back and forth on the wet rocks as intent upon seeing the end of the game as the rest of them.

Casey's head broke water. He swam for the rocks and found a reception committee scrambling down to lift him in. But before he made land, he thrust out his spear, a weird armored captive still wriggling upon it. Hughes automatically grabbed at that. Casey snapped up his mask and drew a deep breath.

"Did it take the bait?" demanded Murray.

Casey's usual lightheartedness was gone. "Something which was mighty hungry did, I didn't see it close—I didn't want to!"

Murray was watching his wrist watch, and now he counted aloud: "—five—six—seven—eight—nine—"

But he never reached "ten." Griff could not have told afterwards whether it was sound, or vibration, or both. There was a tremor, a muffled noise—

"That's it." Casey broke the hush.

"Look out!"

Holmes's shout brought them about to face the cliff wall. A section split off, crashed down into the swirling water. A wave licked knee-high about the men on the rocks. They waited for more. But nothing came, and then Murray gave an order.

"Get into the cutter—we'll take the sea route back."

Griff was crowded against Hughes. The other had out a pocket flash, examining the fish impaled on Casey's spear. It was a new variety to Griff, with a warty, thorned skin, an odd pugged face.

"What is it?"

Hughes replied with more than a little amazement coloring his tone. "Something which does not belong here. Scorpion fish—from the Barrier Reef. If this is what got the chief—" He stopped almost in mid-word. "Maybe we're too late. We're doing much too little, too late. Halfway around the world from where it belongs! Lord, who's mixing us up—or what is happening?"

Chapter Seven
THE *ISLAND QUEEN* DOES NOT REPLY

"You say it's a *what?*" Commander Murray regarded the ugly, spined body of Casey's capture with obvious distaste.

"It's a stonefish—a scorpion fish—We saw enough of them on the Pacific-Banda Sea project. They range from Polynesia to the Red Sea—"

"But not here?" Murray caught him up on that.

"Not known to be here," Hughes corrected cautiously. "But how can we make any definite statements? In 1954 they brought in a live Latimeria Chalumnae near the Comore Islands. And by rights the thing should have been dead more than a million years ago. It was a living fossil. In 1949 fish scales, as large as those from a tarpon, but from a totally unknown fish, were sold to a souvenir dealer in Tampa, Florida. And none of the experts in Washington could identify them. So there might be a whole colony of stonefish cruising about here—"

"They're deadly?" Casey surveyed his catch with open curiosity. "It made a run at the pig, that's why I speared it. Then I forgot about it—I was too interested in the other thing."

Commander Murray leaned back in his chair. "Which, luckily, we don't have to worry about now!"

Casey nodded confirmation. An hour after his exploit Hughes had insisted on making a night dive. He returned with the information that the entrance to the monster cave had been sealed by the landslip they had witnessed and that, living or dead, they need worry no more about attack from the unknown.

Griff stared at the stonefish dully. He knew that the poison from its spines was as vicious as cobra venom. If this was what had struck his father, he could only marvel that Dr. Gunston had survived. But Hughes had an answer to that also. Using a pencil he prodded the warty skin.

"This will be proof for Gongware—"

"Dr. Gongware?" Casey alone recognized the name. Hughes shot him a surprised glance.

"Yes. He's been working on anti-poison serums for divers on the pearl banks. The chief volunteered to play guinea pig. If he was attacked by this, it must have been Gongware's stuff which kept him alive—though it's been over a year since he was inoculated. You sent news about this to the States, Commander? It may give the doctors a lead in treatment."

Murray nodded and then yawned. Griff looked at his watch. It was close to midnight. But he didn't want to leave until they had some word. Holmes came in, blinking at the bright light.

"There's a row going on down island, sir," he announced.

Murray had echoed the word "row" when Griff stepped past the security officer to the door and out into the night. The flood lamps made a harsh white day for a little circle, and there was the clatter of machines to fill it. But some trick of the wind brought another sound, faint enough, but in its very faintness depressing. Griff had heard it before—but never in such volume.

"What is it?" Murray had followed him out.

"The voodoo drums, sir." Griff could feel that beat eating under his own skin. He knew that there were certain rhythms of those ritual drums that were not for the hearing of his race, that would twist and turn emotions to a pitch a paler-skinned northerner could not stand. And this was fast approaching that point. A Seabee near him halted a bulldozer to listen.

"I don't like it!" Breck Murray snapped. "Voodoo, eh?"

"The island brand. But I've never heard it like that before. Not since old Kristina died the week after I came here. She was the Mamaloi, the priestess, a kind of witch, I think. Most of the islanders were afraid of her. She cursed more than she cured—different from Le Marr. And they were drumming out her spirit so she wouldn't haunt them."

"What are they drumming out now?"

"It might be the cave monster, Commander. They considered that to be a dupee—a voodoo devil. Or—"

"It might be us? Le Marr hinted at something of that sort before he faded away this evening."

"Well, the islanders are a close-knit lot. A few of them—Le Marr, Captain Murdock of the *Queen* and his crew, the shopkeeper—have been off island and know more about the world. The rest of them—they are apt to be suspicious of any new thing. It's in their history. They came here as slaves, rebel-convicts, or pirates—fugitives from the law—and they have instinctive distrust for our brand of civilization. I'd listen to Le Marr, sir; he has more real power than the commissioner, though there're still some who follow the spirit of old Kristina and would like to return—"

"To the ways of the bad old days? Such as this for example?" Murray produced a tiny bag of brilliant scarlet calico. In the light of the working lamps it lay a dollop of blood in the hollow of his palm. "What is it?"

Griff did not touch it. "That's a gris-gris, and not a good one, I'd say, though I'm not a student of voodoo. A gris-gris—amulet—can work either for good or evil. A good one you carry as a luck charm for protection. And an evil one you plant on an enemy. Where did you find that, Commander?"

"Lying just within the door of my office."

"Take it back, put it down in the same place, and then get Le Marr to remove it for you," advised Griff.

"Using the right formula?" One of Murray's expressive eyebrows slid up.

"You lost a diver today. Every bit of bad luck you have from now on will be credited to voodoo, and the reputation of the one who made that gris-gris will grow accordingly. It could add up to bad trouble. Listen!"

The beat of those drums was steady, pulsing in time with one's blood, or pulling the blood into rhythm with it. Griff was breathing faster; he found it difficult to stand still. He wanted to be out of this place of light and machines—to run into the quiet dark where he could crouch and cover his ears in blissful silence. And yet that wind-borne sound pulled at him, as if to draw him across the island to its unknown source.

"We don't depend on native labor," Murray pointed out. "Our supplies are brought in from our own ships. I don't see that we have to worry about any trouble with the islanders."

Griff leaned back against a coral slab wall. Maybe the base didn't have to worry about ill will of the men of San Isadore. But he was sure that voodoo or no voodoo, if he were in trouble he would want Le Marr on his side of the barricade. Maybe the islander had no supernatural powers but he had something—something that even the scientist in Dr. Gunston had been forced to acknowledge. And Griff respected Dobrey Le Marr as a man of authority.

"Griff!" Hughes bore down upon him. His eyes were shining and his hands dropped on Griff's shoulders, whirling the slighter and younger man around with him in a circling that had nothing to do with the distant drum, an outburst as foreign to the assistant's usually staid control as Apache war paint.

"They've got it under control! The chief'll pull through! We just heard it by radio. It was the serum that kept him going until they could get the proper antidote."

Griff could never remember afterwards how he got back to the lab. Drugged with fatigue, he made his way up the path from the cutter to his cot at the lab. And then even the beat of the drums, now loud and steady, could not keep him awake any longer.

He did not quite sleep the clock around, but by the slant of the sun across the floor, it was well into afternoon when he rolled over and blinked blearily at the scuttling lizards on the ceiling. Wind rustled in a dry clatter through palm fronds, and beneath that hummed the eternal pound of the surf. He sat up, aware of an aching void in his middle.

The house was quiet. He went down the hall to the shower and saw that the lab door was shut. When he knocked, there was no answer. Hughes must have gone out. Showering was a luxury, dressing a lazy process. He raided the food safe. It was so very peaceful that he decided to visit his spray pool.

But as he stood in the thrust of the wind and looked out over the bay he knew again that vague uneasiness. Something was missing—Carterstown was a deserted town, but that was usual at this hour. Two fishing boats rocked at anchor in the bay. Boats—!

Griff knew now what had bothered him. The *Island Queen* was not at her accustomed berth below. Yet she had been gone three days—and she should have returned that morning. In all the months he had been on San Isadore, he had learned that Angus Murdock, unlike the majority of his compatriots, ran his communication service between the islands with the regularity of a clock. The *Island Queen* had been due to drop her anchor before noon today—yet there was no *Island Queen* to be seen.

Clapping on his palm straw hat, Griff went down to the town. And it was as he threaded his way along the ruts of a side lane that he noticed the second mystery. About one house in three or four was still inhabited. But usually there were signs of life about those. Now—

In spite of the blaze of the sun Griff shivered. Closed shutters, no scrawny chickens scratching half-heartedly in the littered doorways—a brooding quiet. He might be walking through a town waiting for an attack.

The Union Jack hung limp from the pole in front of the Government House, its folds sun-bleached from scarlet to rose. Griff hesitated for a moment and then climbed the three broad steps that set the building on a more imposing level than its neighbors. The wide inner hall was deserted, but echoing loudly through the general silence came the click of an inexpertly pounded typewriter. Someone was busy during the siesta period, and Griff went in search of the worker.

In the second office he found his quarry, a young man of his own age hunched in concentration over the keyboard of an old and battered machine, pecking out some composition letter by painful, two-finger style.

"Henry Grimes!" Griff approached the desk.

The other looked up, startled, but not with the welcome Griff expected from Angus Murdock's nephew. Grimes was due to leave the island in two weeks time on a scholarship the governor at Santa Maria had helped to arrange. But now Henry's square young face, a less tough edition of the pirate Murdock visage, was very sober, and his eyes were both cold and wary. Griff asked the question that had brought him there.

"What's the news from the *Queen?* Didn't she come in on schedule?"

"Did you see her in—the—bay, mon?" Henry counter-questioned, changing in midsentence to the precise diction he tried so hard to use.

"What happened?"

"Ask—the—Navy mons—men—Trouble comes with them. The *Queen*, she don't answer the wireless!" As his agitation grew, Henry lapsed into the island idiom. "The commissioner, he speak to San'Maria. They say *Queen* sail on time, same as always. But she no come—"

Griff stiffened. Those other stories of the mystery ships, the drifting derelicts—he had listened to them, speculated concerning their fate with Chris and Murdock himself. But those reports had never seemed true. They were just something that happened beyond the horizon to strangers, nothing that touched his own world. Only now—what if the *Island Queen* was caught up in that ugly web?

"They've tried to reach her by radio?"

"The commissioner, he expect something important comin' by my uncle's hand—to him from the governor. When the *Queen* do not come, he worry, so he call San' Maria—'cause there be no storm, no thing to keep her back. San' Maria say *Queen* sail like always—calm sea, no winds, no thing bad. But the *Queen*, she do not come. So there is something bad!"

"And her own radio?"

Henry's shoulders hunched as he leaned farther over the typewriter. "They call—they are still callin'. She do not answer."

Griff started for the radio room, the islanders' one link with the outside world. There was the shuffle of hide sandals behind him as Henry followed.

The room was hot and dark, the shutters having been pulled to against the straight glare of the afternoon sun. Commissioner Burrows had shed the white coat he wore in public, but he had made no other concession to the heat. He glanced up as Griff hovered in the doorway, gave a nod, which was both greeting and invitation to enter, and waved to a chair. But he did not remove the earphones clamped across his crisp black hair, nor did he relax his listening attitude.

Henry coughed, and the shuffle of his sandals was unnecessarily loud. The commissioner sighed, slipped up one earphone, and reached for one of the strong island cigarettes lying in a box on the table.

"No news, sir?" Henry asked.

"No news for us."

"And you can't raise the *Queen* at all, sir?"

Burrows shook his head. "Santa Maria has sent out the cutter." His clipped English with its overseas accent still carried a trace of the Indies drawl. "So far—nothing!"

He watched the smoke curl lazily from the tube between his fingers and then added abruptly, "Would you be willing to do something for me, Mr. Gunston?"

"Of course—"

"It may be necessary for me to see Commander Murray at the base—but I don't want to make too much of our meeting. I understand very well the necessity for declaring the installation being erected there restricted territory, but you have a legitimate reason for visiting the base. The plane that flew your father to the States returned this morning. You will desire to have news—"

Griff was already on his feet. Probably Hughes had already gone to the base for just that reason. He knew a twinge of resentment because the other had not wakened him for that trip.

"Present my regards to Commander Murray"—the commissioner's tone became more formal—"and ask him when it will be possible to meet with me to discuss an important matter. Henry will run you up in our launch—"

As Griff went out into the late afternoon with Henry, it was into a still deserted town. A pig sleeping in the rut of a side road, the ever-present humming birds flitting from one flowering spike of aloe to the next, were apparently the only living things in Carterstown.

"Where is everyone?" Griff ventured to ask.

"They wait—"

"Wait? For what?"

"For what comes!" Henry's hand went to the breast of his shirt, in that movement Griff had seen Rob make so many times. So Henry, too, had his gris-gris, his protection against the unseen.

The American spoke boldly. "The drums sounded last night. Le Marr—"

Henry's broad face was impassive; it was as shuttered as the windows of those houses back in town. For all his scholarship, his off-island plans, Henry was of San Isadore. But he did volunteer one strange statement—something that startled Griff.

"Dobrey Le Marr—that mon be not so big-big—" The words trailed off into a mutter as Henry realized that he had made that remark to an off-islander.

Dissension in the island ranks? Griff wondered about that as he cast off the mooring lines of the small boat that was the commissioner's official "launch." Had a segment of the die-hards who had followed the dark beliefs of old Kristina begun to re-establish their brand of the ancient worship? Was that the explanation for the new drumming of the night before?

They headed straight for the Naval settlement. But to Griff's surprise they were warned off long before they reached their destination by the cutter, which had run the laboratory boat from its work two days before. Griff signaled vigorously and shouted across the water that he had a message for Commander Murray from the commissioner. But in the end he had to transfer to the Navy craft and let Henry return alone to Carterstown.

A guard, armed, marched him at a quick trot through the section where construction was in the same frenzied progress to a core of buildings that had sprouted rooms overnight, like cells in a wasps' nest. Once there he ran into Hughes in earnest conversation with the doctor, and Griff broke from his escort to join them.

"He's more than holding his own," the doctor assured Griff. "That serum stemmed the poison until they could pump an antidote into him. But if he hadn't had that—" He shook his head. "Nasty beggars, those stonefish. I'll take one apart scale by scale and see if I can discover what makes them tick. In the meantime, I had them wire Gongware for some more serum. If he has a supply on hand, they'll fly it out to us. Better to be prepared—"

"Two more stonefish brought in this morning," Hughes told Griff. "I want the commander to offer a reward and see if we can get the islanders to hunt them. But how they got here in the first place—halfway around the world from where we thought they belonged—!"

It was a puzzle all right, thought Griff—but no more of a puzzle than a lot of other things which focused on San Isadore at the moment. He saw over Hughes's shoulder the plane bobbing on the water by the improvised landing, and in that moment an idea occurred to him. Visibility from the air was wide. The *Island Queen* could not have drifted so far off her course since she had left Santa Maria that she could not be sighted by a search plane. Could the commander order the machine out to aid in the hunt? No longer attending to Hughes's talk about stonefish, Griff turned to the guard.

"I'd like to see Commander Murray as soon as possible—"

"You've been the one holding up the procession, fella—"

"What's up?" Hughes gathered that there was something else in the world beside fish.

"The *Island Queen* is late—and she doesn't answer radio signals," Griff flung over his shoulder as he trotted after his guide.

Chapter Eight
HOUR OF ULTIMATUM

But Griff was to have no satisfaction from Commander Murray. Scant attention was paid either to the message from the commissioner or to his own idea of using the seaplane in the search for the *Queen.* The atmosphere of the base had always been one of hurry and tension, but now it was building to a kind of controlled frenzy. If the Seabees had been working against time from the start of the project, they now raced with disaster. And Murray had no moments to spare.

Shunted to one side, not knowing how he was going to return to Carterstown, since an overland trek at night was a risky business and Murray had made no offer of a trip in the cutter, Griff watched the scene in bewildered amazement. The lamps flashed on as night closed down.

More lights tonight—this time at sea beyond the broken reef. Then landing craft, a rugged fleet, coming ashore in a steady procession to land quantities of bales and boxes on the beach. Tractors towing flat trucks toiled down to that point, where robots loaded with a speed and efficiency that made Griff tired to watch. He did not understand a tenth of what he saw—he had never known that such machines existed. Most of the labor was apparently done by push-button control over new unmanned cranes and trucks.

The train of goods waddled by, passing the now almost completed administration building to some hidden interior destination. A second tractor with its tow was already pulled up beside the mountain of material on the strand. About him the handful of men were directing only, most of the work was robot. Griff was ignorant of construction work, but surely this precision and remote control was new, though any dullard could have guessed that government brass never published all it knew, nor displayed openly all that it might accomplish in times of stress. Atomic power for machinery had been commonly discussed, and there had been a few timid and costly excursions into that in the civilian field. But Griff guessed now that he was probably surrounded at the present by machines running on atomic power. Perhaps the atomic breakdown also supplied the light under which those various pieces of apparatus went their efficient way.

What was the purpose of the base anyway? He could make a rough guess at a storage depot. The mound of goods moving in a steady and unending stream to an inland pool could not be just for the use of the fifty or so men now stationed here—unless they were only the forerunners of a large garrison.

But the low, heavy-walled building that served as headquarters, barracks, mess hall, and hospital was still the only erection in sight, and there was no indication of another being planned. A sub base? Griff was trying to fit that idea into the general scheme of things when Hughes and the Navy doctor came out. The doctor halted to light a cigarette. In the glare of the working lights his eyes were red and puffy, and he inhaled the smoke with the sigh of a tired man. But Hughes was alert, alive, his fingers drumming on his belt, then moving to ram into the pockets of his slacks.

"Mutant—" Hughes said.

"If you think so. It's your field rather than mine. And I don't remember ever dissecting a fish before. Mutant—? But it wasn't 'hot.'"

"Not this generation—"

The doctor's lips shaped a soundless whistle. "So that's your theory. Well—maybe so." But he didn't look convinced. "Twenty-five years since Hiroshima, and we haven't seen what the horror merchants dreamed up would follow that—no superbrains or monstermen—"

"Not quite a full generation," Hughes pointed out. "And maybe man reacts more slowly to radiation than—"

"Than your fish? You think that thing you found on the beach, and whatever it was in the cave, were mutant forms also? Mutants of what—whales—seals—?"

"There have always been reports of strange things seen at sea, even weird remains washed ashore," Hughes countered. "Dr. Gunston's theory was that unexplained radiation suggested some experimentation in the depths—"

"Which drove Fido up here?" The doctor grinned. "You may have something there. Or maybe the Reds have turned a gimmick loose—just to foul up the picture generally for you brain boys—"

"We could accept that, too, if one of our undercover men hadn't gotten the tip out to us that they're also worried—having trouble with the same red scum off China. They're making their own investigations."

"Which could be a blind—"

Hughes shrugged. "Sure enough. Only we do have it on *our* hands. And sooner or later we'll get to the bottom of it."

"It had better be sooner." The doctor's levity vanished. "There may not be a later—"

"War? But power's too evenly balanced. They know what the retaliation would be if they dared to jump us—"

"They also know what revolution would mean—to them. And there's always the hope that you can move faster than the other fellow—if you jump him without warning. Their grain crop was a failure last season, and they have other internal troubles. They would like to focus their peoples' anger elsewhere than on their own policies. I know—cold war for twenty or so years. We've heard all the rumors and alarms until they don't mean much any more. But that doesn't mean that a spark at the right place at the right time won't set off the blaze!"

Hughes shook his head slowly. "They're not idiots. No one wins an atomic war. Oh, I wouldn't deny that they may be trying some fancy tricks under cover. And maybe we're doing some crowding, too, where it doesn't come out into the light of day. But an out-and-out war—that's suicide!"

The doctor tossed away his half-smoked cigarette. "Let's hope that you're right and we're heading into a half century or so of hot peace. Now I'm going to call it a day—" He yawned widely, but Griff cut in.

"Have you had any more news of my father, sir?"

The doctor blinked at him. "You here, too? Yes, there was a

report about an hour ago. He's got a long pull ahead, but he ought to be back poking into your smelly fish in a month or two. Sooner if the bright boys at the lab there can get that poison broken down." He turned to Hughes. "We'll ship your specimens up in the morning. If Dr. Gunston can identify them as the thing which attacked him, we'll be set—"

Hughes nodded. "I'll do my own report. Thanks for the help—and good night, Doctor."

The Navy man glanced at the brilliant flood around them. "I've forgotten what night's like since I've been here. But there'll have to come an end sometime. Be seeing you—"

Hughes had the solution for their return to Carterstown—the lab launch. As they swung out and away from the light and din of the base, Griff noted that the supply ship was still unloading.

"Looks as if they're getting ready for an army."

Hughes studied the laden craft discharging cargo on the beach.

"Might be preparing for a siege. I wonder—"

"Sub base?"

"Could be that. Well, here comes our escort."

The Navy cutter drew alongside, flashed the search-light beam across them, and then cut throttle, dogging behind the small boat in a warning to get out.

But the radiance that wreathed the base was not the only beacon blazing that night from San Isadore. As they rounded the western bulge of the island and chugged into Frigate Bay, they saw the second illumination, a high leaping column of flame on the cliff head.

"The lab!" Hughes shouted.

But Griff was not sure it was that building. After all, the thatched roof, the wooden interior fittings would burn speedily, and the coral block walls could not feed such a fire as they now saw. Hughes set the motor at top speed, and the small craft bounced along on the surface of the water. It looked as if they might run ashore, and Griff moved toward the controls.

Though the dark bulk of the *Island Queen* was not anchored there, he counted four of the weedy hulks of fishing boats, more than he had ever seen in port together before. And the town, which had been dead when he left it hours earlier, was now alive—windows lighted.

Hughes was out of the launch, stumbling ahead on the wharf as his will moved faster than his feet. Griff made the craft fast before he followed. But when he caught up with Hughes, he found the ichthyologist struggling with someone in the dark.

"Mon—don't you go up there. Not now, mon—"

Only extreme emergency would have set Le Marr to that struggle. Before Griff came up, Hughes was down and the voodoo man crouched over him, trying to hold his flailing body immovable while he talked.

"They's gone wild—those mons up there! The debble out o' the night sits in their minds, an' they thinks wild things. You up there—maybeso more trouble—bad trouble—an' that's not good. They 'fraid—an' 'fraid mons hit out at the first thing they see. They don't think, they do! You come wi' me. The commissioner, he talk. When the wild go—these mons be shamed. Then they listen, they walk small for 'long time."

"Are they burning the lab?" Griff asked. That something he had sensed in the town earlier in the day had now returned a hundredfold. It was thick in the air. He could almost clutch it in his hand, taste it—the fear, the panic of a mob.

"They can't burn the walls—they burn what they find—"

Hughes writhed, and a torrent of raging words poured out of him. But the outburst was short. In a moment he was able to ask in an almost normal voice, "They took everything?"

Le Marr released his hold on the older man and squatted back on his heels. "They missed some things. I tell Heber, Ross, Lechee—take an' hide your papers. They be in my house waitin'."

"But why?" Hughes sat up. He sounded honestly puzzled.

"They 'fraid. The *Island Queen* be missin'. There be debbles in the sea. Before the doctor came, before you came, these things were not. They believe you dive in the sea, stir up bad trouble for island mons. If they burn what is your magic things, then you go 'way and the debble go with you. Now you come commissioner's house, make better plans there. Soon these foolish mons begin to think again—better let them do that then have more trouble now."

Griff aided Hughes to his feet. "You win, Le Marr," the assistant said bleakly. "But all the chief's work—it's criminal!"

"These mons—" Le Marr arose too. His hand twitched in vague

shooing movements as if he would hurry the two Americans on before him to the Government House. “They ain’t thinkin’ now—they is ‘fraid. Mon ‘fraid, he do things what he don’t do when he think. But when you ‘fraid, you do same. Navy mons ‘fraid now—they build, build, hurry-hurry, ‘cause they is ‘fraid.”

Griff could feel it—that net of tension. It had been slowly tightening about the island for days; he had begun to realize that—a feeling that they were all perched on the rim of a steep cliff with a wave rising to lick them into the raging water below.

They found the commissioner still in the radio room. He might not have moved since Griff had left. Braxton Wells, the storekeeper, his grizzled, closely cropped hair a silvery cap, sat by the far wall. Without remembering, Griff glanced around in search of the other two who made up the inner circle of San Isadore. But Captain Angus Murdock and Chris Waite were missing. Instead George Hanson balanced timidly on the edge of a chair, jumping to his feet and jerking his tunic into order as the Americans and Le Marr entered. His topee with its patiently shined constable’s crest hung on a wall peg.

The commissioner might be in the same position as Griff had left him, but he looked years instead of hours older. His face had a drawn expression. He no longer wore the headphones but nursed them in his hand, glancing down at them now and again as if they were totally strange objects.

“What’s going on here!” Hughes burst out. “Those hoodlums smashing up the lab! We’re here under the protection of your government as well as our own, Commissioner. You’ll hear from headquarters about this outrage—”

The commissioner raised his head. “You are perfectly at liberty to file any type of protest you wish, Mr. Hughes, with your government or mine—if either is left by tomorrow morning.” The colorless timbre of his voice, the tone of a dead man, stopped Hughes’s protests as effectively as if he had been slapped across the mouth.

“What’s happened?” Hughes rephrased his question of the moment before, watching the commissioner narrowly. This was more than any outburst of violence on the island, more than the disappearance of the *Queen*.

“We received a message relayed from Santa Maria. Two hours ago Cape Town ceased to be.”

"Cape Town?" Hughes echoed stupidly. What did Cape Town have to do with—

"Cape Town, South Africa, Wellington, New Zealand, Sydney, Australia, Singapore, and"—his tired eyes flickered from one American face to the other—"Seattle—"

"Seattle!" That struck home. "But what—?"

Burrows continued, stating wild facts as if he were repeating the current market prices on conch meat. "There's censorship clamped down tight now, and during the past hour they've been jamming so that nothing at all gets through. But something happened off the coast of China. They blamed it on the Western Confederation, so they have started wiping, out the great seaports one by one until they get what they demand—unconditional surrender—"

"Why not London—New York—Paris?" demanded Hughes.

The commissioner put down the earphones. "Perhaps they don't want to ruin too much before they take over. We've been told enough tales about what will follow out-and-out atomic warfare. The reports which have come in suggest bombardment from hidden subs, not air-borne missiles. And we've heard nothing for the past hour—other cities may be gone by now."

Griff's hold on the back of the nearest chair tightened. He tried not to imagine what might be happening beyond the rim of the sea. Back home they had always sworn they would not fire the first shot. But when they were attacked, there would be a reply the world would remember. Had that attack and reply been already launched?

Hughes was almost shouting. "They said nothing to us about this at the base—but they must have known!"

"Commander Murray said nothing?"

Griff shook his head. "He was speeding up the job there, would hardly listen to me. There couldn't be some mistake?"

"No, the broadcast was official, though we don't know—or they won't tell us—more than a few bare facts. Those cities ceased to communicate—then the ultimatum from the East—"

Hughes shook his head. "They must have gone mad. They know what we'll do in return—"

"They might have gambled on something else," Braxton Wells pointed out in his off-island accent. "What if the Western

Confederation does not reply in kind? What if they won't take the risk of using the big ones—?"

"You mean—surrender on demand? That's pacifist reasoning—"

"Some men think it is better to endure a bad government for a space than to turn the earth into a cinder by retaliation."

"And I say"—Hughes rounded on the little man—"that the men who argue that way should be forced to live in the Eastern Bloc and learn what it means."

"Do you know how many million people signed the last pacifist petition?" countered Wells.

"I know how many million are going to face the firing squads when the Reds take over if we fold up under this! Maybe that's why they've dared to make this move—those mouthy pacifist petitions have the Reds thinking we won't stand up to them."

The commissioner put on the headset and then turned up the volume of the broadcast receiver. From the loudspeaker on the table came a nerve-wracking clamor.

"Jamming—still jamming. Gentlemen"—the commissioner spoke now with a quiet authority—"I believe that we must now assume that a condition of world-wide war may exist."

"And that base may bring it here to us!" Wells snapped.

"Quite true. But it is too late to do anything about that," Burrows pointed out. "And I believe that you will all agree that we have no defense against subs whose weapons can destroy cities such as have already been wiped from the map. Heretofore, wars have been waged and their action has not touched this island. Le Marr, has the real meaning of modern war penetrated to the people here?"

"No, sir. Tonight they fear the sea debbles—they don't fear war. War don't mean nothing."

"Then I must ask all of you here"—Burrows' gaze caught and held the party in the room—"to let it continue that way. We can welcome the disturbance at your laboratory, Mr. Hughes, wanton as that destruction may seem to you. It will occupy their minds. Tomorrow all who took part in it will lie low. But there shall be arrests, fines; we shall be very busy with it. But can we afford a panic—the whole island going mad with fear? You understand that we cannot!"

Braxton Wells opened his lips as if to speak and then closed them. Hughes wore a defiant expression, but reluctantly he nodded.

"All right. I promise to go along. But we must get some sort of news!"

"Most certainly. So I suggest, gentlemen, that the five of us now here will do sentry duty at the radio—but that we alone shall have access to it. Unless the Naval party takes us into their confidence, we have this as our only link with what is happening out there. And since you are homeless, Mr. Hughes, Mr. Gunston, please take quarters here. We shall arrange time for each to be on call here. Do you agree?"

"Do we have any choice now?" Hughes wanted to know.

Chapter Nine
WAR TWO WAYS

Griff swallowed and then ran his tongue over dry lips. He had a stale taste in his mouth; his body ached as he moved stiffly on the hard chair. He must have slept; there was a bar of sunlight advancing from the window. Getting clumsily to his numb feet, he stamped to hurry the return prickle of circulation and went to that window to look out upon Carterstown.

The sour smell of the town hung heavy with no wind to lighten it. He became conscious of that—no wind. A bird chittered in the foliage and was answered by the squalling bray of a distant donkey. But there was no sighing wind, and a dank cloak of heat had fallen heavily on the houses.

His shirt clung to him stickily. Griff wanted a shower, a change. Then he remembered the fate of the lab and all their possessions there. At least it would do no harm to go up and look around.

Not wanting to meet anyone, to have to talk, Griff hurried down the hall and out of the door. A woman in the road outside glanced up at him and then away, staring straight ahead of her as she scuttled by.

But the American strode on unheeding. In the darkness of the previous night he had been able to agree with Le Marr that it was best they stay away from the scene of disaster. But in the brassy sunlight he could not be so moved.

And the sunlight *was* brassy. It glared down with an intensity that kept him in all possible bits of shade. Perhaps it was only his reaction to the past hours, or perhaps there *was* some actual change in the quality of the air. Then, with the memory of what might have happened elsewhere striking home, Griff stopped, one hand against the reasonable, sane roughness of a coral block wall, keeping that touch with reality as he fought a surge of panic. No man could honestly foretell the result of an atomic conflict. There had been so many imaginative constructions, so many learned opinions talked about during the past twenty years. Men had solemnly built ghost towns, peopled the houses with dummies, and then rained this new destruction upon that handiwork to study the consequences. But none of those experiments could equal the real thing!

The burrow of a land crab showed at the roots of a palm a few feet beyond him. If the occupant of that hole were caught in the sun, prevented from seeking the cool dark of its daytime hiding place, it would die—speedily—from the heat baking its shell. Were all of his own kind now caught in the open—without any burrows of safety?

A lizard flashed, a streak of brilliant coloring, jet black, yellow, ultramarine, along the rut of the road. Mechanically Griff began to walk after it. The heat was a flame funneled down upon the island. Without the usual alleviation of the wind, it became torment. Griff's body steamed. He was forced to halt now and then, panting, as he made the climb to the lab.

Now he could smell the stench of the fire, and within moments he came through bushes withered by its heat. Someone else was there before him, digging with an energy that made Griff marvel. To one side lay a pile of wreckage the other had apparently drawn out of the charred mess, and he was pulling out a tangle of blackened metal Griff identified with a flash of anger as one of the diving air tanks. So they had destroyed those too!

Hughes wiped his arm across his face, branding himself with a smear of black. Beneath that he was drawn, haggard. His eyes met Griff's dully.

"They made a clean sweep." He poked the air tank, pushing it to his salvage station. "We're finished here—unless we can get new supplies."

Finished here—that meant return to the States. For a second or two Griff was wildly excited. That was what he wanted. But how could they go to the States now? Was there—was there anything at all left there? If the worst had happened—Resolutely he tried not to think of his father, or others he knew back home. Back home—was there a "home" now?

"Any more news?" The ruin about them had no meaning if what they feared had occurred.

"All wave lengths still jammed, or were when I came up here." Hughes was indifferent. Then he paused, looked straight at Griff with a measuring that held some of his old conscious superiority.

"Maybe everything *has* blown up. But we're still alive."

"No—not dead yet." Griff was wryly amused at the change in Hughes's expression. Did the other believe he was going to have an hysteric case on his hands in the younger Gunston?

Griff stooped, hooked his fingers under the flame-grimed tank, and heaved it over with the rest of Hughes's rescued odds and ends. Who knew—they might just find a use for it sometime.

"Did you get the papers from Le Marr?"

"They're the only thing that was saved. They stole the skull of the sea serpent." Hughes had fallen into the habit of giving that beached monster the traditional name. "I suppose it's on display in their devil-devil sanctum sanctorum! Every other specimen went into this." He toed the malodorous, half-burned rubble.

Griff wandered over to the spray pool. A black and ugly wad lay on the once clean sand of the bottom, and fish floated belly up, washing in a scummy deposit on the surface. He searched for the small octopus. But it was a moment before he saw the limp tentacle trailing from beneath a stone. Chance had crushed the cephalopod. Two of the crabs, whose clan had furnished its favorite prey the day before, were now tearing at its flaccid arms.

A shout brought his attention back to the plundered lab. But Hughes was pointing up—into the molten blue bowl of the sky. Griff saw those white bands of exhaust—four—no—five of them! Jets! He was on his feet, watching those traces of the planes they could not see fade from sight.

"Headed south—"

Sure, they were headed south—South! But why south? Why not north toward the States? Were they in pursuit of some enemy, or fleeing—ships that no longer had home fields—seeking a place to land?

The air trails were lost. Griff's eyes fell to the sea. Down in the bay the full fishing fleet of San Isadore was still moored. No one was to be seen on the wharf or along the beach. But Frigate Bay did not look natural. Though the surf was no higher than it had been, the waters inside the circling reef showed movement. A school of flying fish—and there must have been more than a hundred of them—broke the water so close to the shore that most of them skidded onto the sands.

"What in the world—!" Griff could spot the swirls beneath the surface, but he could see no logical explanation. "Frank—look here!"

Hughes moved up beside him as triangular fins cut the water. Griff began to count aloud. "Ten—twelve—fifteen—Fifteen sharks down there!"

"Fish!" Hughes's wonderment was open. "The whole bay's filling up with them!"

The turmoil under the water was increasing. More flying fish soared aloft, flopping miserably ashore. Someone shouted in the streets of Carterstown, and people ran for the water's edge. A squid launched into the air, struck upon the deck of one of the fishing boats, and lay there writhing. Venturesome children waded into the shallows scooping out fish with their hands. But very shortly they were being snatched back by their elders. There was too uncanny an air about this; the islanders wanted no part of the abundance being driven into their own dooryards.

"What's bringing them in?" Griff asked Hughes, the authority. But the other man only shook his head.

The confused shouting of the islanders was fading to a murmur as they drew back from the shore, retreating slowly, always facing the bay as if ready to defend themselves against sudden onslaught. There was a hail from the sea. The Navy cutter was coming in to the wharf, but the men on board it were striking down into the water, levering off the masses of sea dwellers crowding in. The fins of the sharks drew in about the cutter quickly.

"They're eating those cut to pieces by the propeller," Hughes said wonderingly. "If those Navy chaps don't watch out, they'll be swamped! Swamped by fish!"

Somehow the cutter reached the wharf. And Griff watched the foreshortened figure of the commissioner, his white ducks as rumpled as if he had slept in them, go down to meet the men who came ashore. Then the whole party started toward the center of town.

As they went, the islanders stood aside. It was plain that they wanted no contact with the Americans.

Hughes and Griff came down to the shore line. To Griff's startled eyes, it appeared as if all the fish for miles around had been herded into the circumscribed area of the bay. Yet they had not been drawn naturally as by some oversupply of food—as he had seen them gather so quickly when a diver had broken loose sponge creatures and flat worm cases. But these, now so thick in the water that it was being whipped to froth, had fled in panic from some danger greater than had existed in their world before.

Scaled bodies rose in the air, plumped aboard the anchored boats, to flop over already comatose brethren. And above their heads, the sea birds were screaming themselves hoarse as they dived for such a rich feasting as they had never known before. A flea-bitten mongrel trotted by Griff, nosed at a dying fish, and snapped it up, to go on to the next.

"What brought them here?"

Hughes shrugged helplessly. "I don't know. Never saw anything like this in my life!"

"Mistuh Hughes—Mistuh Gunston—" The constable, his topee pushed to the back of his head, but with his tunic correctly buttoned, bore down upon them. "Commissioner say—please to come along Government House now."

The islanders were in retreat, vanishing into their homes. And shutters were being banged shut in spite of the heat.

"The fish go mad. Now maybe so mons go mad, too," the constable muttered. "This be bad time—"

Like the roll of the sea, the murmur of voices rose and fell in the hall of the Government House. Griff and Hughes entered the commissioner's office. Braxton Wells, Le Marr, and Burrows represented San Isadore on one side of the mahogany table—while facing them were Commander Murray, Lieutenant Holmes, Casey, and a young officer who wore pilot's wings clipped to his shirt front.

"I'm laying it right on the line, sir," Murray was saying as the two Americans entered. "War has been declared. What is going on in the north now is your guess as well as mine. The radio is jammed, and there's interference on all bands. Our supply ship chose to take a chance and head back to the States this morning. She was following her orders. Our orders are—"

Holmes put out his hand as if in protest. Murray did not even glance at him.

"Our orders—the last ones—were to stick on the job here. But it's a hundred-to-one chance whether what we are building will ever be put to use. In fact—I'm being frank with you, gentlemen—I don't honestly know the reason for the base. We have a mountain of supplies and certain installations that cannot be completed—or won't be—unless we get another shipment from the north. Until we get reliable news of some sort—" His voice trailed off.

"That is your problem, Commander," the commissioner replied. "Frankly I feel that it does not concern us. But what is of importance here is the morale of my people. Already they have destroyed the Gunston laboratory. Had there been no further unusual happenings this morning, we could have brought them to order. But now—with this disturbance in the bay—I have one constable, I have the support of Mr. Le Marr, Mr. Wells here. Captain Murdock, upon whose influence we could have depended to a very great extent, is missing, and his disappearance has only added to our burden. In Carterstown we are now sitting on a keg of gunpowder while a lighted match is being applied to the powder train. And, while gunpowder may sound ridiculously old-fashioned in this atomic era, it does explode with unpleasant force. I am going to ask you, Commander, to stay at your own end of the island and keep your men there. You have the right to defend yourselves—but the last thing I want is riot here!"

"Amen to that!" Murray agreed. "All right, we'll stay at home. You won't see us—unless there is need. But I'm going to leave a walkie-talkie unit with you, linking us. It may be necessary to get in touch in a hurry."

"For that I will thank you, Commander. Given a short spell of normality, we of San Isadore will settle down. In the meantime, the unit will suffice to exchange news. I have a steady watch on the wireless here—should I pick up anything—"

"It is the same with us. We'll let you know." Murray arose.

"Commissioner!" The constable hovered in the doorway. "The boat of the Navy mons—it sink! The fish fill it all up!"

"What!" Murray pounded into the hall, but his running strides were matched by Casey. And the rest raced behind them. As they burst out into the day, Griff gasped. Where the brassy sun had beat down, there was an odd greenish light under massing clouds. It was unnatural—somehow horrible. Yet it reminded him of the water world into which he had dived—what arched over them now might not be the sky but the bowl of the sea!

A family party, their belongings lashed to the backs of three donkeys, came out of a side lane and then dodged back swiftly as the men from the Government House ran by. Where there had been an absence of wind, they now plowed through rapidly thickening gloom into the salt spray driven inland by gusts, which almost knocked the runners from their feet.

Clearly a storm was coming—such a storm as Griff had never experienced before. Yet it had none of the characteristics of a hurricane. The greenish gloom was now a dusk as dark as nightfall, yet it couldn't be noon. Griff blundered into a figure, heard Casey swear—an oath that was bitten off to become the muttered words of a formal prayer.

They did not reach the wharf. There was no longer a wharf—no longer fishing boats, Navy cutter. There was a writhing sea, which bore struggling bodies ashore to slam them on the rocks, bash them against the walls of two crumbling houses. The men stopped, and then retreated slowly. An eight-foot shark struck the ground beyond Murray and twisted, its murderous teeth slashing. Someone screamed, the wild cry of panic, and a figure ran back up the street. Griff was engulfed knee-high in a curling wave; a sharp pain scored his leg. He leaped back, dragging the nearest man with him.

A sharp explosion sounded even above the howl of the wind. One of the party was firing into that murk of water—though why, Griff in a moment of rational thinking, could not understand.

They were back again, almost to the open space before the Government House, a knot of men who could not believe the evidence presented by their eyes. Palm fronds torn from buffeted trees were hurled lancewise through the air. Yet it wasn't a hurricane—it wasn't anything San Isadore had ever known!

"Oh, Lord—look!" A voice hardly human in its abandonment to raw fear shrilled weirdly.

This wasn't true, Griff assured himself. Nightmare! It had to be a nightmare! That—that *thing* wallowing down the streaming road, the water curling before it as it came—was nothing for any sane world to spawn. Lightning ripped across the sky, a jagged purple sword. And a monstrous head swung; fanged jaws opened and—closed! A ragged scarecrow thing mewled and squirmed and then hung limp between those jaws, as the dark came down once more.

Griff was running now, but when he felt the lift of the Government House steps, he stumbled and went down painfully. Some inner urge made him twist about. At the foot of the slight rise, which formed the core of the town, four—no—five white-clad figures wavered ghostlike in the dusk. Then Griff heard the crack of side arms. Whatever horror was following them was being met by fire.

But they had not yet faced the worst to be hurled at them that day, for under them the very stuff of San Isadore heaved. Griff, recalling the caves that underlay the island, thought that this was the end—that they were fated to go down with a sinking land. And it was in that moment that light came in a burst—not the lightning of the sky, but a pillar of flame out at sea, hurtling skyward, bathing them all in a bloody glare.

Griff crouched without knowing that he was sobbing. He watched while weatherworn houses collapsed—some in a sudden flattening, some slowly, stone by stone. There were screams lacing the fiery murk. But he remained where he was, seeing the men at the other end of the plaza break and run at what came through.

Death, monstrous because it lived and wallowed forward on flipper feet, death such as no man had faced before. And on its back—! Griff whimpered and buried his face in his shaking hands.

Again the ground rolled and wrenched. There was a trumpeting of anguish, a roar of titanic pain. Griff dropped his hands. From a mound of rubble that horrible neck trailed and wriggled convulsively. The thing was half-buried, struck down. But Griff was only thankful that he could no longer see what had ridden it in.

The blazing torch at sea had not been quenched. And the land was still moving. Then hands fell on his shoulders, jerking him upright. A voice shrieked in his ears words without meaning. But he turned, obedient to those tugging hands. This was the end of the world; why try to escape? Only some instinct far inside him kept him going over the reeling ground, even led him to stop and help claw another staggering figure to its feet. They were out of the town now. Scrub thorn and cacti tore at them as they pushed unheedingly through it. The red fires of hell blazed to light them on—on where? There was nothing left for man—no hole to hide in.

Part 2
OPERATION SURVIVAL

Chapter One
THE GREAT SILENCE

Griff Gunston stood once more on an island cliff. But this was not the San Isadore of the past, and his memories of that peaceful stretch of salted land and reef-bound water were now so dimmed by what lay between that it was difficult to believe that other island had ever existed, or that he, Griff Gunston, had led such a carefree—or reasonably carefree—existence there.

A thick grayish dust covered the ground, clung to tattered bushes, and made a murk in the air through which the sun had not been able to penetrate until yesterday. It packed as mud on the mask he had improvised from salvaged diving materials, and he had to keep scraping it away in order to see. Somewhere not too far to the east a volcano born out of the ocean was still spouting throat-searing fumes, dust, and molten rock into the air. And the same action that had given it birth had rocked and broken San Isadore, bringing a mass of new land from beneath the waves and plunging other sections into the depths. They did not know even yet how many of the islanders had survived the night and day of agony when that change was in progress. Yesterday at the first hint of clearing the Navy party had started overland to discover what had happened to the base, but as yet they had heard nothing from them.

Overland—Griff had crept to the edge of the racked rocks of the cliff to catch a glimpse of the sea. That was the worst—the sea was no longer under the rule of his kind. He knew now that he had not lost his mind in that instant when he had seen the sea monster advance into sinking Carterstown under direction. Under direction! There was a menace lurking out in the bay—about the shallows. A creature with a mind, with intelligence, directing thought-out attacks upon any human being who ventured within range of its weapons. Only yesterday he had seen what happened to an unwary islander who had paused beside one of the inland sea wells. A loop, or it might have been a suckered arm, cast about the man's legs, snapping him into the water from which there was no escape, leaving his two companions to flee in mad panic.

Hughes, the only expert they knew, had no answer for them. He had made a daredevil venture down into the water-logged town to inspect the remains of the thing that had been caught by the falling house. It was of the same species as that found on the beach, but that was all he could tell. Of that which had ridden it he found nothing, for he did not try to dig into the half-awash rubble. Though octopi had been known in the past to exist out of water for short periods, that creature which had directed the sea serpent was a breed with even greater powers of endurance.

There had been no more earth shocks for three days now, and they had begun to hope that the worst of that particular phase was past. The survivors were camping out on the highest point of the interior, the salt plain where the lake of the flamingos had existed a week or so ago.

Luckily, on the second night, there had been a heavy rain. And they had caught the water—which was partly mud and stank of sulphur—but it kept life in them. It was Casey and Murray, with less skilled help from the islanders, who had rigged a crude apparatus for distilling fresh water from salt, and though the yield was small, there were those precious drops garnered to be used for the sick, the women, and the children.

They had organized parties to gather supplies from the town. And the three shotguns found had proved useful in halting the stampede of wild cattle, which had threatened to beat out their camp on the third day. Perhaps fifty people huddled there, fifty out of—how many had Carterstown sheltered—at least several hundred. There might be other survivors in the bush who would eventually drift into the settlement.

Some trick of the wind blew aside the drifting dust, and Griff saw what had once been Frigate Bay. The line of the reef tilted up in one place to form another island, its upthrust rocks slimed with dying sea things. And smashed squarely down upon it was a small boat—an island yawl or a fishing smack. But the dust curtain dropped again before he could be sure.

With a sigh Griff turned to plod along, using a fishing spear to test each suspicious patch of ground as he limped forward. His task was to explore the southern portion of the island, bearing westward, to locate any survivors and start them into the central camp, and, incidentally, to mark down any garden patch, any coconut palm, or other food that could be harvested.

He came out onto a strange strip of land, where the former beach had been raised elevator-fashion several hundred feet into the air. He walked over sand that the week before had been washed by waves now dashing on a new strand far below. His mask kept out some of the stench of the decaying sea life already half-buried under the soft cloak of the dust. But crabs scuttled and tore with clicking claws at the rare feast.

Wind! His head went up as he felt that familiar ripple in his matted hair. Wind! He turned his back to the force of it, very glad for the mask that protected his eyes against the blowing grit. Maybe it would clear the air.

But instead it whipped up the light stuff and thickened the murk until Griff, battling through the soupy substance, fetched up against a rock with a force that brought a grunt out of him. He decided to shelter there. No use fighting through this when a misstep might plunge him to the bottom of a crevice.

He crouched on the lee side, wedging his shoulders against the comforting solidity of the stone, his head down on his knees, waiting with all the patience he could muster for the storm to clear. Rain came—a visible curtain of water, washing the grit from his body in a warm flood channeling the muddy silt away except where it was caught in brown pools.

Griff ripped off the mask and held his face up to that downpour. He drank his fill from a rock hollow, filled the gourd that was his canteen from another. The bushes, the clog of dust washed from them, showed their natural silvery gray. Griff got up, eager to take advantage of this break in the dust fall.

He came to the end of the lifted strip of beach and, faced by a jagged stretch of rock, doubled back to an easier climb. A streamlet born of the rain was already dripping from the upper levels, and twice he stopped to drink for the sheer pleasure of rolling the water in his feverish mouth. It was the stream that guided him into the valley.

Through some freak of the earth's settling, this cup had been born. A ragged row of palms was rooted strongly enough to be still standing. Here the bushes and ground shrubs, washed clean of the dust, were new and green. A trough of rock was turning into a pool of rain water. But beyond that was one of the single-room coral block houses. Its thatched roof had been ripped away, the walls were cracked—but it stood. And against it huddled three donkeys. With them were two of the wild horses, hardly larger than ponies. They stamped uneasily as he came, but they did not bolt.

"Who come?"

Out of the twisted hut crawled a woman. Her ragged dress was plastered to her body; a battered straw hat kept the worst of the flooding streams from her shrewd brown face.

"Oh," she identified him, "Mistuh Gunston, from the fish place. Well, there's a plenty fish now, ain't there?"

"Liz!" He recognized her as the sturdy and independent widow who had done the lab laundry, cooked for them on occasion, and had been their mainstay for general help until the month before when she had been sent for to nurse an ailing daughter-in-law.

"That's me." She smiled. "We done have ourselves a time, ain't we?"

"You here alone?" Griff leaned on his spear to rest his leg. The tear he had received the night of the disaster was healing, but he still had to favor it.

"No, sir. We all done got 'way. Lily—she's ailin'—" Liz jerked her head back at the cabin. "She's got Jamie an' Jess wi' her. Luce—he took the boys 'long him. They go off see they find water." She laughed richly. "They come back an' find water done come to us!" Triumphantly she pointed to the growing pool before her.

"We've a big camp up on the salt flats," Griff told her. "Commissioner wants people to come in there if they need anything." Glancing about the valley, Griff privately thought that Liz and her clan were better off here, and she said so herself.

"This here's a goodly place, Mistuh Griff. Thank you kindly for tellin' us. Now we got us some water we don't need nothin', nothin' at all. Come in, sir, an'have yourself a rest time an' tell the news—"

He allowed himself to be shepherded into the hut. On a pile of palm fronds and dubious bed coverings the ailing Lily lay, her attention all for the answers he gave to Liz's flood of questions, while the two youngest of Liz's grandchildren crawled out of the same nest and crept across the floor to sit staring solemnly up at him. He nursed the thick mug of some herb brew Liz had pushed into his hands and sipped it gingerly as he tried to satisfy her curiosity.

"Carterstown be drownded daid?" She pursed her lips. "An'the fish done gone crazy—"

Griff hastened to pass on the needed warning. The children—he looked down at them—the children of San Isadore had always played along the shore. Most of them could swim almost from the time they could walk. But now—!

"There're worse than crazy fish out there now, mistress." He used the old formal island address to underline the seriousness of what he had to say. "Something's come out of the sea that is dangerous. Keep away from the shore—and above all, keep the children off the beach!"

"Debbles," Liz remarked calmly. "Done raised us a mischief. You needn't fret, Mistuh Griff; nobody in this here family is goin' down near that water! Not 'til those debbles done gone back to where they camed from."

"It be the last days o' the earth!" A thin wail burst from Lily. "This be the end o' all mons!"

Liz swung around, and her voice was sharp. "That's enough o' that foolishment, gal! As long as we has legs to walk on an' hands to work wi'—an' wits in our heads—we ain't daid. We is shook up some an' scared right plenty, an' there's a new world out there. But we ain't daid—an' the good Lord above be bigger than any debble-debble or dupee ever raised! Me—I say we ain't daid, an' we'll git the better o' these bads—"

Griff had the sudden conviction that Liz and her kind would. When he went on, cutting across the countryside where the rain had deadened the dust and brightened the vegetation, he paced almost jauntily. They weren't dead, as Liz had pointed out. And those who had not broken under the extremes of the past few days were all right—as the growing things were straightening up from the buffeting they had taken. There was no use speculating about what was happening—had happened—outside the boundaries of San Isadore. For the time being the world had shrunk to the island and its immediate surroundings, and it was better for them to keep it that way.

The rain continued for the rest of the day, turning some sections into sticky morass, filling pools. Griff came back to the settlement, where the huts, constructed of brush, had to be abandoned to the rising water of a new lake. Bedraggled and dripping, the survivors loaded their supplies on the few donkeys and straggled on across the plain, heading for the base to the north. If any of the construction there had survived the twisting of the island, it would provide the shelter Carterstown could no longer give.

They camped in a weary huddle that night, sheltered by a stand of twisted trees, from which dripped the steady stream of rain. Tins were pried open with knives and their cold contents shared out apathetically.

There was a low keening from where the women and children crouched together. Very few of them showed Liz's spirit, and the constant rain and the lack of fire or protection was beginning to tell on a people already in a state of shock. Griff chewed a mouthful of beef as with stiffening fingers he tried to weave some palm fronds into a leanto. The rain, which in their ignorance they had welcomed as a relief from the scourge of the dust, was becoming as great a curse. During the latter part of their march today he had helped as a rear guard, working with Le Marr and Wells to keep the pitiful train of refugees moving. Several had lain down, refused to keep trying until they were actually booted or beaten to their feet, and Griff knew that anyone who gave up now was lost. Without the will to live, they would, as travelers lost in a snowstorm, drift into unconsciousness and death, some inner spring broken past repair.

Two women, one child, and an old man were lost from the count the next morning—four graves scooped out. The commissioner, showing a skull face with shrunken eyes, walked like a man in a nightmare, but he never ceased to exhort, to urge, to keep that straggling column moving. Griff wondered what Burrows would do, what they would all do, if they had their hope extinguished by finding in the north no remains of the base, only a new desolation as great as the one from which they fled.

But the answer was not to be that brutal. Through the ever-present drone of the rain broke another sound, the crunch of metal over rock. And one of the powerful caterpillar tread haulers he had last seen at work with the supplies on the shore crawled steadily into view, pulling behind it three of the carriers. Men dropped from the tows as the soaked line of islanders was sighted. Donkeys brayed, dug in their small hooves, and refused to approach the monster, while their owners were half-led, half-carried, to be tumbled aboard the platforms as if they also were supplies.

"Hello, Gunston! Hop a ride!" Casey, red stubble still visible on his jaw and cheek, matched step with Griff. He caught the younger man's shoulder and propelled him toward the carrier.

"I take it the base made out all right?"

"After a fashion." Casey lost some of his cheer. "We've a few bad holes here and there, but we're still in running order. Atomic power has its points."

The crawler, with its escort trotting easily beside it, made a wide circle to retrace its trail, the babble of the islanders rising at the novelty of the ride. This had shaken them out of their apathy. Even the men who had elected to walk and lead the donkeys were moving at a smarter pace. And after a short rest Griff slipped off the slow-moving tow to join them.

"Big changes," Casey was saying to Braxton Wells. "I'd say there are some new islands off that way. We've started work on the plane. When she's repaired, Whit'll take her up for a look-see."

"—trouble from the sea, mon?" Griff caught only half of the question.

Casey was sober. "Pretty bad the first night—until the boys got defense wires up. Now we can burn them off when they try it. And they haven't for two days. We've got a landing section cleaned out in the bay, run shocks through the water. But we can't do the whole ocean!"

"This condition may be local." Burrows trudged up to join them.

"Might be, sir," the American agreed, but plainly only because he thought that that was what the other needed to hear. "The radio is okay now—no more jamming. Except what's natural after—after—" He hesitated.

The commissioner stooped more, as if his shoulders were sinking under invisible blows. "After an atomic war—" he supplied in a low voice.

"Well, yes, sir. I guess we have to face that. They've shot the works. So far we can't get any messages through, and we haven't been able to pick up anything except one South American station. The fellow down there sounded hysterical—kept wanting to know what had happened and why someone didn't answer him."

Griff swallowed before he was able to ask his own question.

"Nothing from the States?"

"No. Sorry, kid. The skipper's been asking for news ever since the jamming cleared. He gets a gabble now and then—crazy stuff—but even that stopped early this morning. Today nothing but quiet. Looks as if everything has gone off the air. That's why we're working so hard to get the plane up for an exploring party. They're converting her with one of the new experimental motors—means she can only carry a pilot. But she'll be able to go farther. We certainly can't make a try by sea—not 'til we find some way to brush off those things hiding down there. I'd like to know what they are and why they've got it in for us anyway—"

"The sea have big secrets. Mons, they float about on top the sea, they dive down little way, but how they know what be down there? Mons think they know everything. But they don't. Maybeso other things, they tired of mons an' his big mouth—thinkin' he be the king o' the world." Le Marr dragging at the lead rope of a reluctant donkey had joined their small group.

"Fish with brains yet!" Casey shook his head. "Well, they're mean enough, and they sure go for anything within their reach. Crawl out on the beach—that is, they did, 'til we tickled them up with a rapid fire—then they stopped that. Octopi—only not like those we saw hanging around the reef before all this started. I'll believe they can run us off the earth when I see it done! We'll get their number—drop a bomb and where'll they be—"

"Too many bombs have already been dropped, sir," the commissioner said dryly, and Casey was left without an answer.

The crawler and its laden carriers creaked and crackled down a slope that led into a wide valley. Griff was not very sure of this end of San Isadore, and the recent quakes had destroyed many of the usual landmarks. He thought that they were several miles inland from the original base, but he could not swear to that. A river of rain washed about the treads of the machine and was ankle-deep about their feet. Then they came out where the labor of man was again changing the shape of nature.

White beams from working lamps cut the gloom of the rain, and machines were busy. Shelters of rock blocks were growing visibly as they watched. It was apparent that the builders had cut their losses in the vanished erection by the sea and were in full progress to copy it here. A settlement was coming into being.

They were all shaken out of their own private miseries. The activity before them was in such contrast to their own toilsome harvesting of the shreds disaster had left them. This was a refusal to admit that there was any reason to give in to anything that had been hurled against San Isadore in the past five days.

Griff limped forward, drawn by the burst of light, that aura of confidence that overhung the whole scene. There was that about it which argued that, as bad as the news was, *they* were not licked! Here were Liz's boasts of the day before acted out. No, they were not dead yet.

He was still clinging to that when an hour or so later, under a roof where the rain drummed but could not enter, in a building that was half-erected, half-hollowed cave, he ate and drank, resting in comfort.

Murray was there, Hughes, the doctor, Burrows, Wells, Casey—only Holmes was missing. But the rest were seated on packing cases, poring over the map Murray had pegged out on one wall. The outlines were those of San Isadore as the island had been a week before. And some alterations had been added with a bold black crayon.

"Volcanic action without a doubt—" That was Murray's comment. "Don't know what set it off—might be the result of bombing. At least one new island here." He stabbed with the fish spear he was using as a pointer. "We'll get a plane up."

"No radio yet?" That was Hughes.

"We have men on there—twenty-four hour duty. So far we've heard nothing—"

His words fell into a pool of silence, as for the moment even the outside din was hushed.

"Nothing—" Griff repeated that to himself. His thoughts shied away from all that implied. Did that describe what now lay to the north—nothing?

Chapter Two
NEWBORN WORLD

Griff awoke to lie uneasy in the dimly lighted space. Under the slight movements of his body the hammock swung. But it wasn't the unfamiliar bed that troubled him. Something was missing—and its absence had brought him out of the depths of exhausted sleep. The drum of the rain! That incessant downpour, which they had almost come to accept as the natural order of life, was stilled at last.

He heard a faint snore, a sleepy mutter, and raised his head. Pallets on the floor, hammocks aloft—as many sleepers had been crowded into that room as could find space. Cautiously he slid out of his swaying support and crossed the room with care.

His watch had stopped. He had no idea whether it was now night or day. And as he came into the open, he was even more befuddled. There was still work in progress some distance away. But, though he saw machines building, dragging supplies, he could see no men. Overhead the sky was a frightening, sullen yellow-gray. Not night—but not like any day he had seen either. Except for the clamor of the machines there was an ominous silence. No wind, no rain—even the ever-present boom of the surf was muted.

An eerie call of a sea bird startled him. He could see a single pair of wings wheel and dip overhead. Trouble was on the way, trouble San Isadore could not escape. It was hot, stifling hot, yet there was no sun. Griff was panting; a trickle of moisture crept down his chest.

Somewhere up there, out there—he had turned to face north—danger was building up. The clouds massed like a giant sledge hammer over the wracked bit of land that was the island.

"Nasty-looking, isn't it?"

Griff started. Crepe-rubber soles had made no sound as Breck Murray had come out. The commander wore his uniform cap and a pair of work slacks—with a long tear down one leg. He also had a wide bandage across his upper arm, and about his waist hung a belt supporting a service side arm.

"What do you think is coming now?" Griff asked. The past days had taught him one thing—that one could live through panic—live through the blackness of such fear as he had not known could exist—and come out on the other side. It could only be done by living one moment at a time, by not looking ahead. Yet here he was breaking his own rule for safety.

"Storm of some kind," Murray said. "It'll be the worst yet."

He strode unhurriedly to the side of one of the tanklike machines and opened a door. Griff trailed along in time to see the commander seat himself inside before a microphone.

"All hands!" Murray's voice, magnified into the roar of a giant, split the air. "All hands to work area—on the double! Hit the deck! Assemble at work area—"

Men came, fast enough. And after them followed the islanders until the whole populace of the new settlement was assembled.

"By the looks of this"—Murray went directly to the heart of the matter—"we're in for trouble. The meteorological equipment we've been able to salvage has gone wild. We've got to dig in. As long as the island itself doesn't go, we'll have a chance. Now—on the double—get those diggers going. I want everything undercover—if we can do it. This is Red Alert Two—follow plan Red Alert Two—"

If the activity they had witnessed earlier had seemed frenzied to the islanders, what happened now made them gasp. And they, themselves, found refuge in the new caves into which Burrows and his unofficial committee urged and drove them.

The wind was back, rising steadily. Griff, helping to manhandle boxes, bales, and crates into hollowed storage places, heard the howl of its coming. Though the rain had not returned, spray, whipped out of the sea and borne across the rises between, was a mist in the air.

"That does it here, kid!" A man clapped him on the back, pulled him away from the last stowage job.

The blare of a siren howled across the area as the lamps went out.

Griff helped his unknown co-worker to unhook one and roll it under cover.

"Second warning," the man mouthed in his ear. "We got about five minutes more, kid, then it's hit dirt. Lord, this is going to be a dirty blow!"

Machines clanked by, on their way to such anchorage as had been devised for them. A steady stream of orders, mangled by the scream of the wind, poured out over the loudspeaker in the com truck. Most of them were incomprehensible to Griff, but he ran along with the men he had joined, helping wherever strength to push or pull was needed.

Two blasts from the siren this time. And now the com truck itself crawled through the murk. A Seabee caught at Griff, pushed him ahead with a force that made him stumble.

"Time to go—"

But there were still two lamps—a pile of boxes. However, that grip compelled him to enter the nearest half-built house. He clattered through it, one of a group of four, across the roofless large room, with the wind sucking at them, to a doorway, which was close to a hole, popping through that into light once more—a cube chamber cut in the rock, half-filled with a jumble of hoarded apparatus and supplies.

"—the skipper—?"

"He took the truck out—he'll make it. Listen to that, boys!"

The wail of the wind transcended anything Griff had ever heard before. He half-crouched against a crate, his hands over his tortured ears. Dimly he was conscious of activity by the door, of a chain of men hastily linked hand to hand who edged through to drag a streaming, wind-buffeted figure into their own hiding place. Then came the building of a barrier, heaping up of boxes before the one opening on a world gone mad.

Under him Griff could feel the trembling of the rock, as if the island pulsed with life. Then he remembered—Liz and her small clan! There was no use telling himself that no one could have crossed the island in time to rescue the family in the southern valley. If he had remembered in time, they might have had a thin chance. Now—

"Well, here's where we prove whether the idea boys were right or not." Murray's voice was almost a drawl. He leaned against the barrier they had built to cover the door. Under the light his bare chest and shoulders were glistening wet. His cap was gone, his hair a bushy tangle as if the wind had tried vainly to jerk it out by its too tough roots. "We can see if shelters designed to withstand air attack are going to best old Nature herself."

"Just a buncha guinea pigs," murmured one of the Seabees.

"Live guinea pigs," a fellow hastened to point out.

"Yah—so far!" was the pessimistic answer.

But they were on the move about their constrained quarters, pushing supplies into a line about the wall, dragging other boxes into the open.

"Gunston!" Murray seemed surprised. "Thought you were with the island crowd—What's the matter, son?"

"There was an island family down in a valley to the south. I found them when Burrows sent us out to round up stragglers. They were safe enough then and didn't want to move in. One of the women was ill—so—" That jar vibrating through the rock reminded him of that other valley he had explored with Le Marr, where the contents of the sea's floor had long ago been dumped through a storm's wild fury.

"Nothing we could do for them, Gunston." Murray repeated the same argument his own mind had presented. "We couldn't have brought them here in time. And there's no assurance that we're going to weather this ourselves. Also—this storm is driving from the north!"

Griff's incomprehension must have been plain, for the commander added a terse and frightening explanation.

"If there has been an all-out atomic attack up there—we've got to face the possibility of fall-out. And it may be headed here."

Fall-out! The radioactive debris blasted into the highest heavens to drift or be driven by storms, to settle at last maybe thousands of miles from the site of the actual explosion—but equally deadly to its victims.

"The dust!" Griff blurted out, that gray cloud which had been with them for days—was it—? But Murray was shaking his head.

"Not the stuff that's been dropping here. That was mostly volcanic ash. The counter did a little jittering, but not enough to hurt. Doc's played it safe and taken hourly readings for a while. And we'll play it even safer if we get through this blow."

The hours spun wearily by. All of them wore watches, but, except for that measurement of time, they had no idea whether it was night or day. There were instruments chattering at one end of the rock room. They must have had some meaning for Murray, for the two men who watched them constantly.

Once an ugly serpent of water curled from beneath the door barrier, setting them busy damming its advance. It gathered, crept, and then stopped. Moved by impulse, Griff dipped his finger and touched it to his tongue—salt! Had the sea reached them?

But there was no more water. They slept, ate sparingly of concentrates. A card game ran for hours. Books passed from hand to hand. But Griff was sure that few of his companions were able to concentrate any better than he was. He nodded into a nightmare-tormented sleep, aroused to find himself being shaken none too gently as one of his exasperated neighbors demanded to know why he was groaning.

There was a period when Murray hunkered down beside him to ask a series of questions about the sea life in the lagoon. Griff answered as best he could, with a dull wonder as to why this should matter now.

"Squid—octopus—what are those things after us?"

"Octopi, I think. They could always exist for a short time out of water, and this new breed apparently can do even better. Also those we saw along the reef before the blowup were acting oddly—"

"How oddly?"

"When I was diving with Casey—on that last morning—they ringed us in, watching to see what we were doing. Octopi are normally afraid of divers—they'll slip into crevices and hide—"

"So those were the new super-octopi? Did your father have any explanation—"

"I never had a chance to tell him about them. But those along the reef were much smaller than the type attacking now. The red plague, the dead sea serpent we found were both 'hot.' You've heard the old arguments about mutation forced by atomic radiation. Maybe this new type are mutants. You'll have to ask Hughes—he knows more about it than I do."

"Hughes is with Doc. And I know that they were working on it," mused Murray. "Maybe they *can* give us the dope—if and when we get out of here."

How much later it was that the end came Griff could never afterwards determine. Maybe hours—days were lost in that period of vicious upheaval. But the rocks were stable once more, and men arose to pull aside the barrier, allowing a queerly dressed figure out to explore. The stiff white coveralls, with the windowed cowl covering head and face, made a robot out of a man—a robot who walked with the clang of heavy boots, the rigidity of the thick material weighing down his limbs.

The explorer clanked out as the atomic-powered lamp was switched off. Sun—yellow sunlight—lay in a shaft through the door. Thin and disembodied words came from the walkie-talkie.

"So far—so good, skipper. But—boy, oh, boy, there've sure been alterations! Hey—here's a pal! Out of Doc's burrow—"

"Stanley reporting, Commander," another voice broke in. "All okay in burrow four. But there're 'hot' signals from a drift here."

Murray picked up the small mike. "Bad?"

"Not to danger point. Looks, sir, as if this whole area had been scrubbed right out. Well, I'll be—" The report broke off in a bewildered exclamation.

"What is it?" Murray prompted impatiently.

"Crawler planted right on top of the cliff—upside down! How in the world—!" That was the first explorer answering. "Wait—getting something new, skipper—"

Magnified through the walkie-talkie, they were all hearing that click, click, faint and regular at first and then rising to a furious chatter of warning sound.

"Where's that coming from?" Murray demanded.

"Wreckage, sir. So banged up we can't tell what it was—some sand and dust caught in drifts around it."

Again the counter gave the radiation chant.

"It's the wreckage all right, sir. None of our stuff—"

"That's the tail of a jet!" His partner in exploration cut in excitedly. "What is it doing here?"

"What's anything doing here? Including that half of a horse hung up in what's left of those palms? But this jet can be cleared, skinner—and it's the source of the infection."

"Good enough. But quarter the area and let us know if there is anything else. How about the sand—are there any dust deposits?"

His first answer was a sound that might have been laughter.

"Skipper, except around a few rocks there isn't any sand. This place has been scoured right down to the bottom. If there was a fall-out, it was washed and blown right off our map again. Shall we try to break out one of the crawlers and lug this wreck off?"

"Not yet. Go over the area first. We want to make sure—"

But the report continued to be negative. And the others were free to crawl out and stand blinking at the pallid sun, seeing the scraped world that bore a sharp resemblance to the lunar landscapes drawn by painters of the fantastic.

A working party headed for the place where they had parked the machines that had built this refuge, only to discover that the storm had been there first. There was a jumble of metal, tangled and jammed, thrust into a split in the wall. And there was the single crawler perched upside down on the cliff. Perhaps others would be found later, but for now that was the total machine survival.

In the end the dangerous, radiation-'hot' wreckage was dragged away by hand, the lead-suited explorers fixing the ropes, the others lending their weight at a good distance. It was snaked up and over a ridge and wedged into a crevice, which could be walled up against future accident.

"Jet tail, right enough," was Murray's verdict. "Wonder where it was blown from?"

Decom chemicals were sprayed on the section where it had lain, on the sand pocket that had gathered about it. And then both men in their grotesque suits stood in the heavy stream of cleansing liquid.

Now that the all-clear signal had been given, the other burrows spilled out their inhabitants. But while the Naval personnel poured out eagerly, the islanders came slowly, moving like people caught in a bad dream. The sight of the stranded crawler on the cliff, the changes in the valley, added to their stupefaction.

A child whimpered; a man swore softly in the island idiom. The commissioner came up to Murray.

"Thanks to you, sir, we've been saved. I gather that radiation is not to be feared?"

"There was a piece of 'hot' wreckage, but we've cleared it. Tell your people to take it slow leaving here. We are sure of nothing beyond this valley."

Burrows smiled. "Look at them, sir. They are not yet ready to take up life again. In fact, they must be shaken into it. They are a simple people, Commander, and much which has happened to them in these past terrible days has been beyond their comprehension. Now many of them are in a state of shock. We—" he hesitated and then continued—"already we have two who are totally insane. But the rest—I think that they will be all right. If this last storm is only the end to our misfortunes—"

Murray turned his face to the sky, bright and clear, untroubled. The trade wind was blowing again, although its touch did not dip into the valley where the survivors were gathered.

"We can hope that the worst is over. Luckily we do have supplies—concentrates mainly—which will do for some time. I don't believe that we may expect any help from outside soon—"

"If ever," the commissioner agreed. "But there is no use thinking about that now, sir. I gather we are fronted with the business of taking stock and seeing how we can put to the best use all that can be salvaged."

"Just about that. I'm sending out exploration teams as soon as it is practical. They have to go slow and carefully. We've escaped fallout here, but elsewhere—"

"It may be a different matter? Just so, Commander. Whatever we can do to aid in your plans, please let me know at once. Le Marr has a very intimate knowledge of the island—as it was, of course. There were certain native plants which might be added to the food supply—if they are still in existence." The commissioner smiled ruefully. "One's speech nowadays becomes overburdened with 'ifs.' Men have been accustomed to taking so much for granted, as a part of their personal security. We shall have to learn that nothing can be lightly accepted now. But consider what little we do have to offer at your service, Commander." His hand sketched a gesture close to a salute as he turned away.

Murray gave orders; the Seabees carried them out as precisely as if they were the robots now. But Griff, with no assigned duties, climbed the cliff wall. When he reached the top of the knife ridge, he swung to the north, dreading what he might see, yet forced to that inspection.

He shaded his eyes from the sun. Less than half a mile away he caught the rainbow lights of spray beating into the air against a new coast line. The site of the first base must now be under water. But to the east there was an even stranger sight. He had expected land to disappear—he had not expected it to rise above water. Yet a long strip steamed there under the sun's heat, dotted with clumps of decaying ocean vegetation. It stretched out far beyond where the reef had once encircled this end of San Isadore. Newborn land indeed!

Chapter Three
PORT OF REFUGE

"Well—that's that!" Casey leaned back against a convenient rock and absent-mindedly smeared dark streaks of grease across the shorts that were his only garment. "We can take her all apart, but she'll still be scrap as far as doing her regular job is concerned."

However, he did not appear in the least downcast by his own verdict as he surveyed with narrowed eyes the smashed and twisted wreckage just disinterred from a wind-sculptured sandbank. Undoubtedly he was already mentally tearing the defunct machine to pieces and assembling from its parts a new and efficient tool, which would aid in the reconstruction project. Griff could see no such possibilities. But then, Griff thought bleakly, he had taken on his present role of survivor with very little practical preparation. And the one thing he could have contributed to their general store of knowledge—the lore of a diver—was of no use at present.

"We'll have to dismantle her right here—" Casey was continuing buoyantly. "You know, kid, we have one thing on our side. Maybe it was atomic bombs that got us into this mess, but it's atomic engines that are going to pull us out. In the old days we had to have gallons of fuel to run things. And a slam-down like we had would have finished off all machines—no gas—no oil—we couldn't have run them. But now—we still have plenty of power, and that'll bring us through. Unless—"

He glanced downslope to the distant line of blue. That earlier experimental installation, which had given man a short domination of a strip of that blue water, had gone out in the big storm. Another might be improvised in time. But for the present they were leaving the sea alone, for the menace still lurked there. Two islanders, attracted beyond caution by the jetsam strewn along the strand after the storm, had ventured into the water to haul at a waterlogged boat, to be dragged under shrieking before their companions could move to their aid. And when the others did come to the waves' edge, there was nothing at all to be seen. Hunters and prey were gone.

For a people who had lived on and by the sea for generations, this peril, this divorcement from their usual way of life, was doubly terrifying and at last induced such a shrinking from the boundaries of the ocean that they even avoided the beaches, though the wealth that came drifting in with every thrust of the changing tides was bewildering in its range and value. The inhabitants of San Isadore had benefited from storm salvage ever since the island had been first settled. But now they had to be herded down to the work under supervision and then would go only in full daylight.

The Naval party kept aloof from that task. They had their own repair and rebuilding problems left by the fury of such a storm as this section of the world had never seen before.

And the diversity of the shore gleanings underlined vividly the crash of the civilization that had nourished them. None of the finds were ever approached until after they were checked for radiation. But the pile of loot grew high and pleased both islanders and Americans alike because of future possible uses.

Hughes prowled the dunes on his own project, sharing only with the doctor the secret of his finds, spending long hours afterwards in the improvised laboratory.

Casey dropped down cross-legged, still contemplating the machine they had uncovered. He fumbled in a pocket, pulled out a badly battered pack of cigarettes, regarded it wistfully for a moment, and then stowed it away again.

"It's the little things you miss first," he mused. "Did you hear Lawrence telling off the supply officer this morning when he couldn't promote a tube of toothpaste? We can rebuild old Arabella here—or at least make her earn her keep in some way—but we can't produce a pack of smokes or some toothpaste. Funny to think that there'll be no more zippers, Coke, or disk jockeys—not in this lifetime. The very props of civilization come to dust!

What were you in training for, kid—to be a fish hunter like your old man?"

Griff rubbed his hands together. Blisters were shaping nicely along the palms. He hoped some day that they would be as resistant as Casey's hard paws.

"I was hoping for an appointment to the Air Academy." He was able to mention that dead and gone ambition with a sardonic kind of humor. How long had it been since he had walked along the cliffs above Carterstown pouting at his inability to manage his future? Well, his future had been managed—but good!

Casey chuckled. "Off into the wide blue yonder." He made flapping wings with his hands. "I don't think! Nothing less than a jet, I suppose."

Some tight string within Griff loosened. The apathy with which he had worked, obeyed orders, faced the strange new life, was fading. Casey hadn't changed—there was something easing in his attitude. To be with the islanders was to return to the tenseness, the watchful waiting. With Casey it was like being at home, the home he could not yet force himself to believe had ceased to exist.

"Nothing less than a jet," he echoed. "Maybe some day a space ship—" He laughed self-consciously. "Kid stuff!"

But Casey shook his head. "Maybe yes, maybe no. We had what it took to get us out there—everything but the sense to try that instead of building for the grand smash. Now—no stars—and we start over."

"Casey." Griff dared to put into words the question he had not voiced before. "Do you think it's all gone—everything?"

Casey rested his bristly chin on his fist. "'S funny, kid, you tell yourself that everything went up—smash!—just as all the croakers always said it would. But sitting here you can't really believe it. You're sure inside that off there"—he waved his other hand to the north—"New York still stands—and St. Looie, Frisco—all the rest of them—just as they always have. As long as we don't see the holes, we'll go on with the sneaking feeling that they're there. Maybe it's a good thing we'll never be able to take it in—to see what's up there now."

"As long as we believe in it, maybe it *is* there—in a way—" Griff thought he had not put that into words very clearly, but Casey understood.

"Maybe you got something there, kid." His mouth pulled tight. "Anyway we can keep on an even keel if we keep busy. Our supplies aren't going to last forever, and we have mouths to feed—to say nothing of those jokers hiding in the drink to grab off anyone dumb enough to go fishing. I wouldn't be a bit surprised if they start throwing bait up on land to hook us down to where they can get us. They may be some sort of octopi with brains. But we've had brains longer, and they can't come out here after us, any more than we can go in after them—now. Too bad that last blow got the plane. It'd be good now to have a bird's-eye view of the surrounding territory. I'm betting that this island is half again as big. Whatever spouted fire out there humped us up a lot. Did pretty well for itself too—regular mountain."

With the aid of binoculars the curious had been able to identify a distant smudge as a towering mountain-island, born from the sea in a burst of flame and lava. Steam still arose from its flanks, and there was a curl of smoke at its cap. The internal fires were alive. Whether it was a transient phenomenon that would sink again or whether it was there to stay, they did not know. And so far a closer examination was out of the question.

"Now to work." Casey unstrapped the canvas roll of tools. "We'll pull off her all we can—"

He never finished that sentence, for out of the sky above them came a sound neither had ever expected to hear again—the drone of a plane. Griff was on his feet shading his eyes as he tried to trace that sound to its source.

"Transport! And she's landing here!"

"Where?" Griff glanced around. There was no possible landing strip on San Isadore—unless the pilot in that lumbering ship was headed for what was left of the salt plain, which had been in the interior. Yes—he was trying for that!

Griff began to run, Casey thumping beside him. There was shouting from other points. Griff saw others head inland. He skinned his hand on coral, felt the grit of salt-encrusted sand under his sandals. The plane was overhead now, moving in a wide circle. Something awkward in that suggested that it was either overloaded or in trouble. Then it came in to land.

"Crack-up!" panted Casey. "They're going to crack up!"

There was noise but not the splintering crash Griff had expected. He continued to climb over the sun-heated rock toward the salt-floored basin, where the lake of the flamingos had once rippled. And, thrusting his way recklessly through the thornbrush, which left oozing gashes on his arms and ribs, he came into the open. The plane, undercarriage gone, rested flat on the soil.

"He made it!" whooped Casey. "That bird's something special as a pilot!"

As they ran toward the plane, Griff identified it as one of the passenger ships belonging to the inter-island tourist trade. One of the Seabees was tugging at the hatch as they came up. It gave, and he retreated a step or two as a tall man, his eyes bloodshot and infinitely weary, his once white shirt filthy and spattered with an ominous red, edged through.

"This—is—?" He framed the question slowly.

Before they could answer, they heard the pitiful chorus from the interior of the plane—the crying and whimpering. Casey reached out to support the pilot. The man winced under his touch.

"This is San Isadore, fella." Casey's voice was gentle.

The tall man crumpled, his legs folding under him and letting him down to the sand, his hands covering his twitching face. He was breathing in long, shuddering sobs, which shook his body.

"Never thought we'd make it! Never thought we'd make it!" His words trailed off into sounds that hurt. But one of the others had pushed past to look inside the plane. He came out faster than he had gone in.

"Kids!" He burst out. "There's a whole load of kids in here. Help me get them out, you guys!"

Not all of those handed out of the plane were children. Four women, each holding a baby, staggered out into the sunlight. But some twenty children, ranging in age from toddlers hardly able to stand to three almost in their teens, were led from the confines of the cabin, where they had been lashed for safety in bundles of blankets and foam-rubber pads.

It was from the older children, rather than from the adults, that they got the story. A boy, his grimy hand bandaged in a strip of dirty gauze, held onto Griff.

"Did—did my dad come?"

"In the plane?"

"No. He had to try the boat. The rest all had to take the boats. There was only one plane left, and they made us kids go in that."

Griff knelt so that his eyes were on a level with the boy's. "Where did you come from, son?"

"Santa Maria." He was shivering now. Griff drew him into his arms.

"It's all right, sonny. You got here safe. And Santa Maria isn't far. So your dad'll be along."

"They're things in the sea—" The boy's shudders were a dry sobbing. "They get the boats—"

Griff was silenced. As far as he knew, there was no soothing answer to that one. He could only gather the lad closer, carry him as the cavalcade of children and Seabees moved away toward the settlement in the valley.

"Has the water stopped coming here?" the boy asked suddenly.

"Water? What do you mean, son?"

"It came and covered a lot of Santa Maria. Then it came again, more every day. And Dad said we'd have to get away and get away quick or there wouldn't be any island left! The water just came and came—"

"Well, it isn't coming here! In fact, the water went away and left us a big piece of new land. You can see it from the top of that next little hill. You don't have to worry about the water—"

"And there're no bad things in the water here to get people?"

"You don't have to worry about them now," Griff said firmly. "These men here are from the Navy, and they're preparing some surprises for those things in the water. You're safe. And your dad'll be here soon. You wait and see—"

"What's your name?" his charge asked.

"Griff Gunston. And what's yours?"

"Jimmie Marden. You're an American, too—like Dad—aren't you?"

"Yes." But Griff wondered if it wouldn't be more correct to say now, "I was an American."

"Dad works for the Fruit Company. Are you a sailor—in the Navy?"

"No. I was doing other work here—diving—"

The youngster swung about in his arms to regard him with big eyes. "You go down in the water? But didn't the bad things try to get you?"

"There weren't any bad things here then."

Jimmie nodded. "I remember. It was before the storm. I went out sailing with Hippy. He had a boat—he fished. But I never saw Hippy anymore after the storm. Dad knows how to sail a boat, too. He's about the best sailor on Santa Maria—"

"Then he'll be turning up before you know it," Griff suggested.

But Jimmie's head went down on Griff's shoulder once more, and he felt the boy shiver. "—bad things—" His muted whisper could hardly be heard.

Griff studied the tangled hair and the thin little body with a helpless feeling. There was nothing he could say that might not be a lie. If some desperate party had left Santa Maria by ship—was it possible for them to reach San Isadore? The whole seascape had changed. There were new islands, uncharted reefs—beside the sea enemy. Did such a party have the least chance of winning through?

When they reached the settlement and turned the refugees over to the island women under the supervision of the doctor, Griff and the rest patched together bits and pieces of a horror tale that exceeded anything they had been through. Jimmie's story was only the bare bones.

Volcanic action had wracked Santa Maria to a far greater extent than it had San Isadore. A part of the other island had vanished within an hour as a spouting cone of flame and dust had broken through the outer reaches of the harbor. After that disaster the survivors who had fought to a perilous safety discovered that the doom of the island was sealed. In a series of landslips what was left of Santa Maria vanished hour by hour.

Their escape had been forced upon them. Luckily a section of the airport remained above the water line. There men had labored almost in a panic to cobble together out of the wreckage at least one plane that could take to the air, while others, with little hope of success, fitted up two fishing boats for a try by sea. Most of the island's population had died in the first upheaval, or been lost in the fury of the storm, which had struck when the island was in its death throes. Out of thousands a handful by lucky chance made their way to the last stable land.

The children and three women with newly born babies were given the best odds in the patched-up plane, which a veteran pilot, Henry Forbes, volunteered to fly. Those left behind would take to the boats as the rising water forced their withdrawal. They would try to make San Isadore, though they had not been sure that that island was still above water.

"We're just plain lucky." Casey summed up their own reaction to the news. "Lord, we had it easy compared to them. What're we going to do about those boats, skipper?"

Murray looked in turn to the Navy pilot. "Any chance of getting that plane up again, Whit?"

Hooker shook his head. "Not without a machine shop. Oh, we might do a lot of patching and hope. But it'd take days. You've that one LC 3—"

The LC 3—an amphibian, tanklike vehicle made to plow through water and crawl over coral reefs—which by some freak of luck had survived the storm, was parked on the beach. Just that morning her internals had been checked by mechanics, and she had been proclaimed seaworthy.

"That's a thought," Murray conceded. "If we can rig up some sort of protection—"

"Skipper." Casey leaned forward eagerly. "How about shock waves out from her bow. No," he corrected himself, "we couldn't try that—too risky. But we could mount a couple of spray guns on her fore and aft. And maybe those things wouldn't attack in force if we tried a run by day. They like evening—or when it's gloomy—better."

"How about it, Hughes?" Murray asked the ichthyologist's opinion.

"How can I tell?" Hughes's mouth was set, a permanent nervous tic twitched with clocklike regularity in his thin cheek. "I don't know what makes those things do what they do! Until we can capture one, we won't know anything. And so far none of our traps and bait have worked. They think, I tell you; they can reason out just how to beat us!" His voice rose, and he was on his feet kicking at the packing case that served him for a seat. "Maybe you can shoot them out of the water. If you do, grab a body and bring it back; then maybe we'll be able to get somewhere."

"Commander, you have no idea what course to set." Holmes

entered. There was a bandage turban about his head, and he sat down quickly. "To go out on the mere chance of contacting one of those boats would be acting directly against our orders. We were told to establish this base and wait—" He stopped suddenly as if he realized that he himself had almost committed the cardinal sin of supplying top-secret information.

Casey laughed outright and Murray smiled.

"Wait here for what, Lieutenant?" jibed Casey. "More orders? From where? We're on our own now, and we have to do our thinking for ourselves. That feels kinda good." He stretched.

"You have no real proof of that," snapped Holmes. "Commander, I would suggest that you'd be wiser not to take decisions on yourself so quickly. We have had no official news—nothing releasing us from our original duties—"

Breck Murray levered himself off his crate. "There's such a thing as common sense, Lieutenant. And there're also some people out there, men and women, who have had it worse than we have. If we can make this their port of refuge, then that's for us. All right, Casey, you get Evans, Marshall, Hall, and Koblinski and see what you can do about arming the LC. The sooner you can have her ready the better!"

Chapter Four
SOS AMERIKANSKY

"There's a volcanic island here." The pilot from Santa Maria, propped up on the cot, moved his bandaged hand to mark a cross on the chart Murray had given him. "And shoal water showing here—"

"They'd have to swing to the south then—" mused the commander.

But Griff spoke up. "Who were the captains in charge of the boats?"

Henry Forbes frowned. "There was an islander—Pedro—Pedro Farenez. And Goodrich was slated to take out the other. Farenez knows these waters—he was to lead."

"Pedro Farenez was a runner—at least Murdock always claimed that. He'd head north instead of south; he knows that route better."

"A runner?" Murray was puzzled.

"Smuggler, running contraband to the States, even men who wanted to enter illegally. And he's been busy lately. Murdock said it was common talk among the islanders."

Murray showed Griff the map. "What's the northern route? Did Murdock ever outline it for you?"

"I sailed part of it once in the *Island Queen*. But with these charts no longer accurate—" Griff surveyed the creased canvas and paper square before him with studious attention. He checked place names, the lines of solitary cays and half-hidden reefs. Slowly with his forefinger he traced the course while the commander watched, narrow-eyed.

The route did avoid the recent blocks to navigation that Forbes had sketched in. On the other hand, the pilot had not crossed that section of sea, and more surprises might lie to the north. Murray rubbed his chin thoughtfully.

"And that's Farenez's regular route?"

"Pedro Farenez put in at Carterstown two months ago." The commissioner spoke for the first time. "He was always secretive about his business. Yes, he was known to be operating outside the customs laws, and perhaps against the American immigration laws, but nothing has ever been proven against him in court. However, his knowledge of the northern cays is that of an expert. He might instinctively seek a passage through sea he knew well."

"Like hunting a needle in a haystack! If we head off into the blue northward and they do come in from the south—! No chance of contacting them by radio, I suppose?"

Forbes shook his head. "The boats are old—fishing luggers. One was not equipped with a radio at all, the other had one with parts missing. When we took off, it had not been repaired." His ghostly smile held no humor. "Why should they spend the time on it then? As far as we knew, there was no one left to pick up any calls. After the last day we had begun to believe that we were the only survivors—"

"That makes it tougher. No radio—We could have beamed them in—though there's still a lot of static."

"If we had two LC's—"

Murray snorted. "If we had the fleet and a carrier on tap, we wouldn't have to worry at all." He swung to the commissioner. "What're the chances of picking up a pilot for this northern route from your people?"

"Very poor, I am afraid. The only men who might have assisted you were Murdock and his crew. They're missing. I don't think you could force any of the others to sea now. They have too great a dread of what lies in the water. And superstition adds to that fear."

"I plan on a five-man crew." Murray went to the window to watch Casey and his crew laboring on the LC. "Two on each gun if trouble comes, the other to operate her. But a pilot would be a help—someone who knows these waters—"

"I'll go—" Griff was startled at his own words. But the compulsion to say that had been as strong as the compulsion that had sent him into the inland pool in that reckless dive.

Murray turned around. Griff could read dissent on the commander's face before he spoke, and he had his own argument ready.

"I've been out there with the *Island Queen*. Made the run in her to Santa Maria four or five times, and once we went north along this same course. Captain Murdock briefed me on it, and I know the charts." He thrust the one they had been studying at Murray. "Listen!"

Closing his eyes to picture mentally the lines on the map, he began—first slowly, and then with rapidly growing confidence—to recite sailing directions. Why, he remembered far more than he thought he had! The long sunny days when he had lounged on the deck of the *Queen*, listened to Angus Murdock's unhurried speech, to Chris Waite's stories, were now paying off. When he finished, he found himself the center of a surprised circle.

"All right." Murray re-rolled the chart. "You've proved something or other. I may be five kinds of a fool for letting you go. But maybe you'll provide what we need. I have a hunch about that."

Burrows was nodding, too. "We can—we must depend now on such things—your hunch, I mean. I, also, think that it is meant for this young man to do us this service. But you do not leave tonight?"

Forbes stirred on his cot. "They must have sailed this morning—"

"It would be too easy to miss them in the dark," Murray pointed out. "There's no help for it. We'll have to wait for dawn."

Griff tried to sleep but found it hard. The glow of light from where the LC was being prepared was one irritant. But more important was his distrust of his own proposal. Had he been too sure of Farenez's route? Would the island smuggler try this time for the southern course? Suppose, following Griff's suggestion, they headed in the opposite direction from the party they were trying to help! His fault—it would be his fault.

"Griff—?"

Griff felt a hand touch his arm, slide up to his shoulder, pressing there.

"You have fear—" The words had only a faint touch of the island slur, but he recognized the voice.

"Le Marr?"

"Yes. Griff, you have done what is right to do. There is that which must be done waiting for you. But the end is not failure."

There was conviction in those words out of the dark. Griff had always believed that Le Marr had his own sources of information. There were odd quirks in many human minds that led to a measure of foresight—cases were known, but as yet no one could explain how or why. And the very inability to control such a talent made it more a curse than a gift.

Now he asked without disbelief, "What waits for us—?"

There was a sigh. "That I cannot tell you, my son. But you will return, bringing with you what you seek, also much else."

"Le Marr—who are you?" Griff demanded impulsively.

This time the answer was akin to a chuckle. "Have I not asked myself that these many times, mon? I am a son of San Isadore, also I am a Papa-loi, the ignorant witch doctor of the mixed bloods."

"You're a lot more than that! Dad thinks so anyway."

"Dr. Gunston is a seeker of the unknown. In my small way I walk the same path. Thus are we fellow travelers, owing each other the courtesy of the road. Now do you sleep, for the morning will bring much to be done."

The hand exerted pressure, and Griff yielded to it, sinking back. Then the warm palm went from his shoulder to his forehead unerringly, as if the other could see in the dark, and rested there in a light touch. For the first time Griff was able to relax.

"—can't use the regular stuff. It's not for a job like this." The protest came unmistakably from Casey.

And Griff, as he came downslope through the gray light of predawn, was not surprised to see the chunky Lieutenant, J.G., facing up to the leaner figure of Lieutenant Holmes.

"Sure I told Henley to break open those crates. We gotta know what we have. Maybe some of it can be adapted to this job. All right, all right, so I broke about nineteen dozen regulations when I said rip off the packing! Who in Hades cares now? Go tell Washington, if you can still find it—" His round face was almost as red as the thatch of hair above it as he stood, hands on his hips, a ring of Seabees for an audience and a row of small, sleek, torpedo-shaped canisters laid out on the sand.

"I shall make a full report—" Holmes returned coldly. He must have heard that snicker from one of the group, but he gave no sign.

"Report your head off!" was Casey's hot retort. "I was given a job to do, and I'm doing it—to the best of my ability. I don't care how many reports you make, or to whom. You'd better get it through your head, Lieutenant, that the Navy's washed up. We're on our own—"

"You forget yourself, Mr. Casey." Holmes swung around, his face set in stiff lines. He marched back toward the settlement, passing Griff without any greeting.

"Now." Casey shifted his attention to his working crew. "We'll let this stuff go." He indicated the row of cylinders. "For all we can tell it'd send us to hell and gone if we tried to make it into depth charges. Put in that box of grenades along with the extra ammo. We want to get rolling as soon as the skipper gives us the high sign."

The LC was not trim in line. On shore she had the ponderous shape of one of the crawlers, suggesting brutal power rather than speed or great mobility. During the night the workmen had rigged wire nets along her sides, nets which would offer no deterrent to the firing of the guns now mounted at her bow and stern, but which might give pause to anything trying to clamber on board from the water line. Since the LC was made to carry cargo or a sizable landing party to shore, the six-man crew Murray had designated occupied very little of the cockpit-like interior. But some of the empty space was being filled with boxes of supplies.

"Hello, kid. Come aboard!" Casey had sighted Griff from his commanding position by the wire barrier, where he was now overseeing the last-minute stowage.

As Griff dropped down into the cockpit, the other pointed to the guns.

"Good stuff. They were hush-hush—rapid-fire atomics—something new. Probably planned to use against subs."

"Yeah." One of the Seabees at the nearest gun spoke over his shoulder. "*If* they work. Me, I'm glad we've got a full case of *them* aboard in addition—" He jerked his chin left to indicate a line of automatic rifles of new design leaning barrel-up along the edge of the cockpit.

"Can you handle one of these?" Casey asked.

"I've used a shotgun," Griff returned, willing to admit his own greenness, if it were necessary.

"They've got a kick, but their fire power is great. Here comes the skipper—maybe now we shove off."

Murray's last-minute orders were few enough. Apparently having selected Casey to captain the expedition, he was willing to allow the proceedings to be at his subordinate's discretion. Years of working together in and out of the service had made them a team; each knew and depended upon the abilities and character of the other. The commander's one instruction dealt with time.

"Three days only. Then whether you have made contact or not—come in. We'll try to keep in touch by radio. Any sign of a storm, and you head back at once!"

"That's for true, skipper. We won't try to ride out any blow in this old mud turtle. Okay, Barnes, give her the gun and let's push off!"

There was a snort as the LC motor came to life. She started a slow progress over coral rock and sand, a progress that was close to a waddle but that brought them into the washing waves.

"Come up here to the lookout, kid," Casey called. "You know these blasted fish and how they move. If you see anything coming—sing out!"

"Lookout" proved to be a wide water glass set into the LC itself so that they could watch below the wave line as the amphibian craft took to sea. When the treads no longer caught, she began to chug, a floating tank.

To Griff's surprise the sea world he viewed through the glass was much as it had always been. The rainbow fish, the animal-vegetable foliage of the underworld was, as far as he could tell, normal, apparently untouched by the blasts of storm that had so beaten the island. But he watched alertly for the first hint of trouble.

Sun banners flooded the eastern sky. Was that coming light a threat to the enemy? And who or what was the enemy? Mutants caused by atomic radiation from earlier testing? Such a neat answer, but probably they might never know for certain.

Griff froze. That dark trail—it could be a twist of weed, an extra-long sea plume half torn from its moorings—But it was not!

"Casey!" He gave the alert, still tracing that rippling, ropelike thing back to the crevice from which it protruded. It was a tentacle right enough, but the largest he had ever seen. The squid or octopus it belonged to was far more formidable than any of the creatures he had watched along the reef in the old days.

"What is it?"

"Octopus—very big one. See—it must be holed up there—right behind that big stand of red sponge!"

"I don't—Oh, that's one of its arms waving about. But—Good Lord, kid, that arm must be about twelve-fifteen feet long! I didn't know they grew so big around here."

"As far as I know, they didn't—before. Ink!"

The murky cloud shot out of the crevice, forming a screen through which even the water glass could not aid their vision. Casey went into action.

"Barnes, let's have the best she can do! Hall, you and Briggs stand by—"

The LC's crawl stepped up a notch, but her speed was no better than a snail's compared with the agility that any of the great cephalopods could show, as Griff well knew. He reached for one of the rifles and saw that Casey had already picked one up.

"They shoot that ink when they're afraid, don't they?"

"It can also be a signal. With no speech, no hearing, it's their means of communication."

"Maybe we've alerted a lookout." Casey peered fruitlessly into the glass. "It sure muddles things for us."

Griff watched that murk, hoping that soon the LC would be beyond its fogginess. Minutes passed with dragging slowness. Nothing broke the waves, showed any desire to challenge the LC. Leaving Griff on duty by the glass, Casey went back to control to check their course. It had the look of a calm day. The sea moved in lazy swells. There was only a fair wind, hardly more than a breeze, and the sun was rising into a cloudless sky.

Behind them San Isadore became a black smudge on the horizon. They approached within a mile of the new volcanic island cone and coughed in the sulphur-tainted air blown toward them. Storm wrack, in the form of dead fish, matted weed, and wreckage, floated by, caught along the LC, and had to be pushed away. There was an unpleasant odor, partly sulphur, partly from the flotsam, but alien to the clean scent of salt and sea wind.

Then that cone drew astern, and they were in the open. Gulls beat over them; one of Mother Carey's neat black and white chickens escorted them for a moment or two before tiring of their slow pace and flashing on.

Casey held the headset of the small radio so that one ear could catch any message from shore. At half-hour intervals they tapped back their own monotonous record of no action. As the sun beamed down, they put on dark glasses and covered their heads. But, save for the birds, they might now be traversing a deserted ocean.

"If it's this quiet," Barnes spoke up, "those guys from Santa Maria won't have it so bad. Maybe there ain't all the trouble that we think there is."

"Or else it hangs about land, around the islands," Casey replied. "Wait!" The rifle slipped from his loose grasp. He had clamped the earphone tighter to his head with one hand, and his sun-reddened face was the picture of blank astonishment.

"Something coming in?"

"The Santa Maria crowd? Maybe they got that radio fixed! They can give us a beam to ride, and we'll be right with them—"

Casey held the earphone away, surveyed it as if he could not believe he had heard what he did, and clamped it back in one fluid movement.

"Not Santa Maria—?" queried Griff.

"Not unless they speak Russian there!"

"Russian!" Hall fairly spat out the word, and his hand fell on the mounted gun he was to operate.

"I learned some. That's Russian right enough." Casey was emphatic.

"Expeditionary force—?" Barnes gazed bleaky ahead at the still empty sea.

"Did any expeditionary force ever signal 'SOS Amerikantsky'?"

"They're asking *us* for help!"

"Seems that way." Casey's grin was back. "Sounds as if they'd like to see us quick, too. Well, boys, what do we do? Ride their signal beam in—it's in the general direction we're steering—"

"It's a trap!" That was Lawrence at the bow gun.

But Casey shook his head. "I don't think so. They may not know there's anyone around. Sounds to me like a general appeal. How about it, boys, do we go or don't we?"

"We don't!" Barnes's retort flashed.

"I don't know." Hall fiddled with the ammo belt of his gun. "We're armed, and they can't take us by surprise. After all—if they did plaster us—they must have got it as good. We're both finished—why keep on fighting? Kinda silly to do that, seems to me. And if it's in the same direction, we may run into them anyway. I'd say—have a look."

"Suppose we vote." Casey spit overboard one of the slivers of wood he had taken to chewing in place of the vanished cigarettes. "We ride in on their beam and look them over—Ayes?"

There were five "ayes" to Barnes's still defiant "no," but the dissenter accepted the decision with good grace when Casey pointed out that they would advance ready to open fire at the least hint of treachery.

With the call signal ringing in his ears, Casey set about the delicate task of guiding the LC along the flickering beam, hoping to contact those transmitting it.

Chapter Five
WHO IS THE ENEMY

"What's below?"

With a guilty start Griff looked from the horizon to the glass, which was their spy-hole on the sea. But, though the murk of ink was missing, there was no clear glimpse of what might lurk there. They were out of the shallows, as the color of the waves about them testified. Any ocean flooring now went down to the big deeps, where even the armored divers dared not penetrate. An occasional fish was all he could see, and so he reported.

"How are we doing, sir?" Barnes asked Casey.

"We're still on signal—"

"Do they say anything else?" That was Hall.

"Not so far. The broadcast may be automatic."

"Bait." Barnes still held to his negative opinion. "New type booby trap—"

"Maybe." Casey cupped the earphones closer. "Two points starboard—yes—" As the LC swung on the slightly altered course, he nodded. "That does it—beginning to fade a little. We must have it dead center now."

"Something dead ahead!"

It was a dark smudge on the water.

"Reduce speed," Casey ordered. He produced binoculars from the case hanging on his chest and tried to adjust them with one hand. Unable to do so, he held the glasses out to Griff with an impatient grunt.

"What is it? A wreck?"

Griff dropped his sunglasses and used the binoculars. Rocks, slime-green velvet in places with sea growths, leaped out at him—undoubtedly a newly born islet. But projecting from its crown, as a finger might point to the unclouded sky, was something too sharply edged, too smoothly sided, to be natural.

"Island. Just heaved up, I'd say. Something on it—might be a wreck."

He was still not satisfied. A wreck would be more irregular as to outline. This showed no breaks. He saw something move, flip up from the water's edge toward that smooth pinnacle.

"Look out! Lord—!" Was he really seeing that—that ropy *thing* lift from the water to hurl an object at the structure above! "They're under attack!"

Casey snatched the glasses. But Griff could see the islet without their aid now. And he could distinguish movement along the shore line.

"They sure are! Quarter speed, Barnes. We don't want to hit a reef in these waters."

The LC crept while Griff leaned over the vision glass alert to any movement beneath. The ocean floor shelved suddenly, and now he could see ooze and fish. But the shallows were too new to harbor the life forms of the San Isadore lagoon.

"Port—look to port!"

The thing broke water, its long neck curling up into the sunlight, the dark skin rough and warted, the fanged jaws open. It gave a whistling scream and snaked forward with a speed out of proportion to its bulk. But the guns were ready, and the chatter of their defiance crackled.

A thin steam of red spurted high, the neck twisted, and the head flopped back and forth until the rags of skin, torn by the guns' fire, snapped, and it splashed into the sea on the other side of the LC. The convulsions of the dying monster rocked the heavy craft while Barnes fought the controls and tried to back out of the blood-frothed water.

"Lob an egg over." Casey stood braced in the center of the amphibian. "Anything else bound our way, Griff?"

Griff, clutching the rifle, had an answer. "Plenty! Octopi—big ones—Ink!"

Again that cloudy murk cut off his view.

"Maybe this egg will give them other ideas!" Hall hooked a grenade from the box at his side, drew its firing pin, and pitched it over in the general direction of the islet.

Water—water and other things, grisly flotsam—fountained. But a tentacle flushing yellow as it flipped into the air was planted against the side of the LC. Another joined it, and a third!

"They're over here, too!" shouted Lawrence. Sucker-armed muscle and flesh smacked against the wire netting and shook it.

"Stop the engine!" Casey ordered. "We don't want them wrecking the vanes—"

"We're being pulled down!"

"We are, are we? Well, we'll give them something else to think about. Get out that torch, Briggs. You—the rest of you—plant some more eggs. Nothing like discouraging reinforcements."

The LC was rocking heavily. With the same precision as if he were repairing some part of his beloved machinery, Casey aimed a welding torch at the nearest length of tentacle and let go. There was the stench of burnt meat as muscle and flesh crisped and blackened. The length fell away, the charred strings floating for a second or two on the surface of the water, and then disappeared. Methodically Casey turned and applied the heat to the arms showing on the opposite side of the LC, while his crew obeyed orders with zeal, lobbing grenades out in a circle about the bobbing craft.

How many of the octopi attacked them they were never to know, but, as the sweat channeled in streams from the men in the heat generated by Casey's torch, there came a time when no new arms clutched at the amphibian, no shadows drifted toward them through the ink-tainted water. Casey leaned panting against the combing of the cockpit.

"Did we win the war?" he wondered aloud. "Or are they just withdrawing to rest up for another punch? Better move while we can. Give her the gun, Barnes."

The Seabee moved from his place by the grenade box back to the controls. Cautiously he spun the motor, and a welcome throb shook them.

"Do we head in, sir?"

"We do." Casey had gone to the bow. "When we get close enough, give them three or four more eggs right up along the shore rocks, just to discourage peeking—"

The LC at her own lumbering pace, half-speed to be on the safe side, went islandward. There was a commotion below, hidden by the ink clouds. Griff guessed that the ravenous feeders of the sea had been drawn to the wounded or dying octopi. He was sure of that as the curved fins of sharks cut in. And where the sea serpent had gone down, there was a whirlpool of activity.

"Okay!" Casey snapped. "This is it! Tickle them up, boys. If there're any of them left along there—"

There was a grating noise, and a shudder shook the full length of the LC.

"We're walking," Barnes informed them needlessly. "Shall I keep her going?"

"After we leave our calling cards. Give it to 'em!"

Casey's signal brought five precise throws. A good section of the sea-slimed ledges before them went down with a rumble into the agitated water. Ink and blood, and floating remnants. The water was a horrible soup. "Now—! Take her in—all the way! There's a slope—"

"Aye, aye, sir!" For the first time Barnes sounded as if he were enjoying himself.

The LC shook, dipped, and once, for a wild second or two, slipped on a surface still under water, but her threads caught, and she ground on.

"That's a sub on top there!"

In their preoccupation with the sea battle they had almost forgotten their purpose here. But what Lawrence had pointed out was true. The blunt nose of a sub was slanted into the sky, though most of her lay on the opposite side of the ridge, which formed the backbone of the new land.

"We've gone as far as we can, sir." Barnes switched off the motor.

Ahead the rise was at a sharp angle. If they were to go on, it would be afoot.

Casey was back at the radio, tapping out a call signal.

"International Morse," he explained. "If there's anybody at home and they can answer us—this ought to bring them out of their shell."

They waited a long five minutes by Griff's watch, another five—ten. But there was no sign of life about the bow of the sub.

"Could they have set that call and then got it—all of them?" wondered Hall.

"Sure. Well," Casey shrugged, "I guess we do it the hard way. You and me, kid," he said to Griff, "we're elected to the mountain-climbing act. They'll cover us from here with the guns, and we don't go out of sight unless there's an extra-good reason. Okay?"

"Good enough." Griff slung two of the grenades at his belt, copying Casey's preparations. They kicked off their island sandals, preferring to make the climb barefooted, not trusting any soles but their own on that weed-slick surface.

There was a strong smell of decay, as things never meant to lie in the open air under a tropic sun disintegrated. Linked together, and to the LC, with lifelines, the two made the first jump from the edge of the bow to a reasonably level ledge.

Had it not been for the rotting vegetable and animal remains the climb would have been relatively easy. But all at once Griff, reaching for a new hold, jerked back his hand.

"Look out!"

Casey's head came around. "Some of the snakes after us?"

"No—just watch where you put your hands. See that red stuff—" He pointed to a splotch of crimson, which looked as if it had been hurled against the rock and was slowly slipping from its first point of contact. "That looks to me like the 'plague' weed. And if it is, it may be 'hot'—"

"Oh, yeah?" Casey studied the stain. "Well, there's no use in being a dead hero. What'd'you know, it seems to be rather thick up ahead, doesn't it?"

He was right. The higher reaches of the ledges were dotted with reddish blots, some of which left pink trails where they had struck and then slipped down. Griff recalled his first glimpse of the islet and its besiegers through the binoculars. That arm from the sea hurling something upward—this? But why?

They picked a careful path to avoid the red blobs. Luckily chance had spread most of them up and across walls too steep to climb. With a last spurt Griff reached the top, Casey only seconds behind him. Towering over both of their heads now was the bow of the sub, canting at an angle that fingered it in the direction of the LC.

The surface of the metal was bedaubed with the red weed, which was drying into scabs. It was plain that if the plague stuff *had* been systematically thrown from water level, this had been the target of the attack, and the aim in general had been good.

Though the sub had looked intact from below, what they could see now was a badly crippled ship. Whatever motive power had driven her ashore on the knob of rock had done it with such force as to jam and grind her belly plates, splitting them open as if she were a waterlogged coconut. But all this was inches deep in the red scum. And beyond—downslope so that half its putrescent bulk trailed into the water—was another of the sea serpents, very dead, a ragged hole blasted through its middle.

"They chalked up one hit anyway," Casey observed, "so they must have survived her striking here."

"How can we get down to the hatch?" There was plenty of reason for Griff's demand. The reddened ground was a warning.

"Yeah." Casey pushed back his uniform cap. "Ringing the front door bell is going to be a problem. Ringing the front door bell—" he repeated and then unslung his rifle. "I'm no Daniel Boone, but maybe I can win a cigar on this round. Let's see."

He aimed at the lopsided superstructure of the sub. There was a crack and the answering bong of bullet against metal. Reslinging his weapon, Casey put both hands to his mouth funnelwise and shouted, "Hi! Anybody home?"

There was an answer from the men on the LC, and Griff turned to wave. But Casey's attention was for the sub.

"Give them another shot," Griff suggested when there was movement at last.

In the round entrance to a hatch, a piece of white stuff appeared and was swung back and forth with slow deliberation, proving those within wanted no mistake about their peaceful intentions.

"Hulloooo!" Casey called once more.

"—loooo—" a hollow cry came back. And then framed in the oval hatchway, they saw a figure still waving the parley flag.

"Come on out," Casey urged.

The man on the sub still seemed dubious of his welcome. But he handed his white flag to someone behind him and took in return a swab on a pole. This he pushed before him to clean the sloping deck as he approached a point near the Americans.

"Lieutenant Serge Karkoff!" He introduced himself in understandable, if accented, English and made a stiff little bow. "And this"—he waved his hand over the battered sub—"was the *Volga*. You are—?"

Casey answered for them both. "Lieutenant Bert Casey, United States Navy, C.B., Griffith Gunston. Looks as if you've been having a little trouble—"

The other grimaced.

"Did you come to answer our signal? We could only hope. But where is your ship? Were you not attacked?"

"You didn't hear the battle?" Casey grinned. "Yes, the fish tried to scupper us, but we had their numbers. We're parked on the other side of the island—"

"Parked?" the other repeated dully. "There are but four of us unhurt, Lieutenant. And three with broken bones. We surrender unconditionally. If you can—can get us away from this place—"

Griff saw the Russian's teeth clamp on his lip.

"Leave your arms behind," Casey ordered. "And you'd better bring some ropes, if you have them. There's a stiff climb over here."

"It shall be as you say," Karkoff replied. "We must move with caution. This red stuff—it is deadly. Three of our men have died from it—and those—those *things* keep it all about!"

The rescue of the *Volga*'s crew was a lengthy process. Two of the disabled had to be lowered in slings and then carried to the LC. And those on the amphibian were constantly alert against a renewal of hostilities from the sea.

Now the cockpit quarters were a tighter fit, but the men from the sub were no problem. For the most part they dropped to the deck, staring rather dazedly about them, as if not yet fully realizing that they had been freed from the disabled sub.

"How long have you been here?" Casy asked the Russian commander.

Karkoff shrugged. "Two—three—maybe four days. There was a storm, and we drove into something below which was not on our charts. All compartments but one were flooded. Alexis, Gronmyko, all the rest, they had no chance. We could not tell what was happening. Then—hours later—we were able to cut our way out—and found this. After that—it was a terrible dream. There was the sea beast—we blew it apart with a shell from the deck gun. But the gun burst when we tried to fire a second time. Two men were killed then. Afterwards came the red stuff." With the gesture of a tired and bewildered man, he rubbed his hands across his face, and his cap fell to the deck. "It is very hard to think; you must excuse me. There has so much happened—and all of it strange. There—You are now fighting the war?"

Casey hitched at his rifle strap. "I don't think there's any war left to fight, Lieutenant. We don't know what has happened—"

The Russian was younger than Griff had first reckoned. His broad Slavic face did not register any strong emotion, but his dark blue eyes held a hurt deep in them. He swayed suddenly, and Griff put out a hand to steady him, pushing him down on the edge of the grenade box.

"It has come then—the big end to everything?" he asked in a low voice.

One of his men reached out and touched the officer's dangling hand, asking a question. Almost impatiently the other answered, and the Russian seaman drew in his breath with a hissing sound.

"Seems so," Casey returned frankly. "But our crowd weathered it well—"

"So I see. You were searching for us?"

"We were out on a mission of our own when we picked up your signal. Now," he spoke to Barnes, "we'd better get on course again. Take her out."

"Aye, aye, sir."

With a throbbing motor the LC reversed and crawled back the way she had come.

"Nickov set that call before he died," the Russian explained. "We had only a little hope. You are certain that all is gone—?"

"We don't know. No radio broadcasts have been picked up from the north. But just at present we have other things to think about."

"*Da*," Karkoff nodded. "Keeping alive occupies the mind. But if all is gone, why should we struggle to keep alive?"

"One gets in the habit of it," Casey commented dryly. "And, I, for one, am not going to let any damned fish take over running things!" He spat into the water just as the LC tumbled from her reef footing and became all ship once more.

"Who now is the enemy?" broke out Karkoff. "You and I—or that down there?"

"We haven't settled that yet, sonny boy," was Casey's prompt reply. "But I'm inclined to think that the line-up will be different from this point on—men against fish!"

Chapter Six
THE RETURN OF THE *ISLAND QUEEN*

"We should be sighting the Largo Cays about now," Griff observed but without too much certainty. One northern run with the *Island Queen* had been his only introduction to this particular route, and trying to compare the cruising speed of the *Queen* and the lumbering LC added to his confusion.

The vision glass was no help either. Where, by the old charts, it should have shown shallows, it revealed only the darker gloom of depths. But, after they left the island where the *Volga* had made her last port, they saw no more of the octopi. Karkoff was able to add a fact or two to their information concerning the creatures. It was true that this new breed of cephalopods controlled the "sea serpents" and also that they followed an intelligent pattern in their attack on the sub. But why they should be aroused to that attack in the first place still remained a mystery.

"I see nothing—" Karkoff stood in the bow using his own binoculars. "You seek islands—?"

"Not islands—except as guides. We're after a couple of fishing boats loaded with refugees." Casey outlined the story of the end of Santa Maria.

"A whole island sinking!" Again that strained, dazed expression dulled the Russian's eyes. "But why? Why should islands go up and down?"

"I'm no geologist," Casey replied. "But the balance must have been upset. There's a full-sized volcano off San Isadore—as well as the one at Santa Maria. How do we know what all-out bombing would do? The Atlantic may have poured in over part of the States. And in Europe—"

The Russian shook his head. "I think that I do not want to know."

Casey went back to the radio, still hoping for a signal from one of the fishing boats. But as the LC bore on into the sea, there was no sign that any other craft had been there before it. They did not sight the Largo Cays. Perhaps they had sunk. So finally Casey ordered a circling eastward, to head back to San Isadore. Griff felt their failure the more because he assumed the responsibility for it.

"Getting late—" Barnes observed. And they knew what he was thinking.

Night at sea was a double danger. But in the end it was the darkness that brought success to their mission.

An excited exclamation from one of the Russians drew their attention to port. A fiery trail ascended into the sky, bursting in a shower of stars. That was not born of a volcano!

"Head in!"

Barnes obediently altered course once more, and the searchlight on the bow was turned on, sending a broad path of light out ahead. There was a second starry display and a third. The LC pointed at that dead center. Was that the signal of the boats from Santa Maria—or the call of some other castaway?

When their beam caught the boat ahead, they were reasonably sure they had found what they sought. There was no mistaking the blunt lines of an island fishing smack built for durable use rather than for record speed. It wallowed toward them deep in the water, as if overloaded.

Casey climbed up the netting and, cupping his hands, sent a hail across the waves.

"What ship?"

"The *Felice*, Santa Maria—Who are you?" came the faint reply.

"Navy LC out of San Isadore," Casey boomed. "We've been hunting you—"

The *Felice* and her companion, the *Flamingo*, crept with the beat of hard-driven engines, their pace less than the LC's second speed. Faces, white, dusky, dark, were picked up by the searchlight.

"Good Lord!" Hall exploded. "They've packed them in, standing room only!"

"Can you give a tow?" queried someone from the boats.

"This is a pretty tough old girl, sir," Barnes spoke up. "But she can't haul the fleet!"

But that wasn't required. Behind each of the fishing vessels trailed a string of smaller craft. And that underlined their desperate venture. Only a choice of deaths could have sent the pitiful flotilla into the infested sea so poorly protected against the danger now lurking there.

The LC could and did take tows, three from each of the fishing craft. And then, her searchlight still on, she led the way back, southwest to San Isadore. They were forced to creep, laboring at such a pace that a rowboat ably handled could have outdistanced them. And only the merciful fact that the sea remained calm saved them.

All night long they held course, Casey and Barnes alternating at the controls. And the gray light of predawn was easing across the sky when Lawrence switched off the searchlight. By compass they would approach San Isadore from a different direction than they had left and must parallel the coast northward to the base, being now not far from sunken Carterstown.

Once more they swung to avoid the volcanic cone, and Karkoff, standing beside Griff, exclaimed in Russian before switching to English.

"This is one of those new volcanoes?"

"Yes. The night it broke through, San Isadore had several shocks. See that line over there?" He pointed to a doubly thick horizon. "That's San Isadore."

"Your base?"

"Yes."

"That ship—it is also one of yours?"

"What ship?" Surprised, Griff looked along the line of the other's pointing finger.

Karkoff was right. There was a ship there, a spot of white against the waves.

Before he could ask for the use of Casey's binoculars the other called to him, "Get on the glass, kid. We want to know it if the snakes are preparing a reception party."

Griff went to his post, and the Russian followed him, drawing a deep breath as he shared the vantage point of the glass with the

American. The water was changing color; they were in the shallows—those shallows that were always dangerous now. But, though the usual inhabitants of the reef-protected section were there, Griff saw no signs of the enemy.

Again the LC altered course, now paralleling the outline of land. The fishing boats, with their engines driving heavily, sluggishly, copied her maneuver. When Griff dared to glance up, he saw that the strange ship anchored in Frigate Bay was now hidden by a headland. But it must be investigated when they could.

The flotilla was still some distance from the base when the engine on one of the fishing boats gave a final splutter and died.

"That does it!" Barnes exclaimed. "We can't take *her* in tow!"

From a whirlpool of activity on board the boat, her sails arose, cupping some of the trade. At sea it would not have been enough to give her headway; here it at least kept her moving and manageable.

Casey called across, "Can you keep going for a while? We'll be back as a ferry—"

"It's a case of have to," a voice unmistakably American shouted back.

"So far, so good. Any trouble from below?" Casey demanded of Griff.

But save for the usual dwellers of the shore line he saw nothing.

"Give her all you can now," Casey ordered. "We'll have to be back again."

The other fishing boat had passed them. Now the LC caught up and left her astern. Lawrence hailed a shore landmark with a shout of relief. Over a calm sea they headed straight in to crawl up on the beach. The Russians disembarked, as the other fishing boat anchored as close to shore as her crew could bring her. With a hurried explanation to the waiting Murray and a casting off of her earlier tows, the Navy amphibian took to the sea once more, heading back for the disabled refugee carrier.

"Ink!" The battle signal Griff had been watching for billowed. Undersea sentries were alerted. Did it mean attack?

"Lay a couple of eggs as a discouragement." Casey was cool. "Say one ahead and one behind."

The grenades sailed through the air, splashed, and the LC rocked with the force of those twin explosions. There was another sound carrying clearly across the sea—it could only be the crackle of rifle fire.

Barnes got more speed out of the lumbering craft than Griff would have believed possible. Once her treads bit on a sunken reef, but instead of slowing her spurt, that merely added to her impetus. They rounded a rocky point and saw the white sails of the other ship, heard the steady firing. One of the boats she had towed and had not been able to relinquish to the LC floated bottom up on the water, a water now riffled by more than the morning wind.

"Anything below?"

"Ink mostly. It's all screened out."

"Until we see something we can aim at, just plant eggs."

They tossed grenades at regular intervals as they bore down upon the almost helpless ship. Evidence floated to the surface telling them that they had made at least one direct hit on some gathering of attackers. There were wild shrieks as the second and last of the towed boats began to rock vigorously. The LC was close enough for her crew to see those tough ropes of muscle that had tightened about the small skiff. Men slashed with knives. One tentacle was hacked in two—but there were others.

Lawrence depressed the muzzle of the bow gun, fired an experimental burst, which clipped below the surface, and then sent a steady round into the weltering mass. Luck was with him. The tentacles threatening the boat suddenly fell away and sank. By incredible good fortune one of those bullets had reached some vital spot in the enemy.

Barnes cut the throttle, and the men in the small boat hastily took to their oars, brought it alongside the amphibian, and then climbed the netted sides to drop into the cockpit. They were a mixture of native islanders, English-ancestored planters, and two whom Griff recognized as the manager of the Santa Maria airport—an ex-American flyer—and one of the customs officers.

Casey hardly waited until the last was on board before he called to the larger vessel for a towline. And so linked, the LC began the slow crawl back to the base.

The airport manager crouched beside Griff. His eyes were sunken in dark hollows; his wrist was bandaged, and he carried it thrust into the front of his shirt for the want of a sling.

"What's this thing anyway?" he asked. "A seagoing tank?"

"Something like."

"It sure can do the business! Look here—did a plane get through? We sent one off." His forehead wrinkled in a frown. "It must have been the day before yesterday."

"Yes. It came through. Cracked up when it landed, but everybody was all right. That's why we were out hunting you—"

The other sighed. "A little bit of luck. First we've had. My wife was on that plane. They're all safe—you sure of that?"

"I helped bring them down from the salt flat where they landed, so I can say 'yes' for sure."

The other's hand went to his face and shielded his eyes. "Thanks." His voice was a whisper. "Thanks very much."

Griff was back at his post by the glass. The dark cloud of ink, which had curtained the activities of the attackers, was thinning. Could they hope that the sea things had shot their bolt for this time? Brilliant coral fans, sea plumes bloomed. The unhurried schools of rainbow fish trailed through the drifting threads of weed as they had done for unnumbered years.

"You have any news?" The airport man edged forward. "My people live in Tampa. Any news from the States?"

"No."

The other sank back to stare dully at the flooring of the cockpit.

"Hey!" Lawrence called from the bow. "What's all that red stuff?"

Rippling from wave cap to wave cap, as in more happy days the trails of sargasso weed had moved along the Gulf Stream, as a dull red stain, a splotch that might have been blood draining from some giant wound. But Griff had seen its like before. And he didn't need to sight the fish floating with distended bellies up in the circle of scum to underline its deadliness. The plague!

It had not yet cut across the course held by the LC, but those on board were able to see that it was only the advance part of a vast coat of the stuff, ragged patches of which had split free from the main mass. And from it came the stench of ancient rottenness—of decay fouler than that native to dead sea life.

Insensibly Barnes altered course to avoid those streamers among the waves. But Lawrence's second observation was awed.

"There must be miles of it!"

Yes, they could see that the stain covered the ocean as a blanket. Sea birds dipped, attracted by the dead things floating in its foulness. But then they sheared off suddenly, to rise screaming and baffled. And that which even the birds feared was headed straight for San Isadore. It would be washed ashore all along this end of the island.

They reached the base, and the crippled fishing boat anchored while the LC waddled ashore with her second cargo of refugees. Griff dropped to the sand. It was not until much later that a glimpse of Karkoff talking to Murray reminded him of the ship they had sighted in Frigate Bay, off the now three-quarters submerged Carterstown. Were there survivors aboard her? If so—shouldn't they be helped ashore?

But he couldn't get to Murray. Casey had disappeared. And, although he saw Holmes, he knew better than to try to enlist the aid of the security lieutenant. He had kept the rifle from the LC. Now, after filling a canteen, he went to the caves of the islanders and luckily found Le Marr in the first he entered.

"I think there's a ship anchored in Frigate Bay—near the town. If there's anyone on board her—"

"There be. That has been homin' a long time, many days," Le Marr answered surprisingly. "Yes, we must go to her—"

But he would not explain as they left the settlement and struck southward, with first the cliffs and then the wide beach as their path. The red taint was already leaving its mark on the rocks. He pointed it out to the islander.

"Death," Le Marr said with emotion. "That be death, mon."

The stench of the stuff was thick enough to taste. When they stopped to chew on rations, Griff discovered that, hungry as he had been, he could not stomach food. The odor got between him and every bite he took.

They plodded on into the late afternoon. The mangrove swamp, by some freak of the island displacement, was now higher ground, drained of most of its pools, the mud dried between the knee roots wherever the sun could strike in to suck up moisture. But enough scummy depressions remained to harbor the mosquitoes, which attacked the two so viciously that they had to beat them away, breathing in minute insects, crushing the larger until their shirts were bloody. However, the reek of the dying swamp cut some of the stench of the plague, and they welcomed the change. Crabs scuttled away from their line of march; lizards moved lightning quick along the branches of the trees. It was a dank green world, and Griff wondered if it were now totally doomed by the draining.

It was close to sundown when they came out on the other side. Had it not been for Le Marr, Griff might have been helplessly lost in the mucky maze. In the old days one could have taken to the sea and splashed around such a barrier. But now that path was closed.

They built a fire of driftwood and ate their rations. Griff tired to scrub the slime of the swamp from him with sand. If he could only strip and wash clean in the sea!

A burrowing owl, devoid of ear tuffs so that its head was round, resembling nothing so much as an animated ball of knitting wool, cooed to itself as it appeared in its doorway under the roots of a bush hung with thousands of tiny blossoms. Griff brushed against one of the shrub's outstretched limbs. The owl snapped into cover as a jack-in-the-box. Pollen drifted through the air and with it a strong perfume heavy enough to banish some of the foulness that had clogged his lungs for so long.

They slept there that night, both silent and deep in their own thoughts, the fire at their feet. But the flames died before dawn, and Griff awoke shivering. The red tinge was on the sand here, and the waves brought in the bodies of harmless sea dwellers killed by its poison—lying limp for the tearing claws of the shore crabs, who were not as nice as the birds had been and devoured the dead eagerly.

It must have been close to ten o'clock when they came out on the scrap of road that had once run inland for a half mile or so from Carterstown. The rubble of the dead town lay ahead, three-quarters of it now under water, showing here and there a part of wall or a thatchless roof projecting above the surface.

And there was a ship right enough, swaying at anchor with every rise and fall of the lazy swell, as Griff had seen her so many, many times in the past. The *Island Queen* had come home!

Chapter Seven
CAPTIVE CARGO

She was not the same trim vessel that had put out from that port more than a week before. Her main mast ended in a splintered nub some feet above deck; her white paint was stained and in places ground from her boards. But there was something else! Fastened to that stub of mast, a colored rag beat out in the pull of the morning wind as might a tattered battle standard. Seeing that, Griff turned to Le Marr.

"There must be someone on board! That's a signal! How are we going to get out to her?"

Between them and that deck rolled the oily water that washed over the ruins of Carterstown. Although the red scum was missing here, the rubble under water provided too many good lurking places for the enemy to invite swimming. Yet Griff *had* to reach the *Queen* some way. A dugout? There had been some in the town, used for fishing within the circle of the reef. Could they locate one of those? Only, such a craft would be as easy to attack as a swimmer!

Le Marr moved off around the edge of the flood, where the new shore line was in the process of establishment. Griff fell in behind, hoping the islander could produce a sensible plan of action.

Under them the ground began to rise. It was part of the old cliff line. Soon they were above the level of the anchored ship, for it *was* anchored. Griff could easily picture Captain Murdock, Rob, or Chris, sick and hurt, pent up in her cabin, waiting for help that was too long in coming.

Under the water from this height they could see the lines of walls, those dark pools that were the interiors of roofless houses. Then a triangular fin cut smoothly through the flood, beyond it another—sharks. Griff slipped the rifle strap from his shoulder. He was aiming at one of those dimly seen killers when another idea occurred to him. The sound of a shot might bring into the open anyone on board the *Queen*.

Pointing the rifle out to sea, Griff fired three times and was amazed himself at the roar of sound. Sea birds wheeled and screamed, and inland there was a wild clatter of hooves, a frightened bray. Some of the island's wild donkeys had survived the storm and were raiding garden patches on the outskirts of the town. But the donkeys were not the only life, as the two on the cliff speedily discovered. They were startled by a shout.

"Oheee—mon—"

Tearing through the thorn scrub came a wild figure, which looked to Griff no more than a skeleton barely concealed in flapping rags. And behind the first came a second, even barer, as its full clothing was a twist of drab stuff about the loins.

"What you do here, mons?" Between panting gasps the words broke, as the first skeleton clawed its way up to them, using hands as well as feet on the ground to keep balance.

"Liz!" Griff almost dropped the rifle. The bony figure, the ravished face, was not the confident woman he had seen in the valley. But this was Liz making her way painfully toward them. He ran forward and tried to help her up.

"Mistuh Gunston!" Her hollow eyes fastened on him with a spark of her old energy. "Then the big storm, it don' take everybody like we think! Oh, there's still mons here—there's still mons!" Tears rolled out of her eyes, and she made no move to wipe them away.

"But, Liz, how did you and—and—" He studied the second figure. The man might have been any age from twenty to fifty, but he moved stiffly, favoring his leg down which ran an angry-looking, puckered slash, and his face was dull, beaten.

"This is my boy, Luce. You 'member Luce, Mistuh Gunston!"

Luce! Griff remembered a young giant he had seen win two wrestling matches, a laughing young man with a fine voice for crooning chants of the island. But that Luce and this were not the same.

"What happened?" he began and then wished that he hadn't. Luce stood with hanging head, the vacant look on his face unchanging. But Liz shivered.

"The storm, that's what happened. We found us a cave—but even there—" She faltered. "You got things better, Mistuh Gunston?"

"Yes, you'll come back with us, Liz, and see for yourself," he was beginning when Luce suddenly came to life. Advancing to the edge of the rise, he pointed out to the *Queen.*

"There's the *Queen!* The *Queen*, she done come home!"

Liz was shaken out of her own concerns. She peered down at the bobbing ship. "That's right! Luce, he call it right," she marveled. "That's the *Queen* come home. But"—she surveyed the sunken town—"that home, they ain't goin' to find it no more."

"You haven't been here before, Liz? No one landed from her?"

Liz shook her head in answer to both questions.

"But someone brought her in and anchored here. There's a signal flag on the mast. Someone may be on board—"

"Why you don't swim out?" Luce asked.

"Too dangerous." Griff wondered if the other could understand. "There are things in the sea—"

Luce's skull jaws split in a grin. "They can't touch you if you got yourself jubee oil—"

Le Marr whirled. But he spoke to Liz and not to the grinning Luce.

"You make that?"

She drew herself up with much of her old commanding air, her hysterical welcome to them forgotten. "I found something," she replied. "You can swim in the sea an' nothing—nothing at all touch you."

"You have it here, woman?"

"Done used it all fishin'," she said regretfully. "But we can make us a mess o' it again—do you want it so."

"Do that thing!" Le Marr snapped.

"First we git us a pig. An' they's hard to find now. Luce." She summoned her son. "Luce, we do want us a pig. How we git one—?"

The flash of intelligence still lit his face. He put out a bony hand and drew one finger almost caressingly down the barrel of Griff's rifle. "With this here, it ain't too hard. I show where—"

Liz smiled. "You go with Luce, Mistuh Gunston. Git us a pig, an' we find us what else we be needin'."

"I don't understand," Griff protested, but Le Marr interrupted him.

"It be this way, mon. They's ways the fishermons knows to poison fishes. Not here on the island—but over there"—he made a gesture westward—"where is the big land. Maybeso we find some thing here what will act like that. There's herbs an' there's bad things—poisons—grown here. Do we learn to use them right, we's got us something those sea debbles are goin' to fear. Liz, she knows the plants, better then me she know them 'cause—"

"'Cause," Liz spoke up proudly, "I do be kin to the old wise womons as live here for years an' years. There be's many wise womons in my family, an' they tells to one to the other all they knows afore they die. Me—" She spread her hands wide and then tapped her forehead. "I know much-much. An' this here stuff it work. Luce, he put it on an' walk right in the water—fish they all go 'way fast. You'll see. But first you go shoot us that pig."

Somehow a portion of the animal life of San Isadore had managed to survive the great storm. And Luce led Griff inland to a gully, where the drift of salty sand deposited there by the high winds was pied with the earth that had slipped down in landslides. Luce knew what he was doing, for the slotted pig tracks ran back and forth in trails.

"You stay here with that there gun." He was almost his old-time self again as he swung into action he understood. "I go—git pig—"

Griff stationed himself obediently behind an outcrop of wall to wait while Luce melted into the patch of scrub thorn and cacti that had been rooted against the fury of the tempest.

They really should explore the whole of San Isadore soon, he thought. Water might be a problem. Most of the island had depended upon rain tanks for fresh water. He knew that the base had included a conversion unit in its original installations. But whether that apparatus had been salvaged he could not tell. The storms of the past few days had filled emergency tanks as well as all the rock hollows. And under Murray's orders it had been stored and rationed. Water—and food. Much of the arable land was gone. Around Carterstown the sea had taken the majority of the garden strips. There had been a herd of wild cattle, descended from those left by buccaneers to provision their ships, donkeys, some horses, and the pigs. Surely few of those had come through—

A sullen grunting in the brush alerted Griff. He lowered the rifle. Then came an angry squeal. Two rangy sows burst from cover, behind them an ugly-looking boar, who wheeled and turned its head back toward the cover as if to face up to the danger that had flushed it out of hiding.

The pigs of San Isadore were sorry specimens. Most of them would be considered litter runts by any mainland farmer. But the surly tempers and wily animosity of the small herds made them just as dangerous as their cousins that provided sport for hunters elsewhere.

Griff ignored the sows, setting sights on the boar. He fired, and under the impact of the bullet, the hog appeared to rise in the air before it plunged forward, skidding on its head at the foot of a cactus.

Luce skimmed out of nowhere, a brown shadow, his bare body blending into the color of rocks and earth as he went down on his knees to cut the throat of the still feebly kicking animal.

Together they fastened it to a pole for easier carrying. Thin-legged and spine-ridged as the boar looked, it proved to be much heavier than Griff had anticipated. They got it back to the cliff above Carterstown to find there a fire blazing. An iron kettle brought from one of the yet unsubmerged houses hung on an improvised tripod over it, while Liz chopped silvery leaves into chaff and Le Marr studied an array of other vegetation he held fanwise in his hand. Two land crabs lay to one side on a palm leaf, and a dead lizard hung by its tail on a nearby bush.

Griff found the preparations so grisly that he wandered over to sit on a rock and watch the *Queen*. Since there had been no response from her in answer to his signal shot, he had given up hope of there now being any life on board. But someone had brought her in, had anchored her, and had left that rag of flag flying. And Griff was determined to explore her.

He had little faith in Liz's concoction protecting a swimmer. On the other hand, the native lore of the islanders was surprising, and such a discovery would be welcomed at the base. He was perfectly willing to play guinea pig himself.

The result of Liz's brewing was set out to cool at last. And they ate strips of stingy pork fresh broiled, together with Naval rations, while the thick substance with its base of hog grease congealed, Liz testing it from time to time with a finger tip. When she signified it was ready, Le Marr stripped and rubbed it into his skin. After a moment Griff reluctantly threw aside shirt and slacks to follow the islander's example, smearing it first over his skin and then over the trunks he wore. It was smelly and he hated the feel of it, but he trusted Le Marr's faith.

Luce reached out for the rifle Griff had left leaning against the bole of a palm, but the American caught it up. On impulse he tendered it to Liz. She grinned widely with some of her old-time buoyance of spirit.

"I thinks I'll git me some fresh meats, maybeso. Shark meats—"

Just so he wasn't going to provide fresh meat for some shark in his turn, Griff thought as he padded downslope to the new verge of the bay. Le Marr had waded out along a crumbled, awash wall, water rising from ankle to knee, and then to his waist before he dove to paddle out over what had been the main street of Carterstown, Griff gingerly copied him. Never before, even on that day when he had entered the inland sea pool, had he felt the same reluctance to trust himself to water.

He fell into the effortless strokes of an expert swimmer, heading for the *Queen*'s mooring. The water rolled from his greased flesh. He heard a warning shout and trod water. There was no mistaking the cutting fin coming around in a wide circle. Griff's hand went for the diver's knife.

But there was no need for such defense. The fin sheered off, breaking away in a fury of speed. Griff might have been a sea monster himself. Liz's oil at work?

He had little time for speculation. Le Marr had reached the *Queen*'s anchor line. That must be their means of getting aboard. But the ship was riding unusually low in the water. Perhaps she had shipped a lot of sea in the storm, but from appearances she might have been carrying a full cargo.

Griff clambered up after the islander. The deck was stripped; everything that a high sea could possibly carry away had been torn from its place. There was an odd sucking sound, but otherwise it was very quiet.

The cabin hatch was closed. Griff skidded across the decking, his greased feet slipping. Again Le Marr was before him, prying at that entrance. Under their strength it gave, but Le Marr muttered as he put his shoulder to it, "Locked from the inside—"

With a splintering crash it yielded. Beyond was a thick dusk, too gloomy for their sun-dazzled eyes to pierce at first.

"Anyone there?" Griff called, his heart pounding.

When there was nothing but silence, he climbed over the wreckage of the door to descend the few steps within. There was an evil smell, a sweetish miasma. Le Marr caught at the American's shoulder, checking his advance.

"Wait, mon. There be bad thing here—"

In the murky twilight was a wild state of wreckage. Every object that could be torn loose was piled in a mouldering mess on the cabin floor. And with the gentle rocking of the *Queen*, they could hear the swish of water washing back and forth, trapped in the mass.

"Chris!" Griff could make out the big form sprawled motionless on the stripped bunk. "Chris!"

He stumbled over and through the junk, but he did not reach the mate ahead of Le Marr. The islander pulled at the flaccid body, his hand resting with urgency on the wide chest.

"Chris?" Griff made a question of it this time, looking to Le Marr.

"There still be life. Do we git him out o' here, maybeso we can help—"

Somehow they got the dead weight of the mate's heavy body across the cabin, up those steps, and out into the clean air and sun. Under his dark skin there was an odd greenish pallor, and, in spite of Le Marr, Griff believed that they had brought out a dead man.

"Look for the supplies, mon," Le Marr ordered. "See if you can find food—water. He be not hurt—just sick—"

Griff plunged back into the disordered cabin, digging dog-fashion into the mass on the floor. He found a tin can that appeared intact, though its label was gone, but fresh water was missing.

Back on deck he punctured the can lid with his knife and discovered he had been lucky, as the tart scent of stewed tomatoes came from the battered lid. He passed it to Le Marr and then supported Chris while the other worked pulp and liquid into the unconscious man's slack mouth. As it dribbled out again, Griff's hope sank. They were too late; nothing was going to bring Chris around now.

But some measure of that restorative moisture had helped.

"He swallow!" Le Marr exclaimed excitedly. "This mon not be licked yet. He be tough—"

Griff could see that movement of the throat, too. Yes, some of the watery pulp was getting down. Yet, save for that convulsive swallowing and the very faint rise and fall of his chest, Chris showed no more signs of life than he had when they pulled him from the cabin. And how were they going to transport him to shore?

The contents of the can being at length exhausted, Griff settled Chris gently back on the deck and stood up, studying the disappointing bareness all about. Somehow, somewhere, they must find something on which they could float the unconscious man to land.

"How are we—?" he was beginning when they were both startled by movement in the mate. Chris's eyes opened and passed over Griff as if the American were invisible. His lips, sticky with juice, drew back in a snarl of rage such as Griff had never seen the placid Chris exhibit before. And on his hands and knees he crawled across the decking to the battened-down hatch of the cargo space. There, as if that progress had drained all his energy, he sank down in a heap, but his big hands drummed weakly on the sealed hatch as he collapsed.

"Debble!" His voice was a hissing whisper. "Debble—we done cotched you safe! No more killin' mons. Debble—" His head fell on his beating hands, and they were still.

Griff jumped to help Le Marr pull the mate away from the opening. Then the islander regarded the hatch narrowly.

"I think, mon"—some inner excitement broke his usual calm—"we should look in here. Chris, he goin' be all right. But here—maybeso we find something—"

He was busy at the lashings, and, now that he examined them carefully, Griff saw that the ropes had been wound and tied in a vast network of knots and interweavings—to make very sure that what lay below was safe.

In the end, they had to cut the majority of the ropes in order to clear the opening. And then, together, they pried and tugged until they had the cover up. The same fetid odor so noticeable in the cabin was present to a far greater degree. But there was something else.

Water washed below, swinging back and forth with the movements of the *Queen*. But this was no overflow from the storm as it had been in the cabin. Here was water that almost filled the hold, and in it—

"Look out, mon!"

But Griff had seen it too—that coil of living flesh rising with deliberation from below the surface of the dark flood toward the open hatch. As one, the two on the deck moved, sliding back the hatch, fumbling with the fastenings they had cut loose.

"So he did bring back debble," Le Marr observed as they made secure. "This be a good thing, I think."

Griff stared down at Chris with wondering eyes. How had the mate done it and why? But he had. And now the survivors on San Isadore would have the chance they wanted to study the nature of the enemy close at hand.

Chapter Eight
MAN IS A STUBBORN ANIMAL

"The base—" Griff paced uneasily across the deck. "If they could send the LC—give us a tow—"

"No other way to go," Le Marr agreed. "Night comes—"

Griff caught the significance of that remark. Darkness had always been a factor in the attacks of the undersea things. Did the prisoner below have any way of summoning its kind? If so, could the *Queen* expect an attack? Was it fear of that which had made Chris lock himself in the cabin?

Le Marr arose to his feet. "I go shoreways. Send Liz to the base. We stay here—"

Before Griff could protest, Le Marr dived from the deck and swam inland. He climbed ashore across some half-awash rubble to the cliff. Griff sat down beside Chris. His imagination was painting a vivid picture for him of that thing below, moving sluggishly about its prison. And the secret of how it had been trapped there intrigued him. Where was Captain Murdock and Rob Fletcher?

Chris was asleep, sprawled out on the deck, every rib underlined beneath his skin. Now and then he muttered, but, though Griff listened closely, he could make no sense out of that gabble.

It was nearing sunset, and he felt naked on this battered deck with no other weapon than a knife, no defense against what might rise from the shallows. If one of those "serpents" were to appear now—They could not hope to face up to that menace.

A splash brought him around in a half-crouch, steel in hand. But no fanged head spiraled up from the water. Instead he saw Le Marr paddling back, pushing before him a crude raft hastily cobbled out of driftwood on which balanced the rifle and the iron pot in which Liz had concocted her brew. From the cut lashings of the hatch cover Griff knotted a line to lift that cargo on board. And when both it and the islander were beside him, he discovered that Le Marr had come prepared for a siege. The pot was full of fresh water, and there were their ration tins and some coconuts, as well as the rifle.

"Liz goes to the base. She will tell the commander what be here. Tell him send crawl boat for us. Maybeso come by mornin'—"

Le Marr roused Chris and gave him some sips of the water, while Griff made good use of the remaining sun time to grub in the wreckage in the cabin, locating and bringing up labelless tins, a fish spear, and a lantern. Le Marr shook his head at the last.

"Light bad thing. Light draw eyes in the night. We be better in dark—"

Griff wanted to protest that, but his common sense agreed. He had not forgotten the night he had dived by the reef and the schools of curious fish that had swum into the path of his torch. Yes, a light might draw to them the very attention they hoped to escape.

They ate and drank sparingly. Griff settled down crosslegged, the rifle resting on his knees. The sea was very calm. Save for the half-submerged ruins of the town, the immediate past might not have been. He was almost drowsing when Le Marr's fingers touched his arm, tightened there in a silent signal of alarm.

Griff, now accustomed to the swing of the derelict *Queen*, was aware of it also, the slightly different feel of the ship, a displacement of weight that altered her angle in the water.

Le Marr's soft whisper came. "Debble thing restless. It wake—want to be free—"

The American wished he knew more about small sailing craft. The *Queen* was perhaps in danger, riding so low in the water, her motor useless. Could the movements of the imprisoned octopus capsize them?

The effect of that slightest of changes in the *Queen* was electric as far as Chris was concerned. Pricked out of sleep, he sat up, shivering visibly. His wide eyes stared unbelievingly at Griff, went on to Le Marr, and then back to the American. He shook his head and reached out a trembling hand to touch Griff timidly.

"You be there in true, mon?"

"I'm here, Chris—"

Chris again looked from him to Le Marr. The voodoo man's face wore its usual impassive mask until he smiled.

"You be back—back home, mon."

But when Chris looked beyond Le Marr to the altered shore line, he was plainly puzzled.

"This ain't Carterstown—" he said almost plaintively.

"It's what's left of it," Griff answered.

Chris studied the ruins and then, with a sudden dry sob, buried his face in his hands.

"—never no more—" His muffled words trailed mournfully over the waters of the encroaching bay.

"Chris, what happened to the *Queen?*" Griff ventured to ask. "Where's the captain and Rob?"

At first he thought he was not going to get an answer. But at last, in a colorless voice unlike his own, Chris replied.

"The debble things—they came out o' the sea. Rob, he was took—'fore we really see them. Captain—he shoot—the rest—" He shook his head. "It be all mixed up in my head, mon. No more remember. But"—he brought his fist down on the scarred planking under them—"I got this one debble, an' I think I bring him back to the doctuh—to you father. He know what makes fishes do things. Maybeso he can tell why these fish an' bad things come now to git mons. De doctuh can tell us true! You get the doctuh, Griff—"

"I can't. The doctor isn't here now, Chris. I don't—I don't know where he is." But he was thinking that what he had told Casey was still true. As long as one could not see the disaster, one could keep on believing that it had not happened—that some day, maybe tomorrow, word would come that the worst had not happened—that the north was still clean, its cities standing, its lights bright, its people living. He could not believe that Dr. Gunston would never return to San Isadore, that in time life would not be as it had always been.

"He was poisoned by a fish," he continued steadily. "They flew him to the States for treatment."

"Then we keep this here thing 'til he comes back." Chris slapped the deck again. "But the town—what happened to the town?"

"We had a storm, and an earthquake—and there's a volcano out there." Griff pointed seaward. But Le Marr took up the tale at this point.

"There be war, mon, war with the big bombs. The whole world be changed now—"

Griff wondered if Chris had understood, if he could understand—for the *Queen's* mate sat looking ashore in the thickening dusk, his drawn face a mask of hurt.

"The mons—?"

"They be down island—with the Navy mons—all that be still 'live."

"Everything gone—"

Le Marr nodded briskly. "Everything old be gone. We do other things now. The sea things, they come to fight. We be eaten up 'less we fight back. No more mons fight mons—now they fight other thing—or they don' live no more on this world!"

"Me—" Chris's bowed shoulders straightened—"me, I ain't gonna let no fish thing make trouble for me. I got me one right here. I ain' sayin' fish be smarter nor me!"

Le Marr was only a black blot now in the three-quarter's dark. But his soft chuckle held the approbation they could not see. "There's other mons think that too, Chris. These Navy mons, they ain't shakin' the head and cryin' out 'oh, my, oh, my!' You has done a big thing, bringin' this debble back to San Isadore. We gits it to the Navy mons, an' they makes their own voodoo wi' it. *If* we gits it to the Navy mons!"

"Whyfor you say 'if'?"

"This here debble thing ain't happy. He make his own voodoo. Now he move—"

Le Marr was right. Griff felt the tremor in the *Queen*. Could that creature burst out? Had the ship's sides or bottom been weakened to the point of giving away if the prisoner applied intelligence to the business of winning its freedom?"

"Let him move! He be put in the *Queen* like beef in the can." Chris sounded almost cheerful. "Beef, he don't git out 'til mon takes him. Neither do this—"

"Do he bring help, we have us some things to think 'bout."

"There be debbles here?"

"They be everywhere. They got 'em a sub, didn't they, Griff?"

"Well, maybe they didn't wreck it in the first place, but they sure kept it tied down afterwards!" agreed the American. He spoke almost absently, trying to be alert to every sound about the *Queen*, tense and conscious of that remitting tremor. Could that very faint pulsation carry through the water to summon—?

"There are two kinda debbles," Chris remarked thoughtfully. "There are the long necks and the octopi. The long necks, they stay mostly in the water. These kind"—they heard his hand beat the deck—"can come out a little way. But we gotta teach 'em they better stay in!"

"So we try," Le Marr agreed. "Now we eat ourselves something. Nobody can do everything in one day." He portioned out rations brought from the base and cans hacked open.

Griff ate cold baked beans with his fingers and ended by sucking a square of dark chocolate. He had been watching the incoming waves, and now he pointed out a phenomenon to the others.

"What's that glow—there—along the water?"

He was familiar with the phosphorescence of the southern waters—had seen it fly in foam from the cutting bow of the *Queen* in happier days. But this was different. It appeared to move under the water, not on the surface, and in lines. Then material he had read in the now vanished library of the lab flashed to mind and brought him to his feet in alarm.

The greater octopi from the depths were spangled with bright sparks of luminescence!

"They comin'?" Le Marr sounded neither surprised nor disturbed.

"Maybe—" He had been a fool not to bring some of the grenades, though explosions so near to the crippled *Queen* might have torn the derelict apart.

He was sure his guess was correct. Those odd trails of light were not just slipping along the waves in the aimless fashion of phosphorescence; they were converging on the ship. And her deck was now hardly four feet above the water level. Any of the octopi he had seen about the islet where the *Volga* rested, or which he had watched attack and try to overturn the boats of the refugees, could reach the planking on which the three were huddled. He spoke to Le Marr.

"I think they must have spotted us. And we've got to have the lantern now, for if we don't keep the deck clear—" But how could they do that with only one rifle, a pair of knives, and a fishing spear?

There was a rasping, scraping sound. Griff instinctively moved back from the edge of the deck. It would be only too easy to seize him from below and whirl him over before he could make a defensive move.

A yellow glow cut the thick dark. The three drew together by the cargo hatch. Chris levered himself up on his hands, peering wide-eyed into the dark. Griff nursed the rifle, facing the direction from which that ominous sound had come. Le Marr finished lashing the lantern tight with cord to the hatch cover and then picked up the spear.

If they only had one of the atomic flood lamps from the base, Griff thought, and then forced a twisted grin. As long as he was wishing for tools, he might as well make it a box of grenades or one of the LC's rapid-fire guns. There was a flicker of movement just within the farthest reaches of the lantern's beam, and he tensed.

"They come—" Le Marr straightened.

"An' he know it, too!" The faint tremor of movement below was increasing to a definite shaking, which rocked the *Queen*. Chris's prisoner was either seeking communication with its kind or striving to break out of confinement.

"Can they turn us over?" Griff appealed to his more seawise companions, hoping for an emphatic denial.

But there was no answer except a shrug from Le Marr. Chris continued to stare at the dark. There was a thumping underneath now, regular pounding blows making the planking of the ship ring.

Then Griff saw a brown snake-whip wave above the edge of the deck, as if in blind search for a victim. Would bullets be able to rip that? Anyway he couldn't trust his marksmanship in this light. With a machine gun set to spray, they would have a better chance.

Le Marr was busy, his hands flying as he bound bits of raveled cord about the point of the fish spear. Having provided a wadding that suited him, he pried open the lid of a flat can of sardines, one of the supply cans Griff had found in the cabin. Carefully he smeared the oily fish back and forth across the wadding, working in the greasy liquid.

The battering of the prisoner now shook the deck. With a smack, the rope arm waved through the shadows to the planking. It might be seeking either prey or a secure hold.

Le Marr went into action. He ran his greasy torch into the lantern flame. Fire burst in a sputter of sparks. With the precision of a careful workman he reached out and applied the blaze to the tentacle. For a second or two there was no response. Then Le Marr jerked away his improvised weapon as the arm loosed its hold upon the wood, writhed up, and beat down on the deck with a force that rocked the *Queen.*

The islander stood his ground, and as the arm came to a momentary rest, he was ready to touch it again. Once more the length of stringy muscle and ropy flesh flashed up until they saw the suckers disclike on its length. Then it snapped back into the dark and was gone. In the lantern light Griff saw that Le Marr was laughing silently. And Chris grinned.

"That thing—he don't like the fire."

Le Marr chuckled. "The things of the night, never do they like fire. Fire belong to mons. An' mons, they don't give up fightin' easy. We show these debble things that!"

If they had fought off for the moment the assailant that had attempted to get a hold on deck, they had not settled the captive below. And now Chris showed concern.

"The *Queen*—maybe she can't take this poundin'. Nothing we can do 'bout that one down there?" he appealed to Le Marr.

But the other was forced to reply in the negative. Griff could hear rasping sounds, feel even through the pounding of the prisoner a sucking pull against the sides of the *Queen.* Although no more arms appeared within the circle of light, he could not rid himself of the idea that a net of sorts was being woven about the ship, that the sea things were working with patience and intelligence to overturn the *Queen* as they had overturned with far less effort the tow boat of the refugee ship.

And that was borne out by action as the *Queen* slowly, minute by dragging minute, developed a list to port. There was no more movement in the cargo hold. Perhaps the captive recognized the work of its kind and was content to wait for an opportunity before wasting its strength.

"A little more of this," Griff said between his teeth, "and we'll slide over." It was one of his worst nightmares coming true, and he could do nothing to halt the inevitable. Surely there must be a whole school of the monsters down there lending their weight to the project. The ancient horror stories of mariners were coming true. Here were the kraken who could and would drag down a ship to be plundered at their leisure in the deeps.

"Hellooooo!"

Griff had been so intent upon the immediate scene of action that he had forgotten the shore, the dark waters that washed in upon the deserted town. A band of light, which completely blotted out the feeble gleam of the lantern, caught and pinned the *Queen*.

"Stand by to secure line—"

Griff caught the shout as Le Marr stuck the smoldering spear butt down on the hatch to free his hands and Chris struggled up on his knees.

The line flew in from the dark to fall on the deck. Its weighted end had scarcely landed before Chris had it. Then Le Marr jumped forward, and with fumbling help from Griff they made it fast about the stump of the splintered mast.

But the list of the deck was increasing. They held onto the hatch lashings to keep their balance. Then Chris muttered, caught the diver's knife from Griff's sheath, and with that between his teeth inched his way to the stern.

The anchor! Griff had forgotten about that. Chris sawed at the rope as Le Marr covered him by thrusting the torch-spear into the dark. The tie gave, and the *Queen* bobbed. Perhaps Le Marr had disconcerted the attackers, for the list righted a bit, enough to allow the two to crawl back in safety to the hatch.

Now the line to the shore grew taut. Slowly the *Queen* answered that pull, began to move inland. Once her side grated against a wall, but for the most part they followed along the line of the main street, and, while the roofs of buildings were black blots above the water, they managed not to strike any of them.

For a space the listing continued, even grew. But as the *Queen* took her slow course inland, she began to rise in the water. The attackers were loosing their holds, falling away. At last the bow smashed against a wall with a shock that might have tossed her passengers overboard had they not had a firm grip on the hatch. There was a horrible grating as the pull from the shore continued. Then the line went limp, and they were hailed.

"Can you make it now?"

Griff scrambled to his feet. The wall on which the *Queen* hung canted her up. But within easy leaping distance was a rise of dry land. Yes, they could make it. And with assistance to bring Chris ashore, they did.

Murray and Casey were there—and the smaller towing machine from the base. Karkoff was standing beside that, watching the stranded *Queen* with keen interest.

"How did you—? Did Liz—?" Griff sputtered.

"We heard about this ship from Karkoff and started overland to see her. Met your Liz about an hour ago and heard about your find," Murray explained. Then he spoke to Chris. "So you've one of those things shut up inside that hulk have you?"

"In the *Queen*," Chris corrected sharply. "He sure is, Cap'n."

Murray gazed into the dark bay. "All his little playmates were coming to the rescue, weren't they?"

"They certainly were!" Griff tried to see if those trails of light had disappeared from the waters. He could distinguish none—the enemy must have withdrawn.

"This is round three, and it's still our decision," Murray observed with obvious satisfaction, "If they want to go a full ten, we'll meet them all the way!"

Chapter Nine
THE LONG ROAD BACK

Griff squatted on the edge of a salt-water pool and stared intently into its depths. Save for its size, it might have been the one he had once ruled over near the laboratory—only no one was going to swim lazily in the sun-warmed water cupped there.

Eyes, which were blank saucers without any readable expression, yet which somehow conveyed the impression of implacable hatred, met his. There was no means of communication between the brain behind those eyes and his. More experienced and better trained minds than Griff's had tried to find some common ground of understanding. Here was intelligence to a high degree; they recognized that. But it was a form of intelligence so alien to the human ways of thought that there was probably an unpierceable barrier between.

The Octopus-Sapiens endured captivity. It ate the food supplied; it sank into the same semiconscious state during the brighter hours of the day as had the small cephalopod Griff planted in the spray pool. There were several features about the prisoner, however, that set it apart from the octopi already known. Without dissection they could only guess and deduce from photographs and observation. But it was apparent that the brain had evolved to a higher degree, and two of the great arms had developed at their tips smaller, off-shoot tentacles, which the creature was able to use, if clumsily, with some of the advantage of human fingers.

Whether it was a species old to their world but hitherto dwelling unsuspected in the deeps until roused out by the recent disturbances—by explosions during atomic bomb tests—or whether it was a mutant whose evolution had been forced by radiation from those same tests, was still a matter for dispute.

Islander, refugee, Seabee, sooner or later every present inhabitant of San Isadore spent some time by the pool watching with a fearful fascination the captive brought back in the *Queen*. Hughes hung over it, studying it for hours, raging at times because he could not summon to share his vigil other authorities in his field. Sheer frustration made him blow up in irritated outbursts, which were far removed from his one-time self-satisfied complacency. He pestered Chris with demands as to how the creature had been captured, hoping to add another to their bag. But the mate had replied over and over again that he could not honestly remember—that the horrors of the *Queen's* last voyage did not remain in his memory except as a faint dream. Examination by the base doctor had shown that the island sailor suffered from exposure to mild radiation and that he was lucky to survive at all.

But the captive in the pool was not the only problem. The waves had deposited a thick harvest of the red scum along three-fourths of the island's shore line. And there Hughes had been successful, for his suggestion of using fire to cleanse the beaches and rocks paid off. Ignited, the stuff had burned with a choking oily reek, which set them all to painful coughing but did clear the land.

What was left was a black ash with a sour, nasty smell. This was shoveled and pushed into pits by the base machines, only to prove a disguised blessing—for some of the ash blown into pockets of sheltered earth provided a rich fertilizer never before seen. The pits were then reopened so that this strange sea bounty could be disinterred and put to work increasing the productivity of the garden patches, a move that might mean the difference between life and death in the future as the store supplies dwindled.

It was still not entirely safe to fish—though there were few fish that had escaped the poisonous scum. Thanks to Liz's concoction—which the base doctor analyzed to the last disagreeable drop—small boats well smeared dared venture out along the shore—but there was always the danger of running into one of the "serpents."

"If we could only get into this fellow's think-tank"—Casey came up to the pool behind Griff—"we'd have answers to a lot of questions. You know"—he teetered back and forth, his eyes narrowed speculatively as he studied the captive octopus—"I used to read stories about fellas going to the stars and meeting up with alien life forms. There was a lot of clever mish-mash in some of them about how they established communication. They usually started off with numbers. You know—the old two-and-two-make-four routine. But how are you going to talk to something that probably doesn't give a hoot whether two and two make four or six? Didn't you say once that these things signaled to each other with their ink sacks? Then how are we going to palaver back? With a bunch of paint cans ready to pour?"

"That's already been tried—" Griff pointed out.

Hughes had tried it. The chemical make-up of the ink exuded by the cephalopod clan in moments of emotional disturbance was a matter of record. They had been able to reproduce it in the base medical lab, and it had been introduced in small quantities into the pool—arousing no discernible reaction in the then quiescent captive.

"Sure—Doc's stuff. I saw them try that. But what about some of those native goos—like that stuff your friend Liz cooks up on demand? Did that voodoo doc ever get a chance to try some of his bright ideas?"

Griff had to answer no to that. The island population of San Isadore, or what remained of it, had withdrawn to their own new settlement, spreading away from the base, where the off-islanders, both Naval and refugee, were inclined to remain. In the press of establishing a going concern, everyone was so occupied that even Griff had rather lost track of Le Marr and the others. Casey might just have an idea worth following up. Griff got to his feet. Those black saucer eyes below watched him indifferently.

It was a fine day. In fact, since the great storm, the weather had continued almost uniformly good. Griff watched a flight of birds make a half circle about the new radio tower. Radio tower—perhaps that was the most useless piece of construction they had done since the start of the rebuilding. Yet no one had protested its erection—they all still hoped for news, to learn that some portion of the old life still existed. And among the Naval personnel no one clung more to that installation than did Holmes. He spent most of his time hunched in the hut with the operator, a dogeared wad of messages in his hand, ready to push them through for transmission as soon as contact with the States was once more established. In his way, Griff decided, the security officer was as hopeful in a hopeless position as was Hughes—though it might be easier to awake a response from the pool captive than it would be for Holmes to treat with his superiors in the dim and vanished offices of the United States Navy.

Casey might have been reading Griff's thoughts, for he laughed. "Poor old Holmes, he'd like to do the dirty on the skipper, only he can't get through to the Big Brass. D'you know, maybe Murray's the biggest brass left right now. Only Holmes won't accept that. He's had fourteen fits since we brought the Russkis in here."

"They got it just as hard as we did."

"Sure, kid. And these have turned to and worked like the rest of us. I'm not calling names. And if they plastered us—they got it back as hot and heavy—maybe worse. It isn't going to help matters to shoot Karkoff and his boys—they didn't give the word to start firing. Though you know," he added shrewdly, "if they hadn't been found by us—but by survivors of a bombing—they wouldn't have lasted. We got our bad punches not from the Russkis, but from the sea, the quakes, the storm. If we'd had them from a bomb, we wouldn't feel the same way. As it is now, we're closing ranks—man against nature. If you're human, you're on our side. So they were lucky, darn lucky to end up in our section of the world."

"How about the plane? Any chance of getting it up for a look-see?"

The Navy plane had gone during the great storm, but they held hopes of being able to restore the transport that had brought the cargo of refugees from Santa Maria. Like the mast of the radio station, this plane served as a defiance, a hope. If they could take to the air on an exploring trip—even venture out in a radius of a hundred miles or so and chart the changes—

"Well, Hooker's steamed up about what they were able to do last night. We have a couple of mechanics who can build anything if they have scrap enough. They're trying to fit her with an atomic motor from a wrecked crawler we located. If they can ready her to take off, Hooker's game to fly her."

They had come upslope from the octopus pool and now stood on the crest of one of the heights that had been born during the quakes, giving San Isadore respectable hills for the first time in her existence. The settlement was a ragged circle below—the coral-block, thatched buildings, rather like blocks spilled from some giant child's play box, the half-cave, half-house section of the base, and the islanders' huts, where trickles of smoke arose from cooking fires. It had a hastily slapped-together look but at the same time a vitality that had never been seen in Carterstown.

"There's your voodoo man down there now—taking it easy." Casey pointed to Le Marr seated on the trunk of a dead palm.

The islander was not lazing though. His slender hands moved skillfully as he wove dried fronds into one of the wide-brimmed hats that were the island protection against the sun. And he glanced up with a welcoming smile as Griff and Casey slid down the bank into what was the backyard of his private domain. A cock, tethered by its leg to the other end of the palm log, stopped pecking in the earth and offered crowing challenge.

"Be a good day, mons. Sit you down an' rest your feet." He gave the traditional island greeting. "There's coco-milk for the drinkin'. Shut your big mouth, you crazy bird!" he bade the cock, and astonishingly enough its clamor subsided at once.

"I wish you could do that with the devil." Unconsciously Griff gave the pool captive the name conferred on it by the islanders. "Talk to it, I mean."

Le Marr's swiftly flying fingers paused. "Whyfor you wants to talk with that thing?"

"Not talk exactly. But it is intelligent. If we could find some way of communication, maybe we could—"

"Make peace 'tween ocean an' land? Listen, mon. This here"—he held up a piece of the dried leaf he was using—"is one kinda thing. Once it live, it grow, maybeso it had knowledge. Not like the knowledge in mon's head, but knowledge what was for it. But can you talk with this? All right, all right. This debble, he think good—better nor dog, better nor donkey, more like mons. But not the same way as mons. He don't want the same thing as mons wants—"

"He wants to live, doesn't he?" cut in Casey. "Everything wants to live. Maybe we could get that idea across."

"How you be sure he wants to live more then he wants other things? Mon wants that—but do debble?"

Griff pulled the conversation back from the philosophical to the immediate problem. "But is there any way we could communicate with the thing, Le Marr? That grease of Liz's keeps the things away—or seems to. Is there anything which will attract them?"

Le Marr shrugged. "How do I know? I don't want to talk to this thing. Better we would be if this thing be gone away an' we spend no more time with it. Sea an' land, they never mix. An' they ain't goin' to—You mons, you make the big bombs, you make the plane, the rocket to carry those bombs. Then—" He made an erasing gesture with his hands, and the half-finished hat fell to the ground. "Then you use them! An' what be left? Trouble—death! Mons don't use things right. Maybeso this world be tired o' mons. Now you want more kinda knowledge, you want to start all over again. I say no!" One of his hands came down in a chopping motion as if he were beheading something. "Let mons live quiet, do no thing to learn what will start more bad things."

Casey clasped his hands about his knee, leaned back.

"Brother," he announced, "you've got a good point there. It's one which has been stated before by a lot of earnest souls. There's only one thing about it—it won't work!"

"An' why not?"

"Because, as a species, we're bitten by a queer bug. We've *got* to find out what lies beyond the next range of hills, and not only geographically. Our curiosity is bred into our bones. I'll bet there were those in the cavemen days who deplored the use of this new-fangled fire, who didn't see why tying a stone onto a shaft and making an ax out of it was the right thing to do. You could kill a horse or a deer better that way, sure, but it also was a mighty nasty war weapon. That knowledge which made the bombs gave us the atomic motors which have kept this base going since the bust-up. You can't withdraw from living, Le Marr—unless you want to commit suicide. And we're so constructed that mass suicide does not appeal. There's a long road back stretching ahead of us now. And we have to take it. Perhaps half our globe is uninhabitable. For all we know it is. We haven't yet faced the horrors of a fallout, of radiation sickness. We may be doomed right now. Don't you suppose that every man over there at the base hasn't thought of that? But have you seen anyone stop work and sit around waiting for the end to catch up with him?

"What are you doing here?" He scooped up the half-made hat. "You're weaving a hat—a mighty neat job of it, too. But why do it? Tomorrow you may be dead—we may all be dead. Who'll be left to wear it—that thing over in the pool, one of your donkeys? There's that woman over there scraping up earth to make a garden. She's planting seeds; will she live to see them sprout? She thinks so—or she wouldn't be doing it. You see, Le Marr, inside we all believe that we're going to keep on breathing and walking around. We accept that the more because we *have* already survived some pretty tough treatment. And if we accept that we have to be practical.

"There's the problem of food and clothing. It was lucky for San Isadore that the Navy supply dump was here. We have supplies for several years. But this island is not going to support her present population without some help. And the refugees from Santa Maria may not be the last to reach us, which means we eventually will have to spread out—or import from other surviving communities. And we *have* to have mastery of the sea for that. It's either sit down and die, or it's get up and fight! If we can learn anything useful from the eight-armed thing over in that pool, we have to do it—the sooner the better. It may be a matter of *our* survival, and that is enough to build a fire under any man. You may not agree, but that is the truth as I see it."

For the second time since Griff had known him, Le Marr answered with the speech of an educated off-island man. "You make a good case for your side of the argument, Lieutenant. As you say—this is the truth from your point of view. And for your race it is. We are a mongrel lot, we islanders, and we have certain traits of our own. To our way of thinking, nature has turned against us, and that is a belief rooted in the supernatural. You do not know it in your portion of the town, but some of us have reverted to very dark practices." For a moment his face had the same look of strain it had worn during their weird battle on the *Queen*. "I have some influence with these, my people. I am trying hard to hold that influence—to prevent their falling into the savagery from which they climbed painfully long ago. If once more they turn to certain rites and sacrifices—" He stopped abruptly, his lips thinned as if he tightened them against dangerous admissions. "I can do this only because I do share some of their beliefs and appear to share others. Should I now change in my attitude, should I—as they would see it—attempt to traffic with the devil they fear, I might lose all the control I still possess. Then, Lieutenant, we might have yet another danger to contend with, a situation which might end, once and for all, all your bright plans of a world rebuilt."

"Do they still think that we are responsible for the trouble?" Griff thought of the destruction of the laboratory, of his father's work.

"Some of them do. Others can be readily influenced to join them. Your strange machines, the lights you use, the larger percentage of your belongings"—he was speaking now to Casey—"are sheer magic to my people. It is only since Dr. Gunston and you Naval people have come to San Isadore that our world has changed. We were a century behind history—Now we may have caught up with it, to find the transition not only bewildering but for us—fearful. You believe that you have nothing to fear from us but—"

Griff had a flash of understanding. "You have your own ways of force, of dealing with an enemy—the ways you know, Liz knows—"

Le Marr gave a slow, assenting nod. At the same time he took the hat from Casey and began his work again. "Yes, there are ways my people may make their displeasure felt—if they are pushed too far."

"We have to work together—we *have* to!" Casey brought his fist down on the trunk of the palm. Shreds of dried bark drifted on the wind to the ground.

"Some of us already realize that; the rest must be brought to such an understanding. During the days of the storm we took refuge together. But now you go your own road. You are busy on foreign concerns, and it may appear to you that we have nothing to offer in support of your labors. My people hope that you will go and leave us in peace—that you will repair the plane, ready your seagoing LC's—and that after you are gone, the old world will return. That is what they wait for. If it does not come then—"

"They may take steps to hasten it?" prompted Griff. They had taken steps about the laboratory after it had become suspect—drastic ones.

"We shall hope not."

"Then"—Casey hunched forward on the tree trunk—"can't you use that for an excuse in coming to our help now. We would never leave with the sea closed to us. The plane, if we are ever able to get it off the ground, couldn't carry more than a pilot and a few observers. But if we can free the seas—"

Le Marr made a meticulous business of braiding, of fitting small rough ends into smoothness. To all appearances he was concerned only with that. But a moment later he said, without looking up, "It might be done."

"Can you ask the others to help? Would such a project bring us closer together?"

"That also might be done. But you do not intend to leave—"

"How can we? Maybe not for years," Casey admitted. "We have no idea what's waiting for us out there. Maybe you are right—at your gloomiest—maybe we are washed up, maybe man is no longer top dog. But we won't accept that decision without a fight. I don't think, if it comes right to the point, your people will either. And it's up to you, Le Marr, to see that they fight the right way—on our side, with their minds and their hands—and not their superstitions and their emotions!"

"You are of one kind, my people of another," warned the islander. "Don't try to drive us too hard or too fast. We are like our donkeys—sometimes we may be driven, but other times we must be coaxed, and always we must have our minds and desires considered. Very well, I shall do what I can. If the first step toward cooperation is the study of devils, then I shall undertake the study of devils." He smiled his slow, shadow smile.

The sea wind was rising, beating through the leaves of the standing palms as if the trees applauded him with clapping fronds. Casey stretched.

"Oh, we'll make it back." His confidence was such as drew belief. "I'm not saying 'uncle' to any fish. Just give us time—say a hundred years or so—and you won't know the bloomin' world, you won't for a fact."

"I hope so—with all my heart I trust that that may be true." Le Marr spoke with conviction.

Griff stood up; the wind pushed against him with its old demanding force. Without being conscious of movement, he turned to face north. To him the long road back must always point that way. Would *he* ever tread it openly?

Star Gate

1
INHERITANCE

This had been a queer "cold" season so far. No snow, even on the upper reaches of the peaks, no drifts to stopper the high passes, warm winds over the fields of brittle stubble, though most of the silver-green leaves of the copses had been brought to earth by those same winds. Instead of cold they had experienced a general drying-out to kill the vigorous life of wood and pasturage. And the weather was only a part of the strangeness that had settled over Gorth—at least those parts of Gorth where men beat paths—since the Star Lords had withdrawn.

The Star Lords, with their power, had raised the Gorthians above the beasts of the forests and had thrown over them their protection, as the lord of any holding could now extend the certainty of life to one outlawed and running from sword battle. But now that the Star Lords had gone—what would follow for Gorth?

Kincar s'Rud paused beneath the flapping mordskin banner of Styr's Holding to direct a long, measuring glance along the hill line. His cloak, sewn cunningly from strips of soft suard fur brought back from his solitary upland hunts, was molded about him now by the force of that unseasonably warm wind, as he stood exposed on the summit of the watch tower alert to any movement across the blue-earthed fields of the Holding. Kincar was no giant to boast inches rivaling a Star Lord's, but he was well muscled for his years and could and had surpassed his warrior tutors in sword play. Now he absently flexed one of his narrow, six-fingered hands on the rough stone parapet, while the banner crackled its stiff folds over his head.

He had volunteered for this post at midday, for no other reason than to escape the sly prodding of Jord—Jord who affected to believe that the withdrawal of the Star Lords meant a new and brighter day for the men of Gorth. What kind of day? Kincar's eyes—blue-green, set obliquely in his young face—narrowed as he traced that thought to the vague suspicion behind it.

He, Kincar s'Rud, was son of the Hold Daughter and so ruler by blood as soon as Wurd s'Jastard went into the Company of the Three. But if he was not alive to walk this Holding, then Jord would be master here. Through the years since he had been brought from the city to this distant mountain Holding, Kincar had overheard enough, pieced-together bits of information, until he knew what he would have to face when Wurd did depart into the shadows.

Jord had his followers—men whom he had gathered together during his trading journeys—who were tied to him by bonds of personal loyalty and not by clan reckoning. And he appeared able to smell out advantages for himself. Why else had he come down the long trail two days ago, heading a motley caravan? Ostensibly it was to bring the latest news of the Star Lords' departure, but it was strange that Wurd had just taken to his bed in what could only be that ancient man's last bout with the old wound that had been draining his strength for years.

Would Jord attempt to force sword battle on Kincar for the Holding? His constant oblique remarks had suggested that. Yet outwardly to provoke such a quarrel when Jord himself was the next heir after Kincar was to court outlawing as Jord well knew. And Jord was too shrewd to throw away his future for the mere satisfaction of removing Kincar. There was something else, some other reason beneath Jord's preoccupation with the Lords' withdrawal, behind his comments on the life to come, that made Kincar uneasy. Jord never moved until he was sure of his backing. Now he hardly attempted to veil his triumph.

Kincar could not remember his mother, unless a very dim dream of muted colors, flower scent, and the sound of soft weeping in a shadowed night were to be named Anora, Hold Daughter s'Styr. But he could never reconcile in his mind the fact that Anora and Jord had been brother and sister. And certainly Jord had given him often to believe that whatever lay between them, hate had been its base.

Though he had been born in Terranna, the city of the Star Lords, Kincar had been brought to the Holding when he was so young that he could not remember anything of that journey. Nor had he ever seen the plains beyond the mountain ring again. Now he did not want to. With the Star Lords departed, who would wish to visit the echoing desolation of their city or look upon the empty stretches where their Star ships once stood? It would be walking into the resting place of the long dead who were jealous when their sleep was disturbed.

He did not understand the reason of their going. The aliens had done so much for Gorth—why now did they set off once more in their ships? Oh, he had heard the blasphemous whisperings current among those who followed Jord, that the Star Lords denied to Gorth's natives their great secrets—the life eternal with which they were blessed and the knowledge of strange weapons. He had also heard rumors that among the Lords themselves there had been quarreling, that some had wished to give these gifts to Gorth, while the others chose to withhold them, and that those who would give had gathered a fighting tail of Gorthians to rebel. But since the Lords had withdrawn, what could they now rebel against—the open sky? Perhaps in the hour of their leaving the Lords had set a curse upon this rebellious world.

Though the wind about him continued warm, Kincar shivered. Among his people were those with the in-seeing, the power to drive out certain kinds of sickness by the use of hand and will. How much greater must be such powers among the Star Lords! Great enough to lay a spell upon a whole world so that the cold came not? And later would there follow any season of growing things once more? Again he shivered.

"Daughter's Son!"

Kincar had been so occupied with his own imaginings that his hand went to the hilt of his sword as he whirled, shocked alert by that hail, to see Regen's helmed head emerge from the tower trapdoor. But Wurd's guardsman did not climb any farther.

"Daughter's Son, the Styr would have speech with you."

"The Styr—he is—?" But he did not need to complete that question; the answer was to be read plainly in Regen's eyes.

Although Wurd had taken to his bed days ago, Kincar had not

really believed that the end was so near. The old chief had ailed before, had been close enough to the Great Forest to hear the sighing of the wind in its branches, yet he had come back to hold Styr in his slender fist. One could not picture the Holding without Wurd.

Kincar paused in the hall outside the door of the Lord's chamber only long enough to tug off his helm and drop his cape. Then, with his drawn sword gripped by the blade so that he could proffer the hilt to his overlord, he went in.

In spite of the warmth there was a fire on the hearth. Its heat reached the bed on which was piled a heap of coverings woven from fur strips. They made a kind of cocoon about the shrunken figure propped into a sitting position. Wurd's face was blue-white against the dark furs, but his eyes were steady and he was able to raise a claw finger to the sword hilt in greeting.

"Daughter's Son." His voice was only a faint whisper of sound, less alive than his eyes. It died away in a silence as if Wurd must gather and hoard strength to force each word out between his bloodless lips. But he raised again that claw finger in a gesture to Regen, and the guard moved to lift the lid of a chest that had been drawn forward to a new position beside the bed.

Under Wurd's eyes Regen took out three bundles, stripping off coverings to display a short-sleeved shirt of scales fashioned of metal with the iridescent sheen of a reptile's skin, a sheathed sword, and, last of all, a woven surcoat with a device, new to Kincar, worked upon the breast. He thought that he was familiar with Wurd's war gear, having been set to the polishing of it many times in his younger days. But none of these had he ever seen before, though their workmanship was that of an artist in metal, and he thought that their like could not be equaled save perhaps in the armories of the Star Lords.

Shirt, sword, and surcoat were laid across the foot of the bed, and Wurd blinked at them.

"Daughter's Son"—again that wavering claw pointed—"take up your heritage—"

Kincar reached for that wonder of a shirt. But behind his excitement at the gift, he was wary. There was something in Wurd's ceremonious presentation that bothered him.

"I thank you, Styr," he was beginning, a little uncertainly, when that hand waved him impatiently to silence.

"Daughter's Son—take up—your whole heritage—" The words came in painful gasps.

Kincar's grasp of the shirt tightened. Surely that could not mean what he thought! By all the laws of Gorth, he, Hold Daughter's Son, had a greater heritage than a scale shirt, a sword, and a surcoat, fine as these were!

Regen moved, picking up the surcoat, stretching it wide before his eyes so that the device set there in colorful pattern was plain to read. He gasped in amazement—those jagged streaks of bolt lightning with the star set between! Kincar moistened lips suddenly dry. That device—it was—it was—

Wurd's shrunken mouth shaped a shadow smile. "Daughter's Son," he whispered, "Star Lord's son—your inheritance!"

The scale shirt slithered through Kincar's loosened grip to clink on the floor. Stricken, he turned to Regen, hoping for reassurance. But the guard was nodding.

"It is true, Daughter's Son. You are partly of the Star Lords' blood and bone. Not only that, but you must join with their clan—for the word has come to us that the rebels would search out such as you and deal with them in an evil way—"

"Outlawry—?" Kincar could not yet believe in what he heard.

Regen shook his head. "Not outlawry, Daughter's Son. But there is one here within Styr's walls who will do rebel will on you. You must go before Styr is departed, be out of Jord's reach before he becomes Styr—"

"But I am Daughter's Son!"

"Those within these walls have full knowledge of your blood," Regen continued slowly. "And there are some who will follow you in drawing sword if you raise the mord banner. But there are others who want none of the Star blood in this Holding. It may be brother against brother, father against son, should you claim to be Styr."

That was like coming up with bruising force against a wall when one was running a race. Kincar looked to Wurd for support, but the old lord's still bright eyes held the same uncompromising message.

"Where shall I go?" he asked simply. "The Star Lords have left."

"Not—so—" Wurd's whisper came. "Ships have gone—but some remain— You shall join them. Regen—" He waved a finger at the guard and closed his eyes.

The other moved quickly. Almost before he knew what was happening, Kincar felt the man's hands on him, stripping off ring mail, the jerkin under it. He was reclad in the scaled shirt, over it the surcoat with its betraying insignia. Then Regen belted on the new sword.

"Your cloak, Daughter's Son. Now down the inner stair. Cim awaits you in the courtyard."

Wurd spoke for the last time, though he did not again open his eyes, and the words were the merest trickle of sound. "Map—and the Fortune of the Three with you—Daughter's Son! You would have held Styr well—it is a great pity. Go—while I still hold breath in me!"

Before Kincar could protest or take a formal farewell, Regen hurried him from the room and down the private stair to the courtyard. The mount that he had trapped in the autumn drive pens two years previously and knew to be a steady goer, heavy enough for good work in the press of a fight, and with an extra stamina for long travel on thin rations, stood with riding pad strapped about its middle, saddlebags across its broad haunches.

Cim was not a beautiful larng, no sleek-coated, nervous highbred. His narrow head whipped about so all four of the eyes set high in his skull could survey Kincar with his usual brooding measurement. His cold-season wool was growing in patches about the long thin neck and shoulders, its cream-white dabbed with spots of the same rusty red as the hide underneath. No, Cim was no beauty, and he was uncertain of temper, but to Kincar's mind he was the pick of the Holding's mount pens.

But Cim was not the only thing in Styr Hold that he could claim as his own. As Kincar settled on the larng's pad and gathered up the ear reins, he whistled, a single high, lilting note. He was answered from the hatchery on the smaller tower. On ribbed leather wings, supporting a body that was one-third head with gaping, toothed jaws and huge, intelligent red eyes, the mord—a smaller edition of those vicious haunters of the mountain tops, lacking none of their ferocious spirit—circled once over her master's head and then flapped off. Vorken would hover over him for the rest of the day, pursuing her own concerns but alert to his summoning.

"The road to the north—" Regen spoke hurriedly, his hands raised as if he would literally push Kincar out of the courtyard. "The map is in the left bag, Daughter's Son. Take the Mord Claw Pass. We are blessed by the Three that storms have not yet choked it. But you have only a short time—"

"Regen!" Kincar was at last able to break the odd feeling, which had possessed him during these last few minutes, of being in a dream. "Do you swear by Clan Right that this is a good thing?"

The guard's eyes met his with honesty—honesty and a concern there was no attempt to disguise. "Daughter's Son, by Clan Right, I tell you this is the only way, unless you would go into the Forest dragging half your men after you in blood. Jord is determined to have Styr. Had you been only Daughter's Son, not half of Star blood, none would have followed him. But that is not so. There are those here who will draw blade at your bidding, and there are those who look to Jord. Between you, if you so strive, you will split Styr Holding like a rotten fruit, and the outlaws will eat us up before the coming of green things again. Go claim a greater heritage than Styr, Daughter's Son. It is your right."

For the last time he gave Kincar full salute, and the younger man, realizing that he spoke the truth, set Cim into a lumbering trot with a twitch of the ear reins. But his hurt struck so deep that he did not once turn to look back at the squat half-fortress, half-castle with the cluster of fieldmen's dwellings about its walls.

The wind was at his back as he took the northeast track, which would bring him up to Mord Claw Pass and the way to the interior plains. As far as he knew, he was heading into the broken, aimless life of an outlaw, with the best future he could hope for one in service as a guardsman under some lord who wanted to enlist extra swords for a foray.

Could Wurd's talk of a remaining Star ship—of his joining with the Star Lords—be true? He had half forgotten it since leaving the old man. Kincar fumbled with the left saddlebag and brought out a roll of writing bark. He had been trained to read block characters, for part of his duties at Styr was to keep records. But such reading was not a quick task, and he let Cim pick his own route along the road as he puzzled over the two lines with the small accompanying drawing.

Why—it was clear enough! Those of the half-blood who wished to join the Star Lords had been summoned. And the map was not unfamiliar—it covered a portion of the countryside he had been set to memorize a year or so earlier. Then Wurd had still been able to ride and had carried on the tutelage of the Hold's heir, taking him as far as the passes and pointing out in the wastes below where gatherings of outlaws might exist and where a canny chief of a Holding might well look for future trouble. The map was the heart of such a section, a district of ill omen, rumored to be the abode of the Old Ones, those shapes of darkness driven into foul hiding by the Star Lords upon their arrival in Gorth.

The Star Lords! Kincar's hand went to the device on his surcoat. He had a sudden odd longing to look upon the reflection of his own face in some chamber mirror. Would his new knowledge make any change in what would be pictured there?

To his eyes he had no physical difference from the other youths of Styr. Yet, by all accounts, the Star Lords were giants, their skin not ivory-white as his own but a rich brown, as if they had been hewn from a rare wood. No, if this wild tale were really true, he could have nothing of his sire in face or body. Under his helm his hair curled tight to his skull in small rings of blue-gray. Through the years it would darken to the black of an old man. But it was rumored that the Star Lords also had hair growing upon their bodies—and his skin was smooth. Away from Styr who would know his alien blood? He could discard the surcoat, turn free guardsman—maybe in time raise a following tail and gain a holding of his own by legal sword battle.

But, while he made and discarded half-a-dozen such plans, Kincar continued to ride along the path that would take him over the Mord's Claw and into the wasteland shown on the map. He could not have told why, for something within him shrank from the acceptance of his inheritance. While he revered the Star Lords and had hotly resented Jord's sneers, it was a very different thing to be of off-world blood oneself. And he did not like it.

The day had been half over when he quit Styr. And he did not halt for a rest, knowing that Regen must have fed Cim well. When the track they followed dwindled into a forking trail, he came upon Vorken sitting in the middle of the open space, fanning her wings as she squatted upon the still-warm body of a small wood-suard. He was heading into a country where game might be scarce, and wood-suard was tender eating. Kincar dismounted, cleaned the beast with his hunting knife, giving Vorken the tidbits she hungered for, and slung the body up behind his pad. It would do for the last meal of the day.

Their way up was a winding one. It was a caravan track, only used in times of war when the more western routes were preyed upon by guardsmen. And he was sure that it had not been traveled this season at all—the wastes beyond having too ill a name.

When the slope grew too steep, he dismounted, letting Cim pick a path where the mount's clawed feet found good hold. He scrambled along through scrub brush, which caught at his cloak or the crest of fringed mord skin on his helm. And he knew he was lucky that the season was so warm he did not have to fight snow as well, though here the nip of the wind was keen. Vorken took to hovering closer, alighting now and then on some rock a little ahead of her companions' slow advance to whistle her plaintive call and be reassured by Kincar's answer. A mord, once trained to man's friendship, had a craving for his presence, which kept it tractable even in the wilds where it could easily elude any hunter.

It was close to sunset when the vegetation, dried and leafless, was all behind them and they were among the rocks near to the pass. Kincar looked back for the first time. It was easy, far too easy, in the clear air, to sight Styr Holding. But—he caught a quick breath as he saw that the banner was gone from the watchtower! Wurd had been right—the lordship had passed from one hand to the next this day. Wurd s'Jastard was no longer Styr. And for Kincar s'Rud there could be no return now. Jord was in command—Jord s'Wurd was now Styr!

2
THE BATTLE OF THE WASTE

An overhang of rock gave Kincar shelter for the night. He had crossed the highest point of Mord Claw Pass and come down a short distance to the beginning of the timber line before the daylight faded. But he had no wish to push on into the wilderness beyond during the dark hours. Though the mountain shut off some of the wind, it was far colder here than in the valley of the Holding, and he set about building a traveler's small fire in the lee of the rocks while Vorken settled down upon the pad he had stripped from Cim and watched him intently, spreading her wings uneasily now and again as she listened to sounds from the stunted bushes and trees below them.

With Vorken's ears at his service, and Cim's alertness to other animals, Kincar needed to do no sentry duty. Neither would leave the fireside, and either or both would give him swift warning of danger. He was in more peril from wandering outlaws than he could be from any animal or flying thing. The giant sa-mords of the heights were not night hunters, and any suard large enough to provide a real threat would be timid of fire.

He cut up the meat Vorken had provided, sharpening a stick on which to impale chunks for roasting. And in the saddlebags he found the hard journey cakes of wayfarers, which packed into their stone solidity enough nourishment to keep a man going for days through a foodless wilderness. Regen was an old campaigner, and now that Kincar had time to check the contents of the bags, he appreciated the thought and experience that had gone into their packing.

Food in the most concentrated forms known to men who hunted or raided through waste country, a fishing line with hooks, a darg blanket folded small, its wet-repelling surface ample protection against all but the worst storms, a set of small tools for the righting of riding gear and armor, and, last of all, a small packet wound with a fastening of tough skin that Kincar tackled with interest. Judging by the care with which it had been wrapped, he was sure it must contain some treasure, but when the object was at last bared to view in the firelight, Kincar was puzzled. He was sure he had never seen it before—an oval stone, dull green, smoothed as though by countless years of water action rather than by the tools of men. But there was a hole in the narrower end, and through this hung a chain of metal. Plainly it was intended to be worn.

Tentatively Kincar shook it loose from the hide covering and cupped it in his palm. A moment later he almost dropped it, for as it lay upon his flesh, its dullness took on a faint glow, and it grew warm as though it held a life of its own. Kincar sucked in his breath and his fingers tightened over it in a jealous fist.

"Lor, Loi, Lys," he whispered reverently, and it seemed to him that with every speaking of one of the Names, the stone he held pulsed warmly.

But how had Regen—or was this a lost heritage from Wurd? No one within Styr Hold had ever dreamed that a Tie had lain in its lord's keeping. Kincar was overwhelmed by this last evidence of Wurd's trust in him. Jord might have the Holding, but not the guardianship of a Tie. That was his! The trust—and perhaps someday— He stared bemused at the fire. Someday—if he were worthy—if he proved to be the one Wurd hoped he might be, he might even use its power! With a child's wondering eyes, Kincar studied the stone, trying to imagine the marvel of that. No man could do so until the hour when the power moved him. It was enough that a Tie was his to guard.

With shaking fingers he got the chain about his throat, installed the stone safely against his skin under coarse shirt, jerkin, and scale armor. But it seemed that some measure of heat still clung to the hand that had held it. And when he raised his fingers to look at them more closely, he was aware of a faint, spicy fragrance. Vorken gave one of her chirps and shot forth her huge head, drawing her toothed beak across his palm, and Cim's head bobbed down as if the larng, too, was drawn by the enchantment of the Tie.

It was a very great honor to be a guardian, but it was also dangerous. The Tie could weave two kinds of magic, one for and one against mankind. And there were those who would readily plant a sword point in him to gain what he wore now—if it was suspected to be in his possession. Regen had given him aid and danger tied together in one small stone, but Kincar accepted it gladly.

Without worry, knowing that he could depend upon Vorken for a warning, he curled up with cloak and blanket about him to sleep away the hours of the dark. And when he roused from a confused dream, it was to a soft chittering beside his ear. Vorken was a warm weight on his chest. Outlined against the coals of the dying fire, he saw the black blot of her head turn from side to side. When he moved and she knew he was truly awake, Vorken scuttled away, using the tearing claws of her four feet to scramble to the top of a rock—making ready to launch into the air if need be. Her form of defense was always a slashing attack aimed at the head and eyes of the enemy.

Kincar felt for his sword hilt as she stared into the dark. There was no sound from Cim, which meant that Vorken's more acute hearing had given them time to prepare. What she warned against might well be far down the mountainside. The fire was almost dead, and Kincar made no effort to feed it into new life. His senses, trained during long wilderness hunts, told him that dawn was not far off.

He did not try to go out of the pocket in which they had camped. Vorken still gave soft warnings from her post. But, since her night sight was excellent, and she had not taken to the air, Kincar was certain the intruder that had disturbed her was coming no nearer. The sky was gray. He could pick out the boulders sheltering them. Now he set about padding Cim, lashing on saddlebags, though he did not mount as they edged out of the hollow. Vorken took to the air on scout. Cim's claws scraped on the rocks, but within a few feet the trail began and they walked in thick dust. Kincar chewed on a mouthful of journeycake, giving the major portion of the round to Cim. That must do to break their fast until they were sure they were safe.

The trail came out after a steep descent upon the lip of an even more abrupt drop. But Kincar did not move on. Crouching there, he brought Cim up with a sharp tug at the ear reins, hoping that neither had been sighted by the party below.

His first thought—that he spied upon a traders' caravan—was disproved in his second survey of the camp. There were six larngs, all riding stock—no burden bearers among them. And there were six riders on the bank of the small ice-bordered stream. The larngs bore the marks of hard going, their flanks were flat to the bones, and their cold-season wool hung in draggled patches as if they had been forced through thorn thickets.

But Kincar was astonished by the riders, for three of the figures seated on the bank were women, one hardly more than a child. Women in the wastelands! Of course the outlaws raided the holdings and took women to build up their clans. But these were plainly not captives, and their traveling cloaks were fine garments of tetee wool such as Hold Daughters had. They were on good terms with the men, and their light voices were pitched as if they spoke at ease with clan brothers.

What wag such a party doing here? They were not out for a day's hunting, for each larng bore traveling bags, plump to seam-bursting. Kincar longed to see their faces, but each wore the conventional travel mask under a well-wound turban of veil. For a moment he had a wild suspicion— This was the waste where the Star Lords had ordered their people to assemble. But there was no mistaking the pale skin of the nearest warrior. He was of Gorthian breed, no being from outer space.

As Kincar hesitated, uncertain as to whether he should hail the others, there was a startling scream from Vorken and then the deep, braying roar of a hand drum.

Those below were on their feet as if jerked up by ropes laid about them. The women, tossed by their escorts unto the riding pads of the waiting larngs, galloped off, one man with them, while the other two warriors reined in their mounts with one hand, holding swords free with the other. There was the sound of a running larng, and a war mount burst out of a screen of brush. Kincar, already up on Cim, paused to stare at the newcomer.

His larng was a giant of that breed—it had to be—for the man who bestrode him was also a giant. His wide shoulders were covered with a silvery stuff that drew light even in the gray of early morning.

Both of the waiting warriors rode over to take a stand beside him, all three wheeling to await some attack.

Kincar found the zigzag trail down the cliffside. Recklessly he did not dismount but kept the larng to the best speed possible, as loose stones and gravel rolled under Cim's scrabbling claws. The path took one of its sudden turns, and he caught sight of a battle raging in that river clearing.

Men in the tatters and rusty mail of outlaws, some on foot, a few riding gaunt larngs, leaped out of the brush, a wave to engulf the three who waited. But those three met the wave with licking blades. There was a confused shouting, the scream of a dying man. Cim's forefeet were on the last turn and Kincar leaned forward, whistling into his mount's ear that particular call that sent the larng into the proper battle rage.

They burst through the stream in a spatter of high-dashed water, were up the opposite bank and racing toward the melee. Vorken, seeing that Kincar was on the move, planed down to stab at an unsuspecting face, sending the man rolling screaming on the ground as her bill and claws got home. Cim, as he had been schooled, reared, using his forefeet on the dismounted men, while Kincar clung to the riding pad with one hand and swung his sword to good purpose with the other. There were a few wild minutes, and then the roar of the hand drum once again. A man at whom Kincar had aimed a stabbing thrust broke and ran for shelter into the brush. And when Kincar looked about for another enemy, he found that, except for the bodies on the ground and the three men who had been attacked, the pocket meadow was clear.

One of the warriors dismounted to wipe his blade on the grass before sending it home in its sheath.

"Those scouts have now had their fangs drawn, Lord Dillan—"

The man who had just sheathed his sword laughed, a harsh sound lacking mirth. He speedily contradicted his fellow.

"For the moment only, Jonathal. Were they of the common breed one such lesson would suffice. But these have a leader who will not let us away in peace as long as blades can be raised against us."

The giant in the silver clothing looked beyond his own men to study Kincar, a frown line showing between his brows, though little else was to be seen of his features because of the traveling mask across cheek and chin. Something in that close scrutiny brought Kincar's head up. A thrill of defiance ran through him.

"Who are you?" The question was shot at him as quick as a sword stab and as sharply.

"Kincar s'Rud," he replied, with none of the ceremonious embellishment he should use by forms of holding courtesy.

"—s'Rud—" the other repeated, but his tongue gave an odd twist to the name so that it came out with an intonation Kincar had never heard before. "And your sign?" he pressed.

Kincar had tossed aside his cloak. He twisted a little on the riding pad so that the other could see the device worked so boldly on his surcoat—that device that even yet did not seem right for him to wear.

"—s'Rud—" the giant said again. "And your mother?"

"Anora, Hold Daughter of Styr."

All three of them were staring at him now, the warriors appraisingly. However, he must have satisfied the big man, for now the lord held his hand, palm empty, over his head in the conventional salute of friendship. "Welcome to our road, Kincar s'Rud. You, too, have come at the summoning?"

But Kincar was still wary. "I seek a place in the waste—"

The strange lord nodded. "As do we. And, since the time grows very short, we must ride in haste. We are now hunted men on Gorth."

They might be satisfied with his identification, but he had had none from them. "I ride with—?" Kincar prompted.

The silver-clad lord answered. "I am Dillan, and these are Jonathal s'Kinston and Vulth s'Marc. We are all wearers of the lightning flash and followers of strange stars."

His own kind, the mixed blood. Kincar studied them curiously. The two guardsmen, at first glance, seemed no different from wellborn holding men. And, though they showed Lord Dillan a certain deference, it was that of clansman to close kin and not underling to hold chief.

The physical difference between Lord Dillan and the others was so marked that the longer Cim picked his way behind the leader's mount, the more Kincar came to suspect that he now rode in company with no half-blood but with one of the fabulous Star Lords in person. His great height, the very timbre of his voice, betrayed an alien origin, even though his helm and face mask and the tight silver clothing concealed most of his body and features. Yet neither Jonathal nor Vulth acted as if their leader was semidivine. They displayed none of the awe that kept Kincar silent and a little apart. Perhaps they had lived all their lives in the shadow of the Star-born and knew no wonder at their powers. Yet in the battle the Lord Dillan had not slain his enemies with shooting bolts of fire, as legend said he might do, but used a blade, longer and heavier than the usual to be sure, but still a sword much the same as that now girded to Kincar's own belt. And when he spoke, it was of common things, the endurance of a larng, the coming of full day, matters that any man riding in company might comment upon.

Vorken whistled her warning from above their heads, and all of them glanced aloft to where she skimmed, wings stretched, gliding on the unseen currents.

"You are well served, Kincar," the Lord Dillan addressed him for the first time since they had left the meadow. "That is a fine mord."

"Aye, a battle bird of price!" Vulth chimed in. "She is quick with her beak where there is need. Of your training?" he ended politely.

Kincar warmed. "I picked her from the egg. She has had two years of coursing. The best of Styr's hatchery for five seasons at least."

Those whose presence Vorken's scream had heralded now came into view ahead. The three women on their weary larngs, their escort trailing a length behind with an eye to the rear. He flung up his arm in welcome at the sight of their party and pulled aside to wait, but the women took no heed, keeping on at the best pace their larngs would rise to.

"You have drawn teeth?" the warrior hailed them.

"We have drawn teeth," Vulth replied with grim satisfaction. "They will press us again, but there are now fewer to answer the drum."

As if his words had been a signal, again that ominous roll of sound struck their ears from the back trail. But it was muffled by distance. The hunters had dropped well behind their quarry. Lord Dillan pushed his mount ahead to fall in with the women. They exchanged words in a low voice, and one of the women pointed in a westwardly direction. The Star Lord nodded and brought his larng to one side, letting the women pass. With a wave of his hand he sent their guard pounding in their wake, while the remaining four slackened speed once more—to provide a rear guard.

Kincar saw with woodswise eyes that they were following a marked trail that had been in recent use, its dust churned by larng claws in ragged lines. Lord Dillan must have noted his examination, for he said, “We are the last of the in-gathering. We have come from Gnarth.”

From half the continent away! No wonder their mounts showed bones through thin flesh and the women rode with the droop of weariness in their cloaked shoulders. But certainly they had not been hunted along all that distance? To underscore that thought, the hunt drum rolled again—this time closer. Vorken sounded her war call, but when Kincar did not wheel to face the enemy, she circled over their heads in widening curves, spiraling up into the new day, her keen eyes on the ground, her attention ready for any move from Kincar that would send her once more in a vicious dive against his foes.

The clumps of leafless brush that had narrowed their path since they left the river banks dwindled into patches of small twisted scrub, arid as dried bones in the now waterless land. And the blue earth under foot was pied with patches of silver sand. They were plainly heading into one of the true deserts of the waste. Yet the spoor of those before them was plain to read, and those with whom Kincar now rode appeared certain of the route.

A sun arose, bringing with it the sickly, warmish wind that was so out of season. And, with the wind, the sand came in thin clouds to plague them. Kincar improvised a mask. He was inured to the usual wind grit that bothered city dwellers traveling, but this was something else. Cim closed two of his eyes and veiled the others with his transparent inner eyelids but showed no other signs of discomfort as he trotted along. Vorken soared above the worst of the eddies.

Outcrops of rock, carved by wind and the tempest-borne sand grains into weird sculptures, rose along the trail, as if they were the ruins of some long-sacked holding. And the track wound about among these pillars and towers until Kincar found himself losing his sense of direction, the more so since he could not pick landmarks ahead through the quick flurries of wind and sand.

He was reduced to following Lord Dillan blindly, and only confidence in that leader kept him in control of a growing uneasiness. He was hungry, and water—the thought of water—was a minor torture. They must have been traveling for hours. How much longer would they shuffle on across this barren waste?

Kincar dragged on the reins, forcing Cim to rear up. The roll of the drum had sounded in his very ear! Yet Vorken had given no warning! Then he heard Vulth's voice, muffled by the mask.

"It is the echo, youngling! They stamp yet far behind us—not now have they outflanked our path. But loose your blade in its sheath; it will drink again before sundown—if we find us a proper battleground."

3
NO SHIP—BUT—

The weird echoes of the drum made Kincar edgy. To have it blast from one side and then the other grated on his nerves, and he longed to draw his sword and ride with the blade bared across his knee, ready for attack. But those with whom he rode made no such preparations, and he was ashamed so to betray his own uneasiness.

At the same time he speculated concerning their goal. A sky ship berthed here? Among all the rumors that dealt with the secrets of the wastelands, there had never been one that hinted at such a thing. Those ships at which all of Gorth had marveled had been in the great landing place outside the gates of the now forsaken Terranna. And they were gone, through the pale rose of Gorth's sky, never to return. Had one ship been set here, apart from its kind? When, from time to time, there came short breaks in the force of the grit storm, Kincar held his head high, trying to catch a glimpse of the shaft of metal of a sky ship, which would dwarf all about it.

But, though they bored steadily into the desert land, using the track winding among the pillars, there was no sign—save that same faint road—that man had ever gone that way before. The pillars were growing fewer, and, now that they did not hem in the road, there was the danger of going astray in the fog of wind-driven sand. Lord Dillan slackened pace, sometimes halting altogether for a moment or two, one hand close to his chest, his head bent over it, as if he consulted a talisman. And after each such move he altered their course to the right or left.

Then, as quickly as it had arisen, the wind died, the sand lay once more in dust-fine drifts, and the land about them was clear to the view. They were on an upslope, and far ahead Kincar sighted moving dots of figures, which must be the women and their guard. Those bobbed to the skyline and then were suddenly gone. They might have been sucked down in the sand. A downgrade lay beyond, Kincar surmised, and a steep one or they would not have vanished so quickly.

Jonathal brought his larng up beside Cim, wiping the matted dust from his mouth mask with the back of his hand before he commented thickly, "That was a dry course! And I've never relished a fight without a cold draft to sweeten the throat—"

"A fight?" Kincar had not heard the drum for a time. He had hoped that the storm had shaken their pursuers from the trail.

"They must attack now." Jonathal shrugged. "This is the last throw of tablets in the game. Once we are over that ridge"—he jerked a thumb at the rise—"they will have lost. We are the last of our kind. With us through, the gate will close—"

Kincar did not understand that reference to the gate, but he understood very well the scream from Vorken's long throat, her skimming dive that carried her black shadow back over the sand dunes toward the pillar-studded land from which they had just emerged. And now, at last, he drew his sword, rolling his cloak about his left arm as a shield, ready to snap it into an opponent's face if the need arose.

Figures slipped from pillar to pillar, silent, dark, misshapen. Kincar watched that sly, noiseless advance, set his mouth hard. For five years or more he had ridden in holding spear-festings aimed against outlaws, and once he had served in a real foray against Crom's Hold. In the last two festings, in spite of his youth, he had taken out Styr's banner as Wurd's deputy. He had known such warfare since his small boy's hand had first been fitted to an even smaller sword hilt under Regen's patient teaching. But this was something else—he was sensitive to a change, wary under a threat he did not understand.

Vorken wheeled back above him, shrilling her battle cry, but not attacking since he had not advanced. Cim shifted foot under him. They must feel it, too, this difference, this odd threat that promised worse than slash of sword, thrust of footman's spear, clash of mounted man against his kind.

His sword dangling from his wrist cord, Kincar brought up his right hand to jerk off his dust mask, drawing in more freely the air for which his lungs felt a sudden need. Jonathal was on his left, sitting at ease on the pad of his gaunt larng, a smile curving his mouth as he watched the pillars with a sentry's eye. On the right Vulth was making a careful business of adjusting his cloak about his arm, testing each fold as he laid it ready. But Lord Dillan, his one hand laced in larng reins, his other still held to his breast, had not drawn his weapon at all or shed his travel mask. Above the strip of silver stuff that matched his garments, his odd light eyes were on the pillars and what moved in their shadows.

"Ride slowly," he bade them. "We do not fight unless they push us to it—"

"They will not let us away out of their jaws," warned Vulth.

"Perhaps they will—unless he who leads them gives the order—" Lord Dillan did not relax his Watchfulness or turn his larng after them as the other three followed his orders and headed on.

Kincar was last, reluctant to leave. And at that moment Vorken went into action on her own. Whether the mord misconstrued Cim's movement as an advance, or whether her natural wildness sent her in, Kincar was never to know. But she gave vent to one last whistle and snapped down in a glide toward the nearest pillar.

He did not see the bolt that caught her in mid-air. No one could have sighted the silent, swift stroke. But, as Vorken shrieked in pain, one of her wings collapsed, and she hurtled down toward the sand. Without pausing to think, Kincar sent Cim skimming back to where Vorken lay, beating her good wing in a vain attempt to win aloft again. Her cries were growing hoarser in her pain and rage, and she was hurling spurts of sand into the air with her four feet as she dug fruitlessly with her claws.

Kincar was off Cim. He hit the ground already running, his cloak whipping out to net the frenzied mord. To take her up barehanded was to court deep tears from claws and beak. Somehow he scooped up cloak and struggling creature, cradling her tight against his chest while she snapped and kicked in fury.

There was a shout of triumph from the pillars; a shaggy wave came out of hiding, heading straight for Kincar. He retreated, watchful. His sword was ready, but Vorken's struggles hampered its free use. He was facing spear points, clubs, in the hands of lithe-moving footmen, and in that moment he realized that the uneasiness he knew was truly fear. The openness of their attack was so removed from their usual methods of battle that it alarmed him as much as the stench from their unwashed bodies made his empty stomach churn.

He gave the cry to summon Cim. But, though the larng obediently trotted to his side, Kincar could not scramble up on the pad, not with the still-fighting Vorken pressed against him. Yet he would not abandon the mord.

"Yaaaaah—" The shout of the outlaws echoed about him in a worse tumult than the beat of the drum. And behind the footmen, better clad and armed, mounted men were joining in the rush to ride him down.

Then a larng dashed between him and that advance, the sand fountaining about mount and rider. Vulth thrust and raised a dripping blade for a second stroke. More men boiled from the pillars to get at them both.

With the fraction of breathing space, Kincar had gotten up on Cim, his sword banging from its wrist cord. He let the reins hang. The larng was well enough trained to need no guidance during a fight. The mount was snarling, pawing at the sand, and he reared when he felt Kincar's weight on the pad, clawing down one of the spearmen.

Vorken must be half stifled. She had ceased to struggle, and Kincar was grateful for that as he fell to such sword work as would cut a path for Vulth's withdrawal.

A voice shouted incomprehensible words. Lord Dillan replied in the same tongue with a single bitten-off sentence. His blade was out, and he rode beside Jonathal as if they were the two arms of a single warrior. The outlaws broke, snarling like the beasts they were, and ran, but the mounted men behind them were of a different breed. Jonathal's larng snorted and spun around despite the efforts of its rider to control it. Then it fell with the slack-legged force of an already dead animal and Jonathal was crushed under it, only the soft sand saving him from mortal injury.

Kincar brought Cim up to split the skull of the bareheaded outlaw who had his point at Jonathal's throat as the other fought to pull free of the larng. Then, above the hum of the drum and the cries of the fighting men, there struck a peel as shrill as Vorken's calls. Up over the rise, toward which they had been headed, boiled a group of riders. There were only five of them when Kincar could at last sort them out, but somehow the fury of their charge magnified their numbers into double that score.

They swept past the four, scooping up the outlaws and bearing them along by the force with which they struck into the melee. But they did not pursue past the line of the pillars, wheeling there so shortly as to make their larngs rear and totter on their hind legs. Then they pounded back. One paused to let Jonathal scramble up behind him before they went on, drawing the others with them, over the ridge and down into a deep cup of valley, a bare valley that lay like a giant pock-mark in the desert waste.

As they swept across the crest, Kincar reeled, his knees almost losing their grip on the riding pad. The sensation of bursting through an unseen barrier was part of that shock. But with it, and worse, had come a thrill of white-hot pain. So sure was he that some chance-thrown spear had found its target in his body that he stared stupidly down to where he still clasped the muffled Vorken, expecting to see metal protruding from his breast and wondering vaguely how he had survived a blow of such force. But there was no spear point showing, and, as he straightened again, he knew that he had not been hit. Only—what of that stab of agony, the pulse of heat and pain that he still knew beneath scale coat and underjerkin?

The Tie! For some reason beyond his knowing, its unique properties had been aroused in that second when he had topped the ridge. The why of it he could not guess, and he dared ask no questions. Those who were guardian of a Tie in the Name of the Three held that honor secretly, a secrecy accepted without complaint as one accepted the other burdens and rights such a duty laid upon one. He did not dare to touch the space above his heart where that throb beat as if in promise of worse to come.

In the heart of the valley was a camp—a hasty affair of small shelters put together with blankets and cloaks. These were now being speedily dismantled, men throwing rolls and bundles on the backs of larngs. Beyond the camp stood something else, as different from the primitive shelters as one of the Star ships might be from a trader's wain.

Two pillars of bright blue metal had been based in piles of rocks, the supporting stones being fused into a stability no storm could shake. They were erected some five feet apart, and suspended between them was a shimmering web of some stuff Kincar could not name. It was bright; it glittered with racing lines of rainbow fire that ran ceaselessly crisscross over it—yet it had so little real body that one could see through it to the opposite wall of the valley.

Kincar shifted Vorken's weight upon his arm and regarded this new marvel intently. He had come here expecting to discover a Star ship. He had found a web strung between metal poles. What had his trust in his chance-met companions drawn him into? As far as he could see, they were now trapped. The outlaws need only make one last rush to wipe them out—for there were no more than six men waiting here.

Of those six, four were wearing the silver dress of Lord Dillan, and they were of the same giant stature. They had put off their travelers' masks, and he could see the alien darkness of their hard faces, the features of which lacked the mobility of those he had known all his life. One of them now raised his hand in a salute, which Lord Dillan answered. Then that other lord took in his big hands the leading lines of three of the waiting larngs and moved toward the shimmering web. As they watched, he stepped between the supporting pillars.

There was no discernible break in the web. For a moment the rainbow lines rushed in to outline the figure of the Star Lord—then those colors fled again to the far corners of the screen. But the Star Lord and the larngs he had led—were gone! They did not reappear on the opposite side, and Kincar blinked at the wavy sight of the rocks beyond where no one—no thing—walked at all!

Vorken gave a faint chirrup in his arms; the tip of her beak pushed forth from the wrappings that netted her. Cim blew noisily, clearing the sand grit from his wide nostrils. But at that moment Kincar could neither have spoken nor moved.

It would appear that the tales of the Star Lords' magic, the wildest tales of all—at which sensible men had laughed indulgently—were true! He had just seen a Star Lord walk into nothingness, which perhaps a Star Lord might safely do—but what of the rest of them?

"'Tis the gate, youngling!" Vulth's knee brushed against Kincar's as the other rode beside him. "The gate to give us a new world."

The explanation meant exactly nothing to Kincar. A ship that went out to the stars—aye, that could he understand. He was no ignorant fieldman to believe that the sky over one's head was merely the great Shield of Lor held up between men and a terrible outer darkness without end. And he knew well that the Star Lords had come from another world much like Gorth. But they had come in ships where a man could live, the fabric of which all curious ones could feel with their two hands. How could one seek another world by walking through a veil of shimmering stuff?

His hand flattened over the Tie and his lips moved in the Three Names of Power. This was a magic that the Star Lords had not—a magic native to Gorth. And at this moment it was far better to cling to such a talisman than trust to a veil that took men out of sight in an instant.

It was apparent that Vulth knew what to expect and that this wonder was no magic in his eyes. Cim picked his way through the draggle of tents in the wake of Vulth's mount, but Kincar neither urged him on nor tried to restrain him. Now one of the half-bloods had taken the lead ropes of two more laden larngs. And, as had the Star Lord before him, he went forward with the confidence of one walking a city street into the web where the colors haloed him for an instant of flaming glory before he vanished, the animals after him.

Then it was that Vulth turned and caught Cim's dangling reins. He smiled reassuringly at Kincar.

"This is a venture better than any foray—past even the Foray of Hlaf's Dun, youngling. Past even sky voyaging—"

Kincar, clutching Vorken with one hand, the other resting above the branding heat of the Tie, made no protest when the warrior sent his larng straight on toward the screen gateway. He was aware only dimly of sharp glances from Star Lords who stood nearby, for his full attention was on the web. He could not throw aside the thought that he was about to be engulfed in a trap of some kind beyond his imagining. He braced his body stiffly against the inward shrinking of his nerves, against the impulse that would have sent him pounding away not only from the gate but from those who controlled such a device.

Vulth vanished into nothingness; Cim's head was gone. Kincar was drowning in a sea of color. And on his breast the Tie burned with a force that seemed to char through flesh to his heart. He bit back a whimper of pain and opened dazzled eyes upon a world of gray stone—a world in which life itself seemed alien, intruding, a world of—no, not the dead, for there had never been life here at all—but a world that had never known the impress of a living thing. How he sensed that, Kincar could not have told—perhaps such knowledge came through the Tie.

He straightened painfully, conscious of a party crowded on the stretch of rock plain. But he did not see Vulth's eyes upon him, the odd shadow on the older Gorthian's face as he witnessed Kincar's obvious distress. Nor did Kincar follow when the other dropped Cim's reins and rode on to join the group waiting by a second portal a half mile farther on.

There was a second portal—the same blue metal poles supporting another rainbow web. Only, before this one was a box contrivance where the Star Lords were clustered. One of their number knelt before that box, his hands resting upon it, a tenseness in his position arguing that he was engaged in some act of the utmost importance.

Cim wandered along, his head drooping. Kincar drew a slow and painful breath. The hurt of the Tie had eased a little. Only when he was directly in touch with the Star Lords' magic was it so great an agony. If they were to pass through another such gate, could he stand it? He tried to fix his thoughts upon the Three. The Tie was Theirs, the right to bear it had been set upon him by Them—surely They would aid Their servant now—

He tried to watch those about him, gain some hint of what this was that they must do. There were women here, laden supply larngs, a full caravan of travelers. But in all, the party numbered less than thirty, and only six of those in sight were Star Lords—all the rest must be of the half-blood strain.

There was clearly clan feeling among them, the easy meeting of kinsman with kinsman. Only he felt set apart, torn from all he had known. If only he could know what was happening, where these gates led, what lay before them now! Of one thing he was growing increasingly sure—they were headed into an exile that would be permanent.

A Star Lord burst through the first gate. He ran toward his fellows. Those gathered by the box looked up, their faces strained and bleak. If he bore a warning, they had too little time to act upon it, for through the first gate poured a jumble of mounts and men, swinging bloody steel, and two of them rode double.

The Star Lord at the box moved his hand, bringing down his palm with a smacking force. There was a ripple of green on the second web; the hue became blue, then purple-red as it moved.

Lord Dillan reeled through the first gate. Only two steps beyond it, he staggered about and brought up his hand. What he held Kincar could not see, but from his fist there sprang a spear of light that burned bright in the gloom of that gray world. It struck full upon the first web. The stuff curled, wrinkled, and was consumed as a cobweb fallen into a flame. Between the posts one could see only the barren rocks.

But those who had waited here were now in a hurry to be gone, as if the destruction of that one web was not enough to save them from their enemies. Kincar was caught up in line, and he dared not protest, setting his power of endurance to meet what might chance at his second passage through the magic gates.

It came as an agony worse and deeper than either of the earlier two attacks. He thought he must have cried out, but no one near him took note—perhaps they were too intent upon escape. He was conscious that the sky above was no longer gray but a familiar rose, that Cim's feet crackled through dried field grass. And Vorken stirred in his arm, crying peevishly.

He looked about him dazedly. This was not the wasteland. He saw a roll of wide plain, the rounded mounts of foothills in the distance, and above, the loom of mountains. A chill wind puffed into his face, bringing with it icy particles of snow, and more white flakes were swirling down in an ever thickening fall.

4
NEW-FOUND WORLD

Kincar shivered. Dare he free Vorken from her wrappings in order to bring the cloak about them both? Injured and frightened as she was, the mord might well rend him—for there was a vast, sinewy power in the small body he pressed so tightly against his own. And the burning torment on his breast had sucked from him both strength and inclination to struggle.

So intent was Kincar upon his own problem that the growing clamor about him meant very little. He gathered, only half-consciously, that the Star Lords had been forced by a sudden attack on the outer gateway into action that might prove highly dangerous. And there was a dispute that ended only with the destruction of the second gate, the one that had brought them into this range of open, rolling land. For better or worse, they were now committed to this place, wherever it might be.

Kincar hunched over Vorken, squeaking to her softly in his closest imitation of her own voicings, cautiously loosening the cloak. To his great relief she did not respond with an instant thrust of stiff legs armed with dagger talons. And when he dared to drag the folds entirely away, she crouched, staring up at him, almost as if her fierce nature had for once been cowed by the events of the past hours. She reached out with her forefeet and took firm hold on the breast of his surcoat as she might cling to the bare bole of some tree she had selected for a roost.

Kincar shrugged the cloak about them both, though his movements were slow because of the trickles of pain that ran from the Tie across his shoulders and along the nerves of his arms. It was good that he need not draw sword now. He doubted if he could raise the weight of the blade.

But he did examine Vorken's injured wing, finding across its leathery surface a finger-breath of raw brand, a burn. She allowed him only a moment's inspection and then turned her head and licked at the hurt with her tongue, meeting his further attempt at examination with a warning hiss. And he was forced to allow her to tend her hurt in her own way, only glad that she was content to ride under his cloak without protest.

The Star Lords were marshaling them into line. This open country in a gathering snowstorm was no place for a camp, and they were heading through the swirls toward the foothills where some form of shelter could be expected. To Kincar's eyes the country was oddly deserted. This was too good crop land not to be included in some holding—yet there was no sign of wall, no view of field fort, as far as he could see. By some magic the Star Lords must have brought them into a section of Gorth where there were no holds at all. He was very certain they *were* on Gorth. The sky above them was pale rose, the grass, dried in clumps and edging out of the already covering snow in ragged bunches, was that he had always known. Aye, this was somewhere on Gorth—but where?

At a shout he brought Cim into the line of march. There were no familiar faces near him. And he was too tired, too plagued by the Tie, to try to seek out Jonathal, or Vulth, too shy to look for Lord Dillan in that company.

Luckily the snow did not take on the proportions of a blizzard. Tired, hungry, cold as they were, they could keep one another in sight. But there was little talk along that line. They rode with the suppressed eagerness of those who have been long hunted and who now seek a sanctuary, intent upon winning to such a goal. As the foothills came into clearer view, a pair of scouts broke from the main party and galloped ahead, separating to search the higher ground in two directions.

Cim was only plodding. He had not eaten since they had left the pass camp—had that only been this morning? He must be allowed rest, food, and that very soon. Kincar was debating a withdrawal out of line, to give the larng some journeycake, when one of the scouts came pounding back at a dead run. The excited gabble of his report was loud, though his words were not clear. Some sort of superior shelter had been located—it was ready for them. And, as if to underline their need for just such as that, the wind moaned across the empty land and brought with it a thicker flurry of snow, while heavy clouds scudded in the sky. A blizzard was not far off.

The wind might be a broom the way they were swept by it into a narrow valley. But the gloom of the dying day could not hide—hide or belittle—what awaited them there. Kincar had seen many marvels since he had ridden out of Styr. And this was not the least of them.

Here was a hold such as a lord of limitless acres might dream of building. Its square towers bit into the reaches of the sky; its walls had the same solidity as the gorge rock in which it was set. And it spanned the narrow valley from side to side, as if, massive as it was, it served as gate as well as fortress.

In the hollow of a doorway—a doorway so wide that at least three burden larngs might enter it abreast—stood one of the Star Lords, in his hands a core of yellow-red light blazing as a beacon to draw them on through the murk of the snow. But above, in that dark bulk of tower and wall, there was no other light—only shadows and a brooding silence, which seized upon and swallowed up the muted sounds of their own progress down the valley. Kincar knew that this fortress was a dead, long-deserted pile.

As it was deserted, so was it subtly different from the hold forts he had known, not only because of its size, but also because of some alterations of line. Those who had erected this had not first practiced on the building of such as Styr—they had had other models. Then Kincar thought he understood. This was some hidden hold of the Star Lord. It probably guarded the field on which their last ship stood. He knew that their city of Terranna had been far different from the native holds. And that business of the gates had yet to be made clear. But this then was the goal toward which they had headed. He slid down from Cim, cradling Vorken in his arm. Under him the ground was unsteady, and he was forced to snatch at the riding pad with his other hand to keep his balance.

Still holding to Cim, Kincar went on slowly until the doorway arched above him and he was in a passage lighted by one of the Star Lords' flares. There was no side opening in that passage, and it brought him into a courtyard, ringed in with hold walls, into which some snow was shifting down—though the major part of the storm was kept off by those same walls. Here two more flares showed a stall section under a roof, a structure that could only be a mount pen, and Kincar, through habit, headed for it.

Perhaps it was the effect of the Tie that made him move as if in a foggy dream. Mechanically he went through duties that had been drilled into him in childhood, but his sense of curiosity and his awareness of others about him were oddly dulled. It might have been that only Cim, Vorken, and he were alive in that place.

Cim entered one of the stalls readily enough. There was no blanketing hay for its flooring, and Kincar's boots grated on stone flagstones. As he loosened his cloak, Vorken struggled free of his grip and fluttered her good wing, sputtering her distress, until he lifted her to where she could cling to the top of a stall division, a poor substitute for her roost in the hatchery, but it appeared to satisfy her for the present.

Then he stripped Cim of pad and bags. With an undershirt from his scant wardrobe, he began to rub down the snow-wet flanks, press the excess moisture from shoulder and neck wool, until Cim bubbled contentedly. But with every movement of his hands and arms Kincar's fatigue grew so that he was obliged to lean for long moments against the wall of the stall panting. He kept doggedly to his task, ending by feeding the larng crumbled journeycake in his cupped hands and holding up to Vorken a strip of dried meat from his provisions.

Cim folded long legs in the curiously awkward stance of a larng needing rest. And the coarse crumbs of journeycake were still on Kincar's tongue as he fell rather than lay down beside the mount. He reached for his cloak and pulled it up, and then he remembered nothing at all—for a dream world engulfed him utterly and he was finally lost in a darkness without visible end.

Pain—dull and not biting as he had known it—still centered on his breast. Kincar tried to raise his hand to ease it, and a sharper nip caught one of his fingers, completely arousing him. A toothed bill above his chin, red eyes staring into his, a whistling complaint—Vorken crouched on him. His head rested on one of Cim's forelegs, and the heat of the larng's body kept him warm. But his breath puffed a frosty cloud in the air.

Someone must have closed the door of the stall pens. He was looking now at ancient wood, eaten by insects, splintered by time—but still stout enough to be a portal. Vorken, having seen him fully awake, walked down his body and, trailing her hurt wing, crossed to sit on the bags, and demanded to be fed from their contents.

Some of that strange fog that had dulled his mind since he had dared the web gates had been lost in slumber, but Kincar still moved stiffly as he stretched and went to answer the mord's demands.

Though the outer door of the building was in poor condition, as trails of snow shifting under it and through its cracks testified, the structure itself was in as good repair as if it had been hewn from the mountainside. He marveled at those huge blocks of stone that made up the outer walls, laid so truly one upon the other that the cracks at their joining were hardly visible. The lord who had raised this hold must have been able to command master workers in stone, or else this was more of the Star Lords' unending magic. For all Gorth knew, those from off-world could command the elements and tame the winds, if it was to their desire. Terranna had been a marvel. The only point that puzzled Kincar now was the aura of age that clung to this fortress.

Of course Gorthian time was a matter of little moment to the Star Lords with their almost eternal life. They could die in battle right enough, or from some illness. But otherwise they did not show signs of age until their years had equaled five, even six life spans of the natives—three hundred years was not unknown for men who in that time displayed no outer marks of age at all. And among them before the withdrawal there had still been some who had landed on Gorth almost five hundred years earlier.

But, though they had such a length-of-life span, they did not produce many sons or daughters to follow them. That had been first whispered and then said boldly abroad. And when they took Gorthian mates, the issue of such marriages were also few—two children to a marriage at the most. So their numbers had remained nearly the same as when they had first landed their sky ships, a limited number of births balancing deaths by battle or misadventure.

If they were responsible for the building of this hold, it must have been erected soon after they reached Gorth, Kincar was certain of that. This type of stone exposed to the open air darkened with the passage of time. But he could not remember, save in the scattered stones of a very old shrine, such discoloration as these walls displayed. Yet history had never placed the Star Lords far from their initial landing point of Terranna. And where was this?

His thoughts were interrupted by Vorken's demand, which arose from a hissed whisper to ear-punishing squawks, punctuated by the flapping of her good wing. As he went down on his knees to burrow in the bag that contained his food, the door to the courtyard opened with a protesting scrape, letting in a blast of frigid air and a measure of daylight.

There was a chorus of grunts and sniffles from the larngs in the line of stalls, impatient for feeding and watering. Both men who entered carried buckets slopping over at their brims. In spite of Vorken's protests Kincar got to his feet. And the first man uttered a surprised exclamation as he caught sight of the young man—just as Kincar himself was mildly astonished to see that the other was one of the silver-clad Star Lords setting about a pen task normally left to a fieldman, and no concern of a swordwearer.

"And who are you?"

"Kincar s'Rud." Vorken, completely losing her temper, snapped at his hand, and he tossed her a meat stick from the bag.

"And soon to be an icicle by the look of you," commented the Star Lord. "Did you spend the night here?"

Kincar could not understand his surprise. Of course he had spent the night with Cim. Where else did a warrior sleep on the trail but with his larng? The stone was hard, aye, but a warrior did not notice such discomfort—he must be prepared to accept as a matter of course far worse.

The half-Gorthian with the Star Lord set down his two buckets and chuckled. "Lord Bardon, he but follows custom. In enemy territory one does not separate willingly from one's mount. Is that not so, youngling? But this is not enemy territory now. Tend to your beast and then in with you to the hall. There is no need to freeze in the line of duty." Then he added with the bluff good humor of a captain of guardsmen to a new recruit, "I am Lorpor s'Jax, and this is the Lord Bardon out of Hamil."

Hamil—another far distant district in the west. Indeed this ingathering had caught up those from odd corners of the world.

Having fed Vorken, Kincar fell to and helped the others care for the line of larngs. The animals, used to sparse feeding during the cold months, were given slightly larger rations of journeycake because of their recent hard usage. But most of them were already settling into the half-doze that carried them through the short days of snow-time, unless their services were needed. Cim's upper eyes were fast closed when Kincar returned to his stall to collect bags and Vorken, and his lower ones regarded his master with a dull lack of interest.

Vorken allowed herself to be picked up, but scrambled out of his arm to cling to his shoulder, balancing there a little uncertainly, her injured wing trailing down his back. Lorpor inspected the burn on the leathery skin and whistled softly.

"Best show her to the Lady Asgar—she has healing knowledge. Perhaps she can cure that so this one may fly again. A good mord—of your own training?"

"Aye. From the shell. She was the best of the hatchery at Styr."

Lorpor had fallen into step with him as they crossed the snow-drifted courtyard toward the middle portion of the hold. And now Lord Bardon shortened pace so that they caught up with him.

"You came in with Dillan?" he asked Kincar abruptly.

"Aye, Lord. But I was not of his following. I am from Styr Hold in the mountains—" Kincar volunteered no more information. He found Lord Bardon's sharpness disconcerting—hinting that he had no right to be there. Yet Lord Dillan had received him readily, so perhaps this brusqueness of speech was peculiar to Lord Bardon. Never having been among those of the pure Star blood, Kincar could only watch, listen, and try to adapt to their customs. But he felt no ease in their presence as did the other half-bloods such as Jonathal, Vulth, and Lorpor. In fact, that ease of manner between them and the Star Lords in turn made him oddly wary of them. And for the first time he wondered about his father. Why had he, Kincar, been sent away from Terranna, back to Styr, when still a baby?

True, it was the custom that Hold Daughter's Son lived where he was heir. But neither was such a boy kept so great a stranger to his father's clan and kindred. Kincar had always thought of his father as dead—but— His boot sole slipped on a patch of snow, and Vorken hissed a warning in his ear. What if his father still lived? What if he was to be found among the lords of this company? For some reason

Kincar, at that moment, would rather have faced a ring of swords barehanded than ask information concerning the "Rud" whose name he had always borne.

"Styr Holding—" Lord Bardon repeated that as though trying to recall some memory. "And your mother was—?"

"Anora, Hold Daughter," Kincar returned shortly. Let this Lord know that he was not of the common sort.

"Hold Daughter's Son!" If that had not registered with Lord Bardon, it did with Lorpor. His glance at Kincar held puzzlement. "Yet—"

"Being half-blood," Kincar explained against his will, "I could not raise Styr Banner. There was Jord s'Wurd, Hold Daughter's brother, to dispute."

Lorpor nodded. "With the trouble hot about us, that would be true. And to set brother fighting brother is an evil thing. You did well to seek out another future, Hold Daughter's Son."

But Lord Bardon made no comment, merely lengthened his pace and was gone. Lorpor drew Kincar through a doorway into a hold hall that was twice the size of any he had ever seen. Huge fireplaces at either end gave a measure of heat, not from any pile of well-seasoned logs, but from small boxes set on their hearths to radiate warmth—some more Star magic. Riding pads were stacked to furnish seats, huddles of traveling bags and cloaks marked the occupancy of individuals or families, and there was a babble of sound through which the deeper voices of the Star Lords made an under-thread of far-off thunder.

"Leave your bags here"—Lorpor pointed to a place on the pads—"and bring your mord to the Lady Asgar."

Kincar shed his cloak in the heat of the chamber before Lorpor guided him out of the main room of the hold into a side chamber, which jutted out like a small circular cell. The half-blood halted at a cloak hung curtainwise and called.

"Lorpor, with one who has need of healing skill, my lady."

"Let him enter and speedily," came the answer, and Kincar stepped through to face a woman.

She wore the short divided skirt of a traveler, but she had put aside all head and shoulder wrappings, except for a gold and green shawl caught over her plain green bodice. It was her face that startled

Kincar close to forgetting all manners, for this was the first Star Lady he had ever seen.

In place of the long braids of a Gorthian woman, her hair was cropped almost as short as his own, and it lay in waves of gold as bright as the threads of her shawl, doubly bright about the creamy brown of her skin. The eyes she turned toward him were very dark, under level brows, and Kincar could not have guessed at her age, except that he did not believe her to be a young maid.

She saw at once the purpose of Kincar's visit and held out her hands to Vorken, giving a chirruping cry. Knowing the mord's usual response to any touch, Kincar tried to ward her off. But Vorken surprised him by climbing down along his arm and reaching her long neck, her hideous head, to those brown hands.

"Do not fear, boy." The Lady Asgar smiled at him. "She will not savage me. What is her name?"

"Vorken."

"Ah—for the Demon of the Heights! Doubtless it suits her. Come, Vorken, let us see to this hurt of yours."

The mord gave a short leap, beating her good wing, to the lady's grasp.

She carried the mord over to the full light of the window, examining the drooping wing without laying hand upon it.

"A blaster burn. But luckily only the edge of the ray caught. It can be restored—"

She held Vorken close to the wall, and the mord, as if obeying some unspoken order, caught at hollows in the stone with all four of her feet, clinging there while the Lady Asgar went to some bags and brought forth a tube of metal. This she pointed at Vorken's hurt and held it so for a long second.

What she did or why Kincar did not know. What he was acutely conscious of was the Tie, again awakened to angry life against his flesh. And, perhaps because this was the fourth time he had known such torment, he reeled back against the wall, unknowing that his face was a haggard mask, that Lorpor was watching him with a surprise close to horror. Only dimly did he feel an arm flung about his shoulders, was only half aware of being brought back against a sturdy support that kept him on his feet, while the Lady Asgar spun around, her astonishment altering to deep concern.

5
A QUESTION OF BIRTHRIGHT

Only for a moment did Kincar remain so steadied, and then, the stab of the Tie less, he pulled away, glancing up to see that it was Lord Dillan whose hands still rested on his shoulders. The rigid brown mask, which, to his untutored eyes, served all the Star Lords for a face, had a new expression. And Dillan's voice, when he spoke, was warm with concern.

"What is it, Kincar?"

But the young man freed himself with a last twist and stood, one hand at the breast of his scaled shirt, schooling his body, his nerves under control. He who carried a Tie was honored above his fellows, as well as burdened, but his guardianship was not for the knowledge of others—certainly not for the outland-born Star men. So he fronted all three of them with the same wariness with which he would face a company of strangers in a time of clan feud when enemy was not yet sorted from friend.

When he made no answer, Lord Dillan spoke to the woman.

"What happened?" He used the common speech, purposely, Kincar suspected. Kincar himself wanted nothing more than to be out of that room and away from their prying eyes.

"I used the atomar on the mord—it has a ray-burned wing."

"The atomar," Lord Dillan repeated, his attention once more fixed on Kincar, as if by his will he could force the truth from the young man.

"He fears the Star machines—" That was a newcomer speaking, and there was contempt in his voice. Vulth stood in the door, eying

Kincar as he would some wood creature brought in by a hunter. "It was so that he flinched upon passing the gates—as well I saw. Doubtless at his hold they held to the old belief in night demons and howling terrors—"

Kincar was ready with a hot retort to that, but he did not give it voice. A good enough explanation for his behavior if they had to have one, one that made him less of a man, that was true, but it was better to shrink in the regard of these (though that in its way carried a hurt also) than to reveal what he carried.

A brown hand closed about the wrist of his sword hand, keeping him where he was, and the Lady Asgar was beside him. Something in her manner must have relayed an order to both Vulth and Lorpor, for, after glancing from her now impassive face to that of the Lord Dillan, they went out, Vulth unhooking the upturned corner of the cloak door and letting it fall to give the remaining three privacy.

Kincar tried to follow, but that hand still gripped his wrist. Short of forcibly twisting free, he could not leave. But when the Lady Asgar spoke, he lost his desire to do so.

"The Tie of the Three is a heavy weight for the bearing—"

His hand flattened convulsively against that weight. Mechanically he gave the proper response.

"To the bearer it is no weight, it is a lightener of loads, a shortener of ways, a brightener of both day and night."

Now her hand dropped away. "So did I think!" Swiftly her fingers sketched a certain sign between them in the air, and he stared at her wonderingly.

"But"—that was half protest, half unbelief—"you are wholly of the Star Blood. You do not tread the Road of the Three!"

"To each race there are certain beliefs granted." She spoke as she would to a child under instruction. "We, too, have our powers—though they may not take the same form for our worshiping. But all who follow Powers of Light give faith and belief where it should be. I, who am counted as a wise woman among my people, share in part the learning of the Three. Could I give you these signs were that not so?" Again she cut the air with brown fingers—those ten fingers so alien to his own twelve. "But, Kincar, this you must know for your own protection. Some forces which we bend to our use can in turn make a Tie serve as a transmitter, should one be within the range of their influence. And the greater the volume of that force, the greater its focus upon the Tie. To cross the web—" She shook her head. "You must bear wounds now as deep as if a sword had struck you down. Those must be treated before evil comes of them."

"As you treated Vorken?"

She shook her head. "That force would only add to your torment. The healing of Gorth, not the healing of Star lore, must be brought to your flesh. But that healing is also mine. Will you suffer my tending?"

He could accept her knowledge; she had given him good proof of what she knew. But Lord Dillan? She might be reading his thoughts, for now she smiled and said, "Did you not know that Lord Dillan is also a healer—of our clan? Though his healing reaches out into twisted minds instead of serving lamed bodies. He has taken the Inner Path, been a disciple of the Forest, with the Seven Feasts and the Six Fasts behind him these many years."

"I was a man of Gormal s'Varn." Lord Dillan spoke for the first time. "Though that is indeed now many years behind us—"

Gormal s'Varn! The leader on the Path who had lived many years before Wurd's grandmother! Again that oppressive feeling of the past that clung to these walls and was also a part of the Star people lapped about him. But in that moment he surrendered his will to the two, given confidence by their learning.

It was the Lord Dillan who aided him with the buckles of his scale shirt, helped him draw off the jerkin and soft shirt under it, while the Lady brought out from her bags small jars, two of which she opened, spreading a rich fragrance of dried summer flowers and grasses in the cold, too ancient air of the place.

The Tie swung free, but at the point where it had been cradled tight to his flesh, there was a deep scored mark of angry red, a brand of burning as deep as if white-hot metal had been held there to his torment.

The Lady Asgar produced a skeleton of leaf, which lay like a cobweb across her palm. On this with infinite care she spread creams from her pots, first dipping from one and then the other, blending the oils into the wisp of thing she held, working with the care of an artist applying the last touches of color to some masterpiece. Vorken climbed down the wall and crawled to her feet. The mord's head swayed to and fro on her long neck as she savored the scents that came from the pots. And now and again she gave a beseeching chirrup.

Lady Asgar laughed at the mord's excitement. "Not for you, winged one." But the mord continued to crouch before her with hungry eyes upraised.

The web-leaf with its healing salves was applied to Kincar's breast, adhering there as tightly as if it were another layer of skin. But neither Lord Dillan nor the Lady touched the Tie. But she studied it carefully and asked, "Are you a Looker, Kincar?"

He made haste to deny any such power. "I am nothing, Lady, save Kincar s'Rud, who was once Hold Daughter's Son to Styr and am now a landless man. This came to me from Wurd who was Styr. And it came secretly. I found it among my gear when I was quit of the Holding. I have no power of its bestowing, and I think that Wurd gave it me because by right I was Styr and only ill chance took my inheritance—"

But Lord Dillan shook his head slowly, and Kincar could read the dissent on the Lady's more expressive face.

"A Tie does not pass by chance, Kincar, you know that. If Styr was a guardian, then his was the need to select the one who came later, and the man he chose would not be fitted by birth or kinship, but by what lay within him. Also the Tie is always given secretly, lest evilly disposed ones intercept it and corrupt its use to their own purposes. You may not yet have the powers, but who can say that you will not—"

It was the Lady who interrupted. She stood rubbing her finger tips slowly together and so dispensing a flowery scent to the cold room. "The Tie is of the Gorth we know. I wonder whether it will function in this Gorth also—"

Kincar had picked up his swordbelt. The plaster had not only soothed the burn, he was feeling more vigorous than he had since he had passed through the web gates. "The Gorth we know—this Gorth—" Those two phrases rang oddly. As he hooked the belt about him, he puzzled over their meaning.

"This is Gorth?" he ventured.

And he was relieved when Lord Dillan nodded. But then the Star-born continued bewilderingly, "This is Gorth, but not the Gorth into which you were born, Kincar. Nor is it the Gorth we would have chosen to enter. It is a Gorth strange to us and one in which we are friendless and alone."

"You mean—by your magic, Lord, we have been transported over the bitter water seas to the far side of the world?"

The Lady Asgar sat down on one of the riding pads, and straightway the mord climbed into her lap. She sat there, allowing Vorken to nuzzle her scented hands, and now and then stroking the mord's grotesque head.

"We have been transported, aye, Kincar. But not across the seas. Explain to him, Dillan, for as he joined us so late, he will know nothing of what we have done, and we must all face what comes to us with understanding."

"It is this way." Unconsciously Lord Dillan began with the phrase of a song-smith, but his frowning seriousness said that this was no account of fancy. "When it came time that we must go out of Gorth—"

There Kincar found the courage to ask a question that had puzzled him since the news of the Star Lords' withdrawal had come to Styr. "But, why, Lord, was it necessary for you to go from Gorth? Aye, men of ill will have raised their voices. But we never heard such talk until the Lords first said they were going. You have brought the people of Gorth up from forest-dwelling barbarians. Why do you leave them without the shield of your protection when you have so much to give them? Your magic—could it not be shared?"

Again both of them shook their heads. "Instead of being a protection to Gorth, we may have been its bane, Kincar. When a manchild stumbles about the hall, still unsteady on his feet, do you set in his baby hands a war sword and leave him to his own devices? Or, worse still, do you give him such a weapon and strive to teach him how to use it before his thoughts are formed to know good from ill? In our own world we are an old, old people with a long and dusty trail of years between us and the beginnings of our history. We are the warriors of mature years, though still with many failings in judgment, and in Gorth we have put sharp swords into the hands of little children. We thought we were aiding Gorth to a better life wherein man could have many things he had not. So we taught and wrought with our hands and spread out the fruits of our learning for the plucking of those who wished. But, as children, they were attracted by the hard bright things, the metal which could be forged into blades, the mind-turning which could set one man against another. Had we not landed upon Gorth, had we not meddled, perhaps it would be a happier world, a greater world—"

"Or there could have remained just beasts," Kincar said.

"That is an argument-answer which has come readily these past years," the Lady Asgar answered. "But it is a too ready one. And we have it on our hearts that we may have guided children's feet into false paths. Aie, sadness, sadness—" The words of her own tongue came from her, slow and heavy as tears, and Lord Dillan took up the tale once more.

"So there grew three groups among us. There were those who said that, though it was very late, perhaps even now if we withdrew from Gorth the memory of us, the skills we had taught, would gradually become overlaid by time in the minds of men, and that Gorth could build a world of her own—twisted by some of the gifts we had so rashly given—but still returning to her own heritage, re-fashioned in a way native to her. Then there were those, luckily a very few, who were of a different mind. There will always be born, in every race and species of man, Kincar, certain individuals who have a thirst for power. To them an alien race, should it not be as advanced as they, exists only to serve them. Among us these few were not satisfied with things as they were, but for a different reason.

"They desired full rulership over Gorth, wanted the men of Gorth as servants and slaves. And secretly they began to circulate stories among those landless men, the outlaws, who were willing to form a fighting tail for any lord who would bring them much loot and rich living. Those of them that we could, we brought to justice secretly." His mouth was a thin line and the force of his will was almost a tangible thing as he spoke. "Thus they pushed us into hurried decisions. The major portion of our company voted to take to the ships, to go out once more into space seeking another world, one where there was no native race we might corrupt by contact. But—"

And here the Lady broke in as if this section of the tale was more closely hers.

"But there were others of us, Kincar, who, though we were not of mixed blood, had taken Gorth to our hearts. And when we came to think of raising from her, we could not bear it. So we sought another path of flight. And two men who had been working for many years—lifetimes—on a problem in research thought that they had the solution. It is a difficult one to explain, but it offered us a way to leave the Gorth of troubles for another Gorth in which we might live as we wished. And we labored to turn their theory into fact. This you must tell of, Dillan, since you were one of those men." She smiled at the Star Lord.

He squatted on his heels, and with his forefinger drew lines on the dusty floor as he talked.

"This has been a theory among our people for a very long time, but until this past year there has been no proof of it in fact. To explain it— Well, Kincar, think upon this. Are there not times in a man's life when he has a decision to make which is of major importance in shaping his future? You had the choice of joining with us, or of remaining at Styr to fight for your rights. Thus, at that moment before you rode from that Hold, you had two roads—two separate futures—and probably very different ones."

Kincar murmured assent.

"Then this is true, as we have proven. There now exist two different Gorths for you—one in which you stand here with us, one in which you held to Styr."

"But how could that be?" Kincar's protest was quick. "I stand here—I do not battle against Jord in Styr—or lie dead from his sword!"

"This 'you' stands here—the other 'you' is in Styr."

Kincar blinked, distrusting this new thought. Multiple "yous"—or "I's"—all acting separately, leading different lives? How could Kincar s'Rud be so split? Once more the Lady Asgar came to his rescue.

"The Kincar who chose to remain in Styr," she said softly, "would not be the Kincar who came through the gates in our company, for, by his very decision, he made himself a different person in a different world. He is not you, nor have you now any part in him—for that world is gone."

Lord Dillan studied the lines he had drawn. "But as it is with men, so it is also with nations and with worlds. There are times when they come to points of separation, and from those points their future takes two roads. And thus, Kincar, there are many Gorths, each formed by some decision of history, lying as these bands, one beside the other, but each following its own path—"

Kincar stared down at those faint marks. Many Gorths, existing one beside the other but each stemming from some crossroads in the past? His imagination caught fire, though still he could not quite believe.

"Then," he said slowly, trying to find the right words, "there is a Gorth into which the Star Lords never came, in which the wild men of the forest still live as do the animals? And perhaps a Gorth from which the Star Lords chose not to withdraw?"

Lord Dillan smiled; he had an eager look. "That is so. Also there are Gorths—or at least one Gorth, we hope—in which the native race never came into being at all. It is that Gorth we sought when we came through the gates."

"But which we were not given the time to find," Lady Asgar murmured. "This fortress proves that."

"Had we not been hunted there at the end, had we had but a day—or maybe only an hour more—we might have found it. Still, with the knowledge we have brought with us, we can open the gates once again—just give us a fraction of time."

But even Kincar was able to sense that behind those brave words Lord Dillan was not so sure. And he asked a question.

"Where are we now? Who built this fort? It is not of any fashion that I know. I thought it to be a hidden hold of the Star Lords."

"No, it is none of ours. But it will give us good shelter for a necessary space. Had we only been granted more time—!"

"At least"—Lady Asgar put Vorken gently on the floor and got to her feet—"your destruction of the gates brought one advantage. If it did not serve us very well, it served Gorth—since Herk came to his end in that blast."

Lord Dillan sat back. "Aye, Herk is safely dead. And those he gathered as a following will quickly melt away, their own jealousies and passions driving them apart. He was the last of the rebels, so Gorth is now free to seek its own destiny, while we may seek ours in another direction."

He stood up, and now he smiled at Kincar with a warmth and true welcome. "We are but a handful, yet this is our venture and we shall have the proving of it to the end. Let us seek out the materials we need and we shall have a new gate with time enough to choose which world it will open to us."

"Lord!" Vulth relooped the door curtain. "The gate box has been reassembled—"

"So!" Dillan was away without farewells, but the Lady Asgar put out a hand to stop Kincar when he would have gone after.

"It is not so easy." She was grave. Behind her serenity she was considering some problem. "The time before we can build another gate may be a long one."

"In Gorth—the old Gorth," Kincar commented, "the Lords had all the magic supplies of Terranna to aid them in such a building. They have been forced to destroy some of that. Can they find such magic here?"

She stood very still. "You bear with you that which must give you ever the clear sight. Aye, that is the stone within our fruit—perhaps for us a gate may not rise again. Dillan will try to rebuild, for that is his life. But his efforts may come to nothing. I would know more of this Gorth—for our own protection I would know. How far back in time was the turning which cleaved our Gorth from this one? Who built this hold and why did they forsake it? Are we in a world emptied by disaster—or one only too well peopled? That we must learn—and speedily."

He thought he could guess at what she hinted. "I have not the Sight," he reminded her.

"Nay. But you are closer to Gorth than those of full Star blood. And you wear that which may bind you closer still. If the Sight comes to you, do not deny it, speak aloud—to me or to Lord Dillan. It is in my mind that Herk forced a bad choice upon us and ill shall come here. See, I have not the Sight, either, yet foreboding grows upon one. And you?"

Kincar shook his head. He could not pretend to a sensitivity he did not have, and, privately, neither wanted nor thought he would ever develop. So far the only effect that the Tie had had on him was physical. He could play guardian, but he was willing to relinquish even that task when the time came that he could pass the talisman to one of the proper temperament to make full use of its powers. Wurd had never been a farseer nor seer, yet he had held the Tie in his time. Guardianship did not always accompany use.

He marveled at the tale he had heard of worlds beside worlds. But he had no premonitions and he wanted none. He would give thanks for his healing, for Vorken's, but he was not ready to join forces with the Lady Asgar in that way. And she must have guessed that, for she smiled wearily and did not try to detain him longer.

6
LEGEND COME ALIVE

The gale was brisk, but there was no more snow, and the wind had scoured away the early fall, save where the powdery stuff clung in pockets between trees and rocks. Vorken swung on a high branch, her large head seeming to shake disparagingly above the surrounding countryside as she kept watch. If any creature stirred there, she would mark its path.

Kincar leaned against the bole of the large tree, surveying the domain that their fortress guarded. It was indeed a holding of which any great lord could well be proud. Beyond the narrow neck of the entrance valley, which the hold spanned from wall to wall—an efficient cork to front any enemy—the land opened out into a vast valley ringed about with heights. There might be passes over those mountains, trails out of the valley that did not pass the hold, but so far the newcomers had not discovered them. And all indications pointed to the assumption that the valley of the hold was the only practical entry into the open ground beyond.

From this distance up one of the flanking mountainsides, one could trace the boundaries of old fields, see the straggle of tree stumps, fallen branches, and a few still sturdy trunks marking an orchard. Aye, it had been a rich land, well able to provide a rich living for the hold—once.

But now no harvests from those fields or orchards lay—except as powdery dust—in the storerooms of the fortress. Men must hunt, prowling the wooded slopes of the heights in search of game. So far the results had been disappointing. Oh, now and again one would chance upon a suard or some forest fowl. But they were thin, poor creatures.

This was the first day Kincar had deemed Vorken healed enough to take afield, and he was pinning his hopes upon her aid in a profitable hunt. But, though she had soared and searched in her usual manner, she had sighted nothing. And her rests, during which she clung to some roost well out of his reach, muttering peevishly to herself, grew longer and closer together. The mord might turn sullen with such constant disappointment and refuse to go on unless some success came soon.

With a forlorn hope of flushing a wild fowl, Kincar started ahead, thrusting through any promising stretch of shelter brush. A few scratches and a more intimate, and unwelcome, acquaintance with local vegetation was his only reward. However, he kept to the task.

He heard the stream before he found it—the tinkle of free running water. Then he saw, rising from the narrow cutting in the hillside, misty white tails that might be breath puffed from a giant's lungs.

To his surprise there was no edging of ice on the shore line, and it was from the surface of the water those smoky lines rose. Intent upon the phenomenon, he cautiously slid down the steep slope. There was a disagreeable smell, as well as steam, about him—a strong, acrid odor that made his eyes water as a warm puff drove into his face, setting him coughing. Very warily Kincar put out an investigating finger. The water was not clear, but a reddish-brown, and it was hot enough to sting. He raised the wet finger to his nose and sniffed a fetid smell he could not give name to.

Eager to see from where it sprang, he traced back along the cut until he found the place where the discolored water bubbled out of the mountain's crust. Yet that was not a spring, but a round hole, water worn and stained red-brown, an exit from some depths beyond. Kincar could perceive no immediate use for his find, but, in spite of the odor, the warmth of the water was welcome in the chill, and he lingered, holding hands ill-protected by their clumsy wrappings into the steam.

He was watching the brown swirls of the water, without close attention, loathe to climb back into the cold, when an object bobbed to the surface of the oily flood, struck against a stone, and would have been swept on had Kincar not grabbed for it. He snapped out a pair of pungent words as he scooped it out, for here the water was far hotter than it had been downstream. But he held the prize safely—the thing that had come out of the mountain.

It had begun as a chip of wood, buoyant and fresh enough to possess still the pale yellow color of newly cut zemdol. But it was no longer just a chip. Someone had used it for idle shaping such as he had often seen a man do in Styr, to try out a new knife, or for the pleasure of working with his hands through dull hours in the cold season. The chip now had the rough but unmistakable likeness of a suard. There were the curling horns worn in the warm seasons, lost in the cold, the powerful back legs, the slender, delicate forefeet—a suard carved by one who not only had an artist's skill in his fingers but a good knowledge of suards!

Yet it had bobbed out of the heart of the mountain! And it was not of the fugitives' making, that he was sure of. Where had the builders of the fortress retreated—underground? Kincar was on his feet, searching the wall of rock and earth from which the stream bubbled, striving to see on its surface some indication that there was an entrance here, that someone who was a hunter of suards and had tried out his knife upon a fresh chip of zemdol had a dwelling therein.

They had all puzzled over the history of the hold. There had been no signs that it had been stormed and sacked, no visible remains of those who had reared its massive walls for their protection, tilled the fields beyond. And the Star Lords said that such a place could not have been taken easily, not even by the weapons of which they alone possessed the secret. They were inclined to believe that some plague had struck down the valley dwellers without warning. Except of that there was no evidence either. All the rooms, from nooks in the watchtowers to eerie hollows hacked out of the rock under those same towers' foundations, probably intended for dark purposes the present explorers did not care to imagine, were bare of anything save dust. If the people of the valley had gone to plague tombs, they had carefully taken with them all their material possessions.

Kincar turned the chip over. This was evidence of other life in the mountain land, though he could not be sure how far from its source the water had carried it. But he was inclined to believe that the temperature of the flood, far higher here than it was downstream, suggested a beginning not too far inside the mountain. And it might be at that birth spring that the carver had lost his work.

The desire in Kincar to get to the root of the mystery was strong. But no one was going to move those tons of earth and rock. So at last, having put the chip in his belt pouch, he climbed out of the cut, which held the hot stream, into the frostiness of the upper air, where the wind bit doubly sharp because of his respite in the warmth.

He whistled to Vorken, and her answer came from farther down the slope. As he worked his way along, he saw her take to the air again in an ascending spiral, and he brought out the weapon Lord Dillan had entrusted to him, to be used only if they were sure of a kill. One held the tube balanced—so—and pressed the forefinger on a stud. Then ensued a death that was noiseless, an unseen ray that killed, leaving no mark at all upon the body of the slain. Kincar did not like it; to him it was evil when compared to the honest weight of sword or spear. But in a time when a kill meant food—or life—it was best.

Vorken no longer cried, her circles for altitude were bringing her up level with the peaks. Plainly she was in sight of her quarry. Kincar waited where he was to mark her swoop—there was too good a chance of warning the prey if he went on right now.

The mord brought her wings together with a snap he could hear plainly through the dry, cold air. Now she was at strike, her four feet with claws well extended beneath her as she came, air hissing from her open bill. There was a high scream as she vanished behind treetops, and Kincar ran.

He heard the beat of thumping feet through the brush and crouched. A suard, its eyes wide with terror, burst between two saplings, and Kincar used the strange weapon as he had been instructed. The animal crumpled in upon itself in midleap, its try at escape ending in a roll against a bush. Kincar ran up—there were no claw marks on it. This could not have been Vorken's prey. Had they had the excellent good luck of finding a small party of the animals? Sometimes the suard, usually solitary creatures, banded together, especially in a section where there was poor feeding. Rudimentary intelligence had taught the animals that concentrated strength brought down small trees whose bark proved cold season food.

Kincar paused only to bleed the suard he had killed, and then he sped on—to discover his guess had been right. A tree, its roots dug about, had been pushed to the ground and a goodly part of the tender upper bark shredded away. A second suard lay on the scene of the feast, Vorken's claws hooked in its deep fur. She welcomed Kincar with a scream, demanding to be fed, to have the part of the kill rightfully hers. He set about the gory task of butchering.

The suard Vorken had brought down was prepared for packing back to the hold and the mord was eating greedily before Kincar moved to the other kill. As a trained hunter he walked silently to the place where the second body lay—so silently that he surprised another at work. As he caught sight of the figure hunched above the suard on the bloodied snow, saw those hands busy at the same task he had just performed, he froze. This was no partner from the hold. Unless one of the children had slipped away to trail him—

Then the other turned to strip back a flap of furred hide. This was not a child in spite of the small body, the hands half the size of his own, which worked with the quick sureness of long experience. The face beneath the overhang of the fur hood was that of a man in his late youth, a broad face bearing the lines of bleak living. But when the stranger got to his feet to walk about the suard, his head could not have reached a finger width above Kincar's shoulder. As he himself was to the Star Lords, so was this one to him. The compact body, muffled as it was with furs and thick clothing, showed no signs of malformation—the manikin was well proportioned and carried himself as might a trained warrior.

But had the other been as tall as Lord Dillan himself, Kincar would have jumped him now. To see this dwarfish creature calmly about the business of butchering the suard he had killed, preempting meat so badly needed in the hold, was like waving a bit of fresh liver before an uncaged mord and daring it to snap. Kincar sheathed his Star weapon and crossed the open space in one flying leap, his hands settling as he had aimed on the thief's shoulders. But what happened an instant after that was not part of his plan at all.

The stranger might have the size of a lad not yet half grown, but in that slight body was a strength that rivaled Kincar's. Startled as he must have been, he reacted automatically as one trained in unarmed combat. His shoulders shrugged, he wriggled, and, to Kincar's overwhelming astonishment and dazed unbelief, he found himself on the ground while the other stood over him, a knife blade stained with suard blood held at striking distance from his throat.

"Lie still, lowland rat"—the words were oddly accented but Kincar could understand them—"or you will speedily have two mouths—the second of my making!"

"Big talk, stealer of another man's meat!" Kincar glared back with what dignity he could muster from his position on the ground. "Have you never learned that only a hunter skins his own kill?"

"Your kill?" The manikin laughed. "Show me the wound with which you dealt that death, my brave-talking hunter, and I shall deliver you the meat."

"There are other ways of killing than by sword or spear."

The manikin's lips flattened against his teeth, drawing a little apart in a snarl.

"Aye, lowlander." He spoke more softly still, almost caressingly. "There are such ways of killing. But your sort have them not—only the 'gods' kill so." But he spat after mouthing the word "gods" as a man might spit upon the name of a blood enemy. "And no 'god' would give a slave his power stick! You are naught but an outlaw who should be turned in for the price set upon him—to be used for the amusement of the 'gods' after their accursed way."

There had been outlaws in the Gorth of Kincar's birth. He could readily accept the idea that such men lived here also. But these 'gods' were something else altogether. However, his immediate problem was to get safely out of the range of that knife, and his swift overthrow had given him a healthy respect for the one who now held it.

"I am no outlaw. I am a hunter. My mord flushed the suard in their feeding ground. One she slew, the other I killed as it fled. If you would have proof of that, look behind those bushes yonder where you will find the other made ready for packing. Or, better yet—" He whistled and the blade descended until he felt the chill touch of the metal on his throat.

"You were warned—" The manikin was beginning when Vorken swooped upon him. Only the overhang of his hood saved his face. As it was, the mord hooked claws in his jerkin and beat him about the head with her wings. Kincar rolled away and got to his feet before he called the mord off her victim. And ready in his hand now was the death rod of the Star Lords.

Vorken flapped up to a tree limb, her red eyes holding upon the manikin. But he lay on the ground, his attention all for the weapon Kincar had aimed at him. And his expression was the bleak one of a man facing inevitable death.

"Who are you, wearing the body of a slave, carrying the death of a 'god'?" he demanded. "Why do you trouble the hills?"

Now that Kincar had his captive, he did not quite know what to do with him. To take a prisoner down to the hold, there to spy out their few numbers, their many lacks, would be folly indeed. On the other hand, to turn the man loose on the mountain, perhaps to arouse his own people, that was worse than folly. But to kill as a matter of expediency alone, that was an act Kincar could not commit.

Vorken stirred, uttering her warning, and a moment later they heard a musical whistle, unlike the shrilling of the mord. Kincar answered eagerly with the rest of the bar. The figure who tramped through drifted snow to join them did not come with Kincar's light hunter's tread. And at the sight of the silver clothing the manikin froze as a suard youngling might freeze under the shadow of a mord's wings—seeing raw death above it with no possible escape.

Lord Bardon, leading one of the pack larngs, came to a halt, the animal's head bobbing over his shoulder, the luck of the rest of the hunting party to be read in the small bundle lashed to its back. He surveyed the scene with open surprise.

"What have we here, Kincar?"

"A thief of another hunter's kill!" snapped the other. "Also a teller of tales. What else he may be, I have no knowledge."

The manikin's face was twisted with hate, whitened with something deeper than fear, a dull despair. But he made no answer, though his glance swung from the Star Lord to Kincar as if the last sight he expected to wonder over was such a friendly relationship between the two.

"Who are you?" Lord Bardon came directly to the point, and then added—as if to himself—"and what are you, my small friend?"

But the manikin remained stubbornly silent. There was about him now the air of one about to be put to some torture, determined to endure to the end that he might not betray a weighty secret.

"He has a tongue." Kincar's exasperation broke out. "He was free enough with it before your coming, Lord—with all his talk of 'gods' and 'slaves'! But what he is or where he springs from I do not know. Vorken brought down a suard—a second, fleeing, I killed with the silent death. While I butchered Vorken's kill, he was busy here. And so I discovered him thieving—"

For the first time since Lord Bardon had appeared on the scene the manikin spoke.

"Aye, and but for that mord of yours, you'd have been meat, too, lowland dirt!"

"Perhaps so." Kincar gave credit where it was due. "He is a warrior, Lord, overturning me with some trick of fighting when I closed with him. But Vorken came, and I was free to use this—a threat he appeared to understand"—he held out the death tube—"though how that can be is a mystery—"

Lord Bardon's eyes were like light metal, cold, with a deadly luster in his dark face. "So he recognized a ray blaster. Now that is most interesting. I think it is important that he comes with us for a quiet talk together—"

The manikin had drawn his feet under him. Now he exploded for the nearest cover with the speed of a spear throw. Only this time Kincar was prepared. He crashed against the captive, bringing them both to the frozen ground with the force of that tackle. And when he levered himself up, the other lay so quiet that Kincar was for an instant or so very much afraid.

But the prisoner was only stunned, the rough handling leaving him tractable enough to be stowed away on the larng along with the meat. So encumbered they started back to the hold, making only one short side trip to look at the steam stream Kincar had chanced upon. Lord Bardon examined the carved chip and then looked to the trussed captive on the larng.

"Perhaps our friend here can tell us more concerning this. He is well clad, at home in these ranges, yet we have seen no other steading or hold. If they dwell within instead of without the mountains, that would explain it. But he is a breed new to me. How say you, Kincar; is he a dwarf of Gorthian breed?"

"I do not know, Lord. He seems not to be in any way misshapen, but rather as if it is natural with his kind to be of that size—just as

I do not equal you in inches. There is in my mind one thing—the old song of Garthal s'Dar—" He began the chant of a native song-smith:

"In the morning light went Garthal
Sword in hand, his cloak about his arm.
A white shield for his arm,
And he raised his blade against the inner men,
Forcing their chieftain into battle,
Forcing them to give him freedom of their ways,
That he might come upon his blood enemy
And cross metal with him
Who had raised the scornful laughter
In the Hold of Grum at the Midyear feasting—

"The inner men," he repeated. "They were long and long ago—if they ever lived at all—for many of the old songs, Lord, are born from the minds of men and song-smiths and not out of deeds which really happened. But these 'inner men' were of the mountains, and they were small of body but large of deed, a warrior race of power. Or so Garthal found them—"

"And there are other tales of 'inner men'?"

Kincar grinned. "Such tales as one tells a youngling who would have his own way against the wisdom of his elders, warnings that should he not mend his ways the 'little men' will come in the dark hours and spirit him away to their hidden holds beneath the earth—from which no man ventures forth again."

"Aye," mused the Star Lord, "but in such tales there lingers a spark of truth at times. Perhaps the 'inner men,' who have vanished from the Gorth we knew, are not gone from here, and we have laid hands upon one. At any rate he will supply us with much which we should know for our own safety."

"I do not think this one will talk merely because we bid him."

"He shall tell us all he knows, which is of interest to us."

Kincar measured the greater bulk of the Star Lord. In his brown hands the manikin would be a girl child's puppet to be sure. Yet the half-blood shrank from the grim picture his imagination produced. To slay a man cleanly in battle was one thing. To mishandle a helpless captive was something far different—a thing he did not want to consider. But again it was as if the Star Lord had the trick of reading minds, for the other looked down at him with a hint of smile in his eyes, though there was no softening of the straight line of lip and jaw.

"We do not tear secrets from men with fire and knife, youngling—or follow outlaw tricks for the loosening of tongues!"

Kincar flushed. "Forgive, Lord, the ways of your people are as yet strange to me. I was reared in a hold of the mountains, not in Terranna. What do I know of Star Lord life?"

"True enough. But not 'your people,' Kincar, but 'my people.' We are one in this as in all else, boy. You have an inheritance from us as well as from Styr—always remember that. Now let us bring this song-smith's hero into Dillan and the Lady Asgar and see what they can make of him to our future profit."

7
FALSE GODS

Star Lord ways for extracting information from unwilling captives were indeed strange to Kincar, for questions were not asked at all. Instead their prisoner was given a seat before one of the heat boxes in the great hall of the old hold and left to meditate, though there were always those who watched him without appearing to do so.

After the first few minutes of lowering suspicion, the captive watched them openly in return, and his complete mystification was plain to read on his face. Something in their ways or bearing was too odd for him to comprehend. He stared wide-eyed at Lord Jon who was patiently teaching his half-Gorthian son the finer points of sword play before a fond and proud audience of the boy's mother and sister. They were both busy with their needles at the mending of undertunics—while the younger brother watched with the envious attention of one ready and willing to change places with the other boy at any moment.

And when the Lady Asgar came up behind Kincar and put a hand on his shoulder to gain his notice, the prisoner, seeing that friendly gesture, shrank in upon himself as if fearing some terrible outburst in return.

"This is a new thing you have found for us, younger brother," she said. "Dillan is coming, though he is loathe to leave his calculations. So this is one you think might be straight out of the saga of Garthal the Two-sworded?"

"It is in my mind, Lady, that he is close to the song-smiths' recording of the 'inner men.'"

Vorken fluttered down from her chosen perch high in the roof to claw beseechingly at the Lady's cloak. Asgar laughed at the mord. "Now then, Vorken, would you have me in tatters because of your impatience? Being of the female kind yourself, you should know better than to tear clothing that can not easily be replaced. Ha—up with you then, if that is how it must be." She stooped, and the mord sprang to her arm, climbing to her shoulder where she rubbed her head caressingly against the Lady's and chirruped in her ear.

"You have done very well this day, Vorken," Asgar continued as if the mord could understand every word she said. "More than your part. Now be patient, winged one, we have other business to hand."

But when she came to stand directly before the prisoner, the manikin crouched low, drawing in upon himself as if he would turn his body into a ball under the blows of a punishing lash. Nor would he lift his head to see eye to eye with the lady. His whole position suggested one awaiting death—and no easy passing at that. And it was in such contrast to the spirit with which he had faced Kincar that the latter was puzzled.

"So—what have we here?" Lord Dillan came to them, giving Kincar an approving pat upon the back as he passed. "This is your meat thief, boy?"

"He is more," remarked the Lady. "But there is a second mystery here. Why are we so fearsome to him?"

"Aye." Lord Dillan reached down and, with a hand gentle enough but with a force that could not be denied, brought up the manikin's head so that he could see his face. The captive's eyes were squeezed shut. "Look upon us, stranger. We are not your enemies—unless you wish it so—"

That must have pricked like a sword point upon a raw wound. The eyes snapped open, but none of them were prepared for the black hate mirrored in their depths.

"Aye," the manikin snarled, "the 'gods' are never enemies—they wish the good of us all. Hear me, 'gods,' I give you homage!" He slipped from the pad to the floor, kneeling before the Star Lord. "You may slay me after your own evil fashion, 'gods,' but Ospik will not beg for his life!"

It was the Lady who spoke first. "There are no gods here, Ospik, nor do we have a liking for such titles even in jest. Why do you name us so?"

His broad mouth shaped a sneer he could not prevent, and his inner hatred fought against remnants of self-preservation. "How else should I name you—save as you have taught Gorth? You are the 'gods' from the far stars. Though what you do here in this ruin is beyond the imagining of a simple hunter. What you do here and with them—!" He pointed to Kincar, to the family of Lord Jon busy with their own concerns just out of earshot.

"Why should not kinsmen be together?" questioned the Lady softly.

"Kinsmen!" Ospik repeated the word incredulously. "But the young warrior is a lowlander, a Gorthian, and you are one of the 'gods'! There is no kinship between slave and master. To even think of such a blood-tie is red death for the slave!"

Lord Dillan's eyes had grown bleak and cold as he listened, and the hand that had continued to rest on Kincar's shoulder in the greeting of a comrade tightened its hold, crushing the scales of the younger man's shirt down on the flesh beneath as he stood steady under it. Only the Lady Asgar continued her inquiry with untroubled serenity.

"You are very wrong, Ospik. All those within this hold share a common heritage, at least in part. Those who seem to you Gorthian have also Star blood. Jon, whom you have been watching, is now schooling his eldest son, and that is his wife, his daughter, and his younger son—a large family for us. This is Kincar s'Rud." She indicated Kincar. "And Rud, his father, was brother to Dillan who stands before you. No slaves, no masters—kinsmen."

"Lord Rud's son!" Ospik's teeth showed in an animal snarl, and he gazed at Kincar as if he would spring full at the young man's throat in a mord's murderous attack. "Lord Rud with a slave son! Ho, that is fine hearing! So he has defiled himself has he—the great Rud himself has broken the first law of his kind? Good hearing—good hearing! Though no one shall ever hear it from my telling—" His head moved from side to side like the head of a cornered animal.

Kincar was bewildered, but he clung to the parts he understood. So Lord Dillan was close kin—somehow that was a thought to give warmth, a warmth as steady as if it arose from a heat box. But the manikin's talk of a Lord Rud who had broken the first law? How did Ospik know his father? Asgar spoke first.

"Rud, brother of Dillan, is dead, Ospik. He was killed almost twenty warm seasons ago when he went into a bitter water storm to save seamen trapped on a reef by the floundering of their ship—"

Ospik stared at her, and then he spat. "I am no addle-wit—not yet." Again his shoulders hunched under that unseen whip. "Lord Rud rules at U-Sippar, as he has since the memory of man. No 'god' would raise his shortest finger for the saving of a Gorthian out of the bitter water!"

The Lady Asgar caught her breath. "What have we found?" she demanded, clasping her hands together until the knuckles were hard knobs. "Into what kind of a Gorth have we come, Dillan?"

"To the one of our worst fears, it would seem," he made answer grimly. "The one which we perceived only palely and have always dreaded."

She gasped. "No, chance would not be so cruel!"

"Chance? Do you think that there is chance in this, Asgar? I would say it is part of a large design beyond our knowledge. We have striven to undo one wrong our kind wrought on Gorth. Here is another and far greater one. Shall we always be faced by the results of our troubling?"

Ospik had been looking from one to the other, glancing back at Lord Jon, at the others busy about their chosen tasks in the hall. Now he got to his feet, his hand outstretched to the two before him, his fingers curled about one another in a curious pattern.

"You are no 'gods'!" he accused shrilly. "You are demons who have taken on their seeming. By Lor, Loi, Lys, I bid you be as you really are."

Kincar answered that invocation with one of his own. "By Lor, Loi, and Lys, I tell you, Ospik, that these are Star Lords, though perhaps not of the kind you know. Could a demon remain while I say this?" And he repeated the sacred Three Lines in the older tongue he had been taught, feeling as he said them an answering warmth from the talisman he wore.

Ospik was shaken. "I do not understand," he said weakly. And Kincar would have echoed that, but he had sense enough to turn to Lord Dillan for an explanation.

"Ospik, we are truly of the Star blood." The Star Lord's words had the impact of truth. "But we are not those whom you know. We have come from another Gorth. And in spirit we are opposed to the Lords of this world—or at least I would think it so from what you have told us."

"The 'gods' have done much here," Ospik returned, "but never for the good of Gorth. I do not know what mazed story you would tell me now—"

Later Kincar sat in the ring of warriors, half-blood and Star Lord gathered together, listening to Lord Dillan.

"That is the way of it! In this Gorth our kind brought a worse fate than the one we were fleeing from. Here our breed landed in arrogance and seized the country, making the natives slaves. All our wisdom was used to hold Gorth with a mailed fist. Only a few bands who have escaped to the wastes—or are native to those sections as are Ospik's people—are free. This is the evil Gorth that ours might have been."

"We are a handful against many." Lord Jon spoke musingly. "Yet this is in a manner our ill—"

"Aye, a handful. And this I say—which is only good war wisdom—we must make no moves until we know more of what lies here." That was Lord Bardon. He alone among the Star Lords in the hold had been born in the Star ships before the landing on Gorth. He had chosen to remain with this party because he had Gorthian children and grandchildren—a daughter sat in the circle of women to the left, two boys of her bearing were among the children.

Kincar was only half listening, being more set upon estimating the fighting strength of their party. Fifty in all had essayed the adventure of the gates. Twenty of these were women and young maids, ten were children. Of the remaining males eight were Star Lords, ranging from Lord Bardon to the young Lord Jon— Sim, Dillan, Rodric, Tomm, Joe, and Frans. It was difficult to know their ages, but none of them had the appearance of a Gorthian past his fortieth summer. The mysterious change that had come upon their kind during the voyage across the void had set its seal heavy upon them.

The twelve swordsmen of half-blood were all young, but all tested fighting men, and Lord Jon's eldest son could soon be numbered among them. A good tough force—with such behind him no man would hesitate to foray. And the Star Lords had their own methods of fighting. Aye, had he been faced with an attack on a hold, Kincar would not have hesitated to raise his banner for a spear-festing.

But they were not going up against any hold or Gorthian force, they were to front Star Lords, twisted, vengeful Star Lords who used all of their secret learning to hold the rule of this world. And that was a very different thing. None of them here were so unblooded in war as to vote for a spear-festing before the full strength of the enemy could be ascertained.

However, they had won Ospik's support. The mountaineer, at first without comprehension, was at last forced to accept the evidence given him. Now he was eager for an alliance between his people and the hold party. It had been hard for him to think of Star Lords as friends, but once he could believe that comradeship possible, his agreement was wholehearted. And it was decided that he must return to his own hidden stronghold and promote a meeting between his Cavern Master and the others.

Before nightfall Ospik was on his way. But Kincar had a private puzzle of his own keeping him silent. He was in Cim's stall, spreading dried grass he had brought to bed down the larng, when a brighter gleam of light by the door told him he was no longer alone. Lord Dillan noted with a nod of approval his efforts to make his mount comfortable.

"That is a good larng." There was a hesitancy in that opening. The Star Lord had come to speak on a subject far removed from the care of mounts, and Kincar sensed it.

"He is Cim." Kincar ran his hands caressingly about the pointed ears of the kneeling beast, stroking the callous spots where the reins rested. "I found him in the trapping pens, and he has been mine only since then."

Inside he was as shyly hesitant as Lord Dillan. Since that hour in Wurd's death chamber, when the tightly ordered existence that had always been his world had broken apart, when all security had been reft from him, he had tried to push aside the truth. It had been easier to accept exile from Styr, the prospect of outlawry, than to believe that he was not wholly Gorthian.

Now he did not want to face the fact that his father had been a man such as Dillan—perhaps resembling Dillan closely, since they had been brothers. Why—because he was afraid of the Star Lords? Or was it that he resented the mixture of blood that had taken from him the sure, ordered life of Styr? He never felt at ease in their company as did Jonathal, Vulth, and the others who had associated with the aliens from birth.

Perhaps his reluctance to acknowledge his mixed bloods was fostered by the fact that of all of them here in the hold, he alone had no outward marks of non-Gorthian heritage. Some of the others were taller than natives, others had eyes of a strange color, hair, features— And at a moment such as this, when he was forced to realize his bond with off-world kin, his first and strongest reaction was a wariness, the wariness of a man compelled to imposture and foreseeing exposure.

Dillan set the lamp he carried on the floor and leaned back against the stall partition, his fingers hooked in his belt.

"Rud's son," he said quietly, giving the proper name the same unfamiliar turn of pronunciation he had given it at their first meeting.

"You do not see him in me!" blurted out Kincar.

"Not outwardly." When Dillan agreed so readily, Kincar had a pinch of nameless discontent. "But in other ways—"

Kincar voiced the question that had been in his mind all afternoon.

"Ospik says that a Lord Rud rules this district for the Star Lords. Yet how can that be? For if the Lord Rud who was my father is dead these many years— Another Lord—maybe a son of full Star blood?"

Dillan shook his head. "I think not. This is a tangle we had not thought to find. Perhaps in this Gorth there are counterparts of us—the selves we would have been had chance, or fate, or the grand design taken another road. But that would be a monstrous thing, and we would indeed be caught up in a nightmare!"

"How could a man face himself in battle?" Kincar had followed that thought to its logical end.

"That is what we must discover, youngling. Let it suffice that the Rud who rules here is not he who fathered you—nor could he be—"

"Aye, Ospik made it plain that in this Gorth Star Lord and native do not mate—"

"It is not that only." Dillan brushed the comment aside impatiently. "Nay, it is that the Rud who, by his way of life, his temperament, is content with things as they are in this world is not the Rud of our world. They would have no common meeting point at all. Rud was born in our Gorth three years after the landing of our ships, thus being my elder by a full twenty of warm seasons, the son of another mother. He had four ladies to wife—two of Star blood, two of Gorthian inheritance. Anora of Styr was his last, and she outlived him by less than a full year. He left behind him two sons and a daughter of full blood—they departed on one of the ships—and one of half-blood, you. But of you we were ignorant until Wurd sent us a message three months ago when he foresaw what might be your fate under Jord's enmity. He had kept you apart from us, wishing to make you wholly Gorthian that you might serve Styr the better, so that you have none of the common memories that might help you to adjust now. But Rud, your father, was rightly one to stand sword-proud, and glad we are that his blood lives on among us!"

"But you are of Rud's blood."

"Aye. But I am not as Rud. He was a warrior born, a man of action. And in a world of action that means much." Dillan smiled a little wearily. "I am a man of my hands, one who would build things I see in dreams. The sword I can use, but also do I most readily lay it aside. Rud was a mord on the hunt, ever questing for adventure. He was a sword-smith rather than a song-smith. But it is hard to describe Rud to one who knew him not, even when that one is his son." He sighed and picked up the lamp once more. "Let it rest that the Rud we knew was worth our allegiance—aye, our love. And keep that ever in your mind should fate force us to foray against this other Rud who holds false wardship in this Gorth—"

He lingered at the door of the stall. "You have made Cim comfortable. Come back to the hall now—we hold warrior-council in which each swordsman has a voice."

They ate in company, sharing the fruits of hunting and portions of their dwindling supplies with scrupulous accuracy. A hungry mord, Kincar recalled, was always the best hunter. No one here went so filled that he could not move mord-swift in attack. He chewed a mouthful of suard meat deliberately, savoring its fat-richness to the fullest extent.

The war council had come to a decision. They would hunt for the present, work to stock the hold with what supplies they could garner, perhaps trade with the inner men for extra foodstuffs. For the moment they would not venture forth from the valley guarded by the hold. They were far, Ospik had assured them, from the lowlands where the Star Lords of this Gorth kept control, where the might of strange weapons held slaves in hard bondage. But the thought of those who were their counterparts using such perverted power had driven the Lords into a brooding silence. And Kincar suspected that even were Lord Dillan to produce another gate, a new road to still another Gorth, he might not discover any among his peers willing to use it yet. They felt a responsibility for this world, a guilt for what the false lords did here.

Now they mounted a sentry in each of the watch-towers on the hold, marked out patrol paths for the morrow, divided duties between hunting and scouting among all the company, so that a man would alternate in each type of service.

When the meal was done, the Lady Asgar came to Kincar, in her hands one of the small singing-string boards of a traveling song-smith.

"Kincar, it is said that you have in song memory the saga of Garthal and his meeting with the 'inner men.' Since we have this day proven a part of that story to be no tale but the truth, do you now let us hear all of Garthal's spear-festing and the Foray of Loc-Hold."

He took the frame of the singing-strings on his knee shyly. Though he had played song-smith in Styr Hold, he had never thought to do so in such company as this. But "Garthal's Foray" was a song not too well known nowadays, though it had been a favorite of Wurd's and Kincar had had good lessoning in its long swinging stanzas. Now he struck the two notes and began the rising chant—the tale of how Garthal went forth as a holdless man and came to Loc-Hold, and how he was later cheated of his fight-due so that he fled to the mountains with anger in his heart. Those about him, Lorpor, Vulth, Lord Jon, Jonathal, drew their swords and kept time with the sweet ting of blade against blade, while eyes shone in the lamplight and there were the voices of women bringing in the hum of undersong. Not since he had ridden out of Styr had Kincar known that sense of belonging.

8
FIRST FORAY

They had their meeting with the chief of the "inner men." He came warily and armed, with a covering guard who prudently prepared an ambush. All of these precautions proved to the men from the hold the deep-seated distrust of, and hatred held for, the alien rulers of the plains by the native Gorthians. But at the conclusion of their council, the chief had been forced to admit that there were now two kinds of Star Lords in his land, and the later-come variety were not the wrathful "gods" he had always known. He did not go so far as to reveal any of the details of his own keep, though he did agree to a measure of trade—to supply dried fruits and coarse meal for one of the inexhaustible star torches.

The "inner men" were by long training fine workers in metal. They produced, for the admiration of the hold, coats of ring mail, fine, deceivingly light in weight—but, unfortunately, fashioned only to fit the small bodies of their own race, as were their beautifully balanced swords, which were too light and too short of hand grip for the newcomers. Lord Bardon, surveying these regretfully, went on to other plans. And the next day when he was in the hunting field with Kincar, he suggested that Vorken be set about the business of marking down game, while the younger man aid him in a different search.

"A sapling?" puzzled Kincar. "For a new kind of spear shaft, maybe? But such as we seek now would be too slender, would break at the first thrust which had any power behind it."

"Not a spear. It is intended for another weapon, one from the older days on the Star world from which our fathers came. It was a favorite there of primitive men, but it was so well used that the old tales say it gave him an advantage over warriors clad in mail."

At the end of the day they returned to the hold with a good selection of different varieties of tough yet resilient wood lengths lashed upon the larng-burden of meat for the pot. Vorken, not being under obligation to consider the worth of saplings, had proved a more alert hunter than the men.

Since Lord Bardon had only hazy memory to guide him in the manufacture of the new weapon, they spoiled many lengths of wood, choosing others badly. However, at the end of three days they produced crude bows. Arrows followed. They learned, mainly by mistakes, the art of proper heading and feathering. Now three quarters of the population of the hold had taken a hand in the work, and the hall after the fall of night was a fletcher's workroom.

They discovered that the pull of the bows depended upon the strength of an individual—that the mighty six-foot shaft that served Lord Bardon could not even be strung by any half-blood, while Kincar—with a smaller and lighter weapon—could hit the mark in the trials just as accurately and speedily, though perhaps with not the great penetrating force of the Star Lord.

Oddly enough, only Lord Bardon, Lord Jon, and Lord Frans among the full-bloods showed any proficiency with the bow, and there was much good-humored banter aimed at their fellows who were unable to turn marksmen by will alone.

"Too long at machines," Lord Bardon observed as Dillan's arrow went woefully wide of the mark for the third time in succession. "This is no matter of pushing a button; it needs true skill."

Lord Dillan laughed and tossed the bow to its owner. "A skill not in *my* hand or eye it is certain. But we cannot say that of our brothers."

For, as the full-bloods found it something to be laboriously learned, the half-bloods took to archery with a readiness that suggested that the Three must have given them the gift at birth, to lay dormant waiting this moment. From practice at a stationary mark set up in the courtyard, they advanced to hunting, and the rewards came in an upshoot of meat supplies and the growing pile of suard skins to be plaited into cloaks and robes against the chill of the storm winds.

The cold weather had closed in upon them with true harshness. There was one period when they were pent for five days within the hold, the snow-filled blasts sealing the outer world from them. Any plans for scouting into the lowlands must wait upon more clement days.

Lord Dillan and his assistants had to set aside their work on the machine intended to open a gate upon another Gorth. Too many essential elements had been destroyed with the other gates. And, in spite of their questioning of the inner men's smiths and metal miners, some of those could not be rediscovered even in the crude state of unworked ore. They did not speak of this within the hold, though it was generally known. Instead, men began to plan ahead for a lengthy stay there. Talk arose of working the fields in the deserted valley. Surely land that once had supported a large community would provide a living for their own limited numbers.

At last came a lull between storms, when the sun was dazzlingly reflected from the crusted snow and the trees cast wide blue shadows across the ground. It was a day when the crisp air bit at the lungs as a man inhaled, but at the same time set him longing to be out in the open.

Kincar stood on the crown of one watchtower, with Vorken marching back and forth along the waist-high parapet before him, stretching wide her wings and giving harsh voice to her own private challenge. This was the season when the mords of the hatcheries took mates, and Vorken was lonely as she had never been. It would seem that in this Gorth her kind were either uncommon or had never evolved from the large and vicious menaces of the mountain heights.

She was so restless that Kincar was worried. Should she go out in search of her kind, she might well never return. Yet he knew that if he tried to restrain her by caging, her restlessness would develop into a wild mania centered only upon escape, and she might beat herself to death against the walls of her prison. In order to keep her, he must leave her free, holding to the hope that she would come back at some time of her own choosing.

With another eerie cry, she gave a leap that carried her up and out, climbing in a tight spiral until he could not see her at all. He beat his cold-numbed hands against his thighs, striding back and forth to keep his feet free from the frost-deadening chill as he waited. But there was no Vorken planing down wind, no shrilling whistle. It was as if the mord had gone out through some hole in the sky.

"She is gone?" Snow crunched under Lord Bardon's boots. "I thought the wild fever must be on her when I saw her this morning."

"I couldn't cage her," Kincar argued in his own defense. "Without a hatchery she would have gone mad in a cage."

"True enough. And, though we have not sighted any of her breed here, boy, that is no reason to think that they do not exist. Perhaps in the lowlands she will discover a hold with a hatchery."

That was poor comfort, but it was the only hope he had to hold to. And he knew that in setting her free he had saved her life.

"To lay bonds upon any unwilling living thing, whether it be man or beast, is evil." Lord Bardon rested his hands upon the parapet and stood looking down the cleft of the entrance valley toward the plains. If all they had heard was true, there lay a bondage far worse than the alliance between trained mord and hunter. "Service must be rooted in the need to form part of a pattern. In that way it is security of mind—if not always of body. Vorken serves you in some ways, and you in exchange give her the returns she wants. At present she must be left free for what is important to her, as is right. And now, Kincar," he glanced down with a smile, "I have a service to offer you. After many delays our friends of the inner mountain have decided that they may offer us a measure of trust. They have sent a message that they will show us a sheltered and secret way to look upon one of the main highways of the lower country and assess the traffic that passes there."

"In this weather?"

"It would seem that the cold season does not hit so heavily in the plains as it does here. Also the Lords of the lowlands have their reasons for keeping the lines of communication open. Where men live in distrust and fear, speedy travel is oftentimes a necessity. But, at any rate, we shall be able to see more than we do from here. And if you wish, you may ride with us."

The party from the hold was a small one. Ospik and one of his fellows, Tosi, served as guides. Behind them rode Lord Bardon, his huge bow slung over his shoulder to point a warning finger into the sky, Lord Frans, Jonathal, and Kincar. They were mounted on larngs who protested with muttering grumbles against being urged into the cold, and they led one of the burden breed to carry provisions and additional robes, lest they be storm-stayed out of shelter.

Ospik's trail led to the side of the mountain near which Kincar had charted the warm rill, and then it zig-zagged crookedly back and forth in a dried watercourse where many rock piles made the footing so chancy they dismounted and led their beasts. The path, if so it could be termed, ended in a screen of brush before the mountain wall. But that screen was not what it appeared, for they pushed through it into a dark opening that might have been a deep running crevice.

But, as they advanced and Lord Bardon triggered a torch to light them, Kincar marked the signs of the tools that had turned a fault of nature into a passage for men. However much it had been wrought to provide a way through the mountain caverns, it was not one much used by the community of indwellers. As they threaded their way along it into a cave that fanned far out into deep darkness, their light bringing to life sparkles of answering fire from crystals on the walls, and then to another narrow passage and more caverns opening into one another, they met no one else, heard no sounds save the murmur of water—and those arising hollowly from their own footfalls. The whole mountain range, Kincar marveled, must be honeycombed with cave, crevice, and cavern, and the indwellers had made use of them to their own advantage.

Once they edged perilously over a narrow span set in place to cross a steaming hot flood, their heavier bodies and the bulk of the larngs going one at a time over a bridge made for manikins, choking and coughing as they passed from the fumes of the boiling water. And once or twice they caught a whiff of carrion reek, a distant rustle, as if some nightmare creature had crawled aside from their way, unable to dispute the light of the torch.

Time had no meaning here. They might have spent only hours, or a full day in the depths. Twice they halted to rest and eat, both times in grottoes of prismatic crystal, cupped in a circle of fire-hearted jewels, with the lace-tracery, formed by countless centuries of drip, making palace screens and drapery. It was a world Kincar had never conceived of being, and he explored with Jonathal, each pointing out to the other some particular wonder before or above. Fountains frozen before their spray streamed away, a tree, a fruit-heavy vine, they were all to be found. And in company with those were creatures out of a song-smith's dreams—fair, grotesque, horrible.

Ospik laughed at their surprise, but kindly. "These are to be found many places elsewhere." A pride of possession colored his words. "And many far better. There is our Hall of Meeting—"

"Jewels in the wall!" Jonathal touched a flashing point on a copy of a tree limb.

Their guide shook his head. "Jewels, aye, are to be found. But none of these are real gems, only bits of rock crystal. Take them away from the cavern and you will have nothing remarkable."

"But—" Kincar burst out—"to think of this buried under the earth!"

Lord Frans smiled. He had not moved about, but sat cross-legged, his back against the haunches of his resting larng. However, he had been studying what lay about them with some measure of the same eagerness.

"It is the earth which formed this, Kincar. And, as Ospik has said, tear this out of its present setting and the magic would be gone from it. It is indeed a wonder worth traveling far to see." He drew a small tablet from his belt pouch and with a stelo made a swift sketch of the frozen vine.

When they went on from that last cavern of crystal, the way was again dark, the walls crannied. Kincar forgot his amazement in a growing tension. He glanced now and again over his shoulder. Though he never saw anything but the familiar outline of Cim and, behind the mount, a glimpse of Lord Frans, yet he was plagued with a sense of being watched, a feeling that if he could only turn quick enough he would see something else—and not a good thing.

His hand was at his breast, flattened above the Tie lying there. That touch was not to assure the safety of the talisman but to reassure himself—as if from the Tie he drew a feeling of security against that invisible lurking thing.

The passage now sloped upward, so that they climbed. Tool marks on the walls spoke of the labor that had gone into the opening of this way, but it was a narrow one, so that they went one after the other, and some outcrops of rock in the roof forced both Star Lords and larngs to stoop, the stone brushing the crests on the others' helms.

After one last steep ascent they came into a cave, wide, but with a small opening through which had entered a drifting point of snow and beyond which they could hear the whistling wind of the outer world.

Ospik trotted to this door and stood there, sniffing as might some burrow creature suspicious of the freedom beyond. "Wind up—but no storm," he reported with assurance. "By sunup you will have a fine perch from which to go a-spying. But that is some hours off, so take your ease."

Tosi had already gone to a section well out of line with the cave mouth. And he busied himself there pulling from a crevice a supply of dry and seasoned wood, some light and white as old bones, which he kindled by a coal carried in a small earthenware box, making a fire they crouched about. At last, wrapped in their fur cloaks, the larngs forming a wall of animal heat to reflect the fire, they dozed away what was left of the night.

The cavemouth faced northeast, so that the dawn light was partly theirs, making a warning of gray when Kincar was shaken gently awake by Jonathal. He rubbed smarting eyes and swallowed bites from the journeycake pushed into his hand. They left their mounts in the cave, Tosi volunteering as larng tender. Then the four from the hold, with Ospik still as guide, went out upon a broad ledge and found themselves on a mord's perch above a valley.

There was snow here, sculptured by the wind. But in one strip it had been beaten down, mushed with dark streaks of soil into a grimy path. And it must have required a goodly amount of travel to and fro to leave such well-defined traces. Yet the surrounding country was wild, with no other evidences of civilization.

"Your road to the plains," Ospik pointed out. "For those who use it, you must wait, Lords. Those who travel it do only by daylight."

So they drew lots for the post of lookout, and the rest went back to the shelter of the cave. Kincar, having the first watch, amused himself with the laying out of an ambush plan, such as Regen might have done. This was a proper place for such, armed as they were with the bows. For man-to-man combat after the old fashion it would not have served so well. Here on the ledge one could stand and pick off all lead men in a first surprise, leaving any force below without an officer to rally about.

The snow deadened sound, and a cortege came into view with a sudden appearance, which shamed Kincar out of his notion of himself as a seasoned warrior. His warning hiss brought out the others to creep across the ledge.

Kincar, used to traders' caravans with their lumbering goods wains, or the quick trot of mounted warriors, watched the present party amazed. There were men mounted on larngs to be sure, Gorthians—though there were differences in arms and clothing to be observed. Yet behind that first clot of riders came something else. Two burden larngs clumped along about ten feet apart, and linking the first to the second was a chain of metal. From this issued at spaced intervals—in pairs—other chains, smaller. And each of those—there were four pair of them—ended in collars, the collars clamped about the throats of stumbling, reeling, moaning figures.

A second pair of larngs so linked, towing more prisoners, came into view. One of the captives fell, was dragged along the ground. A rider trotted up, and a whip swung with the intention of maximum pain to the fallen. But, in spite of the blows rained upon him, the fallen one did not stir. There was a shout, and the larngs halted while the riders held a conference.

"Who are those?" Lord Frans demanded hotly of Ospik.

The mountain dweller regarded them slyly from the corners of his eyes.

"Outlaws or slaves—ones who fled from the plains and are now being returned to their homes. The lucky ones die before they reach there."

The rider who had used the whip now slid from his pad and unhooked the collar of the captive. He jerked the body aside, then kicked, and the limp form rolled into a ditch.

There was no need for spoken agreement, for any order, among the four on the ledge. Bow strings came back in unison, twanged as four hands reached for a second arrow, eyes already on a new mark.

A scream, a hoarse, startled cry, the clash of metal against metal as a sword was drawn. But four of the slave guards were down, and one of the chained captives had seized upon the whip, using its stout butt to twist at his prisoning bonds.

It was a slaughter rather than a battle. And the archers proved the worth of their weapons over and over again, shooting larngs so that the riders could not flee. Ospik leaned perilously close to the rim of the ledge watching the deaths below with glistening, hungry eyes.

Twice the guards turned on their captives to kill. And both times they died before their blows went home. In the end only those chained to the dead burden larngs were still alive. Ospik spoke first.

"Now that was a mighty killing, Lords—a mord feeding as shall be remembered long. But it will also bring boiling out those to hunt us down in turn."

Lord Bardon shrugged. "Is there a path down from this sky perch of yours, Ospik? We needs must see what can be done for those wretches below."

"If your head is clear, you can take it!" The mountaineer dropped over the lip of the ledge, hung for a moment by his hands, and then went from one hold to another as if he were a wall insect. The others followed him, much more slowly, and with—at least on Kincar's part—some misgivings.

9
VOLUNTEER

They came out of the brush into the open space bordering the road.

"When the prisoners are loose," ordered Lord Bardon, "collect what arrows you can."

"Now that is indeed wisdom, Lord." Ospik gave tribute. "Let the wild beasts feast here, and no one can say clearly what was the manner of these men's death."

Jonathal had plunged ahead and was prowling about among the bodies of the guards, examining their belts. Now he called and held up a locking rod. But, as they all started toward the chained ones, the man who had worked vainly with whip butt to break his way free gave a wailing cry and crouched, his eyes wild with hate. The whip lash sang out, striking Lord Frans's arm. Lord Bardon jerked his companion out of lash range.

"We should have thought. Take cover, Frans! To these we are the devils they fear the most!"

Jonathal used the lock-rod on the chain, freeing it first from the dead larngs. The half-dazed captives went into action, pulling it back between them, slipping their collar chains out of its hold. They were still paired by the collars, but they were no longer fastened between the slain animals.

For the most part they hunched in the snow, blinking stupidly, their spurt of energy exhausted in that one act, save for the whip wielder who got to his feet and faced his Gorthian rescuers with a spark of spirit. His face was swollen, with angry cuts under smears of dried blood. He might have been of any age, but he handled himself as might a trained warrior, and his head was up. Broken and bruised he was in body, perhaps, but not in spirit.

"What do you?" the words came haltingly, mumbled, as puffed and torn lips moved over broken teeth.

Jonathal wrenched a cloak from one of the dead guards and threw it around a shivering woman before he answered.

"We make you free."

The man turned his battered face so that his one open eye went from Jonathal to Kincar. Apparently all intelligence and curiosity had not been ground out of him by ill treatment. But neither was he willing or able to accept them readily as friends. Kincar gave the best proof of peaceful intentions he could think of, pulling a sword from the scabbard of the nearest guard and holding it out, hilt foremost.

That one unswollen eye widened in disbelief, and then a hand shot out, clawed about the hilt, and spun it out of Kincar's lax hold. The man panted as if he raced up the mountain.

"That is the way of it," Jonathal approved. "Get free, get a blade in your hands. And it is up swords and out at them!"

But Kincar believed that the captive did not hear that at all. He was too busy using the hard knob on the sword hilt to pry at his chains. Most of the others were apathetic, and all bore such marks of ill usage, men and women alike, that Kincar fought a rising nausea as he worked at the stubborn collars. Then Jonathal chanced upon some trick of their locking, and after that they tossed them aside. A few of the released made for the bodies of the guards, raiding for provision bags. And Kincar and Jonathal, much as they disliked the task, had to struggle with the weak creatures to see a fair sharing out of the food.

Kincar was on his knees beside a woman, trying to coax her to taste the coarse meal bread she held in her hand and stared at with a pitiful blankness as if she could not connect it with food, when the man to whom he had given the sword came up. He now wore a guard's armor jerkin and a helmet, and he was sucking a strip of dried meat, unable to attack it with his teeth. But he carried the sword, unsheathed in his other hand. And he watched Kincar warily.

"Who are you?" he mumbled, but in that muffled voice there was the snap of command. "Why did you do this?" The bare blade gestured at the littered road, where the dead were being stripped for the advantage of the living.

"We are those who are enemies to any rule which sets men in chains." Kincar chose his words carefully. "If you would know more, come to our leader—"

"With the point of this resting between your shoulders will I come." The blade caught the light of the rising sun.

"Well enough." Kincar pulled a robe about the woman and stood up. "My hands are open, hold captain." He gave the man the title that seemed to match his manner.

Without looking to see if he did follow, Kincar walked to the screen of bushes where the Star Lords had taken cover. But another had sought that same way before him. As Kincar thrust aside leafless limbs, he saw Lord Bardon and Lord Frans with Ospik, who was passing across arrows he had collected. Only, the three intent upon that reckoning were not alone there. One of the guards had survived the attack, not only survived it but had traced the source of that sudden death.

Perhaps the surprise of seeing who had led it—Star Lords—had kept him quiet at first. But now he crouched behind Lord Bardon, concentrated fury plain to read on his sleek face, a slender needle-knife ready in his hand. And Kincar, knowing very well how that murderous weapon was used by an expert, threw himself forward.

He struck the lurking guard waist high, but he did not carry him to the ground as he had planned. The fellow wriggled in his grasp, loose enough to strike down at Kincar with the knife intended for Lord Bardon's throat. Kincar's hand closed about that swooping wrist just in time, halting the blow when the point was almost into his flesh, kicking out to upset the other's balance. Fire scored down the side of his underchin; then the blade caught in the top of his scale coat and snapped. Before the jagged end of the blade could reach his eyes as the other struck, they were torn apart by a grip neither could hope to break. The hands that had pulled Kincar loose released their hold.

"He got you, boy!"

Blood dripped on Kincar's chest, trickling down over his surcoat. Then Lord Bardon's fingers under his chin forced his head up and to one side as the other assessed the damage.

"A scratch only, thanks be!" the Star Lord exploded a moment later. "We'll get a pack on that to stop bleeding and you'll live, youngling—" There was relief close to laughter in his voice. But when he spoke again, his voice was ice hard. "Put that one in storage, Frans. He can answer some useful questions. And"—engaged in pushing Kincar back against the face of the cliff so he could get at his wound, Lord Bardon sighted the ex-slave who had followed the younger man—"where did *you* spring from?"

"He was one of the prisoners." Kincar got out that much of an explanation before Lord Bardon's fingers, busy with a dressing, pressed him into silence.

"And he would like to see the color of our blood," suggested Lord Frans. He had trussed the guard efficiently, leaving him lying at the foot of the rise. Now he stood empty-handed facing the newcomer.

But if the man had come with swift death for his overlords in his mind, he did not move to attack now. To read any expression on his torn and battered face was impossible, but he stood watching Lord Bardon's hasty work with bandage pack, his eye flitting now and again to the cursing prisoner, his late guard. When he spoke, it was to ask the same question he had earlier made to Kincar.

"Who are you?" Then he made his bewilderment clear in a rush of words. "You wear the guise of the Black Ones, yet you have slain their loyal men, released us who are condemned slaves. Now you tend the wound of a lowlander as if he were a kinsman. And the guard, who is one of your followers, dealing death and torment at your command, lies in bonds. I ask again, who are you?"

"Let us say that we are those who have been sent to put an end to trouble in this land. Though we bear the outward seeming of your rulers, we are not of their kind. Can you believe that?"

"Lord, I have witnessed three great marvels this day. I have seen the despoiling of a slave train; I have seen men of my race and Dark Ones move with a common purpose as kinsmen, with a care for one another as true battle comrades have. And I have seen one set in rule over us laid in bonds by you. Can one who has seen such deeds as these *not* believe? And now that I have looked upon you fairly, I can testify that you are not as the Dark Ones—though you wear their bodies. By Lor, Loi, and Lys—" he went to one knee and held out his sword, hilt extended to Lord Bardon—"I am your man—I who swore by the Forest Altars never to render service to any outland lord."

Lord Bardon touched the sword hilt, but he did not take it into his hand, and the other's eye shone. He was accepted by fealty and not as a bondsman, and Lord Bardon's knowledge of that ceremony impressed him still more deeply.

He was on his feet once more, the sword slammed smartly into sheath.

"I await orders, Lord—"

That reminded Lord Frans of the problem to hand. "We can't just turn these people loose on the countryside. They would die or be scooped up by another patrol."

"What about it, Ospik," Lord Bardon asked the mountaineer. "Will your chief suffer us to take such a party through the ways?"

Ospik plucked at his lower lip. "You have struck a smart blow at the 'gods,' outlander. But, suppose those are taken again, they will blat out all they know and speedily. All men talk when the 'gods' will it. We have kept our land because its secrets were not known—"

"Once they are in the valley of the hold, Ospik, I do not think they will fall prey again."

Ospik nodded. "There is that to consider. But I have not the final word; I can but be a messenger. Come you with me and speak to our chief yourself."

"And in the meantime? What if there is another body of guards along this way?" asked Lord Bardon.

"As to that—get these back into the shelter of a side gulch here. It is a place you can easily defend if the need arises, and it is out of sight."

So they brought the released prisoners, the possessions of the guards, anything that might be of use to the captives, into a small side valley Ospik showed them. Archers on the heights above might well hold that camp against a strong attack. And they remained there as Bardon went back with Ospik into the mountain ways.

The shock of the captives' sudden change in fortune was beginning to wear away and a handful of the men bestirred themselves, under the command of the man Lord Bardon had enlisted, to shepherd the less alert of their fellows and arm themselves from the spoil of battle. Seeing that their leader appeared to have matters well in hand, the three from the hold remained aloof, save when physical help was needed. But when the temporary camp was in some sort of order, the leader came to them, saluting Lord Frans with upheld palm.

"We are at your command, Lord. Though perhaps you do well not to walk among us until those know you better for what you are. For their fear and hate for those you resemble—in outward form—runs high, and it is seldom that we have a chance to approach a Dark One within sword distance. Someone, with dulled wits and a good reason, might well attempt to try your deathlessness with metal—"

"But you do not think as do they?"

"Nay, Lord. I am Kapal, once Band-leader to free men of the wastes—until I was trapped and collar-tamed (or so they thought) by the Hands of the Dark Ones. We have fought, and hid, and fought again ever since the Dark Ones sent to enforce their rule upon the fringes of the Barren Lands. Mostly we die, our blades in hand, cut down in battle. We are very few now. When they took Quaar, they left but a handful of posts, and these can be overrun one by one, as they will do. We die, but we die free! Only"—his eye flickered from Lord Frans to the tall bow the Star man carried—"mayhap with weapons such as these to kill silently and at a good distance, men need not die so hopelessly any more."

"It may be so. We shall see—"

Kapal manifestly took that as a promise of a brighter future, "Let me out into the Barren Lands, Lord, with such a hope to voice, and I shall bring you a hundred hands of good men to ride beneath your banner! I can be gone within the hour if you wish."

"Not so. It is not given to me to have the ordering of this matter, Kapal. And what of these?" Lord Frans pointed to the late captives. "Are any among them minded to raise blade against their late masters?"

"Perhaps they are so minded," Kapal admitted. "But most of them are broken in spirit. Two, mayhap three of them could rally to a battle call. The rest—" He shrugged. "They have worn the collar chain too long."

"So do I think also. But what if they are given a measure of safety, a stretch of land where they may rest without fear, will they sow seed and reap, hunt meat, and work thus for a community that does not ask sword service in return?"

"That they might well do, Lord. If you know of such a place—safe from the Dark Ones' raids. But then you must have come from there!" He glanced from Lord Frans to Kincar and Jonathal. "It is plain to see that these, your guardsmen, have never known the bite of chain or whip, and yet they wear not a Hand's brand upon them—"

"A Hand's brand—?"

"Aye, lord. Those who are one in spirit with the Dark Ones bear their seal for all men's seeing. Look you!"

He crossed to the prisoner. The former guard spat filth, but Kapal stooped to fasten fingers in the other's hair, holding up his head and pointing to a mark just above and between the other's brows. Set deep in the skin was the brand left by hot metal, a small, threefold figure familiar to Kincar, to Jonathal—but reversed! And at that blasphemy both of the half-bloods raised fingers in the blessed sign to repudiate such vileness. Kapal saw their gesture, and when Lord Frans echoed it, he burst forth:

"The Three—you give service to the Forest Ones, Lord?"

"I give service to a belief of my own, of which the Three are another manifestation, Kapal. Good thoughts and beliefs have the respect of any man, whether they be his own by birth, or native to his friends and kinsman. But here, I think, a certain symbol has been deliberately used vilely—"

"That is true, Lord. For those who serve the Dark Ones with their full will allow themselves to be marked thus, and take pride in it—so that all others may see it and fear them. But there are those who do not fear, rather do they hate!" He loosened his hold, and the prisoner's head fell back to the ground.

"It follows a very old pattern." Lord Frans spoke more to himself than to those about him. "Sneer at and degrade what might be a banner of hope to the slave. Aye, an old, old pattern. It is a ripe time for the breaking of such patterns!"

They were never to know what argument Lord Bardon used successfully with the ruler of the inner mountain in behalf of the rescued slaves. But in the late afternoon he returned with the message that they might use the passages to take the company to the hold valley. It was a long, slow trip. And they had left two heaped piles of stones to mark graves in the gulch. The woman Kincar had tried to coax into eating was gone, and with her an old man whose wits wandered so that none of his companions in misfortune knew his name or where he had been taken.

More than a day was spent on that journey, for they had to rest many times, the larngs carrying the weakest when the passages permitted riding. The men Kapal had indicated as being worth recruiting for spear-festing formed a unit under the wasteland leader, accepting his commands readily, and they alone of the rescued were interested in their strange surroundings.

The prisoner stayed in the hands of the hold party, his safety was only assured with them. But, as they penetrated deeper into the winding ways underground, his defiance seeped out of him and he was willing enough to stay very close to his captors, tagging either Kincar or Jonathal as if he were a battle comrade.

At the fifth rest period Lord Bardon called Kincar to him. "By Ospik's reckoning we are now not too far from the entrance in the hold valley. Tosi will go with you as a guide; take your larng and ride for aid. Many of these are close to collapse and we cannot carry them to the hold. Get extra mounts and more food—"

So it was that they brought the weary party into the fortress where the freed slaves, their wounds dressed, their hunger eased, sat for the most part in dumb bewilderment around the heating units, staring with dull surprise at the life about them. But the Lord Dillan called a council of war in the upper chamber he had taken for his own—and to this Kapal alone of the rescued was summoned.

"The guard is wide open to probe," Lord Dillan said of their prisoner. "Doubtless that is used regularly upon him by his masters. The man he was—he might have been—was destroyed when they set that brand upon him. By that act he surrendered his will and they can use him as they wish. It is a horrible thing!"

"So we agree. But we cannot concern ourselves too deeply now with what has been done in the past. We must think of what lies before us. The question is, dare we, with our few numbers, make any move against the entrenched strength of these tyrants?" asked Lord Bardon.

Lord Jon broke the long moment of silence. He was the youngest of the Star Lords, perhaps by their reckoning as youthful and as inexperienced as Kincar had been in the company of Wurd and Regen. Now he asked a simple question.

"Dare we *not?*"

Lord Dillan sighed. "There it is. Being what we are, striving toward the goal we have set for ourselves, we must interfere."

"Aye. But not foolishly, throwing away any advantage we may have," Lord Bardon cut in. "We must make our few count as well as an army. And we must know more of the lowlands before we venture there. Wring that guard dry of all he knows, Dillan. And let us set a post on that road, take what toll we can from other slave trains passing. Then—send a scout into the lowlands— Kapal!"

Soothing dressings about the outlaw's head covered all but one eye and his mouth, but he arose limberly.

"Kapal, what are the chances of a scout into the lowlands?"

"Few and ill, Lord. They have control posts along every road, and all travelers must account for themselves. To one who knows not the land it is impossible."

Lord Bardon corrected him. "Nothing is impossible. It is merely that the right way is not clear at first. Supposing a Dark One was to travel, would any dare question him?"

Kapal shook his head. "Lord, the Dark Ones *never* travel. Death comes not to them through age, but metal enters their flesh as easily as it does ours. They live well protected and only go forth from their hold in air-flying wains, the magic of which they alone know. Just one sort of man would dare such a scout—"

"And that?"

"One bearing the mark of evil—he could pretend to be a messenger."

Kincar's hand sought what he wore secretly. His eyes went from man to man about that circle, studying each in turn. Already he knew the answer. Of all the hold party he was the only one showing no trace of alien blood. The scout could only be his.

"I will go—"

He did not realize that he had said that aloud until he saw Lord Dillan look at him, caught the grim approval in Lord Bardon's appraisal. His hand was at his lips, but it was too late.

10
STORM, NIGHT, AND THE SHRINE

Kincar stood at one of the narrow windows in the Lady Asgar's chamber. The sky as seen through that slit showed clear rose. It was going to be a fair day, and the wind that swept the snow from the courtyard had died away.

"Is it not a matter of time?" he asked without turning his head.

There was no answer, for there was only one they could make, and so far they did not voice it.

"You cannot do it—not and still wear the Tie." Lord Dillan put into words what Kincar had known for long hours since he had made that impulsive offer. "I am not sure you could do it in any case. Such an act might cause an unthinkable traumatic shock—"

Now Kincar faced around. "It is a mark only."

"It is a mark which negates everything in which you believe. And for one bearing the Tie—"

But for the first time in long minutes the Lady Asgar moved. "This devil's mark must be set upon its victims with some ceremony. And the very ritual of that ceremony impresses its meaning upon the new servant of evil. It is a thing of the emotions, as all worship—whether of light or dark forces—is a matter of emotion. If a thing is done without ceremony, or if it is done in another fashion altogether—"

"You mean?"

"That mark is made with a metal branding rod, is it not? Well, it is in my mind to reproduce its like another way—without ceremony. And while it is done Kincar must think upon its falseness and the reasons for his accepting it. Let him hold the Tie in his two hands and see if it repudiates him thereafter."

He crossed to her eagerly. "Lady, let us try!" If this was the answer, if he could have the mark without suffering inner conflict—

She smiled at him. "I have many forms of magic, Kincar. Let us see if my learning reaches so far. Do you hold the Tie now and think upon what you would do for us and why. If all goes well, we shall transform you into the seeming of an obedient Hand."

He was already clad in the alien trappings of one of the slave guards, assembled from their loot of the road attack. Now he brought out the smooth stone that was his legacy and trust from Styr's lord. With it between his palms, he whispered the words of Power, feeling the gentle glow which answered that invocation. And then he closed his eyes.

Concentrating upon the Tie he waited. His flesh tingled under a pressing touch upon his forehead. Three times that pressure. Then nothing at all. The Tie was quiescent, nor had it gone dead as he feared.

"Is that it?" asked the Lady Asgar.

"That is it!" Lord Dillan replied.

Kincar opened his eyes and laughed. "No change. The Tie did not change!"

Lord Dillan released pent breath in a sigh. "You had the right of it, Asgar. He is free to go. Give her the Talisman, Kincar, it will be well guarded—" But he paused at Kincar's shake of the head.

"Not so, Lord. It has not repudiated me. Therefore, it is still my trust and I cannot resign it elsewhere."

"If it is found on you, if they so much as suspect you wear it—! The result might be worse than you can imagine. In our Gorth it must be borne secretly, though there it was an object of reverence. What would it be here?"

But Kincar was restoring it to the usual place of concealment beneath his clothing. "All that may be true, Lord. I only know that I cannot render it up to anyone unless it is ready to go. That is the nature of a Tie. Were I to leave it here, I would be drawn back speedily, my mission unaccomplished. It is a part of me until my guardianship is done, which may come only at my death—or earlier if it is so willed."

"He is right." The voice of the Lady Asgar held a troubled note. "We have never learned the secret of the Ties, as you know. It is his trust and his fate. And somehow"—she hesitated and then added her last words with a rush—"it may be his salvation also!"

Together they went through the hall into the courtyard. It was a very early hour, and no one noted their passing. Cim was padded and ready. And Kapal walked the larng slowly back and forth.

"You have the map?" he asked as Kincar took the reins from him and swung up on the mount. "Think again, young lord, and let me take on a slave collar and go with you!"

Kincar shook his head and smiled a little crookedly. "Back to your wastelands, Kapal, and raise those men for a festing. Be sure I shall take care, and all we have learned from that guard is safely here." His hand went to his forehead, but he did not touch, remembering what was painted there.

The captive had talked, freely, in detail. Lord Dillan, the healer of sick minds, could have thoughts forth when he wanted them. And all that other had recounted was now Kincar's—the passwords for the frontier posts, customs, manners, minutiae that should take him safely in and out of U-Sippar, city of the lowlands.

Now, wishing no formal farewell, he headed Cim through the outer gate and rode out of the hold into the morning, down the cleft toward the openness of the lowlands. He did not once turn to see the fortress. As he had ridden out of Styr, so he now left this new security to face a future that might be largely chance, but in a small part of his own making.

The promise of a fine morning did not last. But at the same time the wind that pulled at his cloak was surprisingly warm. And that was a warning to the weatherwise hunter. He could now be heading into one of the thaws of mid-cold season, when drenching rains blanketed the countryside, making traps of mire for the unwary—rains that turned in seconds, or so it seemed to unfortunates caught out in them, to icy sleet and freezing cold once more.

That map, supplied partly by Kapal and partly by their prisoner and memorized by Kincar, gave him a mental picture of a broad expanse of open plain. But between him and the first outposts of the plains civilization was a stretch of woodland. He had intended to ride south along the fringe of this to a river, then follow the bank of the stream seaward. But perhaps the forest would provide better shelter if the threatening storm broke before the day's end.

This Gorth had a different history than his own, even before the coming of the Star ships. That much they had learned in the past two days. In his Gorth the aliens landed upon a planet where the native race was just struggling out of barbaric tribal wanderings, a world without cities, without villages. The holds marked the first settlements of tribes influenced by the new knowledge of the outworld men. So their customs, laws, ways of life still held many elements of the nomads.

But this Gorth had already been well advanced from the primitive when the Star Lords had come to crush a rising civilization, hunt to extinction the native rulers who had built such fortresses as the hold, proscribe the old learning, the old religion. Where the Star men had striven to raise their own people, here they had reversed the process and attempted to reduce them to a dull level of slavery, not even equal to suard and mord or larng—for those were beasts, and their savage independence was reborn in each new generation.

Far from interbreeding with the natives, the outworlders here considered such a linkage of blood unspeakable, something obscene, so that Kapal found it extremely hard to accept as a fact that the hold men were partly of mixed-birth. But that might work to their advantage in another way, for the ranks of the Dark Ones here were exceedingly thin. A handful of births in a generation, and many deaths by assassination, by duels among themselves, kept the balance uneven.

Between each Dark One and his fellow there was only uneasy truce, and their guardsmen warred for a whim or an insult that had no meaning to the natives. Fear fattened upon night terrors, was not to be sated, even on battlefields or in burnt-out holds. Yet at the hint of an uprising—and in the beginning there had been many as Kapal testified—the mutual distrust and jealousy of the aliens was forgotten, and they combined forces to deal quick death. Of late years the few remaining sparks of freedom were to be found only in the wastes. And now the alien rulers were methodically stamping those out, one by one, as might men bringing boot soles down upon insects scurrying hopeless in the dust.

Cim kept to the ground-covering lope of his best journey pace.

This wide stretch of snow-covered grassland was better going than the crooked trails of the hill country, and by mid-afternoon that same rising land was but a faint purplish line to the northeast. Still the warm wind blew steadily, and the snow melted under its touch, allowing yellow grass to show in ragged patches.

But the mount was not happy. He kept raising his head into the wind, snorting now and again. And twice he increased the length of his stride without any urging from his rider. They stopped for a breather on the crown of a small hillock, and Cim gave voice to a shuddering cry. Shadows moved in the far distance, and Kincar's hand went to his sword hilt. Not for the first time he regretted that he had had to leave his new bow behind. But those distant larngs had the elongated look of riderless mounts. A band of wild ones. There should be good trapping here come warm season. Loose Cim and a couple of other trained mounts to toll the herd into a pen— Why, they should be able to supply all the inhabitants of the hold with a second larng!

But would they still be in the hold at the coming of warm days? Foreboding swept away his hunter's enthusiasm. There had been little said during the immediate past of other gates, new Gorths to come, not since they had discovered the ills of this one. He was sure that the Star Lords were determined to do what they could to set matters right here before they essayed another passage through the ribbon rivers of cross time. And that did not mean that they would be peacefully hunting wild larngs.

Kincar twitched ear reins to call Cim to the duty at hand, and the larng began his steady, distance-eating lope once again. His rider was certain that the thick line of the southwest marked the outer fringes of the forest he sought. And he was none too soon in that sighting, for the wind that wrapped around him now was as warm as a heating unit. The patches of snow were very few, and those grew visibly smaller.

Clouds now came rolling up the rose curve of the sky, driven by that too-balmy wind, clouds heavy and dark with rain, their sides as bulging as the water bags of wasteland travelers.

The first big drops spattered on his shoulders, caught in Cim's cold-season wool. Kincar pulled the flapping edges of his cloak about him and ducked his head, wishing he could pull it down between his shoulders as did a Lacker lizard. Cim shook his long neck, snorted disgustedly, and then fairly flew, an arrow pointed at the promise of shelter, still distant as it was.

They were well soaked before they made it under the trees. In leaf those would have been a good canopy. But now the rain drove among bare branches with a knife-edge force. And the warmth of the wind was gone; rather there was the bite of sleet. Where the moisture ran across bark, it was freezing into a clear casing of ice.

Somewhere they must find covering. Kincar's first annoyance became apprehension. The massing clouds had brought night in midafternoon. Blundering ahead might lose them in unmapped territory, but to halt in the icy flood was to invite freezing.

Kincar tried to keep Cim headed southwest, working a serpentine path that, he hoped, would bring them to the river. At any rate they must keep moving. He was on foot now, the reins looped about his wrist as he picked his way between tree trunks. And he must have unconsciously been following the old road for several minutes before he was aware of the faint traces left by men years before. The larger trees stood apart with only saplings of finger-size growth or low brush between. Then a tearing flash of blue-white lightning showed him smoothed blocks tilted up in the soil—a pavement here!

It appeared to run straight, and he turned into it, knowing that he dared no longer wander aimlessly in search of the river. At least a road went somewhere, and if he continued to grope his way along its traces, he would not commit the lost travelers' folly of moving in circles. A road tying the mountain district to the sea was a logical possibility. If he kept to it, perhaps he could even avoid some of the lowland outposts. And heartened by that, Kincar plowed along, towing the reluctant Cim, showered by the bushes he pushed between.

But very soon it was apparent that to find an ancient road for a guide was not enough. He had to have shelter, warmth, protection against the continuing fury of the storm. And Kincar began to search the gloom for a fallen tree against which he might erect a hunter's lean-to.

It was Cim who ended that. The larng squealed, gave a jerk of his head to bring Kincar's arm up at a painful angle before he could loose the reins. Then Cim reared, threatening Kincar with his clawed forefeet as he had been taught to savage a spearman in a fight. Caught off guard Kincar dropped the reins and stumbled back to avoid that lunge.

Free, Cim moved on, only dimly seen in the thickening gloom. He bobbed aside, struck away between two trees, and was gone before Kincar could catch up. Panting, floundering, the Gorthian hurried ahead, striving to keep the larng in sight. And from time to time he caught a glimpse of the lighter bulk of the mount.

Then Cim disappeared entirely. Half sobbing with frustration and rage, Kincar blundered on in the general direction in which he had last seen Cim, only to come up against a barrier with force enough to rebound into the prickly arms of a dagger-thorn bush.

His outstretched hands slid over stone glazed with the icy skim of the rain. A wall—a building—! Then those hands met nothing at all, and he had found an opening. He hurled himself forward and was out of the pelt of the storm, under a roof he could not see. Cim grunted, having found this shelter before him.

Kincar scuffed through a mass of leaves. Small branches cracked under his weight. Throwing aside his water-sodden cloak, he swept that debris together with his hands, before he brought out one of the mountaineer's clay boxes with its welcome coal.

At first he was too busy with nursing the small fire to life to inspect the structure into which Cim had led him. When the flames took hold, he looked about him for the supply of fuel—and found it woefully limited. Drifts of leaves, aged and a few rotten branches, none of promising size. He had brought in the smallest scraps before he noticed that another door opened into an inner chamber.

There was very little hope of finding any more wood in there, but he had to investigate. So Kincar crowded by Cim and stepped through that other doorway. The firelight did not reach past its threshold. But it was not the dark that made him hesitate—nor was it any visible portal.

When Kincar had passed the alien gates of the Star men, that talisman he had borne had taken fire from their energy, had been to him a burning brand to torment flesh. What he felt now was far different.

There was a gentle warmth—no stabbing heat. But, above and beyond that, a tingling, exhilarating feeling of aliveness, of senses brought to a higher pitch, a new depth of awareness. And with it a belief in the rightness of all this—

How long did he pause there, allowing that sensation of well-being to envelope him? Time had no meaning. Forgotten was the fire, the need for wood to feed it, the drum of the storm on the walls and roof that encased him. Kincar moved on into a dark that was at once warm, alive, knowing, wrapped in a welcoming security as a child is wrapped in a suard robe for sleeping by its mother.

There was no dark now. It hung before his physical eyes, but he walked with a truer sight. His fingers were swift and sure at the throat of his ring jerkin, loosening it, the other leather jacket underneath—his shirt. Then the Tie was in his hands. It glowed green-blue—with the sheen of fertile earth after the growing rains, of newly budded foliage.

Before him was an altar, a square table of stone, uncarved, fashioned with the same rugged simplicity as the shrine—a plain table of stone. But Kincar had seen its like before, though never had it been given to him to awaken what lay there, to summon what might be summoned.

A table of stone with three depressions, three small pockets hollowed in its surface. Its edge pressed lightly against his thighs now, bringing him to a stop. He did not have to stoop to use the Tie as it was meant to be used, a key to an unlocking that might occur only once in a man's life time and that changed him from that moment.

"Lor!" He called the Name clearly as he dropped the stone in the depression farthest to the left. "Loi!" Now that upon the right. "Lys!" The center. And the echo of the Three Names hung in the room, making music of a kind.

Were there now three glowing circles upon the wall? Three heads, three faces calm with a non-human serenity? His mind, coached by hoarded lore, the hundreds of legends, might be playing tricks and seeing things that his eyes in truth did not report.

Lor—He of the Three who gave strength to a man's body, force to his sword arm—a youth of beauty—

Loi—He who brought power, wisdom, strength of mind—a man of middle years with experience deep written on his quiet face—

Lys—She who gave gifts of the heart, who put children into

women's arms, and friendship in the heart of one man toward another. Did a feminine face center between the other two?

What Kincar did see he could never describe. He was on his knees now, his arms on the altar encircling the depressions, with the Tie glowing bright and beautiful in the hollow that was Lys'. His head drooped forward so that the mark of shame he wore touched on the sacred stone, yet there was no deadening of the Tie glow.

And he slept. There were many dreams. He was taken on journeys and shown things that he would not recall when waking, and in his dreams he realized that and was sad. But there was a reason for that forgetting, and that he must accept also.

Perhaps it was because this was a deserted shrine, and the force pent there had not been released for untold time, that it poured forth now in a vast wave, engulfing him completely. He was changed, and in his dreams he knew that, shrank from it as earlier he had shrunk from the thought of his mixed blood.

It was morning. Gray stone walls, a flat table under his head marked only by three small holes, in one of which rested a pebble with a chain through it. Kincar got to his feet and strode out without another glance at that dead room, for it was dead now. What had activated it the night before was gone—exhausted.

11
ILL-CHANCED MEETING

That odd feeling of being cut off from the everyday world passed as Kincar stepped into the outer room of the shrine, just as his now dim memories of the night, of drawing upon the stored power of the Three, faded.

A blackened spot on the floor marked the fire he had started and abandoned hours ago. Cim hunched by the wall, his body heat, now that he was sheltered from the direct blasts of wind and wet, keeping him comfortable. He opened his top pair of eyes as Kincar crossed to him, moving his thick lips to suggest that a sharing out of supplies was now in order. But, though Kincar crumbled journeycake in his hands for Cim to lick away with every sign of healthy hunger, he himself ate only sparingly, more out of a sense of duty than from any inner demand.

The storm had deposited an encasing crystal film over all of the outer world. But the sun was up, and it was chill enough to promise no more unseasonable thaws. Such storms as yesterday's usually meant a space of fair weather to follow. However, the treacherous footing made Kincar decide against riding until they were out of the wood, and he picked a way with care back to the old road, Cim willing enough to follow him now.

It had been indeed a long time since any traveler had used this particular track. The forest was fast reclaiming it each season, uprooting, burrowing under, growing over. Only, those who had laid down these stones had been of the same clan of master builders as the men who had erected the hold, and they had not intended their handiwork to last only a short term of years. So the wild had not yet won.

Kincar guessed by his hunter's knowledge that he was now heading west, if not angling so much to the south as he had first planned. And since he was well concealed on this forgotten path, he determined to keep to it, believing it should bring him through the forest and into the open country about U-Sippar where he would have to travel with greater care.

It was late afternoon before the trees began to thin, and Cim pushed through the last screen of the forest into the country bordering the sea. In fact, this tongue of woodland had run out very close to the ocean's edge. But the port the road had once served was now a tumbled ruin of roofless buildings, battered by storms and time alike, with only slimed stone pillar heads to mark the wharves that had once extended into the brown-gray water.

Ruinous as it was, some life still clung to the place. A battered boat had been hauled well up on the shingle, turned bottom up with the scars of recent repairs on its rounded sides. And from a hut of ill-matched stones came a trickle of cooking-pot smoke.

As far as Kincar could see, there was no sign of any guard post, no suggestion that the mercenaries of the Dark Ones were in command here. Some fisherman, he surmised, had thrown up a shelter in the ancient port to net over grounds so long abandoned as to be worth searching once again.

He had allowed Cim free rein, and now the larng continued to jog along the overgrown, soil-drifted road, winding a way among fallen debris. Kincar, running a knowledgeable eye over the buildings, their windows like the arched hollows given skulls for eyes, believed that the place had been despoiled in battle, a battle in which the inhabitants had fought without hope but with a grim determination, from house to house, wall to wall. Even the beating of many seasons' rains had not erased the stigma of fire. Splintered wood, powdering away, was riven with the blows that had beaten in doors and window coverings.

No wonder this had been abandoned after that day. Not many could have survived the sacking, and if the victor had not chosen to rebuild— Perhaps it had been decided to leave this as a warning and a threat for all time. In his own Gorth, traders had been handy men with a sword. They had to be; most trade roads led across wild lands. And while they did not spout challenges in every man's teeth, they drew blades in their own defense, forcing many an ambitious hold lord to a quick change of mind when he nursed some idea of an illegal tax because a trade route lay across his land. If this had been a town of traders, well then, the attackers had not had matters all their own way. And, Kincar, having no idea of the rights of the matter, but guessing much, was very pleased to think that true.

Seashore birds, scavengers of the tides, shrieked overhead. But, save for that thread of smoke and the boat, the shore was empty of any other sign of life. He did not know how far he was from U-Sippar, though that city being a port, he need only follow the shore line to find it. But—which way—north or south? And to journey on through the coming night was unwise. A lost traveler could, by rights, demand a lodging at the nearest dwelling in his Gorth—perhaps that custom held here.

Kincar headed Cim for the hut on the shore, the hint of food cooking being irresistible at the moment. A fisherman probably lived on the results of his labors. Kincar visualized some dishes, common enough on the shore no doubt, but luxuries in the mountains—shell fish for example—

Cim's clawed feet made no sound upon the sand, but possibly Kincar had been under observation for some time through one of the numerous cracks in the walls of the hut. Before he had time to dismount, or even hail the house, a man came out, shutting the wooden slab of door and taking a stand with his back against that portal that suggested he was prepared to defend it with his life.

In his right hand he held a weapon Kincar had seen only once, and then it had been a curiosity displayed by a trader. A straight shaft curved into a barbed point, resembling a giant fishhook—which in a manner it was. The trader had explained its use very graphically to the astonished men of Styr Holding. Hurled by the experienced in the proper manner, that hook could pierce armor and flesh, drag a mounted man down to where he could be stabbed or battered to death. And this fisherman handled the odd weapon as if he knew just what it could do.

Kincar looped Cim's reins over one arm and held up his empty hands in the old universal gesture of peace. But there was no peace mirrored in the other's set face, in his sullen eyes. His clothing, in spite of the harsh weather, was hardly better than a collection of stained and grimed rags, leaving the scabbed, cracked skin of arms and legs bare to elbow and knee, and the hollows beneath his cheek bones spelt starvation. If he got his living from the sea, it was not a good one.

"I come in peace," Kincar said slowly, with the authority he would have used speaking to a fieldman of Styr.

There was no answer, no indication that the other heard him. Only the hook turned slowly in those hands, the sullen eyes remained fixed on larng and rider—not as if they saw only an enemy—but also food!

Kincar sat very still. Perhaps this was no fisherman after all, but an outlaw driven to wild desperation. Such men were truly to be feared, since utter despair pushes a man over the border of sanity and he no longer knows danger to put a rein on his acts. Somehow Kincar was sure that if he drew his sword, if his hand traveled a fraction of an inch toward the hilt, that hook would swing—

His own eagerness—eagerness and weakness—undid the hook man. Kincar kneed Cim, and the larng gave the sidewise leap of a trained battle mount. He had read aright that twitch of the hands, that stiffening of the other's jaw muscles. The hook scraped across his shoulder, caught in his cloak. Then in a flash he had it and with one sharp jerk snaked its line through the other's hands with force enough to pull him off balance and face down in the sand. There was no sound from the disarmed man. He lay quiet for a moment and then, with more speed than Kincar would have credited to him, threw his body in a roll to bring him back against the door of the hut once again. He huddled there on his knees, his back braced against the salt-grayed wood, his hands on either side of the frame, plainly presenting his own body as a barrier against Kincar's entrance.

Kincar freed the hook from his torn cloak and let the ugly thing thud to the ground. It was well out of the reach of its owner, and he had taken a firm dislike to handling it. But he did not draw his sword.

"I come in peace," he said again firmly, with an emphasis he hoped would make sense to the man at the hut, penetrate his fog of desperation. Again he displayed empty hands. He could ride on, he supposed, find shelter elsewhere. But this other was in the proper frame of mind to dog his trail and perhaps ambush him along the shore. It was too late to keep on riding.

"Murren—?"

That call did not come from the man, but from inside the hut. And at it the guardian flattened himself still tighter, his head turning swiftly from side to side, in a vain attempt to hunt escape where none existed.

"Murren—?" The voice was thin, a ghost of the sea birds' mournful cries. Only some carrying quality in it raised it above the pound of the waves.

"I will do you no harm—" Kincar spoke again. He had forgotten that he wore the clothes of a guard, bore the false brand. He only knew that he could not ride on—not only because of his own safety, but also because there was need to find what lay behind this stubborn, hopeless defense of the hookman, and who called from behind that closed door.

"Murren—?" For the third time that cry. And now something more, a thud ringing hollow against the worn wood, as if one within beat for his freedom. "Murren—dead?" The voice soared close to hysteria, and for the first time the man without appeared to hear. He flattened his cheek against the wood and uttered a queer hoarse call of his own, like a beast's plaint.

"Out—Murren—!" the voice demanded; the beat on the door grew louder. "Murren, let me out!"

But the man held his position stubbornly, hunching his shoulders against the slab as if the disobedience of that order was in itself a source of pain. Kincar flicked the reins, and Cim advanced a step or two. The man shrank, his snarling face upturned, his eyes wild. He must have recognized a larng trained in battle savaging, be expecting those clawed forefeet to rake him down, yet he held to his post.

He could guard the door, but he could not contain the whole hut. There came the sound of splintering wood, and the man leaped to his feet. Too late, for a second figure wavered around the corner of the hut. Its clothing was as tattered as that of its guard, but there was a difference between them.

The man who had fought to protect the hut was a thick-featured, stocky individual of the fieldman breed. He might be a groom of larngs, a guardsman in some hold, an under officer even. But he was no war chief nor hold heir.

The newcomer was of another class—wholly Gorthian, of noble blood as far as Kincar could see, and no beaten slave. He was plainly at the end of his strength as he reeled along, with one hand on the hut wall to support himself. The youthful face raised to Kincar was delicate of feature, wan and drawn, but his shoulders were squared as if they were accustomed to the weight of a scale shirt.

He came to stand by his man, and they both fronted Kincar, weaponless but in a united defiance. The young man flung back his touseled head to speak.

"You have us, Hand. Call up your men. If you expect us to beg for a quick death, you shall be disappointed. Murren has been left unable to plead—if he would—which he would not. And I am as voiceless in such matters as your knives have left him. Let the Lord Rud have his pleasure with us as he wishes. Not even the Dark Ones can hold off death forever!" What had begun in defiance ended in an overwhelming weariness.

"Believe me—I do not come from Lord Rud, nor do I ride as one of any tail of his." Kincar strove to put all the sincerity he could muster into that. "I am a traveler, seeking shelter for the night—"

"Who expects a Hand to speak with a straight tongue?" Weariness weighted each word. "Though how lies profit you, I cannot see. Take us and make an end!"

Murren put his hands on the boy's shoulders and endeavored to set him back, behind his own bulk. But the other resisted.

"This is the end, Murren. Whistle up your men, Hand of evil!"

Kincar dismounted, his empty hands before him. "I am not hunting you."

At last that got through to the boy. He slumped back against Murren, whose arm went about him in support.

"So you are not hunting us; you have not been sent out of U-Sippar to run us down. But then we shall be your favor gifts for Lord Rud. Collar and take us in, Hand, and you will have his good wishes."

Kincar made a move he hoped would allay a measure of their suspicion. He pulled a packet of journeycake and dried meat from Cim's bags and tossed it across the space between them. It struck against Murren's foot. The man stared down at it as if it were a bolt from one of the Star Lords' weapons. Then he released his hold upon the boy and scooped it up, bewildered at what he found within the wrappings.

Murren thrust a piece of the cake into the boy's hand, giving voice to his own avid hunger with a whimpering cry. They crammed the food into their mouths. Kincar was shaken. The captives he had helped to free on the road had been, with the exception of Kapal, so sunk in their misery that they had hardly seemed human. He had tended them as he had tended Vorken when her wing had been singed, as he would have Cim. But these two were no slaves, apathetic, animal-like in their acceptance of degradation and pain.

"Who are you?" The boy had swallowed the cake, was now sucking on a stick of meat, eying Kincar as Kincar might watch Lord Dillan engaged in some Star magic.

"I am Kincar of Styr—" It was better not to claim s'Rud here. And he must keep always in mind that this Gorth was not his Gorth. That Lord Rud, the tyrant of U-Sippar, was not the Lord Rud who had been his father.

"Styr—" The other shook his head slowly; the name plainly had no meaning for him.

"In the mountains." Kincar gave the setting of Styr, which probably did not exist in this Gorth.

The boy, still holding the meat stick as if he had forgotten he had it in hand, came forward to stand directly before Kincar. He studied the half-Gorthian's face with a searching that must have planted every line of it in his memory forever. Then with one finger he touched the mark, dropping his hand quickly.

"Who are you?" he asked again, and this time with a lord's authority.

"You have the truth—I am Kincar of Styr—out of the mountains."

"You dare much, mountain man!"

"How so?"

"To wear that and yet not wear it— Nay"—he shook his head—"I ask no questions. I wish to know nothing of what brought you here. We may be danger to each other."

"Who are you?" Kincar countered in his turn.

The other answered with a wry smile. "One who should never have been born. One who will speedily be naught, when Lord Rud finds me, as he must—for we are close to the end of our wayfaring, Murren and I. I have no name, Kincar of Styr, and you had best forget that our paths ever crossed. Unless you choose to win a goodly welcome at U-Sippar by taking me there—"

"In the meantime," Kincar said with deliberate lightness of tone, "will you grant me shelter this night?"

If the boy was coming to accept him—if not as a friend, at least only a minor menace—Murren was not so disposed. He showed his teeth in a mord's hunger grin as Kincar came forward. Impulsively then the half-Gorthian did something that might have endangered his life, but it was the best example of good will he could think of. He went back, took up the hook, and skidded it across sand and gravel.

Murren was down in a flash, his fingers on its shaft. But as quickly the boy caught his arm.

"I know not how you are tossing your chance sticks in this game," he told Kincar, "but I accept that you will not act after the manner of those whose foul mark you wear. Murren—not this one!"

The older man mouthed a protest of yammered sound, and in that instant Kincar saw the real horror that had come upon him—he was tongueless! But the boy pulled him aside from the hut door.

"If you would claim shelter, stranger, it is yours. Silence can be exchanged for silence."

They had a fire, if they had no food, and in the hut there was a measure of warmth, walls against the night wind. Kincar tethered Cim nearby and gave the larng rations, Murren, ever at his side, turning the hook in his hands, kept only from its use by the influence the boy held over him. When they were all three inside, he stationed himself before the door, his sullen, very watchful eyes daring Kincar to a false move.

But the half-Gorthian was very content to settle down by the driftwood fire, hoping in time to gain some scraps of information from his chance-met companions. If they were outlaws of the coastlands, as the boy's talk of Lord Rud made it clear that they were, then they knew U-Sippar and could set him on the trail for that city. But to ask questions without raising suspicions was a delicate problem.

He was no student of men's minds. It needed the skill of Lord

Dillan or the Lady Asgar to allay others' fears and make them talk freely. And there was very little time in which to work. Oddly it was the boy who gave him a good opening.

"You ride to U-Sippar?"

"Aye—"

The boy laughed. "You could not be coming from there. The search for us is up. Watch how you walk—or rather how you ride—man from Styr. Lord Rud's mords hunger, and they are appeased by those who cannot give good account of their activities."

"Even those wearing this?" His hand arose to his forehead.

"Now perhaps those wearing that. A secret was broke in U-Sippar." His lips twisted again in that smile that was no smile. "Though all its parts were smashed, as a man brings down his boot upon a soil-crawler, yet Lord Rud is not certain that is so. He will question all and everything for many days and nights to come. Think three times before you ride to that city without a tight tale, Kincar."

Had he accented that word "three"? Kincar took a chance. He spread out his hand in the glow of the fire, the red gleam making plain the movements of his fingers as they shaped a certain sign.

The boy said nothing—he might not understand. His features were well schooled, and he sat quietly for what seemed a long period of time. Then his own right hand went up in the proper answer.

"More than ever, it is well that you keep from U-Sippar!"

But already all warnings were too late. Cim did not have Vorken's superlative sight, but he had keen senses, superior to those of men. Now outside he shrilled a challenge to another male larng. The three jumped to their feet.

"This was an ill-chanced meeting, man from Styr," said the youth. "You have been caught with us. But you can still save yourself—" He waited tensely, and Kincar grasped his meaning.

To claim these two as his captives would be his passport to favor. Instead he drew his dagger from his belt and tossed it to the unarmed boy, who caught it out of the air with a skilled hand.

"We shall see ill-chanced for whom!" Kincar returned.

12

A MEETING WITH LORD RUD

To Kincar there was no sense in remaining inside the hut, to be poked out of hiding as a cau-rat would be poked from its nest by a boy. Sword play needed space. But he had to thrust Murren out of the way at the door, and the boy needs must scuffle to follow him. The tongueless man was still making his protesting yammer as they came out into the twilight.

That fading light was yet bright enough to show that indeed their luck had run out. A ring of mounted men was closing in about the hut, and every other one of them balanced a lance ready to use. On Cim Kincar might have fought his way free. His larng was trained and strong enough to override these scrubby animals. But it never occurred to Kincar at that moment to desert the other two.

Only Murren was alert to such a possibility, proving himself more warrior than fieldman. It was he who sprang onto Cim's bare back and then leaned down to swing at the boy. His fist connected with the other's jaw, and the slight young body went limp. Murren got his master across his knees and drove Cim inland, swinging his hook as he charged against the wall of riders. And the very ferocity of his attack disconcerted the enemy as much as it astounded Kincar.

The hook rose and fell, and a stunned man tumbled from his larng, making a break in the wing. Murren used it, Cim leaping through like a hunted suard. Some of the party went after him at the shouted orders of their officer.

But the four or five who remained headed for Kincar, who set his back to the hut wall and waited tensely. Could he bluff it out—say that Murren and the boy had been his prisoners and had escaped? But the facts were too plain. Murren had been armed and Cim had been there for his use.

Lances against sword. It was an unequal contest at the best. He held his cloak ready to entangle a lance point. Had the encounter only come at night, he might have had a thin chance of escape under cover of the dark. But they were between him and the sea—no hope of swimming out—and there was a long open stretch of flat shore before one came to the nearest ruins of the old town. However, surrender without a fight was not to be thought of.

That was what they wanted. The nearest warrior hailed him.

"Put down your sword, stranger! The peace of the Gods between us—"

Not the peace of the Gods. The false gods. And any peace of their offering meant nothing. Kincar made no answer.

"Ride him down!" came a growl from the nearest lancer.

"Not so!" someone objected. "Lord Rud must have speech with any man found in the company of—" The other speaker bit off his words as if fearing an indiscretion. "Take him prisoner if you do not wish the Lord to overlook *you*, lackwit!"

They came at him from three sides. Kincar threw the cloak, shore away one lance point with his sword. Then a larng reared to bring down its raking claws. He flung himself sideways and went down on one knee. Before he could recover, a lance butt was driven against his back with force enough to burst the air from his lungs and carry him down into the sand. They were all over him in an instant, grinding his face into the shingle as they whipped his arms behind him and locked his wrists together. Then they allowed him to lie there for a space, choking and gasping, while they held consultation over him.

For the time being Kincar was occupied with the suddenly difficult job of breathing. And he had not yet given over gasping when he was raised and flung roughly face down over the withers of a sweating larng.

It was a cold ride through the night, for Kincar had no cloak. It seemed that the riders were so well acquainted with the route that they dared travel it in darkness. Or else they were in such a well-founded fear of their overlord that it was worth the risk to carry him a quick report. However, a headdown journey was not an inducement to logical thinking or the forming of future plans. Kincar was only semiconscious at the end of that ride. When he was tumbled from the larng, he was as limp as a pair of saddlebags.

Dull pain reached through the general fog as a boot was planted in his ribs to turn him over. As he lay sprawled on his back, a light flashed blindingly into his eyes.

"—is he?"

"—bears the mark—"

"Whose man?"

Fragments of questions that had very little meaning. And then one order to bring action: "Put him in the cells and then report. If he was with the young one, Lord Rud must know it."

They did not try to get him to his feet. Fingers were laced in his armpits, and he was dragged across a stone pavement, bumped downstairs. The fetid smell of damp underground closed about him along with a deeper darkness. Then he was shoved backwards so that he rolled down a few more steps. There was the slam of a door, and light was totally gone.

He had come to rest in an awkward position, legs higher than his head, and now he tried to wriggle backwards on a level surface until his feet slipped from the stairs. He was bruised, still groggy from the ride, numb with cold. But he had suffered no real hurt, and he was aroused enough to think rationally once more.

They had mentioned Lord Rud, so it followed that he must now be in some fortress of U-Sippar. And he had entered under the worst possible disadvantage—captured while companying with fugitives hunted by the district's ruler. They had noted his brand but had not marked its falsity, so he still had a faint chance to pass himself off as a man following some lord living at a distance. It was a very slender hope, but it was all he had left, and now Kincar made himself go over his story, testing its weakest points.

When that story had first been concocted back in the hold, they had never expected him to face one of the Dark Ones in person. His general instructions had been to enter U-Sippar as an unattached Hand seeking employment, but with enough loot in his pouch to keep him for a space before he had to take service. He was to keep away from the fortress, from the guards on duty there. And here he was in the very heart of the place to be most shunned.

Supposing that Lord Rud—this Lord Rud—was gifted as Lord Dillan with the power of acting upon men's minds. Or if he was not so himself, he could summon those who were. For the first time a new idea broke. If in this Gorth there was a Lord Rud, might there not also be a Lord Dillan? What would it be like to confront a Lord Dillan who was different? That thought spun slowly through Kincar's mind.

Now, he told himself, he had only to remember that these Star Lords were not those he knew, that he must not be misled by resemblance. And he had as yet to see the proof of Lord Dillan's statement that men could have their counterparts in other worlds.

Time in the dark was not a matter of minutes and hours. It was a thing of cold, and growing hunger, and cramp in his pinioned arms, aches in his bruised body. He squirmed across the floor until his shoulders met a wall, and then, with infinite expenditure of energy, he was able to rise to his feet. Now by movement he could fight the cold, be in better shape to meet the ordeal that no doubt awaited him.

Using the wall as a guide he encircled the chamber. It was bare of any form of furnishing save in one corner where he padded over a heap of musty straw, perhaps the bedding of those unfortunates who had preceded him in its occupancy. He came to the stairs again. And for want of a better seat huddled there until the chill from the stone drove him up again.

How many times he circled, rested, and then circled again, Kincar did not try to count. But he was seated when he felt a vibration in the stone heralding the coming of his jailors. He was up and facing the door when that portal crashed back against the wall, and light flared at him from above, blinding him once more.

"Up on your feet, are you, dragtail?" demanded a voice with that sort of hearty humor that is more sinister than a curse. "Have him forth, you stumble feet, and let his betters see if he's ripe for the skinning—!"

Figures plunged out of the source of the light, hands fastened on him, shoulder and elbow, and he was propelled up the stairs and out into a stone-walled corridor. More stairs, then the light of a fair day, as they issued into a courtyard.

The men who hustled him along were guardsmen of the common sort, with flat, brutal faces, the spark of intelligence low behind their uncaring eyes. Their officer was a huge man. Kincar almost believed him of off-world breed until he saw the Gorthian features and the devil mark between his eyes. He grinned, showing tooth gaps, leaning over Kincar until his foul breath was thick in the younger man's nostrils. One big hand dug deep in Kincar's hair, pulling his head back at a painful angle.

"The mark right enough," remarked the giant. "But you'll find that will not save you here, youngling."

"Do we pin him, Sood?" inquired one of the guards.

The giant loosed his grasp on Kincar and slapped his open palm across the questioner's face, rocking him so that he stumbled against the prisoner.

"Tighten your lip, dirt! He's pinned when Sood says pin and not before. But he'll cry for pinning before we get the irons to him, so he will! Nay, larng scrapings, he goes to the hall; you get him there! You know who is not ever pleased to be kept waiting!"

The man who had been slapped spat red. But he made no protest at his rough disciplining, not even the inarticulate one of a glare at Sood's back as the giant marched ahead. Kincar was pushed on across the courtyard and under a second archway into the living quarters that were officers' territory.

They shuffled under an arch of rough stone into another world. Here was no stone, no native cloth arras as were stretched across the walls of Styr's Hold to keep out cold-season drafts. On either hand the walls were smooth with the sheen of a sword blade. They might have been coated with metal. And over their pale gray surfaces there was a constant dance and play of rainbow color, which appeared, until one focused steadily upon it, to form pictures in an endless and ever changing series of ghostly scenes.

It was totally unlike anything Kincar had ever seen or heard described, and he guessed it was born of the off-world magic of the Star Lords. But he kept his surprise under control. He must appear to be familiar with such if he would carry out his pose as the ex-retainer of another lord in search of a new master.

A curtain of shimmering stuff fronted them. Without any touch from his guards, it parted, drew back against each wall to allow them through. Now they had come into a wide room. Sun flooded it from the roof, filtering through an intricate patterned crystal, which threw more rainbows on the floor. Evenly spaced about were a number of doors, each veiled with the strange curtains, while in the center was a square pit, some benches beside it. On those nearest Kincar, two Gorthians sat stiffly. There was no ease in their manner. They might have been fieldman bidden to eat at a hold lord's table because of some whim of that lord, wary at what would chance should that whim change. They did not turn their heads to look as Sood and the others tramped in but kept their attention upon the man at the other end of the pit, as a novice swordsman watched a master-of-blades during a lesson.

Here Sood, too, was dwarfed for all his giant's brawn, made to dwindle in an odd fashion. He was no longer a roistering bully to be feared, but a servant attendant on a lord of power. He advanced no further than within a foot or two of the occupied benches and stood waiting to be noticed.

The lord of this fortress, he who held in a child's discomfort fighting men and who dwarfed Sood, lounged at ease on a couch removed from the Gorthians by the width of the pit. He was lying full length on the padded surface, his head supported by his crossed arms as he watched something below. And there was no mistaking *his* birthright. This man was of the Star breed.

Hitherto Kincar had seen the off-worlders only in their silver battle dress, simple clothing designed for hard usage. This man wore a robe of some light fabric under which every movement of his muscles was plainly visible. He was as massive as Lord Dillan, but the clean, fine lines of Dillan's body were here blurred as if someone had tried to copy him from the same mold but with no master touch. There was a curve to a jaw line that should be square and sharp, a rounded softness of lip and chin. His hair was the most alien—a dull dark red, thick and straight.

Kincar had time for that appraisal because the Dark Lord was intent upon the pit. Then there came a thin squeaking from that opening, and he laughed, levering up his head to see the better.

"Well done!" He might have been cheering on some warrior duelist. "I win again, Calpar!"

There was a duet of agreement from the two Gorthians. But they were still watching their lord rather than the pit. Now he looked up—to sight Sood's party.

"Ah, Sood—" His voice was rich, almost caressing, only Kincar felt a sensation of cold as if he had walked barebodied into an ice storm. Here was something he had never met before. He had known awe with Lord Dillan, and to a greater degree with the Lady Asgar. With Lord Bardon he had felt the admiration of a warrior in the train of a noted chief. But none had given him that daunting of spirit, that feeling of being less than a larng in their sight. From this man he did not even strike the interest he would give to Vorken—he was less than a well-trained beast.

But that realization was consumed by a growing heat within him, a heat that flamed outward, as the heat of the Tie had eaten inward when it had been so cruelly activated by the Star Lords' magic. Perhaps the men of this Gorth had been beaten long ago into accepting that valuation of themselves—but he had not. Kincar fronted the Dark Lord straightly, striving to keep under control both his aversion and his defiance.

"What have we here, Sood—" The purr lapped across the pit.

"The one who was taken at the hideout of *those*, Lord."

"The one who aided in their escape, aye. Bring forward this hero—"

Kincar was shoved ahead, to the very lip of the pit. But those who pushed him remained a little to the rear, sheltering behind him from their ruler's attention.

"And who may you be?" The Lord addressed Kincar directly.

"I am from the mountains, Lord—Kincar of Styr who was lately Hand to Lord Seemon—" He had chosen the lord who had ruled the captured guard, and hoped it would prove a good choice.

"And why, my good Hand, did you leave the service of Lord Seemon?"

"There was a sword quarrel set upon me, Lord. I killed my man, but he had brothers who took blade oath to meet me one by one—"

Lord Rud laughed. "You are an unlucky man, are you not, Kincar of Styr? First you kill a man with brothers to be active in his favor and then you make a long journey only to meddle in what concerns you not, so you come to an ill fate in U-Sippar. Tell me, Kincar of Styr, why did you befriend those dirt-eaters you met upon the shore?"

"Lord, I knew nothing of them, save that they said they were flying also from a blood feud—"

"*They* said? Ah, but I think that one of them was incapable of saying much, or had he miraculously grown once more a certain important piece of his body which had been stricken from him?"

"The young man said it, Lord," Kincar corrected himself. He knew very well that Lord Rud was playing a game with him, that sooner or later the alien would give an order to finish him.

"So they were flying from blood vengeance were they? Apt enough. But they will discover that one does not fly from some kinds of vengeance. They are within my hand, even as these—"

He made a gesture at the pit, and for the first time Kincar looked down into it. What he saw was a Gorthian scene in miniature—a thread of stream, trees no higher than his tallest finger, clearings he could cover with his palm. Yet water ran, trees and grass grew, and other things moved. A suard the size of a flying beetle grazed on open land. And on a trampled bit of ground lay—

Kincar swallowed. Great was the Star magic—but this! He could not believe what his eyes reported. The inner men of the mountains were manikins, but what were these tiny things? Manlike in form, manlike in their deaths, but surely they were not, had never been living things! Then he knew that his astonishment had betrayed him, for Lord Rud was watching him closely.

"One could almost believe," his silky words came deliberately, "that you had never seen the 'little ones' before, Kincar of Styr. Yet it is in my own knowledge that Lord Seemon has a fine company of such and that pit wars are the leading amusement in his hold. How odd that one of his men should be so ignorant of them! Perhaps we should ask you again, and with greater persuasion, just who you are and what you do in U-Sippar, Kincar of Styr. Not only do you keep very ill company for a loyal Hand, but also your past seems hazy, and that will not do at all. Not at all—"

"Lord, not all the men who serve one of your greatness are admitted to the inner chambers." Kincar seized upon the only argument that might save him. "I was no chieftain, nor a captain, but a young warrior. What amused my betters was none of my affair."

"Your wits are quick enough, that is certain." Lord Rud yawned. "Quick-witted natives are good sport. Sood, we have a puzzle here—"

The giant quivered in his eagerness, as a mord quivers before being signaled to the hunt. "Aye, Lord, shall we have him forth to the pins?"

"Sood, Sood!" The other laughed. "Always impatient. Break a man and then expect answers from the bloody bits. No, Sood, here are quick wits and perhaps something else." Lord Rud paused. His eyes—hard, dark, and yet with a fire in their depths—raked over Kincar. "I wonder, now, I wonder. Could Seemon have made a mistake in the dark?" He chuckled softly, as if nourishing some amusing idea. "Not the pins, Sood—at least not yet. It is a wearying business, this living ever penned within walls. I need amusement. Remove this Kincar but keep him in good condition, excellent condition, Sood. I want him whole of body and mind when I summon him again. Meanwhile, Kincar of Styr, you had best examine your conscience, reckon up the number of times you have twisted the truth to your own profit, for we shall have another time for questions and then I shall have straight answers! Oh, aye, I shall have them, Kincar of Styr, for am I not a god?"

He had a breathing space, if a limited one. Kincar clung to that. Every hour so won was a small victory for him. He presented a problem to Lord Rud, and as long as he continued to interest the bored ruler, so long might he hope for a slender measure of safety.

But Kincar breathed easier when he was out of the rainbow-walled inner chambers into the open day. Sood did not return him to the foul underground cell where he had been pent on his arrival. Rather he was marched up a flight of stairs into a tower room, which, bare as it was, had a crude bed, a table, and a bench, and might have been the quarters of a very junior officer. They loosened his wrist bonds and slapped coarse provisions on the table before they left him. Rubbing his wrists and wincing at the pain of returning circulation in his blue, swollen hands, Kincar crossed to the window to look out upon U-Sippar.

13
ORDEAL BY MORD

Though he was viewing it from an unusual angle, looking down upon those roofs and towers instead of up, still U-Sippar presented the unreal aspect of some city visited in dreams, where the most commonplace is linked with the bizarre. Here were ancient stone buildings, the work of the native Gorthians who had reached for the stars with their towers and sharply slanted rooftrees before the stars came to them with such devastating results. And from that honest stone sprang other structures, excrescences frankly alien to this earth. There were not many of these, only enough to distort the general outline of U-Sippar into something faintly corrupt and debased.

The fortress was part of it, a monstrous hybrid crouched upon an artificial rise, so that its shadow moved menacingly across the packed houses below with the climbing and setting of the sun. Half of it was of the stone, the rest of it new. And that portion flashed metallic, cold, smooth, like a sword pointed to sky.

Kincar could count four—no—five similar structures in U-Sippar. They could not all be dwelling places of Lord Rud. But surely each housed some measure of Star magic. The one farthest from him was planted so that sea waves washed about its foot. Though there were ships in the harbor, anchored there for the cold season when no trained mariner attempted passage into the freakish winds, none were tied up near the tower, and what purpose it might serve was beyond Kincar's powers of speculation.

Having seen U-Sippar, or as much of that city as could be viewed through a window slit, he set about the more urgent business of seeking a way out, not only of that room, but of the fortress itself. Unless he could shrink to less than Vorken's size—and possess her wings into the bargain he could not attempt that window. And a single testing told him that the door was secured from the outside. An examination of the bed made it plain that bare hands could not rip loose any part of it for an improvised weapon, and the same was true of table and bench. He had been stripped by his captors of his outer ring-sewn jerkin and his belt, so even the empty sheaths of his weapons were gone. And since he was no hero of the song-smith's creation, he could not blast his way out with a well-tried spell.

But at least he could eat. And coming back to the table Kincar did just that. The fare was coarse, rations such as were given to the rank and file of guardsmen. But it was not prison fare, and he finished it to the last crumb of soggy milt-bread, the last swallow of sour frangal juice. Then he threw himself on the bed and tried to prove his right to Lord Rud's charge of quick wits.

Lord Rud! Was this the man his father had been in that alternate Gorth? Strange— His hands folded over the comforting bulge of the Tie. Had a change in history also wrought a change in a man's nature, the way Lord Dillan insisted that it would? This Lord Rud could not be the man he had heard extolled in the hold. This ruler was corruption, evil power, fear and death; the odor of his character was an evil smell throughout his stronghold.

Kincar wondered what would happen if the truth were made plain to this Dark One. And in the same instant he knew that no act, no betrayal, would be more fatal. No matter what chanced with Kincar of Styr—as long as he could, he must lock lips and mind alike against telling what he knew.

Had Murren and the boy escaped? Cim was better than any of the larngs he had seen in the troop that had captured him. And Murren's desperate dash might just have broken through the circle with enough force to give them the necessary start, since Cim had had a period of rest and was fairly fresh, and the troop mounts were weary at the end of a long day. That escape had been wholly Murren's improvisation—the boy would not have deserted another to the Hands of Lord Rud, though, because he bore the mark he did, the fugitives might have believed Kincar was in no great danger. What was the crime held against those two? From the bits he could piece together, it was enough to stir up all U-Sippar. He wished that they could have been picked up earlier by men from the hold.

So, in place of planning, his thoughts drifted from place to place, until, at last, the needs of his body could no longer be denied and he slept, while outside the sky over U-Sippar darkened into night and it seemed that Kincar of Styr was forgotten by his guards.

He was aroused by a cry so familiar that he lay blinking at the roof overhead, hazy as to where he was, certain for the space of an instant or two that he lay on his pallet within Styr's walls. That shriek, ear-torturing, came from the hatchery on the watchtower, where Vorken was doubtless exerting her authority over some rebel. Vorken was ruler of the Styr hatchery; let any other mord challenge her at its peril.

Vorken! Kincar sat up as he remembered. Vorken was gone and Styr, too, was farther away than if the whole of Gorth's sea lay between him and its towers! There was a square patch of sun on the floor of his prison. It must be hours late into the morning. And he had been visited during sleep, for a jug and a plate, both filled, stood on the table. Apparently, if Lord Rud had not yet made up his mind concerning Kincar's disposal, his men were still under orders to treat their captive well.

Kincar ate as a duty. There was no reason to believe that such coddling of a prisoner would continue, and he'd best take rations while they were still coming. It was again fare of the most common sort, but it was filling and designed to satisfy men who were ready for a spear-festing.

While he munched away, he twice more heard the challenge call of a mord. But his window gave him no sight of any. The hatchery might be at the crown of the same tower in which he was locked, but mords always sought the heights when they took wing. That cry set him to a restless pacing, and, as time passed with a bar of sun creeping from crack to crack across the rough slabs of the floor, his impatience grew.

There was no doubt at all the Lord Rud planned some unpleasantness for him. And, knowing so little of U-Sippar, of this fortress, there was very little he could do on his own behalf. He would be as a child in Sood's paws, and the giant would be very pleased for a chance to subdue him physically. As to matching wits—who could match wits with the Star men?

The shaft of sun crawled on, disappeared. Kincar was by the window again, studying his knife-edge view of the city, when the outer bar of the door was drawn. He faced Sood and the two who had brought him there the previous day.

"Have him out!" Sood bade his underlings with the loftiness of a Star Lord, or his own interpretation of such. And he stood aside sucking his teeth while the other two roughly rebound Kincar's wrists and gave him a shove doorwards as a reminder to move.

When he would have passed Sood, the giant put out a hand and held him. Fingers bit into flesh and muscle as Sood pawed at him, as a man might examine a larng for sale. And from that grip there was no wrenching away.

"There's good meat on him," Sood remarked. "The sky devils will not pick bare bones after all."

His two followers laughed nervously, as if it were very necessary to keep their officer in a good humor. But neither of them ventured any comment upon Sood's observation.

They went down the stairs and crossed the court. As they went, the majority of the men in sight fell in behind. And they did not reenter the inner section of the fortress but trudged on through another gate and down a road, past three encircling walls with watch-towers and ramparts.

U-Sippar's fortress had not been built in the center of the town but straddled the narrow neck of land that extended into the sea bay from the main continent. Apparently those who had first planned the city's defenses had had nothing to fear from the ocean, but wanted a sturdy barrier between their homes and the interior. Now the party went inland, from the fringes of the town to a wide stretch of open field.

There was snow here, but the drifts had been leveled by the wind. And it was open for the maneuvering of mounted troops or for the staging of a spectacle. Kincar suspected that it was to be the latter use now. There was a gathering of Gorthians about the edges of that expanse, with mounted guards to keep a large center portion free.

As the party with the prisoner approached from the road, there was another arrival. Out from the upper parts of the fortress shot a flying thing. It had no wings, it was not living, but some magic kept it aloft, hovering more than a man's height—a Star Lord's height—

overhead. It circled, and as it passed over the natives, they fell face down on the ground. Then it swept up to confront Kincar and his guards. Lord Rud sat in one of the seats upon it and in the other—

Kincar had been warned—but until that moment he had not truly believed! That was Lord Dillan! But not, he told himself fiercely, not the Lord Dillan of the hold. *This* world's Lord Dillan. If he had not been prepared, he would have betrayed himself in that moment. Lord Rud was smiling down at him, and that smile, gay, charming, was colder than the air in which their breath smoked blue.

"A fit object lesson, brother," Lord Rud said to his companion.

But Lord Dillan leaned forward in his seat to study Kincar with a searching intensity. He spoke, his deep voice a contrast to Lord Rud's.

"He is no Hand."

"He bears their mark—"

"Then it is no proper mark. You!" Lord Dillan spoke to Sood, at the same time tossing to the giant a small box he had taken from his belt pouch. "Use that upon a piece of cloth and see if you can rub away that mark."

Sood ripped loose an end of Kincar's shirt and, dipping it into the paste in the box, scrubbed away with vicious jabs at the mark on the prisoner's forehead. The brand sign, which had resisted the rain and withstood all inadvertent touching since the Lady Asgar had set it on him, yielded. Sood's astonishment became triumph, and Lord Dillan—this Lord Dillan—nodded in satisfaction.

"As I told you, brother, this is no man of ours. Best keep him for questioning. If someone has dared to plant the mark, they will dare other things. And the fault which you hold against him is relatively minor. What if he was found in the company of escaping slaves—do not all outlaws tend to herd together, until we gather them up? Or was there something about these particular slaves?"

He was eying his fellow lord sharply. And there was a dull flush on Lord Rud's face. He flung up his head.

"You rule in Yarth, brother, I in U-Sippar. Nor did I ask you hither; this visit was of your own planning. In another man's lordship one does not ask questions concerning his dealing of justice. This is an outlaw, come into our land to seek out knowledge to aid that rabble which others seem unable to beat out of their mountain holes. I will deal with him so that there will be few willing to follow him. Sood, make ready!"

Under his control the flier bounded higher into the air, so that Lord Dillan must clutch at his seat to keep erect, and then swerved to one side to hover.

However, Kincar had no attention to spare for the actions of Lord Rud and his brother, for the guards were on him, stripping away his clothing. His jerkin was slashed so that it could be drawn off without unpinioning his arms, and the shirt ripped in shreds to follow. But the man who tore at that paused, his eyes round and questioning, and he drew back hastily.

Sood, too, had sighted the talisman on Kincar's breast. The big man stood, his mouth working curiously, as if he must suddenly have a double supply of air for laboring lungs, and a dull stain crept up his thick throat to darken his weathered cheeks. These men wore a brand that divorced them utterly from the Tie, but the awe of that talisman held them as much, if not more, than it would a true believer. Perhaps, Kincar had a flash of insight then, perhaps it was because they had ritually denied all that the Tie represented that it now possessed the greater power over them.

The giant was tough-fibered, far more so than the man who had pulled off the last of Kincar's shirt, for that guard's retreat turned into panic flight. He threw the rag as he was holding from him as he ran blindly down the field.

His comrade was not quite so moved, though he took his hands from the prisoner—Kincar might have been a fire coal—and shuffled back, his terrified eyes watching the captive as if he expected the latter to assume some monstrous guise. And he cried out as Sood's hand came up slowly, his fingers reaching to pluck away that round stone.

Sood had his brand of courage. He had to have an extra measure of self-confidence to hold his leadership among the bullies of U-Sippar's fortress. It was not by size and weight of arm alone that he had won his under-officership in Lord Rud's service. Now he forced himself to a task not one Gorthian in a hundred—in a thousand—would have had the will power, the hardened fiber, to attempt. Wearing that mark, proclaiming himself so to be what he was, yet he was prepared to set hand upon the Tie. From a barracks bully he was growing to a far more dangerous man.

"By Lor, by Loi, by Lys," Kincar said, "think what you do, Sood."

The gentle warmth that had answered his invocation of the Names told him that the stone was alive. What it might do to a branded one he could not guess, for to his knowledge such a happening had never occurred in the Gorth of his birth.

There were oily drops gathering along the edge of Sood's helm; his mouth was twisted into a skull's grin of tortured resolve. His fingers came closer. About the two there was a great silence. The wind had died; there was not even the plop of a larng's foot in the snow. The men of U-Sippar were frozen by something other than the cold of the season.

Sood made his last effort. He clutched at the stone, tugging at it so Kincar was dragged forward, the chain cutting into his neck. But that chain did not break, and the stone fell back against Kincar's skin, a blot of searing fire, to cool instantly.

Rud's under-officer stood still, his hand outstretched, the fingers bent as if they still held the Tie. For a second longer than normal time he stood so; then, holding that hand before him, he began to roar with pain and the terror of a wounded beast, for the fingers were shriveled, blackened—it was no longer a human hand. Being Sood, he was moved to kill as he suffered. His left hand brought out a knife clumsily; he stabbed blindly with tears of pain blurring his sight.

The sting of a slash crossed Kincar's shoulder; then the point of the blade caught in the Tie. Sood screamed this time, a high, thin sound, too high and thin to issue naturally from that thick throat. The knife fell from a hand that could no longer hold it, and the giant swayed back and forth on his feet, shaking his head, his hands before him—the one shriveled and black, the other red as if scalded.

Wounded he might be, but the blind hatred of the thing—of the man who wore the thing—that had blasted him, possessed all his senses. Kincar, his hands bound so that he could move only stiffly, was forced into a weird circling dance as the giant lurched after him to accomplish by weight alone what he had not been able to do with steel. Sood might lack the use of his hands, but to his slighter opponent he was still formidable.

The fate of the giant must have bewildered the rest of the guard. None of them moved to interfere with the two on the field. Kincar was so intent upon keeping away from the other that he heard a whistle only as a distant sound without meaning.

But the answer to that whistle had a great deal of meaning for both circling men. Lord Rud, baffled by the happenings of the past moments, but in no mind to lose control, had chosen ruthlessly to sacrifice the crippled Sood in company with this captive who knew too much. Where it had been planned that one naked prisoner would be exposed to certain death, two men moved. But the death was already in the air, and it would strike. Perhaps it would be all to the good. Sood was something of a legend in U-Sippar and should he be struck by a supernatural vengeance and the tale of it spread, it would put the countryside aflame. Let him die quickly, by a familiar means, and all that went before could be forgotten.

Kincar had not understood his fate at the whistle, but seconds later he knew it well. There was no mistaking the cry of a mord sighting meat—alive and moving meat—but yet meat for a hungry belly. And he guessed the type of death to which he had been condemned. Had his arms been free, had he a sword in his hands, he could have delayed that death—for a short space. But he could not have kept it away long. Against one well-trained mord an armed man, providing he was mounted and had a cloak, had a bare chance. Against a full hatch of them, that mounted warrior was lost, picked to the bones before blood had time enough to flow to the ground.

Sood was deaf, blind, unheeding of everything but Kincar. All the pain and shock of his hurts had crystallized into the urge to kill. He moved ponderously with deadly purpose. But, because he tried to use his hands time and time again, Kincar managed to elude his hold. The giant cried aloud, a wordless noise that was half plaint from pain, half demented rage at his inability to come to grips with his prey.

Perhaps it was that sound that drew the mords to him first. By rights the scent of the blood welling from the cut on Kincar's shoulder should have brought them down upon the younger man. However, the rushing wings centered on Sood, and they struck.

The giant's cry welled into a roar once more as, still only half aware of his peril, he beat at the swarming flesh-eaters. First he tried only to brush them aside so that he might attack Kincar. Then some spark of self-preservation awoke, and he flailed his arms vainly, his face already a gory mask.

Kincar, backing away from that horror, caught his boot heel on a turf and went down. His fall attracted several of the wheeling mords, and they swooped upon him. Claws bit into his upper arm, a beak stabbed at his eyes, and he could not restrain the scream torn out by his repulsion and fear.

But that beak did not strike him; the claws were sharp but they did not open gashes. There was the hiss of an aroused and angry mord, and the one on his body struck upward with open bill at another come to dispute her perch.

"Vorken!"

She chirruped in answer to her name. Vorken who had sought her kind in the mating season had found them—in the fortress hatchery of U-Sippar! And, knowing Vorken, Kincar could also believe that during her stay there she had with the greatest possible speed assumed rulership of the perches. Now it was only necessary for Cim to come trotting onto the field to make this truly an adventure of a song-smith's devising.

Only it was not Cim who came to take him away from the murderous, horrible heap of twisting, fighting mords. It was the flier of the Dark Lords. And the false Lord Dillan with his own hands dragged Kincar onto its platform before it flew back to the fortress.

14
THE PLACE OF TOWERS

There was the crackle of speech in the alien tongue of the Star Lords. Kincar, seemingly forgotten for the moment, pulled himself up against a pillar, while Vorken chuckled throatily and waddled in a half circle about his feet, very proud of herself.

The wrangle continued. Lord Rud sat on a bench spitting out angry answers to a stream of questions Lord Dillan shot at him as he paced up and down that end of the hall, sometimes bringing his hands together with a sharp clap to emphasize a point. At first Kincar was so bemused by the wonder of his own escape from a particularly grisly death that he did not speculate as to why he had been lifted from the field. Now, from the gestures, from the sullen attitude of Lord Rud, the aroused state of this Lord Dillan, he guessed that his rescue had been made against Rud's will.

And this was borne out as the false Lord Dillan came striding away from his brother to stand before Kincar, looking him up and down.

"You are a priest of demons, fellow?"

Kincar shook his head. "I have not followed the Threefold Way," he replied as he would in his own Gorth.

That face—he knew every line of it, had believed that he could recognize every expression its muscles could shape! Yet to look upon it and know that the man who wore it was not the one to whom he had given his allegiance was a mind-wrenching thing, much harder than he had imagined such a meeting could be.

"So—we have not yet stamped out *that* foolishness!" Lord Dillan whirled and shouted a stream of angry words at Lord Rud. The other did not register only sullen denial this time. He walked toward them alertly.

"This one is from the mountains," he said in the Gorthian speech. "Look closely, Dillan. Has he the appearance of a lowlander? Without a doubt a creeper from some one of those outlaw pockets, trying to spy upon his betters. He should have been left as mord food—"

"Mord food, you fool!" Lord Dillan's exasperation was so open that Kincar looked to see him strike the other. "After what he did to Sood in the face of all this city? We have gone to great trouble to rout out this pestilent worship. Do you not see that the tale of what happened out there is going to spread and grow with the telling? Within days we shall have secret altars sprouting up again, spells being mouthed against us, all the other things to tie rebels together! You cannot erase from a thousand minds the manner of Sood's death. No, this one must be handled by the council. We must have out of him every scrap of knowledge, and then he must be reduced to groveling slavery before the eyes of his own kind. Abject life, not a martyr's death—can't you see the sense of that? Or, Rud, is it—" His speech slipped once more into the off-world language, and brother glared blackly at brother.

"We shall take him ourselves," Dillan stated. "We want no more natives seeing what was not meant for their eyes, hearing things certainly not intended for their ears. Send a message that we are coming by flier—"

Lord Rud's jaw jutted forward. "You are mighty free with your orders in another man's hold, Dillan. Suppose I do not choose to leave U-Sippar at this moment. As you pointed out, that scene on the field will doubtless provide fuel for rebellion. And my place is here to stamp such fires to ashes before they can spread."

"Well enough. Remain and put out your fires, though if U-Sippar was under proper control, I should think there was no need for such careful wardenship." Lord Dillan smiled slyly. "I shall take the prisoner in for questioning—"

It was very plain that that was not to Lord Rud's taste either.

"He is my prisoner, taken by my men."

"True enough. But you did not assess his importance until it was driven home to you. And your reluctance now to turn him over to the authorities argues that you may have some hidden reason to wish him quickly dead." Lord Dillan fell to studying Kincar once more. "What is this great secret, fellow, for which your lips must be permanently sealed? I wonder—" His hand closed about Kincar's upper arm, bringing the younger man up to stand under a clear shaft of light. He eyed him with an intensity that had something deadly and malignant in it.

"The Great Law, Rud," Dillan spoke very softly. "I wonder how many times it has been broken and by whom among us. The Great Law— Usually the fruits of its breaking can be early detected. But perhaps now and again such cannot. Who are you, fellow?"

"Kincar of Styr—"

"Kincar of Styr," the other repeated. "Now that can mean anything at all. What is Styr, and where does it lie? Should it not rather be Kincar s'Rud?"

He had guessed the truth, but in the wrong way. Perhaps some shade of surprise in Kincar's eyes convinced his questioner he was on the right track, for Lord Dillan laughed softly.

"Another matter for the council to inquire into—"

Lord Rud's face was a mask of rage. "For that you shall answer to me, Dillan, even though we be brothers! He is not of my fathering, and you cannot pin law-breaking on me! I have enemies enough, perhaps of close kin"—he eyed his brother hotly—"who would be willing to set up a tool, well coached, to drag me into trouble by such a story. Look to yourself, Dillan, on the day, in that hour, when you bring such an accusation before the council!"

"In any event, he needs be shaken free of all information. And the sooner the better. It is to your own advantage, Rud, that he tells the full and complete truth before all of us. If he is not the fruit of law-breaking, let us be sure of that and speedily."

As if to draw his brother away from a dangerous line of investigation, Lord Rud asked, "But why did Sood suffer? Let us have a closer look at that thing he is wearing—"

He reached for the Tie. Kincar pulled back, the only defensive movement he could make. But before those fingers closed upon the stone, Lord Dillan had slapped down that questing hand.

"If you value your skin, you'll leave that alone!" he warned.

"Do you think that I'll be burnt as was Sood? Why—I'm no ignorant native—"

"Sood's fate was aggravated because he wore the mark," Lord Dillan explained almost absently. "But we have no inkling as to the power of these things or how they can be used against alien bodies. And until we do know more, it is wisest not to meddle. I have only seen one before, and that was just for an instant before its destruction by the witch doctor who had been wearing it. We'd overrun his shrine at night and caught him unawares. We'll have plenty of time to deal with this—and its wearer—when we get them to the towers. And that is where we should go at once."

They were talking, Kincar thought bitterly, as if he had no identity or will of his own except as a possession of theirs—which, he was forced to admit bleakly, was at that moment the exact truth. The only concession his captors made to the fact that he was flesh and blood was to throw a cloak over his half-bare body after they had put him aboard the flier, to lie, bound wrist and ankle, by their feet.

Vorken had protested such handling, and, for an instant or two, it appeared that she would be destroyed for her impudence. Then the false Lord Dillan decided that her link with Kincar must be thoroughly explored. She was muffled in another cloak and bundled in beside Kincar, where her constant tries for freedom kept the improvised bag bumping up and down.

To fly through the air was a terrifying experience. Kincar had ranged the mountain heights since he had been large enough to keep his seat on a larng pad and follow Wurd hunting, in the years before the old lord of Styr had been reduced to level country riding and at last to his bed. And Wurd's acquaintance with sheer ledges, far drops, cliff edges had been wide. But to stand with one's boots planted on solid rock and look out upon nothingness was far different, Kincar discovered, than to rise into that nothingness knowing that under one was only a flat platform of no great thickness.

He fought his panic, that picture his imagination kept in the forepart of his mind of the platform dissolving, of his helpless body turning over and over as it fell to the ground below. How had the Star men been able to travel the sky and the depths of space? Or were they alien to this fear he knew? He wriggled about, but all he could see of the two were their feet. The Star Lords of his own

Gorth had had no such fliers. However, they might well accept such traveling as natural.

There was a windbreak on the front of the platform, and he was lying behind the control seats. Yet the chill of that journey bit deep, and the cloak was but small protection. As the minutes passed, Kincar's panic subsided, and it seemed to him that from the Tie spread a gentle heat to banish the worst of the cold. He had been afraid on the field when the mord hatch had turned their attention to him, but that was an honest fear to be fully understood. Now he knew a queer apprehension, the same quiver of nerves and tenseness of muscles that a swordsman knows before the command to charge is given at a spear-festing. He tried to school himself with the knowledge that for him there would probably be no return from this flight.

Against Gorthian captivity a man could plan, foresee. But among the Star Lords what chance had he? There was but one thing—Sood's amazing experience with the Tie and this Lord Dillan's wariness of that same token. A slim advantage—perhaps. He had listened to talk in the mountain hold. There were unseen powers—"energies" the Lord Dillan he followed called them. Some of these energies had activated the between-worlds gates through which they had come into this Gorth. And during that passage the Tie had also proved to be a conductor of energy, as Kincar could prove by a scar he would carry until he passed into the Forest.

The Tie, in addition, might have its own "energies," which would be inimical to the aliens. That night in the forgotten shrine, the talisman had been recharged with the power native to it. It must carry a full supply. If he only knew more of its potentialities! But he had had no desire to follow the Threefold Way, to train as a Man of Power—for he had understood that he could not have the Way and Styr together and his heart had lain with Styr. So all he had to guide him were the mystical invocations of any believer, the legends and half-whispers. Had he been adept with the Tie, what might he not have accomplished—what could he not do?

The flier swooped, and Kincar fought sickness from the resulting flare of panic. Was it falling, coming apart to crash them to the earth?

But the swift descent slowed. Walls flowed up to cut off the light. They might be dropping down the mouth of a well. The flier came to a stop with less force than that with which a foot is set upon the floor, and both Star men arose. They had reached their destination.

Lord Rud made no move toward the captive. It seemed that he disliked laying hand upon Kincar. But Lord Dillan pulled the half-Gorthian up, cut the thongs about his ankles and, surprisingly enough, those about his wrists also. His arms fell heavily to his sides, his hands swollen. Lord Dillan picked up the bag containing Vorken and thrust it at him. He caught it clumsily, making a silent resolve not to display any sign of the intense pain any movement of hands or arms cost him.

"You will walk quietly where you are told." Lord Dillan spoke with the exactitude of one giving orders to a slow-witted child. "For if you do not, you shall be burned with this force stick." He had taken from his belt a rod not unlike the one Kincar had used in suard-hunting. "It will not kill, but the pain will be worse than death by mord, and you shall never be free of it. Do you understand?"

Kincar nodded. He could believe that the Dark One meant exactly what he said and uttered no vain bluff. Could he hope for a speedy death if he attempted flight? Would he flee if that were the end? As long as a man was alive, he could nourish hope, and Kincar had not yet reached the point where he would try for death as a hunter tries for an easy thrust at his prey. Carrying Vorken, he obediently followed Lord Rud out of the chamber where the flier rested, down a sideway, while behind tramped Lord Dillan, weapon in hand.

The living quarters of the fortress at U-Sippar had been of alien workmanship and materials. The narrow passage in which they now walked was as unlike that as *that* had been from the Gorthian architecture upon which it had been based. Here were no flitting rainbow colors, only an even sheen of gray, which, as he brushed against it, gave to Kincar the feel of metal. And the passage ended after a few feet in a stair ascending in a spiral, the steps no wider than a ladder's treads. Kincar grasped the guard rail, Vorken in the crook of his left arm. He kept his eyes resolutely on the legs of Lord Rud going up and up, refusing to yield to any temptation to look down into the dizzy well beneath them.

They passed through a series of levels from which ran other passages, emerging from the floor of such a level to climb again through its roof. Kincar could not even speculate upon the nature of the building in which so unusual a staircase formed the core. On the third such level Lord Rud stood away from the stair, turning into a side corridor, and Kincar went after him. So far they might have been in a deserted building. Though the noise of their climbing feet echoed hollowly up and down that well, there had been no other sound to break the quiet, no sign of any guardsman or servant on duty. And there was a queer, indefinable odor—not the dank emanation of the hold walls, of U-Sippar's fortress, but in its way as redolent of a remote past, of something long closed against the freshness of wind and cleansing sunlight.

The passage into which Rud had turned was hardly more than a good stride long. He set his palm flat upon a closed door, and under that touch it rolled back into the wall so that they might enter an odd chamber. It was a half circle, a curved wall ending in a straight one—the shape of a strung bow, the door being in the straight wall. Spaced at intervals along the curved surface were round windows covered with a clear substance strange to Kincar.

A padded bench ran along the wall under the level of the windows, and there was an equally padded covering on the floor and over the walls. Otherwise the room was bare of either inhabitants or furnishings. Lord Rud glanced around and then stepped aside to allow Kincar to enter. When the Gorthian had passed through the door, he went out and the portal closed, leaving Kincar alone.

He pulled loose the covering about Vorken and evaded the exasperated snap of her bill, loosing her on the bench where she waddled along with her queer rolling gait, her claws puncturing its padding and having to be pulled out laboriously at every step. Kincar knelt on the same surface to look from one of the windows.

No U-Sippar lay without. The structure he could survey was totally unlike anything he had seen on either Gorth. Beyond were several towers, not the square stone ones he had known all his life. Fashioned of metal, they caught the sun and reflected its beams in a blaze of fire. All were exactly alike, round with pointed tips that stood tall in the sky. Kincar surmised that a similar building harbored him. Linking all of them together—by pressing tight to the transparent pane he could just make them out—were a series of walls—walls thick enough to contain corridors or rooms. But those were of the native stone. Metal towers—pointed—

Kincar's swollen hands closed upon the edge of the window until he felt the pain of that grip. Not towers—no, not towers. Ships! The sky ships of the Star men—here forever earthbound, built into a weird fortress. He had heard them described too many times by men who had visited Terranna on his own Gorth not to recognize them. Was this the Terranna of this Gorth? It could be nothing less than the heart of the Dark Ones' holdings.

On his own Gorth those ships had gone forth again—out to the stars. Here that must be impossible. They had been anchored to the earth. They had rooted their ships, determined to possess Gorth for all time.

As he studied that strange mating of ship and stone, Kincar could spot no signs of life. Nothing moved along those walls, showed at any of the round ports that now served as windows. And there was a sense of long absence of tenantry about it all. A storehouse—Kincar could not have told why that particular thought took possession of him nor why the conviction grew that he was right. This must be a storehouse for the aliens. As that it would be well guarded, if not by warriors, then by the magic the Star men controlled. A race who flew through the air without wonder would have weapons mightier than any sword swung by a Hand to protect their secret place.

The age-old thirst that arises in any man at the thought of treasure tempted Kincar. This whole city, fortress, whatever it was, must be thinly populated. If he could get free of his present lodging and explore—! But the door was sealed tightly. Vorken hissed from the bench. She was uneasy in this closed room as she had never been in the hold. Kincar went from one window to another. Three merely showed him other aspects of the tower-ship building, but the other two gave him a view of the countryside.

There were no trees, but odd twisted rocks. Some, with a puff crown of snow, were vaguely familiar. He had certainly seen their like before. Then the vivid memory of their ride through the wasteland desert to the first gate returned. There were no signs of vegetation here, unless its withered remnants lay under the snow. But in the distance was the bluish line of hills, the mark of mountains. And seeing those, Kincar's hopes rose illogically.

Vorken's head bumped against him. She raised a forefoot to scrape his arm and draw his attention. Though none of his race had ever believed the mords lacked intelligence, it was generally conceded that their mental mazes were so alien to that of mankind that communication between the two species was strictly limited to the recognition of a few simple suggestions, mostly dealing with food and hunting. But it was plain that now Vorken was trying to convey something in her own way. And he did what otherwise he would have hesitated to try, since mords were notoriously averse to handling. He sat down on the bench and lifted her to his knees.

She complained with a hiss or two. Then she squatted, her red eyes fastened upon his as if she would force upon him some message. She flapped her wings and mouthed the shrill whistle she gave when sighting game.

Kincar's preoccupation with Vorken was broken by the sudden heat on his breast. The Tie was glowing. Somewhere within the ship-tower an energy was being loosed to which that highly sensitive talisman responded. He hesitated. Should he take it off lest he risk a bad burn and incapacitate himself—or should he continue to wear it?

To his overwhelming surprise, Vorken stretched her skinny neck and butted her head against him, directly over the Tie, before he could fend her away. She pressed tightly to it, lifting her claws in warning when he would have moved her, giving voice to the guttural battle croaks of her kind.

The warmth of the Tie increased as the mord pressed it tightly against him. But that did not appear to disconcert Vorken. Her battle cries stopped. Now she chuckled, the little sound she made when she was very content with her world. And Kincar himself felt relaxed, confident, fast losing his awe of both surroundings and captors.

15
TRIAL OF STRENGTHS

That sense of well-being persisted. Vorken's beak gaped in a yawn. Her eyes closed as she huddled close, her grotesque head still resting against him. But Kincar felt far from sleepy. Instead he was alert mentally and physically, as he had never been before that he could remember. The feeling that there was no task beyond his accomplishing grew. Was this how the full blood of the Star breed lived? It must be! This supreme confidence in one's self, the certainty that no difficulty was too great—

Kincar laughed softly. And something in that sound struck below the surface of his present well-being, brought a tinge of doubt. Perhaps because of the Tie he was doubly alert to any hint of danger. Did that emotion, the self-confidence, stem from the energy in the talisman, or was it more magic of an alien sort? It would be very easy to work upon a man's mind—if you had the Star resources—to give him an elevated belief in his own powers until he was rendered careless. So very easy.

There was one way of testing that. Kincar lifted the Tie by its chain, slipped the chain over his head, and put down the stone at a short distance from him on the bench. The warmth on his flesh was gone. Vorken stirred. Her head arose as she regarded Kincar with an open question. But he was too preoccupied to watch the mord.

Pressing in upon him, with the force of a blow from a giant's fist, was an overwhelming and devastating panic, a fear so abject and complete that he dared not move, could only get air into his cramped and aching lungs in short gasps. His hands were wet and slippery, his mouth dry, a sickness ate him up inwardly. In all his life he had never known such terror. It was crushing all identity from him, turning him from Kincar into a mindless, whimpering *thing!* And the worst of it was that he could not put name to the reason for that fear. It was inside him, not from without, and it was filling all of his burnt-out body shell—

Vorken squalled, a scream that tore at his ears. Then the mord struck, raking him with her claws. The pain of her attack broke the spell momentarily. He made a supreme effort, and by its chain drew the Tie back into his hands. In those sweating palms he cupped it tight as Vorken ripped at him. But once he had it, the panic was gone, and when the chain was again over his head, the Tie resting in its old place, he sat weak and shaken, but whole and sane once more—so whole and sane he could not quite believe in what had struck him as viciously as the mord.

Blood trickled from the scratches Vorken had given him. Luckily she had not torn deeply. Now she crouched once more on his knees, turning her head from side to side, giving voice to a whimpering complaint as one of her punishing forefeet raised to the Tie. It was that talisman that had saved them both from utter madness—the why and wherefore of that deliverance being more than Kincar could understand. He could only accept rescue with gratitude.

Kincar had left Styr with no more training than any youth who could confidently aspire to the lordship of a holding, and a small, mountain holding at that. He had ridden away under the shock of the abrupt revelation of his half-blood, unable to quite accept that heritage. Wurd's secret gift of the Tie, with all that meant, had been an additional push along a new path of life. His painful experience at the gates, and his acceptance thereafter by Lord Dillan and the Lady Asgar as one who had rightful guardianship of a power they respected, had tempered him yet more. Perhaps his volunteering for the expedition into the lowlands had been born of a spirit of adventure, rooted in the quality that sent any young warrior to a spear-festing. But with it had gone the knowledge that he alone of the hold was fitted for that journey—

What had happened that night in the forest shrine he did not understand. He was no adept to be able to recall the work of the Three. But now he believed that he had ridden away from there subtly altered from the Kincar who had taken shelter. This last ordeal might be another milepost on his road. He would not be as the Star Lords, nor as the ruler of Styr that he might have been had Jord not taken from him that future—but a person he was not yet able to recognize.

Kincar was sure he was no mystic, no seeker of visions, or wielder of strange powers. What he *was*—now—he did not know. Nor did he have the time to become acquainted. It was better to accept the ancient beliefs of his people—his mother's people—and think that he was a tool, mayhap a weapon, for the use of the Three, that all he did was in Their service.

There was a security in that belief. And just now more than anything else he desired security, to trust in something outside his own shaken mind and body.

He had been right in his surmise that he would be allowed scant time for self-examination. The door of the chamber rolled back into the wall. Vorken hissed, flapped her wings, and would have taken to the air in attack had not Kincar, fearing for her life, made a hasty grab for her feet.

Lord Dillan stood there. He did not speak at once, but, though he did not display surprise by any sign readable to Kincar, the latter thought his alertness astonished the other.

"Slave—" The harsh grate of the Star Lord's voice was meant to sting, as the whips of the Hands had stung their miserable captives.

Kincar stared as steadily back. Did the Dark One expect from him a cringing plea for nonexistent mercy?

Now the wand of power was in Dillan's hands as he spoke again.

"We have underestimated you it seems, fellow!"

"It appears that you did, Lord." The words came to Kincar as if someone else who stood apart and watched this scene selected them for his saying.

"Rud's offspring in truth!" Lord Dillan laughed. "Only our own kin could stand up against a conditioner set at that level. Let him try to deny this to the council. Come—you!"

He gestured and Kincar went. Vorken had struggled free of his grip and now balanced on his shoulder, a process made painful by her claws. Yet he was glad to have her with him, a steadying reminder of that other Gorth where a man could not be so beset by magic.

"Up!" The single word set him climbing once more, up the ladder spiral of the stairway. On the next level they came upon something he had not sighted from the windows. Connecting one ship with another, strung far above the ground, was an aerial bridge—temporary, Kincar judged, for so light-weight a creation could not survive the first real windstorm.

But frail as it was, it was also now their road. Kincar clung with his full strength to the hand rope, some of the fear he had known on the flying platform sweeping back. To stop at all, he guessed, would be fatal. So he made the crossing, step by step, his attention all for the port door ahead.

He was within a foot of two of that door when he remembered Vorken. He had no way of escape—that he could see now—from the towers, not with the armed Lord Dillan ready to blast him. But perhaps Vorken could be saved. Still holding to the guide rope with his left hand, he half turned, flicking out with his cloak, at the same time giving the hunter's call for a sky search.

Was it by luck alone that the edge of the cloak entangled with the Star weapon? He had been well trained in the swordsman's art of using the enveloping fabric to bewilder and disarm an opponent, but he had never attempted such a throw under these adverse circumstances. Skill or luck, he engaged the rod until Vorken was up and away, rising cannily not in her usual spirals but headed in an arrow's flight for the distant hills.

Oddly enough, Lord Dillan made no effort at retaliation. He loosened the cloak, and it went flapping down into the chasm below them, where Kincar dared not look. He had not been lucky or skillful enough to have dragged the weapon from the other, and now it was centered upon him.

"Go on," Lord Dillan ordered, and Kincar, sure of Vorken's escape and treasuring that small triumph, went ahead, passing through the port into the second of the Star ship towers.

Two more of the Star Lords awaited him there—but neither were doubles of those he had known in the hold. To be faced by a Lord Frans, a Lord Bardon, a Lord Jon who were not what they appeared would have added to his burden at that moment. These men were all younger than Lord Dillan, if he could judge the age of the Star breed rightly, and both looked soft, lacking that alertness of mind and body his captor possessed—traces of which Lord Rud had displayed. They had that inborn arrogance that comes not from the authority of a man who has rightfully held leadership over his fellows through innate traits of character, but that which is based instead upon never having one's will disputed, and having absolute power over other intelligent beings by birthright alone.

Neither concealed his amazement at Kincar, one asking Lord Dillan a question in their tongue. He snapped an impatient answer and motioned them on.

"Follow!" he told Kincar tersely.

They were about to descend another of the spiral stairways. Descend it! A glimmer of a plan was born—a fantastic plan—perhaps so fantastic that it would work! Success would depend upon how quickly Kincar could move, whether he would be able to take his guards by surprise. He did not think too highly of the newcomers, but Lord Dillan was another matter. However, the cloak trick had worked against him. Kincar could only try, desperate as the plan was. And, making his first move, he clutched at the hand rail of the stair. What he intended might well burn the flesh from his hands. He must have some protection for them— He was bare to the waist; there was no way to tear any strips from his hide breeches. If he only had the cloak again!

One young Star Lord was already passing through the first of the well openings. He was the only barrier between Kincar and the realization of his plan. And he was wearing not the tight weather suit of Lord Dillan but a loose shirt of some light material.

Kincar started down the ladder with a meekness he trusted would be disarming. The steps were so narrow, the incline so steep that he hoped Lord Dillan would have to give a measure of his attention to his own going and so might be a second or so late in attacking when the prisoner moved.

The young lord was disappearing into the well at the next level now and Lord Dillan was waist-deep in the first, Kincar on the stair between them. The Gorthian threw himself forward, his weight on his hands. To the watcher it might seem he had missed a step. His foot swung out and caught the young lord on the side of the head. The other gave a choked cry and caught at the floor. It was that instinctive move to save himself that aided Kincar. He landed beside the alien and tore at his shirt, the thin stuff coming away in his hand. He pushed through the well opening, pulling over the half-conscious man to block it after him, and slid down the spiral, with only his hands on the rail as support.

He whirled about, wondering if he *could* brake his descent now. There were shouts behind, perhaps calls for help, and the clatter of boots. Friction charred the cloth under his hands, pain bit at his palms, but he held on. Two more levels, three; there was a regular din behind him now. Beneath him, two levels ahead, was solid floor, and he made ready as best he could to meet it. With dim memories of how he had taken falls in his first days of riding, he willed his muscles to go limp, tried to ball together, and prayed against the horror of broken bones.

There was blackness, but even in the semiconscious state he still strove for escape. When he was again truly aware of his surroundings, he crawled on smarting hands and aching knees down a narrow corridor.

Praise be to the Three, he had come through that landing unbroken, though his body ached with bruises. Wincing at sharp stabs, Kincar got to his feet and lurched on, only wanting now to put as much distance between himself and the noise as he could.

The walls about him changed as he stumbled over a high step. They were stone, not metal, now. He must be within one of the walls that tied together the ship-towers—far nearer ground level. Surely here he could find a door to the outer world.

Though he did not know it until afterwards, Kincar was perhaps the first prisoner within that maze who was in command of his mind and body, unbroken by the conditioner. To the men who hunted him, he was an unknown quantity they were not prepared to handle. They did not give him credit for either the initiative or the speed and energy he was able to muster.

The stone-walled corridor wove on with no breaks of either windows or doors. He sped along it at the best pace he could keep, nursing his scorched hands against the Tie, for it seemed to him that there was some healing virtue in the talisman. At least it drew away the worst of the pain.

To his dismay Kincar came to a second of the ridge steps, marking the entrance to another ship-tower. But there was no turning back, and, with all the chambers that must exist in the ships, he could either find a hiding place or access through a port window to the top of a connecting wall. The dim light that radiated from both walls of stone and of metal showed him another spiral stairway. He made a complete circuit below. Two doors, both fast closed, and neither would open. He dared not linger there. Necessity sent him climbing.

The first level gave upon more doors all closed, all resisting his efforts to force them. Another level, the same story. He leaned, gasping, against the hand rail, fearing that he had been driven into a trap with the Dark Ones able to pick him up at their leisure.

The third level, and as his head arose through the well, he could have shouted aloud his cry of triumph—for here a door gaped. In his eagerness he stumbled and went to one knee. And in that moment he heard the unmistakable pound of feet below.

He fell rather than sprang through the door. Then he set his hand flat against it as he had seen Lord Dillan do. It moved! It fell into place behind him! He could see no way of locking it, but the very fact that there was now a closed door between him and the stairwell gave a ghost of safety.

The corridor before him was a short one, and he burst into a small, round room. The walls rose up to the open sky— He had seen it—or its like before—for here was berthed a flier like the one that had brought him here.

He was trapped. There was no climbing the smooth walls of the well that held the flier. Soon—any moment now—the Dark Ones would be through that door he could not lock, would take him as easily as one roped a larng in the spring trapping pens. Why they had not already been upon him he did not know. As he hesitated there, he heard, more as a vibration through the walls than a sound, the pounding feet. But there was no fumbling at the door. Kincar guessed that his pursuers had gone to the next level, that the closing of the door had momentarily hidden his trail. Should he—could he dodge out now and backtrack while the hunters were on the higher levels? He could not bring himself to that move. The wild slide down the well ladder in the other tower and his run through the passages had worn him down; his energy was fading fast.

What did he do now? Remain where he was until they searched

from chamber to chamber and found him? He swayed to the flier, dropped on one of the seats within it, his hurt hands resting palms up on his knees. If he had only the proper knowledge, he could be free—away without any difficulty at all. The buttons on the panel before him were frustrating—if he only knew which ones—

The vibration of the hurrying hunters reached him faintly. They were coming back down again—or could that be reinforcements arriving from below? Dully Kincar studied the controls. Nothing in his dealing with the Star men he knew had given him a hint of their machines. But he could not be taken again—he could not! Better to smash the flier and himself than to sit here tamely until they broke in.

Kincar closed his eyes, offered a wordless petition to those he served, and made a blind choice of button. Only it was the wrong one. Heat walled up about him as if a cloak had been flung about his shivering body. Heat answered that button. He counted one over, relieved that disaster had not resulted from his first choice.

A shaft of light struck upon the rounded wall before him, flashing back into his dazzled eyes. It startled him so that he triggered the third button before he thought.

He grabbed the sides of his seat in spite of the pain in his hands. His gasp was close to a scream, for the flier was shooting up, out of that well, at a speed that almost tore the air from his lungs. The machine broke out of the well, went on and on up into the sky. It must be stopped—or he would reach star space. But how to control it he had no idea.

With the faint hope that the function of the button next to the last one he had pushed might counteract it, he thrust with an urgent finger. He was right, inasmuch as that sickening rise stopped. But his flight was not halted. The flier now skimmed forward with an equally terrifying speed, as might an arrow shot from a giant bow. But for the moment Kincar was content. He was not bound for outer space, and he was headed with breath-taking speed away from the towers. He crouched on the seat, almost unable to believe his good fortune.

When he grew more accustomed to flight, he ventured to look below, keeping a good grip on the seat and fighting vertigo. The same chance that had brought his finger to the right button had also dictated the course of the flier. It was headed across the waste plain, not for the sea lowlands and the cities ruled by the Dark Ones, but toward the distant mountain range—only not so distant now—where Kincar might have a faint hope of not only surviving but eventually rejoining those at the hold.

There remained the problem of grounding the flier. Just at the moment he had no desire to experiment—until at least one mountain lay between him and pursuit. And, thinking of pursuit sent him squirming about to look behind. The Dark Ones must have more than just one such flier—would they take to the air after him? But above the rapidly diminishing dot of the fortress he could see nothing in the air.

What might have been two—three days' travel for a larng flashed below in a short space of time. Then he was above the peaks he had seen from the ship-towers, skimming—just barely skimming—over snow-crowned rock. If he only knew how to control the flier! Its speed was certainly excessive. His elation gave way once more to anxiety as he imagined what might happen should the machine crash head-on against some peak higher than its present level of flight.

16
RESCUE

If no other flier arose from the ship-towers to intercept Kincar's runaway transport, something else did. He first knew of his danger when a piercing shriek of rage and avid hunger carried through the rush of air dinning at his eardrums. Compared to that challenge, Vorken's most ambitious call was a muted whisper. Kincar stared aloft and then shrank in the seat, for what swooped at him now was death, a familiar death, well known to any Gorthian who had ever roamed the mountain ranges.

Vorken was a mord, but she was counted a pygmy of her species. Among the frigid heights lived the giants of her race, able to carry off a larng at their pleasure. And their appetites were as huge as their bodies. They could be entrapped with a triple- or quadruple-strand net and men well versed in the tricky business to handle it, but such a netting meant days of patient waiting, luring the creature to the ground with bait. Once on the surface of the mountainside or plateau, they were enough at a disadvantage to be snared, though it was always a risky business, and no one was surprised if such a hunting party returned minus one or more of the hunters.

No one had ever faced a sa-mord in the air. No one had lived through an attack made when the attacker was wing borne and free. And Kincar had no hope of surviving this one.

With the usual egotism of a man, he had reckoned that *he* was the aim of those claws, whereas, to the sa-mord he was merely an incidental part of the thing it attacked. It made its swoop from the skies, talons stretched to grasp the flier, only to discover it had not properly judged the speed of this impudent air creature, missing its strike by a foot or more.

It plunged past in an instant, screaming its furious rage, and was gone before Kincar could realize that he had not been pierced through by those claws. Had he then been able to control the flier, he might have won free or tired the creature out to the point where it would have given up the chase. But such evasive action was beyond his power. He could only stay where he was, half sheltered by the back of the seat and the windbreak, as the flier bore straight ahead, while behind, the sa-mord beat up into the sky for a second strike.

Like their smaller relatives, the sa-mords had intelligence of a sort, and most of that reasoning power was centered upon keeping its possessor not only fed but alive. The sa-mords were solitary creatures, each female having a section of hunting territory where she ruled supreme, ready to beat off any of her kind who threatened her hold on sky and earth therein. And to such battles each brought accumulated knowledge of feint, attack, and the proper use of her own strength.

So when the sa-mord now struck for the second time, from a yet higher point, she had recalculated the speed of the flier and came down in a dive that should have brought her a little ahead and facing the enemy with waiting claws, a favorite fighting position.

Only again mechanical speed proved her undoing, for she hit directly on the flier's nose. The windbreak was driven into her softer underparts by the force of that meeting. Claws raked across the shield, catching on the seats, as she squalled at her hurt. Kincar, wedged in as flat as he could get, felt rather than saw that gaping beak that snapped just an inch or two above him as blood spurted from torn arteries to flow greasily.

The machine faltered, dipped, fought against that struggling weight impaled on its nose. It was losing altitude as the sa-mord beat and tore at it. Only the fact that the flier was metal, and so impervious to her attack, saved Kincar during those few moments before they were carried into a thicket of snow-line scrub trees. There the sa-mord's body acted as a shock absorber and cushion as they slammed to a final stop.

Kincar, the breath beaten out of him by the sharp impact, lay where he was, the stench of the torn creature thick in the air. Gone was the heat that had enfolded him. Shivering in the lash of mountain wind, he at last fought his way out of the grisly wreckage and staggered along the splintered swath the flier had cut. One sa-mord to a hunting territory was the custom. But there were lesser things that could scent blood and raw meat from afar. Weaponless he could not face up to such carrion eaters. So, guided more by instinct than plan, he reeled downslope.

Luckily the flier had not crashed on one of the higher crests, and the incline was not so straight that he could not pick a path. Here the scrub wood was thin. It was possible to set landmarks ahead to keep that path from circling.

It must be far past midday, and he would have to find shelter. From upslope there came a muffled yapping, then a growling, rising to roaring defiance. The scavengers had found their feast, and there was no hope of returning to the wreckage. In fact, that din spurred Kincar to a faster pace, until he lost his footing and fell forward, to roll into a snowdrift.

Gasping, spitting snow, he struggled up, knowing that to lie there was to court death. Only by keeping on his feet and moving did he have the thinnest chance. Fortunately the sky was clear of clouds; no storm threatened.

That fall and slide had brought him into a valley with a trickle of stream at its bottom. The water was dark, flowing quickly, with no skim of ice. He wavered down to it and went on his knees. Now he could feel the faint, very faint warmth exuding from the riverlet. This must be one of the hot streams, such as he had discovered in the hold valley. He had only to trace it back to its source and that heat would grow, promising him some protection against the cold of the coming night.

It was an effort to get to his feet again, to flog his bruised body along. But somehow he kept moving, aware through the fog of exhaustion that there were now trails of steam above the water, that the temperature in the valley was rising. Choking and coughing from the fumes, he fell against a boulder and clung there. He had to have the heat, but could he stand the lung-searing exhalations of the water?

Slowly he went down beside the rock, certain he could go no farther, and no longer wanting to try. It all assumed the guise of a dream, and the inertia of one caught in a nightmare weighted him. There was the grit of stone against his cheek and then nothing at all.

The sa-mord loomed above him. He had been very wrong. It was not killed by the flier, and now it had tracked him down. In a moment he would be rent by claw and beak. Only it was carrying him up—higher than the mountains! They were swinging out over the waste to the ship-towers. A flier bore him—no sa-mord but a flier! The machine was rising at the nose—it would turn over, spill him down—

"Get him up if you have to lash him! We can take no chances on this climb—"

Words coming out of the air, words without meaning. Warm—it was warm again. He had not been killed in that fall from the flier. Now he was lapped in the waters of the hot riverlet, being borne with its current. Watery, he saw the world only through a mist of water, and before him bobbed another dim figure. Then that shadowy shape turned, and he saw its face and knew that there was no escape. Lord Dillan! They had traced him, and he was once more a prisoner.

"Not so!" He heard his own cry as shrill as a mord's scream as he tried vainly to win free of the current, away from the Dark One. But it was no use; he could not move and the riverlet carried him on.

It was night, but not the total dark of the U-Sippar dungeon, for stars swung across Lor's Shield resting above him. And those stars moved—or did he? Dreamily he tried to work out that problem. The homely smell of larng sweat had driven away the stink of the river. But he was still swinging as if cradled in water.

"There is the beacon! We are almost in now—"

In where? U-Sippar? The ship-tower fortress? He had solved the mystery of the movement around, under, about him, realizing that he was lashed securely in a hunter's net swung between two of the burden larngs. But how much was real and how much was a dream he could not tell. He closed heavy eyelids, worn to a state of fatigue in which nothing at all mattered.

But perhaps he was too tired for sleep, for he was aware of arriving in a courtyard, and roused again to see the one who loosed the fastenings of his net.

It had been no use, that wild attempt at escape, for it was Lord Dillan who gathered him up and carried him into light, warmth, and sound. They were back at the ship-towers, and now would come the questioning—

They must have returned him to the padded chamber. He was lying on the softness of the bench there. Feeling it, he kept his eyes closed obstinately. Let them think he was unconscious.

"Kincar—"

He tensed.

"Kincar—"

There was no mistaking that voice. They might duplicate Lord Dillan but—the Lady Asgar? He opened his eyes. She was half-smiling, though watching him with a healer's study. And she was bundled in cold-season riding clothes, her hair fastened up tightly beneath a fur hood. Vorken sat on her shoulder appearing to examine Kincar with a measure of the same searching scrutiny.

"This is the hold?" He doubted the evidence of his eyes; he had been so sure he was elsewhere.

"This is the hold. And you are safe, thanks be to Vorken. Is that not true, my strong-winged one?"

Vorken bent her head to rub her crest of bone peak caressingly against the Lady's chin.

"We were hunting in the peaks and she came to us, leading us to a feast—" Asgar's expression was one of faint distaste. "And from there it was easy to trace your path, Kincar. Now"—she stooped over him with a horn cup in her hand while someone behind raised his head and shoulders so that he might drink—"get this inside of you that you may tell us your story, for we have a fear that time grows very late indeed."

It was Lord Dillan who supported him. But his own Lord Dillan and not the dark master of the ship-towers. Braced comfortably against that strong shoulder, Kincar told his story, tersely with none of a song-smith's embroidery of word. Only one thing he could not describe plainly, and that was what had happened to him in the ruined shrine. And that they did not ask of him. When he told of his meeting with the fugitives at the shore, Lord Dillan spoke for the first time.

"This we have heard in part. Murren could not master Cim, and the beast took his own path. He brought them to our gates, and they were found by Kapal and a foraging party. We have heard their story, and it is a black one." There was a dark shadow of pain in his eyes. "It will be for your hearing later. So—you were taken by the ruler's men," he prompted, and Kincar continued.

There was Vorken's providential appearance on the field where he had been condemned to death, and then the interference of the Dark Lord Dillan—

The man who held him tensed at his description. "Not only Rud—but *I*—here too?"

"Did we not know that it would be so for some of us?" queried the Lady Asgar. "And in the end that may prove the one weapon we have. But where did they then take you, Kincar?"

His memories of the ship-towers were so deeply etched that his account of the action there was more vivid. Both of the Star-born were moved by his recounting of his trial by fear.

"A conditioner!" Lord Dillan spat the word. "To have perverted that!"

"But that is a small perversion among so many," Asgar pointed out, "for their whole life here is a perversion, as well we know. Because that particular machine is a tool known to you, Dillan, it may strike more deeply home, but it is in my mind that they have made use of all their knowledge—our knowledge—to weld slave chains. And mark this—the conditioner was defeated by something native to this Gorth! Kincar believes that he was sent on this path, and it seems to me that he is right, very right! But you escaped from these earth-bound ships, and how was that done?" she demanded of the young man.

In retelling, his flight from the weird fortress sounded matter-of-fact and without difficulty, though Kincar strongly doubted that he could face it again. Action was far easier to take in sudden improvisation than when one knew what lay in wait ahead.

When he had done, the drink they had given him began its work. The aches of his bruised body faded into a lethargy, and he slipped into a deep sleep.

He woke again suddenly, without any of the normal lazy translation from drowsiness to full command. And when he opened his eyes, it was to see the youth from the seashore hut seated not far away, his chin cupped in both hands, studying Kincar as if the other held some answer to a disturbing puzzle. The very force of that gaze, thought Kincar, was enough to draw one out of sleep. And he asked, "What do you want?"

The other smiled oddly. "To see you, Kincar s'Rud."

"Which you are doing without hindrance. But there is more than just looking upon me that you wish—"

The boy shrugged. "Perhaps. Though your very existence is a marvel in this world. Kincar s'Rud," he repeated the name gravely, not as if he were addressing its owner, but more as one might utter some incantation. "Kincar s'Rud—Kathal s'Rud—"

Kincar sat up on the pad couch. He was stiff and sore, but he was alert and no longer weary to his very bones.

"Kincar s'Rud I know well," he observed. "But who is Kathal s'Rud?"

The other laughed. "Look at him! They have told me many things, these strange lords here, and few of them are believable, save to one who will swallow a song-smith's tales open-brained. But almost I can trust in every word when I look upon you. It seems, though we can both claim a Lord Rud for a sire, it is not the same Lord Rud. And that smacks of truth, for you and I are not alike."

"Lord Rud's son—" For a second Kincar was befuddled. Lord Dillan had spoken of brothers—no, half brothers—who could name him kin. But they had gone with the Star ships. Then he understood. Not his father—but the Lord Rud of this Gorth, that man softened by good living, rotted with his absolute power, whom he had fronted in U-Sippar. "But I thought—"

"That there were no half-bloods here? Aye!" The boy was all one bitter protest. "They have even spread it about that such births are impossible, like the offspring of a mord and a suard. But it is true, though mostly we are slain at birth—if our fathers know of it. To live always under a death sentence, enforced not only by the Dark Ones, but by your other kin as well—it is not easy."

"Lord Rud found out about you; that was why you were running?"

"Aye. Murren, who was guardsman to my mother's kin, saved me twice. But he was handled as you saw for his trouble. Better he himself had knocked me on the head! I am a nothing thing, being neither truly of one blood or the other."

As he had studied Kincar, so now the other reversed the process.

This was no duplicate other self, no physical twin, as were the two Dillans. So some other laws of chance and change had intervened between them. Kathal, he judged, was the younger by several birth seasons, and he had the fine-drawn, worn face, the tense, never-relaxed body of one who, as he had just pointed out, lived ever with danger. No happy memories of a Wurd or of the satisfying life of Styr were behind him. Would *he* have been as Kathal had he been born into this Gorth?

"You are safe now." Kincar tried to reassure him.

Kathal simply stared at him as one looks at a child who does not understand how foolishly he speaks.

"Am I? There is no safety ever for one who is s'Rud—no matter how it may be in the world from which *you* came."

"The Lords will change that—"

Again that bitter laugh. "Aye, your Lords amaze me. I am told that all here are full or half-blood—save for the refugees and freed slaves you have drawn in. But what weapons have your lords? How can they stand up against the might of all Gorth? For all Gorth will be marshaled against this hold when the truth is known. Best build another of these 'gates' of which they speak and charge through it before you feel Rud's fingers on your throat!"

And Kincar, remembering the ship-towers, the flier, could agree that other weapons and wonders must rest in the hands of the Dark Ones. His confidence was shaken for a moment.

"—and a deft server you shall find me!" That half sentence heralded Lord Dillan, who pushed through the door curtain, walking with exaggerated care because he held in both of his hands an eating bowl, lacy with steam and giving off an aroma that immediately impressed upon Kincar how long it had been since he had eaten. Lord Bardon was close behind him, his fingers striving to keep in one bundle several drinking horns of different sizes. Following on his heels came the remainder of the Star Lords, dwarfing the younger half-Gorthians with their bulk.

Kathal slipped from his seat and backed against the wall. He gave the appearance of a man about to make a lost stand against impossible odds. It was Lord Jon who put down the leather bottle he was carrying and smiled.

"Both in one netting. Feed yours, Dillan, and I'll settle this one and see that his tongue is properly moistened for speech." His clasp on Kathal's shoulder was the light one he would have used on his own son, and though the half-Gorthian fugitive had not lost his suspicion, he did not try to elude that grip.

Kincar spooned up the solid portion of the stew and drank the rich gravy. He had had no such meal since he had ridden out of Styr. Journeycake and dried meat were good enough for travelers, but they held no flavor.

"This," announced Lord Bardon, but his tone was light enough to war with the sense of his words, "is a council of war. We have come to learn all you can tell us, sons of Rud."

Perhaps Kathal flinched at a title that in this world meant shame and horror. But Kincar found it natural and was pleased at that link with the soft-spoken but sword-wary men about him. A measure of that confidence that had been frayed by Kathal's suspicions was restored. He had seen the Dark Ones, and to his mind none of them were matches for the Star men that he knew.

"We shall begin"—Lord Dillan took charge of the assembly as he was wont to do—"with a naming of names. Tell us, Kathal, who are the Dark Ones—give us a full roll call of their number."

17
INVASION

"It can never be set one piece within the other properly again!"

Kincar sat back on his heels. There was a broad smear of suard fat across his cheek where his hand had brushed unnoticed, and before him lay a puzzle of bits of metal salvaged from the broken flier. Brought from the point where it had cracked up, the machine was in the process of being reassembled by the Star Lords and half-bloods alike, neither certain of the ultimate results.

Lord Dillan sighed. "Almost it would seem so," he conceded. "I am a technician of sorts, but as a mechanic it appears I have a great many limitations. If I could only remember more!" He ran *his* greasy hands through his close-cropped dark-red hair. "Let this be a lesson to you, boy. Take notice of what you see in your youth—it may be required of you to duplicate it later. I have flown one of these—but to rebuild it is another matter."

Lord Jon, who had been lying belly-down on the courtyard pavement to inspect parts of the frame they had managed so far to fit together, smiled.

"All theory and no practice, Dillan? What we need is a tape record to guide us—"

"Might as well wish for a new flier complete, Lord." Vulth got to his feet and stretched to relieve cramped muscles. "Give me a good sword tail, and I'll open that box for you without this need for patching broken wire and shafts together."

Lord Bardon, who had earlier withdrawn from their efforts to fit the unfitable together, protesting that he had never possessed any talent for machine assembly, laughed.

"And where do we recruit a tail for spear-festing, Vulth? Lay a summoning on the mountain trees to turn them into warriors for your ordering? From all accounts any assault straight into the face of danger will not work this time. I wonder—" He was studying the parts laid out on the stones. "That gear to the left of your foot, Dillan—it seems close in size to the rod Jon just bolted in. Only a suggestion, of course."

Lord Dillan picked up the piece and held it to the rod. Then he observed solemnly, "Any more suggestions, Bard? It is plain that *you* are the mechanic here."

Kincar was excited. "Look, Lord. If that fits there, then does not this and this go so?" He slipped the parts into the pattern he envisioned. He might not know Star magic, but these went together with a rightness his eyes approved.

Dillan threw up his hands in a gesture of mock defeat. "It would seem that the totally unschooled are better at this employment. Perhaps a little knowledge is a deterrent rather than a help. Go ahead, children, and see what you can do without my hindrance."

In the end, with all of them assisting, they had the flier rebuilt.

"The question remains," Lord Bardon said, "will it now fly?"

"There is only one way to test that." Before any of them could protest, Lord Dillan was in the seat behind the controls. However, even as his hand moved toward the row of buttons, Kincar was beside him, knowing that he could not let the other make that trial alone.

Perhaps Dillan would have ordered him out, but it was too late for that, as inadvertently the Star Lord had pushed the right button and they were rising—not with the terrifying speed Kincar had known in his last flier trip, but slowly, with small complaints and buzzes from the engine.

"At least," Lord Dillan remarked, "she did not blow up at once. But I would not care to race her—"

They were above the hold towers now. And Vorken, seeing them rise past her chosen roost, took to the air in company, flying in circles about the machine and uttering cries of astonishment and dismay. Men walking, men riding larngs she understood and had been accustomed to from fledglinghood. But men in her own element were different and worrying.

Kincar, with only too vivid memories of the mountain sa-mord, tried to wave her away. Vorken could not smash the flier with her weight as had the giant of her species. But if she chose to fly into Lord Dillan's face, she might well bring them to grief. Her circles grew closer, as she swung in behind the windbreak, her curiosity getting the better of her caution. Then she made a landing on the back of the seats and squatted, her long neck outstretched between the two who sat there, interested in what they would do next.

"Do you approve?" Lord Dillan asked her.

She squawked in an absent-minded fashion, as if to brush aside foolish questions. And seeing that she was minded to be quiet, Kincar did not try to dislodge her.

Dillan began to try out the repaired craft. It did not respond too quickly to the controls governing change of altitude or direction. But it did handle, and he thought it could be safely used for the purpose they planned. After flying down the wide valley guarded by the hold and making a circle about the mountain walls, he brought the machine back for a bumpy but safe landing in the courtyard.

"She is no AA job, but she will take us there—" was his verdict given to the hold party and the natives from four liberated slave gangs. The hold archers now kept a regular watch on the mountain road and freed all unfortunates dragged through that territory.

Kapal had assumed command of these men, and out of those who still possessed some stamina and spirit, he was hammering a fighting tail of which he often despaired but bullied and drilled all the more grimly because they fell so far below his hopes. He had taken readily, greedily, to the use of the bows and was employing both the men and the few women from the ex-slave gangs to manufacture more. Now he insisted that it was time for him to lead his band in some foray on their own.

"It is this way, Lord," he had sought out Bardon the night before to urge. "They have been slaves too long. They think like slaves, believing that no man can stand up to the Dark Ones. But let us once make even a party of slave-driving Hands surrender, or rather let us blood our arrows well on such eaters of dirt, and they will take new heart. They must have a victory before they can think themselves once more men!"

"If we had time, then I would say aye to that, Kapal, for your reasoning is that of a leader who knows well the ways of fighting men. But time we do not have. Let the Dark Ones discover us, and they have that which will blot us out before finger can meet upon finger in a closing fist. Nay, our move must be fast, sure, and merciless. And it should come very soon!"

Kathal had given them the key to what might be their single advantage. Occasionally the Dark Ones assembled at the ship-tower fortress. In spite of their covert internecine warfare, their jealousies and private feuds, they still kept to some fellowship and a certain amount of exchange of supplies, news and man power.

Though they laughed at native traditions, stamping out any whenever they found them, they themselves were not wholly free of the desire for symbolic celebrations. And one such, perhaps the most rigidly kept, was that marking their first landing on Gorth. For this anniversary they assembled from all over the planet, making a two-day festival of the gathering. It seldom ended without some bloodshed, though dueling was frowned upon. The natives, excluded from the meeting, forbidden even to approach within a day's journey of the ship-towers, knew that often a Lord did not return from the ingathering and that his domain was appropriated by another.

"It has been our hope that they would continue to deal with each other so," Kathal had said, "using their might against their own kind. But always it works to our ill, for those Dark Ones who treated us with some measure of forbearing were always the ones to return not, and the more ruthless took their lands. Of late years there have been fewer disappearances—"

"How many Lords are there left?" Lord Frans had wanted to know.

Kathal spread his fingers as if to use them in telling off numbers. "Who can truthfully say, Lord? There are fifty domains, each with an overlord. Of these perhaps a third have sons, younger brothers, kinsmen. Of their females we know little. They live secretly under heavy guard. So secret do they keep them that there are now rumors they are very, very few. So few that the Lords—" He had paused, a dark flush staining his too-thin face.

"So few," Lord Dillan had taken that up, "that now such as your Lord Rud has a forbidden household, and perhaps others do likewise. Yet they will not allow their half-blood children to live."

Kathal shook his head. "If the Lords break that law, Lord, then they are held up to great shame among their kindred. To them we are as beasts, things of no account. Mayhap here and there a half-blood, who was secretly born, lives for a space of years. But mostly they are slain young. Only because my mother had a sister who kept her close did I come to man's age."

"Say perhaps one hundred?" Lord Bardon had kept on reckoning the opposition.

"Half again more," Kathal replied.

"And they will all be at the ship-towers twelve days from now?"

"Aye, Lord, that is the time of the in-gathering."

The hold began their own preparations, working all day and far into the night, for if at no other time all the Dark Ones would be together, then they must strike here and now. They dared not wait another whole year, and they could never hope to campaign against fortresses beaded clear across Gorth.

As soon as they were certain the flier could take to the air again, the first party, mounted on the pick of the larngs moved out, armed and prepared for a long ride across the mountain trails that the inner men had shown them.

Kapal and his ragged crew, or the best of them, padded through the secret ways of the mountain with Ospik for a guide, heading for the agreed-upon point overlooking the waste plain on which the ship-towers stood.

Kincar had expected to ride with the other half-bloods in the mounted party. But, as the only one who had ever been at the ships, he was delegated to join the Star Lords.

The flier would carry four at a time—reluctantly—but it *would* rise and, at a speed greater than a larng's extended gallop, get them over the ranges to the last tall peak from which they could look down upon their goal. All wore the silver clothing insulated against the chill, giving them more freedom of movement than the scale coats and leather garments the Gorthians and half-Gorthians were used to. And Kincar, clad in a suit hastily cut to his size, moved among them looking like a boy among his elders.

On the heights they took cover, but four pairs of farseeing glasses passed from hand to hand, Kincar having them in his turn. And so they witnessed the arrival of swarms of fliers at the towers.

"That makes one hundred and ten," Lord Bardon reported. "But each carries several passengers."

Lord Dillan had the glasses at the moment.

"I wonder, Bard—?"

"Wonder what?"

"Whether those ships were ever deactivated?"

"They must have been! Surely they wouldn't have built them into those walls otherwise—"

"Ours were not. In fact, Rotherberg said that he didn't believe they could be."

"Do you mean," Kincar demanded, "that they could take off in those ships right now, as the Star Lords did in our Gorth?"

"It would solve a lot of our problems if they would do just that, but I hardly think they will oblige us by trying it."

Lord Dillan did not answer that. He continued to hold the glasses to his eyes as if memorizing every detail of the ships.

"No arrivals for a long time now," remarked Lord Bardon. "Do you suppose they are all here?"

"It would appear so. We'll wait until morning to be sure." Lord Dillan was still on watch. "We'll camp and leave a scout to keep an eye on them."

The camp was a temporary affair, set up in a gulch, with a heat box to provide them with the equivalent of a fire and journey rations to eat. Kincar took his turn at scout duty close to dawn. There had been no more arrivals at the ship-towers in the darkness, and the party from the hold concluded that all the Dark Ones must be in the fortress.

"We could use double our numbers," Lord Bardon remarked as they broke their fast.

"I could wish more for Rotherberg of Lacee."

"Hmm." Lord Bardon gazed hard at Lord Dillan. "Still thinking of that, are you? But none of us are engineers—we would not stand here if we were. Those who had that in their blood chose to go with the ships."

"Nevertheless, I believe we should keep the idea in mind!"

"Oh, that we shall do." Lord Bardon laughed. "Should I chance upon the proper controls, I shall set them for a takeoff. Meanwhile, the escape hatches seem the best entrances—we should be able to reach them from the tops of those walls. Shall we head for the nearest?"

"We shall. And before it grows too light."

Again the flier was pressed into ferry service, transporting their small band across the waste to the base of one of the corridor walls close to the foot of the nearest ship-tower. Lord Sim swung overhead a rope with a hook attached—twin to the weapon Murren had used. The prongs caught on the top of the wall and held against his heaviest tugs, and by the rope they climbed up.

Lord Tomm planted himself with his back against the smooth side of the ancient ship, bracing his feet a little apart to take weight, and the lighter Lord Jon stood on his shoulders, facing inward so that he could touch an oval outline that showed faintly on the ship. With a tool from his belt he traced that outline carefully, and then pushed. It took two such tracings to cut through the sealing, but at last the door came free and they were in the ship.

Kincar was the third inside, sniffing again that odd musty odor of the silent tower. But Lord Frans, following him, gave an exclamation of surprise as he stood in the corridor.

"This is the *Morris!*"

"*Their Morris*," corrected Lord Dillan. "You can guide us, Frans. This is twin to your father's ship—"

"The control chamber—" Lord Frans frowned at the wall. "It has been so many years. Aye, we'll want that first!"

"Why?" Lord Jon wanted to know. He was looking about him with some of Kincar's curiosity. Himself two generations younger than the original space travelers, the ships were almost as strange to him as they were to the half-Gorthian.

"If she is still activated, we will be able to use the scanner."

While that meant nothing to Kincar, it apparently did to the others.

Lord Frans guided them, not to a center well ladder-stair such as Kincar and his captors had used, but to a narrower and more private way, hardly large enough for the Star men to negotiate. The steps were merely loops of metal on which to rest toes and fingers. They went up and up until Lord Frans disappeared through a well opening and Lord Bardon after him. Then Kincar climbed into one of the most bewildering rooms he had ever seen.

There were four padded, cushioned objects, which were a cross between a seat and a bunk. Each was swung on a complicated base of springs and yielding supports before banks of levers and buttons to which the controls of the small flier were the playthings of a child. Above each of these boards was a wide oblong of opaque stuff, mirrors that reflected nothing in the room. Kincar remained where he was, a little overawed by this array of Star magic, with a feeling that to press the wrong button here might send them all off into space.

Lord Dillan walked across the chamber. "Astrogator." He dropped his hand on the back of one of those odd seats, and it trembled under the slight pressure. "Pilot," he indicated another. "Astro-Pilot." That was the third. "Com-Tech." The fourth and last was the seat Lord Dillan chose to sit in.

As soon as his weight settled in the chair-bed, the bank of buttons slid noiselessly forward so it was well within his reach. He was in no hurry to put it to use, deliberating over his choice before he pressed a button. Above the control bank that square mirror flashed rippling bars of yellow light, and Lord Jon broke out eagerly, "She is still alive?"

"At least the corns are in." Again the words meant nothing to Kincar. But he would have paid little attention to any speech at the moment. He was too intrigued by what was happening on the screen. It was as if Lord Dillan had opened a window. Spread out there was a wide picture of the wastelands and the mountain range as they existed outside the ship.

He had only an instant to make identification before that picture changed, and they were looking at a room crowded with a mass of metal parts and machines he could not have set name to—

"Engine room," breathed Lord Jon softly, wonderingly.

Another movement of Lord Dillan's finger, and they had a new view—a place of tanks, empty, dusty, long disused.

"Hydro—"

So they inspected the vitals of the ship, cabin to cabin. But in all their viewing nothing was living, nor was there any indication that anyone had been there for a very long time. At last Lord Dillan leaned back, sending his support jiggling.

"She is not the one—"

Lord Bardon was studying the banks of controls fronting the pilot's seat. "They would be more likely to hole up in the *Gangee.*

After all she was the flag ship. Hm—" He did not sit down in the pilot's place but leaned across to move a lever. There was a brilliant flash of red in a small bulb there, and from somewhere about them a voice rasped in the speech of the Star ways.

"She's still hot!" Lord Jon exploded.

Lord Dillan smiled, a chill smile that Kincar knew he would not care to have turned in his direction.

"And she will be hotter." He arose and crossed to join Lord Bardon. "Five hours ought to give us time enough. Let us see now—" He counted levers and studs, peered closely at dials, and then his hands flew, weaving a pattern over the board. "Let us be on the way now. We'll try the *Gangee* next."

"She'll lift?" demanded Lord Tomm.

"She'll certainly try. In any event she'll wreck this part of the building."

They made their way back to the wall top, out into the early morning sunshine. Lord Dillan pivoted, examining each of the other towers.

"Might as well split up now. Jon, you and Rodric, Sim and Tomm, get in those other end ships. If they are empty, set them to blow—five hours from now or thereabouts. Bring with you any of"—he rattled off a string of queer words incomprehensible to Kincar—"you come across in their store rooms. We'll try for the *Gangee*."

They nodded and separated, heading for different ships.

18
ONCE MORE A GATE—

There was a different "feel" to the *Gangee*. They made their entrance through the old escape port of the ship without opposition or discovery. But, as they clustered together at the foot of the ladder to the control cabin, even Kincar was conscious of a faint heat radiating from the walls about them, a lack of dead air long sealed in.

"This is the one." Lord Bardon was satisfied.

"Controls again?" Lord Frans wanted to know.

"Just so!" The words were bitten off as if Lord Dillan was reluctant to make that climb. Did he think they might find others occupying that chamber?

But he sped up the ladder, Lord Bardon at his heels, and the rest strung out behind. They climbed by closed doors on every level. And twice Kincar, brushing against the inner fabric with his shoulder, felt a vibration through the ship, like a beat of motive power.

The control cabin, when they reached it, was, at first inspection, very little different from that of the *Morris*—the same four chairs, the same banks of controls, the same vision plates above them. Once more Lord Dillan seated himself in the Com-Tech's place and pressed a stud. They glimpsed the outside world, and then the picture changed. The engine room—but this one was not silent, dust-shrouded. Rods moved on dials set in casing. The Hydro garden was stretches of green stuff growing, and the Star Lords were surprised.

"Do you think they are planning a take-off?" asked Lord Jon.

"More likely they keep the *Gangee* in blast condition as a symbol," Lord Dillan replied. "Which may be their salvation now—"

Once more the picture flickered and cleared. Kincar started. It was so vivid, so clear, that he had the sensation of looking through an open window into a crowded room, for it was crowded.

An exclamation in his own tongue burst from Lord Frans, echoed by one from Lord Jon. It was an assemblage of the Dark Ones they spied upon.

"You—Great Spirit of Space! Dillan, there you are!" Lord Bardon's voice shook as he identified one of those men. "And Rud—that is truly Rud! Lacee—Mac—Bart—but Bart's dead! He died of the spinning fever years ago. And—and—" His face was a gray-white now beneath its weathered brown, his eyes wide, stricken. "Alis—Dillan, it's Alis!" He flung away toward the other door of the chamber.

Lord Dillan barked an order, sharp enough to send Kincar moving. The other Star Lords were frozen, hypnotized by what they saw. Only to Kincar to whom it was just a company of aliens did that command have meaning.

"Stop him! Don't let him leave this cabin!"

Lord Bardon was a third again his size, and Kincar did not know how he could obey, but there was no mistaking the frantic urgency of the order. He hurled himself across the door, clasping the stay rods on either side imposing his body between Lord Bardon and the portal. Lord Dillan was hurrying to them, but he did not reach there before his fellow had crashed into Kincar, slamming the half-Gorthian back painfully against the ship metal, before he began tearing at him, trying to drag him away.

A hand caught at Lord Bardon, brought him partly around, and then a palm struck first one cheek and then the other in a head-rocking duo of slaps.

"Bardon!"

Lord Bardon staggered, that strained stare in his eyes beginning to break. Lord Dillan spoke swiftly in their own language until Lord Bardon gave a broken little cry and covered his face with both hands. Then Lord Dillan turned to the others.

"They are not there, understand?" He spoke with a slow and heavy emphasis, designed to drive every word not only into their ears, but also into their minds. "Those down there are not the ones we know—knew. I am not that Dillan, nor is he me."

Lord Jon caught a quivering underlip between his teeth. He was still watching the screen longingly, and Lord Dillan spoke directly to him.

"That is not your father you see there, Jon. Keep that in mind! This I know." He swung upon them all. "We must have no speech with these, for our sakes—perhaps for theirs. There is only one thing to do. They have poisoned this Gorth, as we to a lesser extent poisoned ours. And now they must go forth from it—"

He had laid his hand on the back of the pilot's seat when Bardon spoke hoarsely.

"You can't blast them off without any warning!"

"We will not. But they shall only have enough to ensure their lives during take-off. There must be payment for what has been done here—the risk they shall run in entering exile will be toward the settlement of that account."

The Star Lords were occupied with their problem, but Kincar had been watching the screen again. Now he ventured to interrupt.

"Lord, are they able to see us, as we do them?"

Dillan whirled, his head up, to front the vision plate. There could be no mistake; the party they spied upon were quiet, all heads turned to face the screen. And the blank astonishment of most of their expressions was altering to concern. That other Lord Dillan moved, advancing toward them, until his head alone covered three-quarters of the plate.

It was something out of a troubled dream to see one Dillan stare at the other, if only from a screen. A huge hand moved across the corner of the plate and was gone again. Then a voice boomed out above them, speaking the Star tongue. Dillan, *their* Dillan, snapped a small switch beneath the plate and made answer. Then his hand swept down breaking contact, both eye and voice.

"We have little time," he said unhurriedly. "Dog that door so that they may not enter until they burn through—"

It was Lord Frans and Lord Jon who obeyed. Lord Bardon remained by the pilot's chair—until Dillan turned on him.

"We shall give them more than just a slim chance, Bard. Once in space they can make a fresh start. We are not dooming them—"

"I know— I know! But *will* the ship lift? Or will it—" His voice faded to a half whisper.

"Now," Dillan told them all, "get out—away from here—as fast as you can move!"

Kincar was on the ladder. The fear of being trapped and torn skyward was very real. Lord Jon and Lord Frans came after him. All three were in the outer air before Lord Bardon joined them. And he lingered in the hatch, one hand on the rope, waiting.

They were hailed by the other parties. Lord Jon waved them off with wild arm signals. Then Lord Bardon dropped from the hatch and a last silver figure appeared in the oval opening. He brought that door to behind him and slid down the rope.

"Run, you fools!" he shouted, and Kincar found himself pounding away from the *Gangee* along the top of the wall. He had no idea how a space ship, especially one built up by masonry would take off, but he could guess that the results would be earthshaking at ground level.

A large arm clamped a viselike grip about his waist, and Lord Dillan gasped, "Jump now, son!"

He was borne along by the other from the top of the wall. They hit hard and rolled. Then he was punched into a ball half under the other's bulk as the ground under them rocked and broke. There was the clamor of mistreated metal, the rumble of a world coming to an end, and a flash so brilliant that it blinded him—to be followed by a clap of noise and a silence so complete that it was as if all sound had been reft away.

Broken lumps of stone rained noiselessly from the sky. There was no sound at all. Kincar struggled free of a hold that was now only a limp weight. He sat up shakily, his head ringing, red and orange jags of light darting back and forth before his eyes when he tried to focus on his surroundings. His groping hands were on warm flesh, and then on stickiness that clung to his fingers. He rubbed impatiently at his eyes, trying to clear them. But, above all else, the dead silence was frightening.

He could see now, if only dimly. Red crawled sluggishly over a silver back beside his knee. Dazed, he rubbed his eyes again. A ringing began in his ears, worse when he moved, making it very hard to think—

But he could move. Kincar bent over the quiet body beside him.

There was a gash on the shoulder, a tear in both the silver clothing and the flesh beneath it. Already the bleeding was growing less. Cautiously he tried to move the other, exposing Lord Dillan's face slack and pale. The Star Lord was still breathing. Kincar steadied the heavy head on his arm and ripped open the sealing of the tunic. Under his fingers there was a steady heart beat, though it seemed too slow. The flier—if he could find the flier and the supplies on it—

Kincar settled Dillan's head back on the ground and stumbled to his feet. He had an odd sensation that if he moved too suddenly he might fly apart.

Before he could turn away, another silver figure hunched up from the ground. He could see Lord Jon's mouth open and shut in a grimed face, but he could not hear a word the other said. Then others ran toward them. Miraculously they had all survived the blast-off of the *Gangee*, though for long, anxious moments they were afraid that Bardon had been lost. He was discovered at last, stunned, but still alive, on the other side of a cracked and riven wall.

Kincar was deafened, unable to understand the others as they gathered at the flier. Dillan, revived, bandaged, and propped up against a heap of rubble, was giving orders. Both Jon and Bardon were unable to walk without support, and the rest were busy exploring the remaining ships and coming back to report to Dillan. Twice they brought boxes to be piled at the improvised camp site.

Lord Frans used the flier to ferry their spoil and the injured to a point well out in the waste, several miles from the ship-towers. Where the *Gangee* had formed the core of the queer structure, there was now a vast crater, avoided by the Star men, smoking in the morning air. And the walls that had tied it to its sister ships were riven, reduced to gravel-rubble in places. Studying the remains, Kincar marveled that any one of them had survived. He might have been even more deeply impressed by their good fortune had he possessed the information shared by the men around him.

"—took off to the mountains—"

He had been watching soundlessly moving lips so long, with a growing frustration, that at first he did not realize he had caught those words, faint as a whisper, through the din in his head. Lord Frans was making a report of some importance, judging by the demeanor of those about him.

Men scattered to the ships at a trot, and the flier returned. Lord Dillan and Kincar were motioned aboard her, to be transported to the mid-point camp. Then the others came in groups until they were all well away from the ship-towers. They must have triggered the other ships, all of them. Those slim silver towers would follow the *Gangee* out into space, untenanted and derelict.

Again his ears cleared, and he caught a sharp hail. A string of mounted men were riding out in the waste, the party from the hold. They rode at a full gallop, as men might go into battle, and Vulth spurred well ahead, a Vulth shouting news as he came. He threw himself from his mount and ran up, to skid to a stop before Lord Dillan, his aspect wild.

"That demon—the one with your form, Lord—he has turned the freed slaves against us!"

Kincar noted an empty saddle among the oncoming party. Where was Jonathal? Two of the other men were wounded.

"They will circle back to the hold—"

Lord Dillan cut through that crisply. "Aye, that is his wisest move. So we must get there speedily. Frans, you take the controls—Sim—"

"Not you, Dillan!" That was Lord Bardon's protest.

"Most certainly me! Who else can face him so successfully and reveal him to be what he is? And"—his eyes went to Kincar—"and you, Kincar. This may be the time, guardian, for you to use that power—"

Dillan's energy got them on the flier after a flood of orders had sent the mounted party around to come at the hold from the plains side with the remainder of the Star Lords in their company, leaving the wounded, Lord Bardon and Lord Jon to stay at the waste camp and check on the blast-off of the rest of the ships.

The flier lifted over the ridge, heading straight for the hold. Lord Frans pushed the limping motor to its utmost, and there was no talk among the men in her. A familiar peak cut the sky before them—they were almost to the valley.

"He'll use your face as his passport," Lord Sim commented.

"Asgar will know the truth."

Aye, the Lady Asgar would be able to tell true from false, but could she distinguish that in time? And how had the false Lord Dillan managed to get out of the *Gangee* before she blasted into space? Kincar speculated concerning that, but, having seen the preoccupation of his companions, thought it better not to ask for any explanations.

From the air the hold appeared to be as it always had been—until one marked a body lying before the door of the main hall in the courtyard. Save for that grim sight there was no other sign of life—or death.

Frans brought the flier down in the courtyard. Now the ringing in Kincar's ears could not blot out the clamor issuing from the hall. He was on his feet, his sword in hand, but he had not moved faster than Lord Dillan. And running side by side they entered the core of the hold.

A handful of Gorthians, a women among them, were backed against the far wall—but they were aimed and waiting. Towering among them stood the Lady Asgar. And she faced a silver figure who was the duplicate of the man beside Kincar. Fan-wise behind the false lord was a rabble of ex-slaves. Kapal, writhing feebly as if he would still be on his feet to match blades, lay with the Lady Asgar's people. And beside her, half-crouched to spring at the false Dillan's throat, was Kathal s'Rud.

The hold people were at bay, held so by the weapon the false lord fingered—the blaster with which he had once threatened Kincar. One of the slaves in his tail caught sight of the new party. His mouth opened on a scream of undisguised terror, and he flung himself to the floor, beating his fists against the stone pavement and continuing the yammering screech, which went on and on. His fellows cowered away, first from him, and then from their erstwhile leader as they saw the other Lord Dillan.

Even one with an iron will could not keep his attention from wandering at that interruption. The false lord glanced once to what lay behind him, giving those he held in check their chance. The Lady Asgar was at him in a fury, striving to wrest from him the blaster, while Kathal and Lord Jon's eldest son leaped to her support.

The rest of the party from the flier rushed in. Dillan, fresh stains of red seeping out on his bandaged shoulder, faced himself—but the likeness between them was no longer mirror-exact, for the Dillan of this Gorth snarled, his face awry in a grimace of rage. Asgar had torn the weapon from him. Now his bare hands reached for his rival's throat.

Kincar, as he had done to save Lord Bardon from the needle knife, clove through the distance between them, his left arm striking hard against the false lord's thighs, his sword tripping the other up. And they smashed down on the pavement as others of the half-blood piled upon them.

When the false lord was safely pinned by Kathal and two of the others, Kincar sat up.

"Who are you?" demanded the prisoner of his standing double.

"I am the man you would have been had history in Gorth taken another path—"

The false Lord Dillan lay rigid; his mouth worked as if it were a struggle for him to force out the words. "But who—where—?"

"We found a path between parallel worlds—"

Dillan was alert to the Gorthians more than to his captive. Those of the ex-slaves who had followed the false lord were shrinking back. One or two whimpered. And the one who had howled and beat upon the floor was drooling as he stared vacantly at nothing. They were close to the breaking point.

It was the Lady Asgar who spoke to Kincar, drawing him to his feet with both hands and the urgency of her orders.

"This is a task for you, guardian. Give them something—a sign—they can fix upon. Or they may all lose their wits before our eyes!"

He tore open the sealing of his silver tunic and brought out the Tie. On his palm it emitted that soft glow of awakened power. And he began to chant, watching the glow brighten. Those of the half-blood took up his words. The sonorous sound filled the high vault of the hall. The stone warmed in his hold. He held it out to the Lady Asgar, and her larger hand cupped over it, sheltering the talisman with her alien flesh for a space as long as the chant of a line. There was no alteration in that glow, no harm to her.

Kincar turned to the Lord Dillan of the hold. In turn, that man's hand, broader, darker, arched without hesitation over the stone. Once more one of the Star blood passed that test.

Last of all the guardian stooped to the false lord. That Dillan, too, was not lacking in courage. His mouth set in a mirthless smile as the hand Kathal freed reached for the stone.

But in spite of his courage, his determination, he could not cup the Tie. It flared, pulsing not blue-green but a malignant yellow, as if some strange fire sent a tongue out of it at the encroaching hand.

"Demon!"

A bow cord sang, and a feathered shaft stood from a broad chest. The man on the floor arched his back and coughed, tried to fling some last word at his double. It was Kapal, clasping his bow to him, who laughed.

"One demon the less," he spat. "I care not if all his fellows be on the trail behind him. There is one demon less!"

"There will be none to follow him." The live Dillan spoke above the dead. "They have returned to the stars from which they came. Only this one broke from the ship just before it blasted—taking a flier. Gorth is now free of his breed."

From somewhere words flooded into Kincar's mind, began to pour from his tongue in a wild rhythm. He knew he had never learned them by rote, and together they formed a fearsome thing, a curse laid upon men in this world and the Forest beyond, upon their coming and going, their living and dying. The very beat of those words upon the air invoked strange shadows, and as he uttered them the ex-slaves crept about his feet, drinking them in.

Then from curse the words turned to promise, a promise such as the Three sometimes set in the mouths of those inspired by their wisdom.

"Lord—" It was Kapal who broke the silence that fell when he ended. "What is your will for us?"

"Not my will." Kincar shook his head. "Do you live like free men in an open land—" But that fey streak still possessed him. He had one more thing that he must do. The Tie was dead now, a lifeless stone. For him it would never again grow warm or live. His guardianship was at an end. It must pass to another, perhaps one better fitted to use it as it should be used. He was but a messenger, not a true wielder of the Threefold Power.

"I show you a man of your own to lead you—" He turned slowly to face that other who was also s'Rud.

Kathal's hands came up slowly, as if they moved by some will outside his own. Kincar tossed the talisman into the air. It flashed straight across the space between them into those waiting hands. And as the stone touched flesh once more, it glowed! He had been right—the Tie had chosen to go from him. He could not, if he wished, take it again.

A faint promise of the coming warm season mellowed the stone at his back. Kincar breathed the fresh air from the courtyard. Vorken squatted on his shoulder, chirruping now and again.

"Stay with us, Lords—we need you—"

They had heard that plea repeated so many times during the past months. And, as ever, the same patient answer came.

"Not so. Us you need least of all. This is your world, Kathal, Kapal; shape your own roads through it. We did not sweep away one set of alien rulers to plant another. Take your fortune in your two hands and be glad it is truly yours!"

"But—where do you go, Lords? To a better world?"

Out in the valley was the shimmer of the now complete gate, erected from materials looted from the vanished ships. Did they seek a better world through that portal when on the morrow they went into a second self-imposed exile? Kincar reached for his bow. Would they ever find a Gorth to fit their dreams? Or did that greatly matter? Sometimes he thought that an endless quest had been set them for some purpose, and that the seeking, not the finding, was their full reward. And it was good.